A
B(

"*Borrowed Time* is so many things. Epic, thrilling, suspenseful, beautiful. There are horrors in this story that are truly monstrous, and I'm a sucker for a brutal, complicated villain. But it was the love story that got me. When I finished the last page, I actually had to take a moment to breathe."

—**Victoria Dougherty**, Bestselling Author of
The Bone Church and the *Breath* series.

"Longtime journalist John Nolte's compelling and moving *Borrowed Time* is no mere first novel. It is the first fictional work to forcefully dramatize the terrifying world we live in today—what Nolte calls the All at Once—while showing us the way out through God and love. Read this extraordinary book now!"

—**Roger Simon**, Oscar-nominated Screenwriter,
Prize-winning Mystery Novelist

"John Nolte's *Borrowed Time* is a story-telling breath of fresh air. With a deft touch, Nolte tells a tale that is at once magical, and is yet rooted in a kind of Dickensian naturalism. This novel is a high-wire narrative that meditates on life and death and God's eternal presence. The novel is also an unabashed love letter to America. An absorbing story of love and the role history plays in our lives, I read this book in one sitting and look forward to reading it again, out loud, to my grandchildren. This is, quite simply, a great American novel."

—**Robert Avrech**, Emmy-winning Screenwriter of
Body Double and *A Stranger Among Us*

"John Nolte has written a fine page turner of a novel. Sure to be a fun summer read. A love story with a cinematic almost Capra-esque throwback to its feeling and passion, which at the same time is a smart thriller jumping along at a fun clip. I really enjoyed it."

—**Mike Binder**, Comedian, Screenwriter, Director of
Upside of Anger, Reign Over Me, and Author of *Keep Calm*

"I will read anything John Nolte writes. He's sharp, he's fearless, he's hilarious. But *Borrowed Time* is something special. The idea at its center is ingenious, and seeing where he takes this concept is a thrill. I couldn't put it down."

—**Alex Marlow**, Editor-In-Chief of Breitbart News
and *New York Times* Bestselling Author

"John Nolte has achieved something on which many Christian fiction writers fall short: he's produced a riveting, fast-paced novel without sanitizing the characters or the gritty reality of our modern world and without preaching. Though this book cannot fairly be categorized as Christian fiction, it expresses Christian themes as surely as if it were, and more effectively. I marvel at Nolte's creative imagination and his facility for storytelling. This is a fun but provocative read."

—**David Limbaugh**, Author and Lawyer

BORROWED TIME

JOHN NOLTE

BOMBARDIER
BOOKS

Published by Bombardier Books
An Imprint of Post Hill Press

Borrowed Time
© 2023 by John Nolte
All Rights Reserved

ISBN: 978-1-63758-928-1
ISBN (eBook): 978-1-63758-929-8

Cover Design by Conroy Accord
Interior design and composition by Greg Johnson, Textbook Perfect

Post Hill Press
New York • Nashville
posthillpress.com

Published in the United States of America
1 2 3 4 5 6 7 8 9 10

For Julie—
my wife, my muse, my Doreen...
and
for Mom, my faithful reader.

"Even the immortals live on borrowed time."

—ORIGIN UNKNOWN

Prologue

1

The year was 1849 and Joshua Mason had just discovered he was an American.

For the better part of two decades Mason had been roaming Northern Mexico. Then sometime last year, and without anyone asking his opinion on the matter, Mexico and the U.S. signed a treaty. Now both he and the land he called home were American.

Mason was puzzling out what this might mean as he entered his adobe hut. There he unloaded supplies purchased at the same trading post that had apprised him of his updated citizenship status.

It was after dark and he was exhausted from the twelve-mile walk. The bed looked inviting, but so did his purchases.

He was outside sipping steaming coffee and enjoying the aroma of sizzling bacon when a heavily accented and exhausted voice croaked from the dark, "Hello, the camp!"

Mason tensed. His flintlock pistol was some ten paces away in the hut. But then the stranger was hit with a brutal coughing fit. Mason used the distraction to step away from the firelight and into the black. Moments later he returned with the flintlock. The stranger was still hacking away. After the coughing quieted, Mason called out: "How many?"

"Just I, sir! Semyon Mikhailevich Akhrosimov! And I can assure you I am alone, sir—unless you wish to consider the company of this godforsaken mule."

"Come on, then. There's coffee and bacon."

If Semyon Mikhailevich Akhrosimov wasn't so obviously near death, his presentation would have been comical: while trying to remain straight-backed and dignified, the sick man bounced atop a truculent mule with no saddle. One bony hand held tight to the reins and the other held a dented top hat in place. The ensemble was completed with a dusty, oversized black suit that included a vest and string tie. Swimming in all that black cloth was the withered body of a man who looked to be about forty and had no chance of reaching forty-one.

The man's face was sweaty and yellow with death. Mason had seen the ravages of consumption before, but never like this—at least not outside of a casket. The exertion required to dismount the mule gave the visitor another coughing fit.

The sick man coughed and coughed until his legs trembled. Mason jammed the flintlock in his belt and eased his guest to sit on the ground. There the stranger gasped and hacked into a piece of ragged cloth already stained with blood. Then he caught his breath just long enough to express some sarcasm: "Just a moment, kind sir, while I inhale the miracle desert air my esteemed doctor assured me—" the coughing returned.

Mason retrieved a blanket and water from the hut. He draped the blanket over the dying man's shoulders like a cape. A few sips from the canteen allowed Semyon Mikhailevich Akhrosimov to gather himself.

"It's a noble kindness you've shown this weary stranger."

"Don't talk, mister. I'll take care of your animal."

"Ach," said Semyon Mikhailevich Akhrosimov, "shoot the cursed beast and I will repay you the price of the bullet."

2

After Mason had fed, watered, and hobbled the mule, he returned to find his guest near the fire stretched out on his side and propped up on an elbow. His free hand poured whiskey from a silver flask into a cup of coffee that sat on the ground.

"I do hope you don't mind me helping myself," he said, referring to the coffee.

"Nope," Mason replied and picked up the canteen. "There's bacon."

"Your coffee is generous enough," he said and offered Mason the flask. Mason thanked the stranger, and instead took a long pull from the canteen.

"Out there in the dark," Mason said, wiping water from his mouth with the back of his hand, "what was that name of yours you called out?"

The visitor smiled, and like a conductor about to go to work, he lifted his hand in the air and flicked the silver flask to and fro to the beat of each syllable: "Sem-yon Mik-hail-ev-ich Ak-hros-i-mov. But since we are about to become very good friends, you and I, you may call me Simon."

"You sound Russian."

"American, sir. One hundred percent American. Born and bred. It was my parents who escaped the brutality of serfdom under Alexander the First. And it was here, in this great country, where they turned swampland into a thriving ranch and left it to a worthless son who squandered it on roulette and young whores."

The speech cost Simon his wind. He replaced it with raspy breaths. Then he coughed a few times into his cloth, downed some more whiskey from his flask, and gathered himself enough to offer Mason a rakish grin.

Mason responded, diagnosing him. "Consumption. Pretty far along."

Simon's grin remained, but sad eyes and a small nod confirmed his tragedy.

From the oversized clothes and all the loose skin hanging from his jowls, Mason guessed the sickness had melted at least fifty pounds of robust living from this man.

"I am dying, Joshua Mason. Which is why I followed you—" Suddenly, a wet cough fired out of Simon's mouth. Mason heard a spray of blood sizzle when it hit the fire.

Simon got to his knees and hacked away, until all pretense of dignity disappeared. He bent over and the top hat tumbled from his head. The flask fell from his hands. He coughed and moaned and coughed some more, all the while holding onto himself as though the coughing might break him apart. This went on until he toppled over unconscious.

Mason carried his guest into the hut, laid him on the bed, and wondered why the stranger's name sounded familiar. Then he wondered why, so near death, the stranger had ridden all this way.

While spreading out a blanket for himself on the floor, Mason put those wonders aside. He'd met all kinds of Russians over the years, all kinds of people. Names tended to blend together after a while.

3

Early the following morning, Mason was awakened on the floor by Simon's coughs. He sat up to find his new roommate lying in bed lighting a freshly rolled cigarette.

"I see you live life on your own terms," said Mason as he stood and folded his blanket.

"Is there any other way, sir?" replied Simon. Then he took a puff, and began hacking away.

Mason could only chuckle at the man's stubbornness.

Still coughing, Simon pulled the cigarette from his mouth and offered it to his host. Mason gently eased the folded blanket behind Simon's head to prop him up, accepted the smoke, took a couple of satisfying puffs, and let it hang from his lips.

"A vicarious smoke is better than none," Simon said with an edge of self-pity.

"You gonna want some coffee?" asked Mason before he stepped outside.

Shivering, Simon pulled the blanket up to his chin and said nothing.

4

The coffee was just boiling when Simon, trembling and wrapped in a blanket, shuffled out of the hut. He would not have made the last few paces without Mason's help.

"You should stay in bed, friend," said Mason.

"If you're going to allow me to die, sir, allow me to die beside the warmth of a fire."

Mason eased his guest to the ground and then retrieved a pillow for his head. Then he lifted a lid to check on the biscuits, poured coffee, and offered his guest the cup.

Simon didn't respond. He stared at something beyond the desert as his ravaged lungs rasped and wheezed.

Nothing was said for a long while, not until the biscuits were brown and removed from the flame.

Mason broke the silence. "You know my name," he said.

Still lying on the ground, Simon kept his eyes locked on the horizon. "When I was a boy, Joshua Mason, you died in my bed. My father dug your grave. My mother spoke prayers over you."

"You're feverish," said Mason. "I'll fetch you some water just as—"

Simon cut in: "I suspect that to a man like yourself, it was not so long ago." He downed the last of his whiskey and turned to look at Mason with the soft eyes of remembrance. "I was a child then, ten or eleven, and Joshua Mason was in my father's employ clearing the swampland in Alabama that would become the ranch I would lose with the unjust bounce of a white ball. Yes, you died in my bed. A terrible death. Unforgettable. My father laid you there after you stepped into a nest of water moccasins. Thirty years later, I am lying in my own deathbed, a filthy cot in the back of a trading post run by a greedy pig waiting for me to die so he can steal my clothes and feed my naked corpse to the coyotes. And then, in answer to a prayer I did not make, I hear your voice—I am very good at remembering voices. I peer through the curtain and there you are, alive and unchanged. I rub my eyes. 'This cannot be true,' I tell myself. But there *you* are. An angel? The Devil? I care not who you are in league with. I refuse to die on a filthy cot from a disease given to me by a fifteen-year-old whore. She was a beautiful whore, I must say. A lovely Polish girl. Stefania. And in that regard, I have no regret. But after catching her condition from a railroad worker, Stefania grew bitter and told no one of her illness until it was too late.... Until many of us were doomed. She doomed even those like myself who were kind to her, who were gentle and brought her small gifts. She's dead now, Stefania...poor little Stefania.... Although still unsure I was not deluded by fever, I removed myself from that deathbed, stole that dreadful mule you must promise me to shoot, and followed you here. And very soon after, I *was* sure. Here you are. *You.* Joshua Mason. Who else could you be? You answer to 'Joshua Mason,' and although you correctly diagnose my condition, you still risk a terrible death carrying me, giving me your bed, sharing a canteen, and finally, accepting a cigarette that has just touched my consumptive lips."

Finished making his case, Simon rolled over and gave his back to Mason. There was no sound other than the terrible wheezing.

Without a word Mason stood, grabbed the canteen, and walked away.

Exhausted from his monologue, Simon fell into a deep sleep.

5

When Simon woke, it was night, the stars shone like diamonds, and he was warm—warmer than he'd felt in many weeks. With some effort, he managed to roll himself over and found Mason a few feet away stoking an oversized fire. The dying man tried to sit up. He didn't have the strength. His smile was just as weak. "You are a good man, Joshua Mason. I am warm."

"And the water's cold," Mason said. Then he snatched up the canteen, pulled its cork, and knelt so Simon could drink. The water made the sick man cough some. Mason wiped his visitor's mouth with a cloth, sat down next to him, and absently poked at the fire for a while. Then he said, "If I could give you more time, Simon, more years, I would."

Simon nodded a little. "So you can only save yourself from death, ah? Not Semyon Mikhailevich Akhrosimov?"

"No, I could save you. I could. But I won't. Not you. Not anyone. Not ever."

Simon coughed a few times, but the strength had now left even his cough.

"I see," was all he said.

"A good man who cannot die, who lives forever, is cursed," said Mason. "And an evil man who cannot die is a curse on everyone else."

"And you are a good man, Joshua Mason?"

"No...no, I'm not. I'm both cursed and a curse, so I keep to myself."

"I see," Simon repeated.

Then Mason turned to his guest and said, "But I won't steal your suit of clothes, Semyon Mikhailevich Akhrosimov. And I promise the coyotes won't get to you. And if you ask me to, I'll speak prayers over your grave."

Simon's rakish grin returned. "And you will shoot that mule?"

Mason closed his eyes and let out a laugh, something he'd not done in a long time.

PART ONE

THE LOVE STORIES

Mason

1

In the busy parking lot of a Starbucks still celebrating its grand opening, Joshua Mason leaned against the sun-bleached hood of his pickup truck as the world did what it always did: went about the business of not noticing him.

There was nothing to notice. Guys like Mason were scattered all over Southern Arizona: lean, late-fortyish, brown skin, dark eyes, scuffed cowboy boots...

If people noticed anything, it was his 1981 Chevy pickup, which looked as weathered and used up as he did.

Beneath a low sun that promised a blistering day, Mason stared at a tall hospital building directly across a road choked with four lanes of morning commuters. Only, he wasn't staring at the building. Not really. In his mind's eye, he was sitting quietly with Doreen while she slept.

This daily ritual gave him some comfort. Not much, some. Enough to make the thirty-five-mile trip worthwhile.

Although he was early today, Mason still hoped Doreen would sense he was out here. The last time he'd seen her was two weeks ago, on that inevitable day when she'd told him he could never come back. He'd known that day was coming, and when it did, he promised to be outside her window every day at noon. She declared the idea silly, but did so in that way only a wife can—in that way that said she still saw her husband as the impulsive young man who'd won her heart.

The idea wasn't silly to her, not at all.

A noon visit wasn't possible today. Mason was expected in Las Vegas before dark and it took most of a day to get there.

2

Vegas was necessary because Doreen's dying hadn't changed their money situation, hadn't changed the fact that the Rebel Yell, their rundown little motel in the middle of nowhere, was operating deep in the red—a fact that had to be kept hidden from Charlie.

Charlie was Doreen's thirty-six-year-old grandson. At age seven, he'd been forever brain-damaged in a terrible car accident after Charlie's father—who was high on acid and died instantly—deliberately drove into the oncoming headlights of a dump truck. Also killed was Charlie's mother, Doreen's daughter Maya.

Charlie's brain damage was so extensive it halted his ability to mature. He still hasn't matured. Not by a single day. Mentally and emotionally, twenty-nine years later, Charlie remained a seven-year-old with a terrible stutter encased in a grown man's body.

Through his marriage to Doreen, Mason became Charlie's step-grandfather, but the marriage has been kept secret—even from Charlie.

The secret marriage meant that to the rest of the world, Mason was just another one of the faceless handymen Doreen had hired over four decades. The truth, though, was that there was only ever one handyman: Mason. To know that, you'd have to notice him. But no one did, and that was how he wanted it.

3

Mason was off to Vegas to make some desperately needed cash. Not at the craps tables or roulette. What he was about to lay down was something more than money.

From Vegas, he would be taken someplace else. He didn't know where, only that it would be a place where the rich and powerful play... those rich and powerful enough to cough up $50,000 for the privilege of murdering him using whatever method entertained them most.

The All at Once

1

Mason guided his exhausted pickup through that part of the desert where there were no problems, just two lanes of blacktop with government barbed wire hanging on either side. Here the world remained the same: endless miles of wasteland unchanged since the beginning. But then, as though his vehicle were a time machine barreling towards the future, he'd suddenly find himself in a town or city, and there it sat, the suffocating banality of contemporary life, a world filled with sameness and surveillance.

Mason used to enjoy driving through the desert. Its timelessness calmed him, anchored him. The desert had always been his home. He was here before the Americans, before the Navajo and Apache, even before the Aztecs. But these days, nothing calmed him, not with Doreen's dying digging a hole in his guts.

Still, if he couldn't be with her, couldn't visit her, if he couldn't even stand across the street at noon in the parking lot of that stupid Starbucks, driving through the desert was something. A little something.

2

Although it always found its way back to her, the drive gave his mind a chance to meander and enjoy refuge in thinking through troubles that hadn't yet arrived, but would. Although the stakes were as real as Doreen's old age and cancer, puzzling out how he'd continue to survive in a future rapidly closing in on him, distracted and even intrigued him.

The modern world had arrived so quickly it caught Mason unprepared. For thousands of years, human civilization hardly advanced, and then—just like *that*—it was bursting with marvels that would've been labeled science fiction or witchcraft only a generation before.

Mason didn't have a name for this explosion of wonderment, this era of modernity that suddenly arrived and then hit light-speed, but if he did, he might've called it the *All at Once*.

3

Mason had seen more change in the last hundred years, maybe even the last fifty, than all the previous years combined. Millennium after millennium of almost no change and then *all at once*, the world was choking on neon, asphalt, rock 'n' roll, super highways, satellites, mass media, plasma TVs, Roombas, and iPhones.

For thousands of years, fire lit the dark and animals provided transportation, and then *all at once*, there was electricity, automobiles, computers, internet, drones, Netflix, air travel, laser surgery, smart weapons, and skyscrapers.

Mason could hardly comprehend how it came about so quickly, how in such a short period this society went from worrying about harvesting enough to eat to thinking nothing of whole establishments devoted to selling only ice cream, chicken, pizza, bagels, donuts....

The bounty.

4

Back in the early '90s, right around the time Charlie came to live with them, local flooding left a woman named Connie Shields and her children homeless. Until the government found them a new place, state vouchers covered their stay at the Rebel Yell.

Being on welfare all her adult life embarrassed Connie, so she'd buried that shame the only way she knew how: by convincing herself the world had singled her out for indignities.

"Can't believe they're making me live in this shitbox," she'd snort whenever Mason passed within earshot, something he couldn't avoid with her always sitting outside puffing on a Lucky Strike.

Seemed like every day she had a new complaint. One time it was the air conditioning. Another time it was the mattress. One day she berated him over the weather, which he had no control over.

The final time she lashed out was the day he stopped holding his tongue. "You got cable TV, plenty to eat, clothes everywhere, even a swimming pool," Mason said to her. "What's enough?"

He hadn't said it to be mean or even to argue. It was just that this society's stubborn refusal to appreciate the bounty bewildered him. He hoped some perspective might make her feel better about her situation. But all he got in return was a death stare—which she held onto as she dropped her smoke, stubbed it out with a slippered toe, and strolled over to the office to complain about the uppity handyman.

Doreen assured her she would have a word with him.

Boy, they had themselves a good laugh over that one.

Keeping the marriage secret was difficult, but sometimes things happened that made that secret kinda special, something all their own.

The two of them stole away as many nights as they could. Those nights became fewer after Charlie came to live with them.

5

The door behind the motel's front desk gave way to the small apartment Doreen shared with Charlie. Mason lived in Room 14, the room at the end of a tired row of fourteen rooms.

Room 14. That was the one she'd given him the night they met.

Mason realized he was thinking of Doreen again.

Driving through the desert helped, just not much.

Doreen

1

Three months ago, seventy-seven-year-old Doreen was told she had three months to live. After receiving this death sentence, Doreen's mind turned to her Aunt Patsy.

Everyone liked Doreen's father. He'd been a handsome, charming, successful corporate attorney—also a hopeless gambler. Doreen was only ten when she saw him for the final time.

Doreen's mother might've survived her husband's death, but the fact he'd disappeared—the not knowing—was too much. Doreen was only eleven when she saw her mother for the final time, in a bathtub.

What happened next remained a bit of a haze. Doreen had never met Patsy, her mother's older half-sister, but by way of familial machinations she took no part in, Doreen was sent to live with her.

Goodbye, Connecticut.

Hello, Arkansas.

2

Doreen would never understand why her aunt agreed to take her in. Patsy was never cruel, just indifferent, and seemed to tolerate her orphaned niece as though she were a lodger.

Aunt Patsy didn't work—didn't do much of anything. She'd won a small house and a pile of alimony by way of a bitter divorce. Afterward, she decided real life wasn't for her anymore and cocooned herself with a TV and homemade baked goods. From morning to night, year after year,

Patsy sat on a plastic-covered couch devouring pastries and what she called "her stories": soap operas, sitcoms, detective shows, Westerns....

Artificial comfort is still comfort.

Doreen hadn't been unhappy. She was fed, clothed, even received an allowance. Her aunt simply didn't care. Not about Doreen's grades (which were pretty good), how late she stayed out (never late), or who she stayed out with (boys would come after high school, when Doreen's baby fat melted away).

3

The final time Doreen *spoke* to her aunt was the day she left for college. Aunt Patsy gave her a peck on the cheek, a check for one hundred dollars, and never took her eyes off a *Father Knows Best* rerun.

The final time Doreen *saw* her aunt was two decades later. There Patsy lay dying of colon cancer in a god-awful hospital room with pea-green walls. Patsy wasn't watching TV, not anymore. Instead, her artificial comfort came from morphine, a sight that outraged Doreen— the very idea of wasting life's final moments in a drug-induced stupor.

And this was why, after receiving her own death sentence, Doreen's mind fritzed out and hopped through every moment of her life before landing on the memory of Aunt Patsy, lost in that morphine haze.

4

Here on her deathbed in the hospice wing of the Santa Cruz County Hospital, Doreen's lifespan was no longer measured in months or weeks. It was measured in days, perhaps hours. Nevertheless, until the pain became so agonizing it threatened to cloud her mind as much as the morphine, she refused to press the button that delivered the narcotic. Instead, she was determined to live every moment of life she had left, to honor her past by remembering it, and to honor God by praying with a lucid mind.

It was Doreen's fear of God that kept her sane. She couldn't imagine facing death without this fear. Without it, she would dive into a vat of morphine. Those without faith would never understand the comfort and peace that came with a terrible fear of God.

Mason, her husband of some thirty-five years, surely didn't.

5

Doreen found Christ in a tired, old church during those dark days just after Rodrigo, her first husband, abandoned her and their baby daughter Maya.

It was then when Doreen came to understand that the only way to gain acceptance into Heaven was through *belief* in God. The Bible made it clear good deeds and repentance weren't enough. You must *believe*.

For decades this knowledge brought her only stress and agony. Every doubt about God's existence—and there were many—came with the paralyzing fear this doubt would send her to Hell. And then one day, not long after her seventieth birthday, the most significant breakthrough of her spiritual life came to her. She realized her fear of God was *itself* proof, not only of her faith, but that her faith was instinctual and came from a place deep down inside.

If I didn't believe in God, she reasoned, *I wouldn't fear* not *believing in Him.*

To Doreen, it was that simple, and this comforted her like nothing else.

There was comfort too in Mason, in the angel God had sent her. Mason would always protect Charlie, her only grandchild. If that weren't the case, if she were leaving Charlie to an uncertain future, there'd be no hope for a peaceful death. The thought of any harm coming to Charlie, of his innocence being shattered or even pricked, was a thought as intolerable to Doreen as Hell itself.

6

Loving Mason had been both easy and not. There was nothing easy about growing old while your husband remained the same age, remained young and virile. Doreen had her vanity—a woman's vanity—and things became especially difficult after she arrived at that place beyond growing old, to that place where she *was old*.

Even so, she understood that was a small price to pay for the love of a good man and the knowledge that Charlie *will always be protect—will be—will alwa—aw—*

She could feel the cancer now, the rot.

The pain was all-consuming. It slashed away at her insides and derailed her train of thought.

She had no choice now but to press the button, so she did, and the serene warmth of the narcotic immediately marched to her pleasure sensors.

She surrendered to it, closed her eyes and drifted on it.

God will understand, she told herself. *God loves me. God brought me Mason. Maya was still alive then. My Maya.... The accident hadn't yet killed her or damaged Charlie's brain. Everything was just about to fall apart...and just in time, there he was, looking for a room in the middle of the night. No suitcase, only those saddlebags filled with books—like a cowboy out of one of Aunt Patsy's Westerns. He was so handsome and sexy. And he was nice—nice and gentle like a man should be.... Like Mr. Arthur was.... An angel....*

7

Time vaporized into a cloud and hovered beside her like a lover. Together, she and time prepared to drift beyond the sterile stench of noisy hospices, beyond the wrinkle in a bed sheet that would've given her a bedsore had she lived to see tomorrow.

Over the times of her life she would drift, through the good and the bad....

The Rebel Yell

1

Even at its inception, the Rebel Yell Motel was nothing special: a single strip of fourteen rooms with an attached office and manager's apartment. It sat all alone in the middle of a desert thirty-five miles north of the Mexican border and twenty miles from anything that might pass as a town.

Originally called the Sleep-Inn, the Rebel Yell was built in 1928. The All at Once was just getting started then, so there were no hotel or motel chains, just what were called motor inns and roadhouses. Most were owned by individual proprietors.

Those driving along the single lane Highway 661, which was then a well-traveled artery between Rio Rico and Tucson, would come upon the Sleep-Inn and the restaurant next door.

Both establishments had the misfortune of launching a few months prior to the market crash of '29. The restaurant went bankrupt in '31 and the owner, an otherwise honest man with a large family, burned it down for the insurance money. He was never caught.

Between 1933 and the end of World War II, the Sleep-Inn closed and reopened four times under four different owners.

It was Benito and Marina Medina, the parents of Doreen's first husband, who changed the motel's name to the Rebel Yell.

2

Although born in Mexico, Benito obtained legal entry into America during the war and earned a Purple Heart machine-gunning Nazis for Uncle Sam in Europe.

Benito loved America. Even more, he loved being an *American*.

After his honorable discharge, he was granted citizenship, married his high school sweetheart, and purchased the shuttered Sleep-Inn for the price of the back taxes.

To prove how American he was, Benito changed the motel's name to the Rebel Yell and decorated the office with American and Confederate flags, along with photos of Robert E. Lee, Ulysses S. Grant, and his own personal hero, Emiliano Zapata. This was his way of saying, *There's room for everyone in America* and to disarm those suspicious of immigrants with shaky English.

It worked. One look around, and a smile would creep across the face of even the hardest of men. "You're alright with me," that smile said.

Benito and Marina worked eighteen-hour days and their only time off came with the births of their five children. Rodrigo was the youngest.

All that dedication combined with the post-war boom and America's exploding car culture allowed the Medinas to comfortably retire in the late '60s. This was just after Rodrigo graduated college and brought home his new bride: a pregnant Doreen, fresh with her own degree in Hospitality Management.

3

Rodrigo and Doreen had taken over the Rebel Yell with the idea of someday purchasing it outright from his parents. The plan didn't last two years. Just after Maya was born, Doreen discovered she'd done what too many young women do: married a version of her father, a handsome charmer with no sense of family or responsibility.

Doreen had also married too young. Rodrigo was the first boy to stir her up sexually and the marriage ensured she would never have to return to Aunt Patsy's indifference.

She'd loved Rodrigo. She really had. It had taken effort, sure, but she'd loved him. Even more, she loved the idea of running his parents' motel. That was all she'd ever wanted—a place where families came to make memories.

It was true that she'd never respected Rodrigo. He was lazy, arrogant, and a bit of a peacock. He sure was sexy, though. Problem was—he knew it. Still, she'd never tried to change him. Figured he'd grow up as they grew old, and convinced herself there was a fine man in there and that time would keep whittling away until he stepped out.

Then he up and left. Just like that. No anger, no fights, no resentment, no warning. *Don't hate you,* he said. *It's not another woman. I just want out.*

This second helping of indifference exploded her all over the place. The little pieces were everywhere.

Rodrigo ran off to California and the bank repossessed the Rebel Yell. Her in-laws stayed in touch and offered to help, but Miami was a long way from Arizona and Doreen couldn't bring herself to ask for money.

After the foreclosure, she was forced to rent a room in a boarding house on Dankworth Road just off Route 202.

"Bathroom's down the hall," the landlady told her.

4

The shame Doreen felt applying for welfare wouldn't allow her to finish the application. With Maya in her arms, she walked out and wandered around Browning's small downtown until exhaustion and heat drained her of that pride. She was on her way back to finish the application when she came upon the Church of the Holy Mother and its wide-open doors. She needed to sit down out of the sun, so she went inside.

The place was cool, dark, and empty; not a soul in it. The sanctuary was small, worn out, right on the edge of used up: eight wooden pews going up one side, eight going down the other; white plaster walls, wobbly ceiling fans, plain wood floor....

Seated in a back pew feeling like a trespasser, Doreen was satisfied just being out of the heat. But, when she peered down at her sleeping child, at fragile little Maya, despair arrived.

Tears streamed down her face, and since she didn't have a better idea, she decided this might be a good place to give prayer a try. She'd never prayed before, or even thought much about God. So she swallowed her pride to do something she'd not done before: ask for help. She admitted she didn't know what kind of help to ask God for, so she asked if He could figure that out for her.

Praying in this clumsy way embarrassed her, made her feel small and silly.

She did it anyway.

Over time, prayer would come to feel like settling into a warm bath. But that time was a long ways off.

By the time she left the church, Maya was hungry, the welfare office was closed, and Doreen's head felt like an unmade bed.

5

There was no place in the tiny rented room for a crib, so Doreen pushed the bed into a corner and used pillows to make a sleeping spot for the baby. After Maya was fed, Doreen stretched out next to her in the dark, sipped a can of beer, and began to sort through everything wrong in her life.

The beer was nearly drained before she was able to stop feeling sorry for herself and zero in on the real problem: she couldn't afford to work *and* pay for daycare.

Sure, she could tread water on welfare or look for a man to bail her out. She could also lay down and die. There was no shortage of bad ideas.

She was chuckling over the hopelessness of her dilemma and wishing she'd picked up a second can of beer when she was hit with the idea of getting a job *at* a daycare center.

The one that hired her was right on Highway 661, about three miles past the Rebel Yell. Coming and going, there it sat, a monument to Doreen's failure as a wife and businesswoman.

After months of driving past this taunt twice a day, Doreen decided she'd have to live with being a failed wife, but not a failed businesswoman.

6

So it wouldn't fall into disrepair, Doreen convinced the bank to allow her to move into the motel as its caretaker. After that, all of her daycare earnings went into fixing the place up.

Come hell or high water, she was determined to repurchase the Rebel Yell and make a go of it.

A couple years later, her luck took a turn when she landed a good-paying job as the night manager of Monument Resorts, an upscale hotel on the outskirts of Tucson that had just gone national. The hotel allowed Maya, who'd just turned three, to sleep in the back office.

At night, Doreen managed someone else's hotel. During the day, she willed the Rebel Yell back to life. You should've seen the look on the bank's face when she walked in and made a serious offer to buy it back.

After the deal closed, her work had just begun, and so had the good years.

Those years would be so good that even as she lived them, Doreen would sometimes stop right where she was and take a long look around so she'd always remember.

No one had ever told her that remembering the good times made the bad times worse.

Charlie

1

The welder's gloves worked perfect. Made of thick leather, they nearly reached Charlie's elbows. As Misty struggled, slashing away with her sharp claws, she didn't leave a mark on him.

Charlie held tight until the terrified cat went limp. Then, filled with childish excitement, Charlie held the dead animal by its neck in one hand and shook the glove off the other. He then transferred the dead cat to his bare hand and shook off the remaining glove.

The next part was his favorite.

With both hands now bare, Charlie squeezed the cat's neck until he felt it...*give.*

He lifted Misty's lifeless body and looked into her eyes, into the void *he put there.* This filled him with a sense of superiority.

Charlie was so happy with his accomplishment, he skipped in a circle and whipped the dead cat around like a Fourth of July sparkler. He liked knowing he had the power to do whatever he wanted to Misty, the name he'd given her last week. Naming the animals made the kill more personal, more rewarding.

2

Misty was one of the countless strays that made their way out of the desert to the Rebel Yell looking for water and someone to trust. Charlie was well-practiced at earning that trust and then betraying it.

And for a time, Misty did have a loving home, warm bed, and saucers of milk. She'd been purring and rubbing a figure eight around Charlie's legs when he suddenly stuffed her in a sack and tore out the back of the Rebel Yell deep into the desert, to *his den.*

3

Charlie adjusted the thick, horn-rimmed glasses that had slid down his sweaty nose and dropped Misty's slack body into a ghoulish pile of kills. The dead animals—primarily dogs and cats mixed with the occasional desert creature—were sacrifices to Charlie's rage, something that had been expanding within him ever since he realized he was trapped inside of a *fat fucking retard.*

4

After the car accident killed Charlie's mother and father and mangled Charlie's brain, Doreen maxed out every credit card she could get her hands on to take Charlie to the country's top experts.

The verdict was always the same: the damage was permanent. Those parts of Charlie's brain that controlled reasoning, problem-solving, decision making, and personality would never heal. This meant Charlie would never mature. His ability to learn and to develop emotionally had been destroyed forever.

"Developmental incapacity," they called it, and so, twenty-nine years later, Charlie still had the mentality of a seven-year-old—only now it was entombed in the tubby, bespectacled body of a thirty-six-year-old man in frequent need of a shave and shower.

5

What the doctors failed to foresee was what happened after Charlie turned fourteen. This was when something in the unsolvable mystery of the brain winked open and took a good, long look around.

This wink was a spark of self-awareness. Charlie was suddenly aware of the fact he was mentally disabled. Before that, you would've described him as innocent, happy-go-lucky, forever seven, and blissfully unaware of his disability or how the outside world saw him.

Then he wasn't.

This self-awareness initially seemed like it might be a solution. Now that Charlie knew there was something wrong with him, he could work on improving himself—*except, he couldn't.*

No matter how much he struggled, nothing improved and he could only watch helplessly as everything came out of him in the bumbling, stuttering *blah, blah, blah* of an overexcited seven-year-old, of a *fat fucking retard,* which was how he came to see himself.

No matter how long he stared at a book written above a second-grade level, he couldn't comprehend it. Worst of all, *he knew* he couldn't.

No matter how much he concentrated, something as simple as replacing a faucet washer was beyond him, and *he knew* it was beyond him.

Charlie was mentally disabled and *aware* he was mentally disabled, and when you mixed that tragedy with all the psychological and chemical complications that come with puberty, the result was toxic.

Charlie once saw a movie where a man fell into a covered swimming pool. The more this man struggled, the more he got tangled and trapped. That was how Charlie felt in his disabled brain: trapped, suffocating, and forever drowning. Only his pool was filled with black oil.

At first, that wink of self-awareness frustrated him. Then it depressed him. Now it had turned to rage, and Charlie's rage was blacker than the oil.

6

Charlie was fifteen the first time he killed—his own dog, Wolfie. The pup had been a birthday gift. Charlie had named him after Wolverine, his favorite comic book character. He loved Wolfie. He loved strangling Wolfie even more. Killing soothed the intolerable frustration and rage, and mollified the self-hate...at least for a while.

Murder was an act that hit Charlie's sweet spot. Killing animals required a level of cunning and it was the one thing he could execute in the precise way he visualized it. Strangling a cat or dog never came out in *blah, blah, blah.*

The *fat fucking retard* finally discovered something he was good at.

Most of all, outsmarting the animal and stealing its life force satisfied Charlie's need to feel special, which came from a sense of entitlement that was itself downstream from a raging current of self-pity mixed with victimhood.

Like any seven-year-old, Charlie was efficient at lying and not getting caught. He knew the difference between right and wrong, so he concealed his wrongdoing from his Grandma Dory and Mason. All they saw was a thirty-six-year-old good boy who did his chores, brushed his teeth, and didn't argue too much over bedtime.

Bamboozling them was part of the thrill that made him feel superior.

7

With Misty already forgotten and his rage temporarily soothed, Charlie strolled back to the Rebel Yell feeling sunny about things.

Mason was away on one of his work trips and wouldn't return until later tonight or tomorrow. Grandma Dory was in the hospital preparing to go to Heaven. So, today, Charlie was running the place, the whole operation. It even said so on the badge pinned to his wrinkled shirt: *Charlie Breslin: General Manager.* He was good at it, too. Sure, he struggled with credit card payments—*stupid machine*—and any repairs that required more than a plunger had to wait for Mason. But that was Mason's job. He was the handyman. He reported to Charlie.

Much of Charlie's rage was caused by Mason. Not that Mason treated him wrong or anything. Mason loved Charlie and Charlie loved Mason. Heck, Charlie loved Mason almost as much as he loved Grandma Dory— and he loved Grandma Dory a whole lot. Charlie would someday like to *be* Mason: a capable, confident, easygoing guy who could fix anything, someone people like and respect. Yep, if Charlie could be anyone, he would be...well, his first choice would be Wolverine, and then Mason.

But sometimes Mason was so self-assured and competent, he made Charlie feel like a *fat fucking retard*, and sometimes Charlie resented that.

Sometimes he resented it a whole lot.

8

Still sated from strangling Misty, Charlie stood behind the motel's front desk feeling every inch the proprietor, the man in charge. This was *his* motel. Grandma Dory told him so. He knew that wasn't entirely true. She still vetoed a lot of his decisions. Like the licorice.

Charlie had wanted to advertise free licorice with every night's stay. Charlie loved licorice. If he ever had to choose a motel, he'd stay at the one that offered free Twizzlers.

Grandma Dory said no.

She said no a lot. But once she was in Heaven, there would be no one to say no to him. That meant things were going to change. He wouldn't be advertising Twizzlers. He loved his grandma and had no intention of defying her after she was gone. That wouldn't feel right. But there were other things he wanted to do that he'd never brought up because he knew she'd say no.

Mason couldn't say no. Mason worked for him. So after Grandma Dory went into the hospital, he had told Mason to reopen the swimming pool. That was why Mason was out on one of his business trips—to make money to repair the pool.

Another of Charlie's new ideas was already in full swing: the continental breakfast. On an old TV tray, in a corner of the office, sat a box of powdered donuts and warm pitcher of Hawaiian Punch. Charlie ended up consuming most of it.

The motel's sign needed repainting. He would start on that tonight. He wouldn't do a good job; Mason would make it right.

Then there was the website. Every motel needed a website. Out of frustration, Charlie had smashed two laptops trying to build that stupid website. Maybe he'll hire someone to do that.

9

As the proprietor of a crumbling motel in the middle of nowhere that averaged fewer than twenty guests a week, Charlie managed to keep himself busy. He patrolled the grounds every hour, wiped dust off the front desk with his sleeve, sharpened pencils, straightened stacks of scrap paper, and ate the continental breakfast.

There were only two customers today. He wanted to knock on their doors and ask if they needed anything, but his Grandma Dory had told him to stop doing that.

Instead, he snatched up a couple of donuts, shoved one in his mouth, and headed outside to pick up litter and make sure no marauders were lurking about.

10

Charlie strolled aimlessly around the motel grounds until he saw a candy bar wrapper. He picked it up and thought of his dad. His dad's favorite movie was about a boy who spent a day in a chocolate factory. Charlie was named after that boy, his dad had told him.

Sometimes Charlie hated his dad for killing his mom and mangling his brain, hated him more than anything. Other times, he missed him more than anything. He'd been a pretty cool dad until he ruined everything.

Charlie always missed his mom, even though she'd spent most of her time in the back bedroom and only came out to yell at him to be quiet. That was how it seemed, anyway.

They'd been dead a long time now, his mom and dad, a real long time. Charlie was just a little kid then. He remembered how they'd planned to go and see the new *Lethal Weapon* movie. That's how long ago it was.

11

Thinking of his past, of who he was before the car accident and the unfairness of it all, angered Charlie. So he turned around and headed for the garbage cans. That was where he left out food and water for all those poor, helpless animals that got lost in the desert.

It was never too early to start making a friend.

Valhalla

1

Mason slowed and pulled into a gas station. Outside, the sign said "Qwik-Shop." Inside was Valhalla, the mind-stopping miracle of a convenience store dropped right in the middle of a desert.

The door announced Mason's arrival with a pleasant *ding* and the cool, dry air instantly washed over him.

The air conditioning in Mason's pickup died a while back and was the one thing he hadn't repaired on a truck he'd kept running all these decades. There was a leak in the cooling unit and the Freon required for the 1981 cooling system had been outlawed long ago to save the planet or something. He could still get it, but only if he signed a bunch of government forms.

Government forms—one of the countless ways the All at Once found and tracked you.

Just like that, the world got computerized, everyone was assigned a number, and loaded into a central government databank to be labeled, cataloged, archived, and inventoried.

The digital age complicated Mason's life to no end.

2

Mason was in possession of the one thing this spoiled society didn't have, the one thing that those who have everything would still want more than anything else: immortality.

He didn't hold the secret to immortality and had no idea how it had happened to him. He found the whole thing confusing. But this ignorance wouldn't protect him, not in a world where people riot over a TV sale the day after something called "Thanksgiving."

So he remained hidden.

Prior to the All at Once, hiding had been easy. For centuries, he'd lived in what was now called the Sonoran Desert. That great expanse had belonged almost exclusively to him. After people arrived, he sometimes lived among them, first with the Indian tribes, then with the Americans whose government had wiped out those tribes. His only fear was someone noticing his agelessness, so he moved on every few years.

At one time or another, Mason had lived all over North America.

Life had been simple then. Drifting here to there, meeting different people, working various jobs, never becoming too attached to anyone or anyplace.... Those were good days. And he was never lonely.

He knew nothing of loneliness before Doreen.

Then the federal government confiscated much of the desert, called it a preserve, put up barbed wire, and sent out patrols. What the government didn't take got smothered in asphalt, office parks, and strip malls.

After that, the computers arrived, followed by a world where everyone carried a camera.

The All at Once, with its databases and social security numbers, with its fingerprinting and DNA, had relentlessly stalked Mason and now had him cornered in a crumbling motel that sat on a piece of land so barren and lonely, the wind and dust didn't bother to stop. They just blew on through looking for a better place to land.

3

Should I risk driving without a license or risk breaking the law to get one? Will Charlie someday notice I haven't aged, and how will a grown man with a seven-year-old mentality keep that secret?

Those were some of the problems Mason tried to work out on his long drives.

There were more problems, plenty more. Mason had a backup plan, a place to wait out this thing called Western Civilization—a safehouse. Nevertheless, he still signed nothing.

What if those Freon forms are scanned into a computer and eighty years from now I sign something else and the matching signatures are flagged?

Everything required to be in someone's name was in Doreen's name: bank accounts, deeds, insurance, license plates. After Doreen died, they would transfer over to Charlie.

Charlie could sign for the Freon, but what if someone discovered Charlie shouldn't be signing anything?

It made his head spin.

A mere hundred years ago, he didn't have to worry about any of this. Hell, thirty years ago, it was manageable. Now, even here in Valhalla, security cameras hovered like gargoyles, like snitches.

4

Mason had no credit or debit cards, so he didn't pay for gas at the pump, which was fine by him. Any excuse to enter Valhalla. *Good heavens, what a place....* Indoor plumbing, fluorescent lights, music piped in from somewhere, refrigeration, enough food and drink to carry a man for years, games of chance, and pre-rolled cigarettes.

Mason missed smoking more than anything. Doreen wouldn't allow it. Not around her and never around Charlie. She wasn't a hard woman, so he knew it mattered when she was firm on something.

Mason always gave himself time to walk Valhalla's aisles. *Look at all this stuff.* Most of all, he enjoyed the air conditioning. He dare not get used to it. Like everything else, like all civilizations, the All at Once and its conditioned air would someday disappear. Getting used to it would make him soft. He didn't turn it on in his room. Probably for the best it died in the pickup.

There was one exception: those times when he and Doreen snuck away. Then there was air conditioning and love-making and cold drinks and soft skin and hot showers and crisp sheets and intimate talks spoken in whisper and....

And all the roads of his mind led back to her.

5

"Yes, sir?" the cheery clerk asked as Mason approached the register. She was in her late fifties and her smile was no put-on.

Why would it be in Valhalla?

"Here's forty for pump six," he said, handing her the bills. "And I'll need a prepaid phone with international minutes."

"'International minutes,'" the clerk repeated with a wink in her voice as she searched the shelves behind her. "You must be a spy."

Mason told her the truth: "Overseas bank account."

She laughed, enjoying the most exotic moment of her day. The nametag said her name was "Angie."

Mason liked Angie. He liked all the world's Angies, those who appreciated the bounty.

If asked, Angie would probably say, *I don't know why; I guess I'm just a naturally cheerful person.*

That wasn't it. Angie and her unspoiled, everyday decency instinctively understood how good life was and appreciated it—appreciated what she had and didn't worry about what others had. She was what you'd call *good people*. There were plenty of good people in the All at Once. Mason knew that. He also knew they were losing ground to the not-so-good ones.

Vegas

1

Mason's trip through time reached its zenith in Vegas. *The bounty of bounties*. A city devoted to excess: casinos, showbiz, neon, hookers, restaurants, pawnshops, limos, and hoards of people all in a hurry to experience everything before they died.

What had been nothing but desert for millions of years was now a shiny, noisy, electrified Mecca of Want.

2

He'd been here before. This wasn't the first time Mason sold his life, not by a longshot. Things had been desperate for a while. It took money to build a safehouse and to hold onto the failed motel that served as Charlie's Potemkin existence.

Luckily for Mason, the bounty had made obsolete the very struggles that give one's life meaning. Everything came too easy in the All at Once. Men were hardwired to protect and provide for a family through problem solving. Then modernity solved all those problems. Women were hardwired to nurture a family. Then society told her to award that honor to daycare, schools, and electronic screens. Without a purpose, people began to wander. Some found meaning elsewhere. Too many went astray and lost themselves in self-worship and nihilism. So, yeah, there were plenty of buyers for the one thing Mason had left to sell.

Las Vegas was a key part of the deal he worked out with his buyers. Using black market software, Mason advertised his life on the Dark

Web with four conditions: 1) the price was $50,000, 2) the meet takes place in a hotel, 3) the buyer chooses the hotel, but 4) the hotel must be in Las Vegas.

Mason understood that someone willing to pay $50,000 to commit a cold-blooded murder was the most dangerous person in the world: someone with everything to lose and the resources to leave nothing to chance. Vegas was far enough away to keep Charlie and Doreen safe from a buyer paranoid about loose ends—but only temporarily. All Vegas could really do was slow down the hunt. With all the electronic footprints in the All at Once, there was no question a determined buyer would eventually find and kill Doreen and Charlie, and in the process, they might stumble across Mason's secret.

While Mason knew that not every buyer was a threat, it was a chance he'd never take. He killed them all.

3

With its two airports, multiple bus terminals, and countless parking garages, Vegas made it impossible for the buyer to monitor everything. If no one saw Mason arrive, no one could trace him back to where he'd started by way of a license plate or talkative cabbie.

And it was in one of those garages ten miles from the Strip where Mason parked his treasured pickup, Doreen's wedding gift to him.

At this point, the routine was the same: Mason separated the pickup's ignition key from the key ring and carefully emptied his pockets. Except for that key, the just-purchased burner phone, forty dollars in cash, and a hotel key card (mailed by the buyer to a post office box Mason would never use again), everything else was locked in the glove box.

Mason exited the truck, secured it, and hid the key in the parking garage. Before hailing a cab, he walked two miles so the driver couldn't connect him with the garage.

He further covered his tracks by having the cabbie drop him about a mile from the hotel.

Mason didn't mind the walk. If he could, he'd walk everywhere. Once, he had.

4

He entered the hotel's elevator, another modern miracle, a thing made entirely of glass.

You can see everything.

He pressed *12* and the doors closed, but before he could take in the view, the giant bubble leapt twelve stories in the air and immediately ordered him out.

He'd wanted to savor that view but was outvoted by a world in a hurry.

5

In front of Suite 1212's large double doors, Mason double-checked the key card. Scrawled on the back in black marker was "FOUR SEASONS 1212."

He was in the right place.

From here, he would use the alias "Mike Stark."

He paused a moment to gather himself, because once again he was about to pay the price for having never cared about money.

Making money was something he'd never considered. Too much hassle. Too much risk. Sure, had he opened a simple savings account a few hundred years back, he'd be a wealthy man today. He knew that now. He knew that then. But it had always been him alone.

Well, now he wasn't him alone. He had a wife, Charlie, a mortgage, responsibilities.... So he slid that card into the slot and the little red light on the locking mechanism switched to green.

Mason pushed open the door.

"Mike Stark" disappeared on the other side.

The door slammed shut.

6

In that empty hallway, the little green light switched back to red. And in that luxury room, Mason would unknowingly take the first step into the events that would bring about the end of the world.

Ernest

1

The morning of "Mike Stark's" arrival, Ernest showed up at the Las Vegas Four Seasons a few hours before check-in time.

The hotel accommodated him. When you're paying $2,700 a night for a suite, the hotel accommodates you.

Suite 1212 was everything Ernest had hoped for during his noisy, crowded coach flight from D.C. After tipping both bellboys for hanging up the suits, Ernest escorted them out, locked the double doors, and beheld the luxury: mammoth rooms, high ceilings, full bar, hot tub, fresh flowers, whole wall of windows, and one helluva view of the Strip.

"Fuck yeah," said Ernest as he kicked off his shoes.

2

The early flight hadn't been his idea. Ernest wasn't allowed to have ideas. Still, he'd been happy to be on it—thrilled, if you must know. Before this Mike Stark fella arrived, Ernest was determined to enjoy every minute of his time alone.

"Mike Stark" wouldn't be his real name. Ernest didn't care about that. It was none of his business. Besides, he had bigger things to worry about, like the grudge the universe held against him. He knew the universe would soon smite him, so he kept his focus on grabbing hold of life's pleasures while he could.

One pleasure he would *not* be grabbing hold of was the hotel's amenities: room service, pay-per-view, or that full bar. Like many wealthy and powerful men, Ernest's employer was petty and greedy and would personally scrutinize the bill (while smoking a two-hundred-dollar cigar). If so much as a candy bar was missing from the mini bar, Ernest would go to prison—not for stealing the candy bar, for something far worse.

That's why Ernest brought along his own candy bars: eighteen Almond Joys in a cooler loaded with Orange Gatorade. He also brought along his favorite movies and a laptop computer to watch them on.

Yes, for one blissful afternoon, and for the first time in months, Ernest would not be on 24/7 call to the Old Rich Prick—as he called him, but never out loud, not even when alone. With all the hidden and not-so-hidden cameras and microphones in the Old Rich Prick's world, were he to even whisper, *You old rich prick*, he'd die in prison.

This luxury suite sure wasn't for Ernest. Nope, it was for this Stark fella. You see, the Old Rich Prick believed that wowing his Sacrifices kept them calm. What's more, the only reason Ernest was set free so early today was to ensure a thorough search of the suite for electronic devices. After finishing that search, he was under strict orders not to leave the room for any reason. Well, that was fine by him. Ernest intended to settle into the luxury bed of this luxury suite, gorge himself on candy bars, and watch his favorite movies: *The Goonies*, *The Sandlot*, and *Stand by Me*.

Yes, for a few hours, Ernest would forget all about the universe, all about the horrors that were in store for this Mike Stark fella tonight, and his own dreaded role in those horrors.

It wasn't that Ernest was squeamish about body disposal. It was that he weighed 350 pounds, and body disposal was fucking exhausting.

3

Ernest was fifty-one years old, felt every day of it, and earned his living as the Old Rich Prick's "body man." This meant he drove the limo, ran the errands, killed people, got rid of bodies, and pulled down the Old Rich Prick's pants every morning to give that wrinkled, old pimply ass a shot of "vitamins" that were really amphetamines.

For his loyalty, Ernest received $100,000 a year plus room and board. His girth testified to the quality of the board. The room was lovely and large and located...right next to the Old Rich Prick's room.

"Ernest, goddammit, get the car!"

"Ernest, goddammit, where's my Viagra!"

"Ernest, goddammit, vodka tonic!"

Ernest, goddammit! rang in Ernest's ears. Sometimes he heard it when it wasn't shouted. Mostly it was.

The alternative was prison. No, the alternative was *death* in prison, and the Old Rich Prick never let him forget it.

"Murderers in prison murder child rapists in prison," the Old Rich Prick was fond of saying.

So Ernest did everything he was told, and every year—on the anniversary of the day the Old Rich Prick enslaved him with videos of his crimes—the Old Rich Prick wired $100,000 into Ernest's bank account.

Except for small expenditures, like Almond Joys, the money sat untouched. Ernest was a millionaire. Barely, but still: *a millionaire!* He could hardly believe it.

4

After the Old Rich Prick died, Ernest would be free *and* rich. Except he wouldn't be and he knew it. He knew the Old Rich Prick would double-cross him in death because the Old Rich Prick double-crossed everyone in life. Ernest knew, *just knew*, that after the Old Rich Prick croaked the videos of his crimes would be forwarded to the authorities. Ernest hadn't figured out what to do about that. He spent a lot of time thinking on it. Once, he'd even confronted the Old Rich Prick.

"Why would I betray you?" was the Old Rich Prick's response. "If people were to discover I employed a child buggerer, it would sully my legacy!"

Liar. The Old Rich Prick didn't care about his legacy or his family— which was comprised of one daughter: Anne, a woman who so unsettled Ernest he locked his door at night.

But now was not the time to cloud the mind with stresses and puzzles. Before the universe struck, before this "Mike Stark" fella showed up, Ernest would enjoy Almond Joys, Orange Gatorade, and a trilogy of movies starring young boys.

Stark

1

It was dusk when Mason entered Suite 1212.

In a winged-back chair, dressed impeccably in a dark business suit, sat an expressionless fat man. The only sign the fat man lived a life outside of one where he sat around in winged-back chairs waiting for people was his hair, which was still damp from a shower.

Mason found the presentation—complete with intertwined fingers settled on a mountainous belly—a little too mannered. *Posing for effect*, he thought. Not that it mattered. He had no intention of giving this cheesy Bond villain any trouble.

"I'm Stark," Mason said.

The fat man lifted himself from the chair.

2

This wasn't Ernest's first go-round with the Old Rich Prick's *Sacrifices*, as Ernest called them. The Old Rich Prick had already purchased five lives, so Ernest knew what to expect. These sorry bastards always showed up a real mess. Sometimes high as hell, sometimes bitter and resentful, always stressed, and *always* some combination of freaked the fuck out. That's why Ernest made sure to always present himself as *The Man You Don't Fuck With*.

The Sacrifices had to be *handled*, you see, and finding Ernest naked in bed singing "Stand by Me" made the wrong impression. So in plenty of time for "Mike Stark's" arrival, Ernest had picked up, showered, dressed, and sat waiting.

3

Mason was surprised by the fat man's physical grace. Despite his heft, in a single fluid motion, he'd effortlessly removed himself from the chair and approached with ease and confidence. He didn't offer to shake hands.

"Name's Ernest. I need to see your key card."

Mason handed over the card for inspection and Ernest compared it to his own, which also had "FOUR SEASONS 1212" written on the back in black marker. The writing matched and the fat man seemed to relax a little.

"Go ahead and empty your pockets on the desk," Ernest said. It wasn't an order—more matter-of-fact, like the two of them had an understanding. This surprised Mason. He'd expected more of that Bond villain shit—*If you would be so kind as to empty your pockets, Mr. Bond, we have had the desk brought in for your convenience*—and admonished himself for underestimating his host.

Mason emptied his pockets of the flip phone and the twelve bucks left over from the cab ride. Then Ernest impressed him again by conjuring a handheld metal detector, seemingly from nowhere. Then, like it was a religious ceremony, the fat man scrupulously passed it over every inch of Mason's body—twice. He then passed it over the former contents of Mason's pockets.

"You're good," the fat man said and returned to the winged-back chair, where he settled in and opened a laptop. He began typing and without looking up relayed a message: "You can still back out, pal. My employer won't hold it against you. But you have to decide now."

Mason didn't believe that, not after he'd seen the fat man's face. But even if it were true, his ticket was for the full ride.

"Didn't come all this way to turn myself around," said Mason.

Ernest grimaced. *Great, more body disposal.*

The only sound now was Ernest's typing.

Ta-tap-tap-ta-ta-ta-tap-tap-tap.

Mason patiently waited.

Tap-tap-tap-ta-tap-ta-ta-tap.

Tap-tap-tap-ta-tap-ta-ta-tap.

Without taking his eyes from the laptop, Ernest finally spoke: "Gimme your bank wire info."

Mason recited the routing and account numbers from memory. After a few keystrokes, Ernest slammed the laptop closed and announced: "Transfer's done. Now I need you to—"

Mason calmly lifted the "not-so-fast" finger on one hand and his burner phone with the other. "Gotta verify the transfer."

"Yeah, okay, pal. Just put it on speaker."

Mason hit the flip-phone's "on" button, and as it took its time to power up, the ensuing silence grew more and more awkward.

4

Ernest loathed silence. Silence made him think about things. He didn't want to think about things. Like before, when he'd been sitting in all that terrible quiet waiting for Stark. He hated that—where his thoughts went. But he still did it because that was the job, because *The Man You Don't Fuck With* doesn't sit around watching TV. Nope, *The Man You Don't Fuck With* sits in silence.

At home, Ernest kept the TV on. Always. Especially at night. All night. Even while he slept that TV was on, because the worst thoughts in the world come when you're just lying there in the dark.

So while the Sacrifice's fucking phone took its fucking time to warm the fuck up, Ernest started to think about his drunk old man and then killed those thoughts by pointing his chin at that wall of windows and their garish view of the Strip.

"Some town, huh?" asked Ernest.

"Yeah, some town," answered Stark.

The phone came to life.

The man Ernest knew as Stark punched in a phone number, activated the speaker as ordered, and placed the flip-phone on the desktop where it sat like a miniature deckchair. The bank announced itself after the first ring.

Ernest listened closely.

"I'm calling to verify my account recently received a fifty-thousand-dollar deposit," Stark said. "The account number is 568X-X8NE-9Q21."

The bank confirmed the wire.

"Okay, I want that total amount transferred into another account. Do you see the instructions I left earlier?"

The bank did.

"I'll hold until you confirm that transfer's complete."

It was at this point when Ernest realized Stark was talking to an offshore bank. He hadn't expected that and didn't like it.

5

Mason received his confirmation, said goodbye, and used both hands to twist and break the phone into two useless pieces of plastic. For an encore, he snapped the sim card in half with his thumbs.

Mason pointed to a pitcher of water. "Alright?" he asked.

Still seated, Ernest replied by pulling a pistol from somewhere and leveling its over-sized silencer at Mason's chest.

Mason scoffed. "Hey, like I said, I didn't—"

"No, you didn't," Ernest told him as he effortlessly rose from the chair. "Open that middle desk drawer."

Mason did. The only thing inside was a plastic capsule.

"Get your water and swallow that. Then we're *alright*."

With a shrug that said, *You're the boss*, Mason removed the hotel's fancy paper cover from a glass, poured two fingers of H2O, and drank it down with the capsule.

"Open wide," Ernest demanded with a flick of that big gun. Mason opened his mouth to prove he had indeed swallowed the capsule.

6

Now it was time for the *Point of No Return* speech.

"That capsule has a receiver in it," Ernest said, his voice firm and tight, "and somewhere on me is the transmitter. If you're ever more than twenty feet away, my transmitter blows open your capsule and the acid inside burns straight through your guts. So stay close, pal."

Ernest braced himself for the four-alarm freak out that always followed the *Point of No Return* speech, but Stark only narrowed his eyes and asked: "Is that bullshit, Ernest? Because that sounded like bullshit."

Before he could catch himself, Ernest chuckled and holstered the big gun inside his coat. *This guy's alright.*

Stark dropped the cell phone pieces into the pitcher's icy water and inquired, "Now what?"

Ernest answered with a stroll across the room, where he opened a large closet filled with dark suits.

"We have a couple hours before the flight," Ernest said. "Find one in your size, also shoes. There's a shaving kit in the bathroom."

Old Highway 661

1

Four years after losing it, twenty-nine-year-old Doreen Medina became the sole owner of the Rebel Yell Motel. She and five-year-old Maya moved into the manager's apartment and immediately went to work.

Doreen wanted to create a family place, so she added a playground and converted the garage into a gameroom with a pool table and pinball machines. Out back, and all on her own, she built a picnic area with grills, tables, and a volleyball court. In the office, she sold sandwiches and candy. She couldn't afford a liquor license, so she kept cold beers in a cooler for her regulars and charged them only a half-buck.

Families came.

Doreen herself was a selling point. She was polite, accommodating, had a sense of humor, and now that her chubbiness had melted away to reveal a lovely and mature woman, she attracted more than a few regulars—men who made a solitary living on the road.

She didn't mind when they flirted, or even when they made a pass. She could handle herself. Besides, they were lonely—not aggressive—and really only wanted the buzz that came from making a beautiful woman smile.

The wedding ring she still wore ensured no one's feelings were bruised.

The Rebel Yell became a flourishing getaway for working people and families; a place with station wagons in the parking lot, children yelling and splashing, and parents sunning themselves around the pool with one eye on the kids and the other on a magazine.

This was all Doreen had ever wanted, and although she would never make the connection, it was something she'd wanted ever since Mr. and Mrs. Arthur took her on that camping trip when she was a girl.

Best of all, it was just her and Maya, who was blossoming in Catholic school and who looked so beautiful in her First Communion dress, Doreen could hardly believe that was her child.

They were more than mother and daughter. They were girlfriends comfortable in each other's company. And as they teamed up to make beds, wash linens, scrub toilets, and check-in guests, the Rebel Yell belonged to them both.

Doreen's cup runneth over.

But real life doesn't stop at *happily ever after*. Real life keeps on keeping on....

The official notice the good times were over arrived in the mail.

2

The letter from the post office said, *This is a reminder your address will change at the beginning of the year*. Doreen knew what it meant: everything she'd worked for was about to be located on "Old Highway 661" instead of "Highway 661."

There'd been talk for years of the county widening the single lane 661 into two lanes. This notice meant the county had instead decided to build a brand new 661 somewhere else and that her 661—the artery that kept her business alive—was about to become a back road.

A little over a year later, the reality proved worse than the imagined. The new route was two miles away and the All at Once had stormed in with a cluster of chain hotels and a shopping mall, all built right on New Highway 661.

The Rebel Yell was now *out of the way* and *off the beaten path*. On top of that, the culture had changed. In the popular imagination, Rural America was no longer Mayberry. Instead, it was *Deliverance* and *Texas Chainsaw Massacre*.

No one at the Holiday Inn ever made you squeal like a pig.

3

Doreen hung on, barely. Families were replaced with bikers, transients, adulterers, and drug dealers. The Rebel Yell gained a reputation as a "rough place" and attracted a rough crowd.

Catholic school became an expense Doreen could no longer afford, and, after being enrolled in a public high school, Maya fell in with losers—including a boy three years older, a seventeen-year-old named Tate Breslin.

Under his influence, the daughter Doreen loved disappeared forever.

What Maya saw in Tate—with his dirty yellow hair and pale face—Doreen never understood. He had red eyelids and always wore the same clothes, including a dirty baseball cap that said something about *Catching you on the flip-side.*

He was a quiet boy, skinny, always in ripped jeans. When he wasn't quiet, he'd try to win you over with obnoxious proclamations about how "Real men honor their word and treat women with respect."

God forgive her, Doreen hated Tate. He'd stolen the one person she loved—her only family—and twisted her precious daughter into something sullen and removed. When Maya wasn't out with Tate doing heaven knows what, she was locked in her room doing heaven knows what.

Maya was into drugs now, and not just pot.

4

Doreen's biggest mistake was borne of desperation. Maya turned sixteen and dropped out of school. Tate was nineteen then and unemployed. Maybe they just needed some responsibility. So, Doreen invited them to move into Room 1 and manage the motel at night.

By this time, the lack of customers had forced Doreen to work a second job: the closing shift in the food court of the same mall that had stolen her life.

After another long night of cleaning bathrooms and mopping floors, Doreen came home to find Maya and Tate handcuffed in the back of a sheriff's cruiser.

Tate had expanded his marijuana business to Rebel Yell customers. This expansion was actually Maya's idea, a truth Doreen refused to accept.

Doreen mortgaged the motel further to pay for a lawyer, who earned every penny. Both walked away without so much as a wrist slap.

Doreen wondered if she'd made another mistake. *How would they learn without facing consequences?*

They learned nothing.

Maya begged to move back in; swore up and down she'd changed and deserved a second chance. Doreen knew it was just another lie and kicked them both out.

5

Two years passed before Doreen saw Maya again, when, out of the blue, she showed up with a baby in her arms. The baby's name was Charlie.

Maya explained that they were all living about forty miles east in the Redstone Trailer Park just outside Littleton. Tate was working now, she added. Somehow the former pot dealer had landed a job as a prison guard. He didn't make much, Maya said, and they needed money for the baby.

Doreen fell in love with baby Charlie on sight and an unspoken agreement was brokered between mother and daughter: as long as Doreen sent money she would be allowed to see her grandson.

There had been a time when the TV news reminded Doreen things could be worse. Now, no matter how bad the news was, she'd still wonder if it got any worse than being blackmailed by your own daughter.

A few weeks later, Doreen would finally consent to be baptized, and it would be one of the darkest days of her life.

Baptism

1

In a frumpy white frock that smelled of stale incense, forty-two-year-old Doreen Medina, who'd just discovered she was a grandmother, stood waist-deep in a muddy pond just behind the church.

The Church of the Holy Mother, her church of some twenty years now, was more like a big ol' shed than a church. Doreen liked that. She liked the chipped white paint and how the whole building sagged like it was getting ready to sit down after a tough day.

It was humble. Christ was humble.

Although she'd found God some twenty years earlier, Doreen wasn't able to commit to this baptism until she'd felt closer to God and had overcome her resentments toward Him.

For so long she'd wondered, *Why does God allow so many terrible things to happen? How can God stand idly by like this?* It wasn't just the things that had happened to her; it was all the horrors of the world.

For two decades, the sharp edges of that question rolled around inside her, vexed her, and distanced her from a God she was desperate to embrace. She prayed and prayed for an answer that never did come.

In the end, she'd managed only to come to terms with it by accepting the natural world as exactly that: *natural*, painfully natural, and created by God for the good of His children....

God refuses to definitively reveal Himself because He wants us to seek Him, not worship Him blindly out of fear of some giant head in the sky, she told herself. *And it's in this awful world where we gain wisdom, emotional strength, and maturity through our suffering. In the perfect world everyone thinks they want, a world without tragedy, death, pain, adversity, and failure, we would never mature or grow. We'd be spoiled, ungrateful, and entitled babies forever and appreciate nothing—especially Heaven.*

It was the best she could come up with, and that would have to do.

2

The forty or so people gathered to witness Doreen's baptism were mostly strangers. While she wanted to attend services every Sunday, running a motel—even a failing one—was a 24/7 responsibility. And even when she could attend, she still had to scoot out as soon as services ended. Sheets always needed changing; ratty carpets always needed vacuuming; customers always had a complaint....

Doreen covered her nose, Father Samuel cradled her shoulders, bent her backward, and into the water she went, all the way in. She was submerged into the Holy Spirit and returned to the natural world soaked to the skin.

Her fellow parishioners clapped politely, as though she'd sunk a short putt.

Maya wasn't there. There'd been no point in asking.

Doreen felt alone going into the water and just as alone coming out. That scared her. Here she'd just been baptized and still she wasn't sure if God was beside her. And if He was, she couldn't sense Him.

That was probably worse.

3

There'd been no one since Rodrigo, her first husband. Eighteen years was a long time to be alone.

She hadn't always been lonely those eighteen years, not during the good years when she and Maya were building something together. She'd been full up then. But those years were gone now and weren't coming back, and with their absence came a loneliness she'd never before experienced.

After she'd kicked Maya out, she didn't miss the tantrums and arguments. She also didn't expect the quiet to feel so empty.

There was no chance of meeting a decent guy at the Rebel Yell, a place that had turned seedy. *Seedy.* That fact broke the part of her heart that Maya hadn't. You also couldn't meet a good man in bars or supermarkets. She could surely bear witness to that.

Sure, church can be a desirable place to meet a guy. But you better join committees, attend potlucks, and serve Cokes on bingo night. She had no time for that.

Doreen knew she still had something to offer—lots to offer. Plenty of single guys would like to help her serve Cokes on a bingo night. Some of the married ones wouldn't say no to that offer, either.

Yeah, she sagged here and there. Having a kid and sprinting past forty does that to a woman. *Men sag too, you know.*

On those nights when she didn't mind being alone so much, she'd sometimes switch off the light above the back door, drag a kitchen chair out there, look up at the stars, and contemplate the evening.

Lightning storms were the best. You haven't seen lightning until you've seen it dance over the desert.

But when the loneliness felt like it might crush her, she'd sit out under those same stars and compose a letter in her head, a whole letter that started with "dear" and ended with "sincerely yours." An affectionate letter describing her day and thoughts. And she never forgot to ask how everyone out there was doing.

Doreen wished she had someone to send letters to; she'd always wanted to be a letter writer.

4

With her hair still wet from being bathed in the Holy Spirit, Doreen drove alone along the dusty and empty Old Highway 661 feeling cheated. Here she'd just been baptized and still her only companion was fear—fear for Maya's eternal soul, of her business going under, of rough customers, of being alone forever. Worst of all was the fear her loneliness meant she lacked faith and what that meant for her own soul.

Suddenly she pulled the van over onto the dirt so she could lay her head on the steering wheel. She'd had a powerful urge to do exactly that, so she did.

God was supposed to put her back together. That's what Father Samuel had told her that one time she'd talked to him about things. Well, she'd gotten the Rebel Yell back from the bank and kept it going all on her own. No miracle caused that, just a single mother's hard work and—

She stopped her blasphemy right there and squeezed the steering wheel until her knuckles went white. Then self-pity slid in next to her and tugged at her sleeve: *Remember that hotel bar, the dark one outside Rio Rico? That's where you'll feel wanted and desired. Go on, lady, treat yourself!*

Yep, here she was still damp from accepting the Holy Spirit and she'd opened herself up to the Devil.

It was time to get her head off the steering wheel.

5

A car passed going the other way, a station wagon, so she decided to stop thinking about the pieces of herself all over the place and remembered a ray of sunlight, the one that had once woke her up in the back of a station wagon. She was only fourteen then. Orange soda, warm days, sunburn, and a big, fluffy dog named Kiefer...

Kiefer must've died more than twenty years ago, she thought, and then pushed the thought aside. Instead, she focused her memory on Mr. and Mrs. Arthur and wondered if they still remembered her and where they might be now.

That same evening, after all the work was done, Doreen dragged that kitchen chair outside and composed a letter in her head, this one to the Arthurs. She told them how much she missed them and what those two weeks still meant to her.

She told them everything.

Even the stuff about Maya that made her feel like a bad mother.

6

A few nights later, Doreen was dreaming of orange soda, warm days, sunburn, and a big, fluffy dog named Kiefer when the night buzzer woke her. She sat up, and just as she told herself to remember the dream, she forgot it.

She slid into slippers, grabbed her robe, and felt some relief the buzzer hadn't gone off again; a good sign that whoever it was might be sober.

She was right. Mason was sober and looking for a room.

Room 14

1

No one would ever convince Mason fate had anything to do with bringing him and Doreen together. He didn't believe in such things. In his mind, there was only one reason the two of them met on that night more than thirty-six years ago: the ever-encroaching All at Once.

A couple of federal rangers had stumbled on his desert camp and made it crystal clear that if he was ever again caught on federal lands, he'd be arrested and charged.

Sure, they'd been polite—in that way authority figures often are, with their flurry of passive-aggressive "sirs."

"You need to move along, *sir*." "Don't let us catch you again, *sir*." "Have yourself a good day, *sir*."

That spot had been his home for nearly four years, a comfortable spot right up against the shade of a butte. Books had kept him company, kept his mind occupied. Watering hole was only a half day's walk.

He sure hated to lose it.

2

Mason didn't require food or drink to survive, which was something else he didn't understand. If he didn't eat or drink, as the day progressed, he got as hungry and thirsty as any man. But sometime in the night, the hunger and thirst disappeared. Next day, the cycle started fresh.

The hunger wasn't so bad. He could live with that. The thirst got uncomfortable. So he always made sure a watering hole was near his camp. Not too near. Watering holes attracted people.

Those had been four peaceful years, but now a couple of swaggering beer guts with badges had him on their radar. Time to move along.

Carrying large saddlebags so stuffed with clothes and books he could barely tie them down, Mason was headed to Mexico when he stopped at the Rebel Yell for the night.

3

To remain inconspicuous, Mason made a practice of following the rules, all the rules, everyone's rules big and small. The faded sign said "Press Button after Midnight," so, since it was well after midnight, he pressed the button. On the other side of a closed door behind the front desk, a buzzer sounded off. Figuring he was getting the proprietor out of bed, Mason waited.

No need to buzz again right away.

Not being an asshole was another way to keep a low profile.

He filled the time looking around the small office.

Cheap paneling covered the walls. A puppy dog calendar said it was April when it was June. The design on the front desk's Formica had been rubbed almost entirely away. A yellowing state map was thumb-tacked to a wall. Stuck among water-stained ceiling tiles, a fluorescent bulb buzzed in a way that was kind of comforting.

4

Doreen entered through the door behind the desk, snugged the knot in her light-blue robe, and ran a hand through her long black hair.

Her first impression of Mason was the impression he desired: none whatsoever. Another drifter. *Not bad looking, though, and he's not afraid of books.*

"If you're looking for a room, that's fine," she said. "If it's directions you want.... Well, at this time of night, I'm about to be a little less pleasant."

Her eyes were softer than her voice. It was banter. Drifters, truckers, salesmen looking for a bed in the middle of the night appreciate when a mature woman who's held on to her looks doesn't act like a cash register.

"Well, then, I guess I'd like a room," he replied dryly.

At that, she smiled the practiced smile all beautiful women smile; a polite smile no man can confuse with a come-on.

The limit on his return smile told her he understood.

She slid him a registration card and a pen plucked from a Disneyland cup, a place she'd never been.

"How many nights?"

"Just the one," he said, filling out the card.

"That'll be eighteen dollars."

He stopped writing.

"Afraid I don't have a home address or license plate number to put down." With an apologetic shrug he added, "It's just me."

Doreen was used to that. Usually, they lied and wrote something like *123 Schlitz Malt Liquor Lane*. She appreciated honesty.

"Still eighteen dollars," she said. "Check-out's at eleven, but due to the late hour, I can give you some leeway." Then with sympathy for a man traveling alone on foot, she added, "If you're hungry, you'll find some vending machines right around the corner of the office here. Coffee's not very good, but it's only a quarter."

"'Not Very Good' happens to be my brand," he replied.

He slid her the eighteen dollars.

She slid him the room key.

"I put you in number fourteen at the end. No one's in thirteen, so it'll be quiet. If you're in no hurry to move on, I can give you a second night for ten dollars."

"The one night'll do, thanks. That's a pretty good offer, though."

"Not really," she confessed before she could stop herself from saying more than she wanted to a stranger. "With me being two miles from the highway and all those chain hotels...."

Doreen had no idea why she was sharing her problems. "Anyway," she said, putting an end to the foolishness, "business can always be better."

"Maybe it's the coffee."

As the unguarded smile made its way across her face, it felt strange, foreign. *Has it been that long since I smiled?*

"You need some change for the machines?" she offered, suddenly wanting to extend the transaction.

"Not hungry. Thanks again, though."

"Have a good night, then."

5

Gripping his room key and saddlebags, Mason was almost out the door when he hesitated for a moment and then turned.

"You know, maybe I will stay for another—"

Doreen was gone.

But Mason did end up staying that second night, and every night thereafter.

Casa de Despair

1

Clean-shaven and sharply dressed in a black suit (the shoes were a bit tight), Mason politely pretended to sip his drink and watched the Washington Monument, White House, and U.S. Capitol glide across the limo's tinted windows.

Every society builds pyramids to itself, he thought.

Mason hadn't asked for the drink. Nevertheless, the moment they'd settled into the back of the limo, Ernest made a big deal of mixing it up for him. In fact, from the moment the private jet that brought them here lifted in the air, Ernest had eagerly taken on the role of a gracious host.

Sitting across from Mason, Ernest gaped out the window at those mammoth monuments to American democracy. "I never get used to this," he confessed with disarming sincerity. Then he shot Mason a quick look and shrugged off his embarrassment. "I don't know. It just gets me," he admitted. "I love this country. You ever been to D.C.?"

Mason took another pretend sip and answered honestly, "Lived out here a while back."

Ernest perked right up. "Really? What'd you do?"

"You know we can't get into that."

"Oh, yeah. Gee, sorry," Ernest said with real remorse. "I wasn't trying to—I was just...."

"This where you live?"

"Not far. You'll see."

On the other side of the divider, whoever was driving turned onto a dark street. With no more monuments to awe him, Ernest leaned back in the leather seat and finally gave Mason *The Look*.

Every time he sold his life, Mason got the look, the same one that asked the same question: *You don't look sick. You're obviously not crazy. Why in the world are you doing this?*

Mason knew the question was driving the fat man to distraction, and since the fat man had been pleasant, he decided not to make him ask. "Suicide," Mason said.

Ernest slowly nodded and then repeated the word as though it contained a profundity. "'Suicide,'" he echoed.

"If I kill myself," Mason volunteered, "people who mean something to me get nothing, no insurance. This way, they get something."

It was a good answer. Ernest accepted it, leaned back, and in a single gulp downed what was left of his mojito.

Mason focused his attention out the window and memorized the route.

2

Ernest had sure enjoyed the private jet that took them from Vegas to D.C. He surely had. What a difference from that miserable morning coach flight.

The Old Rich Prick wasn't paying for private jets to be generous—to give the guy he was about to murder a little bonus. The Old Rich Prick didn't want the Sacrifice getting second thoughts or any kind of ideas on a commercial flight, that was all. So the pilot and co-pilot remained up front as ordered and with no pretty young thing to serve drinks, Ernest happily filled the role.

High above the clouds, Ernest tried not to stare, but the Sacrifice intrigued him. *Nothing like the others*, he thought. *Knows what's coming, has no idea how it's coming, and still cool as Steve McQueen. Look at him thumbing through a magazine like he's headed to a business meeting. And that bank wire move, the offshore account, slicker than slick.*

Ernest worried for a moment Stark might be a cop. He always worried over stuff like that, dumb stuff like, *Maybe the government invented an electronic bug that doesn't give off a signal.*

How dumb was that?

Nah, a cop wouldn't be all cool, Ernest reasoned. *Cop would play up the twitchy act thicker than thick.*

The Old Rich Prick's previous sacrifices had all been a bundle of twitches: oiled in sweat and driving Ernest crazy with the same goddamned questions. Those men were the walking dead pre-embalmed with despair; the type who never would've covered their tracks through an offshore bank.

Those poor bastards, their backs weren't up against a wall; for them, there was no wall—nothing to prop 'em up. Drugs, drink, lunacy, whatever it was, it inched them right over the abyss and still they didn't know enough to cry out. Their *presence* was a cry, a cry no one wanted to hear. The Old Rich Prick, he heard that cry and made the criers his Sacrifices.

3

Ernest quickly learned how to handle these desperate men. First, he gave them whatever they wanted to take the edge off: downers, whiskey, heroin, coke.... He also mixed a powerful anti-diarrhea powder into their drinks. First guy taught him that the hard way. Stunk up the whole plane.

They all got the nervous-shits something terrible.

He also made sure to answer their questions with well-rehearsed lies. Whoppers like, *Don't worry, pal, you won't feel any pain.*

But this Stark fella didn't ask questions. Didn't ask for anything. Didn't drink his drink. Never once used the bathroom. Ernest sure was intrigued by him, especially that slick-ass bank wire move.

Three of the previous Sacrifices had asked to be paid in cash and then mailed the money on the way to the airport. Dropped it in a mailbox. *You believe that?* Finding and killing their people had been *easy peasy japanesey.*

Ernest couldn't remember how he'd tracked down the fourth's family.

If you can believe this, the fifth guy had them stop at his mother's house so he could personally put the money into her greedy hands.

Parked across the street watching, Ernest could tell the old lady only cared about the cash. Didn't give a damn about her son, even though he was a veteran. Two tours in Iraq. You had to respect that. Ernest did, so he kept the war hero's drinks fresh, listened to his sob stories, and put some real effort into making the lies reassuring.

That old ballbreaker snatched up the money from her war hero son and then, like they were celebrities, smiled and waved to Ernest and the limo driver.

Ernest considered it his patriotic duty to kill her slowly, so he did.

4

Stark's bank wire move would make it a bit more challenging to find and kill the money's recipients. Not even the Old Rich Prick had the juice to squeeze secrets out of an island bank. Ernest would have to trace Stark though that burner phone, which he'd had the foresight to retrieve from the water pitcher.

The brand would tell him who manufactured it. The manufacturer would use the model and lot number to track down the retailer. The retailer would probably have security cameras. If not, the sales receipt's time and date stamp would make it easy to check other cameras in the area.

Whole fucking country was full of cameras. The Old Rich Prick had access to all of it, to everything, and one would catch Stark and whatever it was that delivered him to where he'd purchased that phone.

Ernest would eventually find and kill Stark's people, *easy peasy japanesey*.

5

The limo stopped in front of an estate wrapped in eight-foot walls. The wrought-iron gates opened slowly. The limo crept through and then glided down a long, winding driveway lined with trees covered in white lights.

Mason caught a glimpse of a pier and boathouse, along with a whole lot of high-tech security. Security wouldn't be a problem. Security systems all had the same flaw—a human flaw.

As they slowed to a stop, a red glow penetrated the limo's windows and slowly crept across the car's insides until it saturated everything.

Ernest didn't seem to notice. Mason found the glow disorienting, like he'd entered a dream on the verge of a nightmare.

The limo stopped.

"You ready, Mike?" Ernest asked like they were pals.

Mason said he was.

Ernest opened the door and the red glow burst inside.

Again with those elegant moves, Ernest extricated himself from the car and held the door open.

Mason stepped out into a world far removed from his own.

6

The mansion resembled a demented version of Scarlett O'Hara's Tara. Thick vines strangled white columns. Black curtains shrouded large windows. The mammoth entranceway was blanketed in thousands of tiny but powerful red lights that corrupted everything in their reach.... *Like the insides of arriving limos.*

Two parking attendants stood straight as soldiers in crisp white shirts, red vests, and goat masks complete with long horns. Two armed men guarded the entrance. Mason hoped the two mercenaries had only been hired for tonight's festivities. Full-timers would complicate his return.

Right before Mason reached the front steps, she appeared out of nowhere.

7

She had long black hair, pale skin, and a womanly body fraught with curves that poured out of a low-cut dress. She was leaning hard into forty, with glassy eyes and a slur in her voice.

"You must be Mike Stark," she said to Mason.

"I am."

With theatrical flourish, she spread her arms wide, bent her pretty bare knees, and said, "Welcome to Casa de Despair. I'm your hostess. My name's Anne. I'm completely fucked up. And not only on narcotics."

In about a half-second he'd read her and tossed her aside like a waiting room magazine. Welcome to tonight's performance, where the leading lady seduces unsuspecting men onto the rocks of their doom with a well-rehearsed portrayal of a beautiful maiden in need of saving. Ten, maybe even five years ago, she'd undoubtedly been something else. Now she was all fucked-out with too much makeup and eyes as empty as dry wells.

After her "fuzzy end of the lollipop" act flopped, she fired torpedo number two: what had once been a dazzling smile. Mason saw only creases in a face edging into ragged and the somewhat comical sight of red lipstick smeared across her front teeth.

She offered him a sparrow-sized hand. He found it repulsive, cold with sweat.

8

Casa de Despair's interior was all whites and golds, like they'd never left Vegas. With Ernest trailing in the shadows, Anne led Mason down a wide hallway decorated with expensive paintings and mirrors. Their footsteps echoed off oak floors.

Frustrated by his indifference toward her, Anne looked back, hoping to catch the man she knew as Stark checking out her ass.

He stared straight ahead.

Over a strapless shoulder, she tried again with that lipstick-smeared smile.

Stark replied with a tight nod.

Jesus Christ, is this guy a homo?

She added more shake to her fries and hoped for the best.

The previous Sacrifices had all appreciated Anne's presentation. Two even begged for a goodbye quickie, which she was happy to provide. Nothing turned her on like losers who reeked of fear and death.

She'd once considered doing Ernest, or letting Ernest do her. He was as disgusting as anyone she'd ever met. But her father—the Old Rich Prick—informed her of Ernest's preference for young boys and showed her the movies to prove it.

9

"That smell you smell," the lost maiden said as she strolled on, "that's the Potomac, which is right over there." She pointed to the left...and then slowly stopped walking.

Unsure about something, she stood and chewed a fingernail.

"Or it might be over there." She pointed the other way.

"Anyway," she said as she started walking again, "I hate that smell. I hate the water and boats, or ships, or whatever you call them. Probably because my daddy loves that stuff. I hate my daddy. This is his place. My daddy's, I mean."

High as a kite, Anne chattered on about how much she hated these parties, hated the people at these parties, and then she stopped so suddenly Mason almost bumped into her.

Just as sudden, she wheeled around to look him over—head to toe and back to head. Then she rendered a verdict. "You're not like the others, are you? You're, you're...."

She paused to hunt down her thought, faltered, and then tried again hoping Mason would bail her out. "You're, you know, you remind me of, *you know*...."

Mason knew what she wanted to say. What they all said. Something about how he seemed too normal to volunteer for something like this. Yeah, he could've bailed her out, but this dead-eyed bitch was gonna kill him, so he let her hang.

Failing to finish the thought, she shrugged, twirled herself back around, and the three of them continued their long march down this endless hallway.

With some hallway still left to go, they arrived at a slender door. Using a key tied to her wrist, Anne unlocked and opened it to reveal a narrow, wrought-iron staircase that circled down to the floor below.

10

Ernest hated those goddamned stairs almost as much as body disposal.

Anne bounced down the steps and chirped, "Hope you brought your autograph book."

The Color of Madness

1

The light was dim, the air chilly and damp, and the reds and blacks every bit as twisted as the stairway that had delivered them here.

Anne led Mason and a lurking Ernest down a corridor with a red floor and black walls covered in art depicting sexual torture. They breezed past a dozen red porcelain figures spaced every few feet. Each figurine sat alone, elegantly placed on a black pillar, and was lit from above by a small spotlight. The figures depicted people engaged in depravities.

Mason knew what such a display might mean and felt his insides tighten.

2

Mason didn't mind dying and would suffer the pain of death for the simple reason that if the buyer believed everything had gone as planned, the buyer relaxed. A relaxed buyer was easier to kill. But Mason wouldn't allow himself to be raped. No way in hell.

What's more, he couldn't allow Doreen to sense that kind of a change in him. She could never know about any of this. A man who made good money delivering expensive automobiles to wealthy collectors didn't return home someone else. So, if that's what was in store tonight, if things got even a little kinky, he'd choke on his tongue. He'd done it before, and from the looks of this place, he might have to do it again.

3

Anne made an abrupt turn down a short corridor that ended at a steel door painted white.

This must be it, Mason figured. His anxiety shifted into a higher gear.

Anne stopped at the door. She didn't move or speak. She just stood there with her back to Mason, who waited and waited, until....

"I got it," she announced quietly, and then turned to face him. Her eyes were full of mirth.

"You remind me of a mailman. *That's* what you remind me of. Are you a mailman, Mr. Stark?" Her grin was seductive. This was her last chance and she was really pouring it on.

He would never let these people see him sweat, so Mason swallowed that anxiety and popped off something glib. "Nope. Sea captain."

The answer caught her off guard. She believed him. "Oh, my.... Well, I hope you don't hunt whales. This crowd wouldn't like that. They would not like that at all."

"More of a pirate, really."

A pause before her grin blossomed into a genuine smile. She was impressed. "You're teasing me."

"Afraid I am."

"You seem nice," she admitted. Her smile was marred only by that lipstick smear and for the first time Mason saw a maiden almost worth saving. *Almost.*

"You really do seem nice," she added with a tone that suggested it was almost a shame he had to die tonight. *Almost.*

4

There was no need to knock or signal. As soon as Anne turned around, someone somewhere unlocked the white door electronically.

Without Mason noticing, Ernest had caught up with them.

Fat man moves like a cat.

The cat offered his hand. "I'm not.... Well, I don't go in there."

Mason accepted his handshake. "What about the acid and transmitter?"

Ernest almost smiled, but the weight of the moment was too much. "Houdini couldn't get out of there," he said. "So, ah, so long, pal."

"Yeah. Thanks for that drink."

Mason watched Ernest disappear around a corner.

"Come on," Anne said as she pulled open the door. "I'll introduce you around." And like they were off to the prom, she hooked her arm through his and led him into the enveloping sounds of laughter and ragtime.

5

An outsider would've been dazzled by what Mason witnessed as an animated Anne led him through a well-dressed crowd gathered in a ballroom decked out like a 1920s speakeasy.

Mason went out of his way to avoid media, celebrity, and politics. They warped a person's worldview, he felt. Still, even he recognized any number of faces from those rarefied worlds.

Over the jaunty sounds of Scott Joplin, a murmur of animated conversation from the fifty or so guests filled the air. Most were seated in an elegant sea of small, round tables.

By candlelight, they sipped drinks, smoked, chatted, chuckled, and backslapped.

Those not schmoozing were cutting a rug on the far side of the room near a ragtime band situated at the very edge of a stage. On the actual stage was a live sex show which the jaded crowd hardly noticed.

"Meet tonight's special guest," Anne said to no one and everyone as she threaded their way through the tables towards the stage. The curious ones stared at Mason. Some nodded as though they were friends. The honest ones grinned like he was dessert.

"He's a pirate who kills whales," she blurted into the face of a humorless couple who'd long ago lost their battle with plastic surgery.

No one paid attention to Anne's tired provocations. She wasn't one of them. They tolerated her only because of her father and him because of his money. They tolerated each other because that's what was required to retain their status. The one thing they couldn't tolerate was themselves, and that was why they were here: the stimulation of depravity distracted the conscience.

6

The party was over.

The phony speakeasy was deserted.

The ballroom was all stillness and shadows—except for the stage.

In the center of that stage, under a spotlight and handcuffed to a pole, stood Mason.

He could hear them whispering in the dark, working up the nerve, savoring the anticipation.

Mason closed his eyes to focus on Doreen and Charlie; on his home, on his life and the people he loved. But his mind rebelled and led him down the path he most hated, the one where he tried to imagine the unimaginable: life without his wife. And like the size of the universe, it was something impossible to comprehend.

He'd lost her once before. Those two years after her daughter Maya was killed, Doreen disappeared into a place where she blamed herself. A terrible and lonely place where no one could reach her. But she'd come back to him. She was never quite the same, but she'd come back.

His thoughts shifted to Doreen's Christian faith, something he couldn't help but resent. How could he not resent the superstitions that stopped her from accepting his gift of eternal life, something he'd never dared offer anyone before? All it took was his touch, she'd be healed, and they'd be together forever. But she refused. Over and over, even on her deathbed, in deference to her God, she refused.

He blamed himself for not finding the words.

Mason took a deep breath and decided that this time he would find the words. This time nothing would stop him from getting to her with the words that would spare him from losi—

Anne stepped from the dark holding a dagger. Her face was blank, robotic. She stared at Mason for a beat, and then another, and then her heels *click-clacked* on the wood floor as she strode up to him and jammed four-inches of blade into his shoulder. Mason groaned. Blood sprayed her face. She licked it from her lips, extracted the dagger, and then, like a curious child, tilted her head for a closer look.

"I'm sorry," she whispered without emotion.

"You've got lipstick on your teeth," he said through gritted teeth. She didn't hear him. She heard only the color red, the color of madness.

She stuck him again, this time in the gut, and twisted the blade.

He let out a cry.

His knees buckled.

His head flopped forward.

7

Gripping their own blades and cloaked in red smocks to protect their finery, the Beautiful People, one by one, like shy groundhogs, emerged from the shadows. Some were hesitant, at least at first. Murder was still new to some of them.

Mason died as the stabbing turned into a frenzy, and as he died, he was still searching for the words....

Goodbye

1

After the morphine lost its hold and she'd stopped drifting over the times of her life, Doreen's eyes opened to a present where she was a dying old woman; where her daughter Maya was dead and Charlie's brain was mangled; where two weeks ago she'd told her husband he could never come back.

Her mouth was dry. She licked her chapped lips and reached for water with bruised, rail-thin arms. The reaching was painful. Her joints grinded like gears with no grease. The cup was out of her grasp.

She tried to sit up and kept trying until the trying exhausted her.

Yesterday she could sit up.

She lay there a while listening to the sound of her own breathing. She drew air in and then exhaled. In and then out. In and then out.

Deep in her back, beneath a shoulder blade, there was a new ache, a fresh spot of rot that wasn't there yesterday.

Keep breathing, she told herself. *Keep breathing.*

Her eyes felt heavy. Something told her if she closed them, they'd never open again.

Don't close your eyes.

Keep breathing.

Doreen hit the call button for the nurse.

Keep breathing.

In...out.

In...out.

The nurse entered and gave Doreen a drink of water.

As she sipped the cool liquid through a plastic straw, Doreen remembered that she was supposed to remember something. *What was it? What am I supposed to remember?*

The nurse asked Doreen if she needed anything else.

Doreen asked for a priest.

The nurse left.

Keep breathing.

In...out.

In...—Then she remembered: *What time is it!? Maybe he's out there.*

Her dry lips cracked as she smiled at the idea of Mason, her husband, standing outside her window at noon. With some effort, she managed to turn her head to look at the time. But along with the rest of her, her eyes were dying and the clock was a blur.

Yesterday, she could see the clock.

Not today.

Keep breathing.

In...out.

In...out.

Thinking of her husband kept her mind off death, so she concentrated even harder on him, risked closing her eyes, and pictured him—the way he moved, the gait of his walk, his hands on her bare skin, his taste—and then she felt something...*strange.*

What is this? This wasn't the rot, this was...different. And then she released a laugh. Not a laugh that might prompt someone to say, *You must be feeling better*—more of a throat clear mixed with a sigh. But it was still the laugh of a woman shocked by what she felt....

Doreen was horny.

Here she was, seventy-seven-years-old, rotting out, and horny as a newlywed. Her laugh became a cough, harsh and painful, a wracking and wet thing. When it was over, she wiped her mouth and found blood, which made her angry.

The chemo had stolen everything. Even at age seventy-six, she'd been a striking woman, but the poison plundered her looks along with her sex drive. She'd hired the chemo to hunt down and kill the rot, and instead it embezzled her womanhood.

Doreen started to cry, and cried harder than she had in a long time, right up until the sin of despair announced its arrival.

That's enough of that.

2

She decided to focus her thoughts on what was good in her life: Mason again, always Mason. But her thoughts chose instead to punish her and insisted on returning to two weeks ago, to the last time she saw him, to that look on his face.

Why did it have to end that way?

She'd never hurt Mason before, not like that, not in a way that couldn't be fixed. And now there was no way to explain or to apologize. To protect Charlie, Mason's secret had to be kept, especially *from* Charlie, who'd never be able to keep it.

And so, because it made no sense for the motel handyman to sit by his dying employer's bedside, that was that. A visit now and again, sure, but no vigil. And at the very end, he could never come back, not when she'd be too drugged to remain discreet. This included telephone calls a nurse might overhear.

Why did it have to end that way?

Doreen had never asked God for a miracle. But Mason had offered her one, a real one, and she'd turned him down. Again and again, he'd pleaded and then badgered until it became a sore spot in their marriage. Still, to honor her faith, she'd refused.

The way Doreen saw it, accepting eternal life would be the ultimate act of someone who lacked faith, something she could never risk. Well, for Maya she would have risked it. If Mason could have brought back Maya, she would have done anyth—

Doreen's tears returned.

Why did it have to end that way?

3

Two weeks earlier, Mason had been asleep in a chair by Doreen's bed. When he'd walked in, he was again overcome by how she looked like someone trapped in a science-fiction world of beeps and tubes; of wires, machines, pumps, and monitors.

After a few minutes, he'd dozed off while reading. The book slid from his lap and slapped onto the floor, waking them both.

She stirred a little. He bent to retrieve the book and then eased himself forward.

After her eyes focused on him, she smiled.

"Hey you," he whispered.

She tried to mask it, but her pain was obvious. Mason reflexively reached for the magic morphine button. She shook her head. "No, no, don't. It's okay. I'm fine. Just raise me up."

Mason pressed the other button, the one that lifted the head of the bed. *More science fiction.*

"That's good," she said, now that she was upright.

4

As she sipped some water, he watched her and realized: "You look...I don't know...you look more like yourself today."

"That's because I'm not drugged into oblivion," she replied, which was the truth. For the first time in a long time, she felt clear-eyed instead of fuzzy-headed. But she knew she wouldn't be able to hold out much longer.

"Yeah," he said with a false hope he was determined to make real through the saying of it. "You're *you* again." His smile widened. "This is good. You must be feeling better if you're off the meds." He expressed that last part in a way that wasn't a question. When your wife's dying, you don't ask questions you don't want answered.

She answered anyway, as gently as she could. "No, I'm not feeling better, and I'm not going to get better."

She then willed herself to the next part, to the hard part: "I told the doctors to stop the pain meds, so we can.... Well, you and I, we knew this...." Her voice trailed off.

Mason stared off somewhere and said nothing.

"We talked about this day," Doreen finally said. "How we would...." Her voice disappeared again.

Mason knew what this meant and felt his insides fall through a hole in the floor.

Doreen said what was necessary, "Charlie's all that matters."

A terrible silence was created around the fact they would never see each other again.

A housekeeper entered to empty a wastebasket.

A fly buzzed against a window.

A nurse took Doreen's blood pressure.

A siren passed outside.

On the other side of the closed door, some nurses laughed over something.

Mason swallowed hard and tried again. "We can *both* protect him," he said.

Doreen wasn't going to have that conversation—not now, not again. She was too old and too sick to argue over exhausting things.

5

All Mason could do was sit there strangled by the now-familiar frustration brought on by his wife's ridiculous religious faith. He closed his eyes so tight he saw colors and tried to conjure the words that would convince her to join him. Sure, she'd be seventy-seven forever. He couldn't turn back the clock. But she'd be in perfect health, and, well.... It was too late. It was too goddamned late, and the truth of that made him so brittle, he was sure that if anything touched the hollow shell that had once been his body, his body would shatter like glass and follow his insides down that hole.

Doreen touched his hand and he didn't shatter, and the fact he didn't reminded him of how her love worked on him, like white magic. That was when he told her of his plan to be across the street every day at noon, and that was when she called the idea silly.

"I'm going to kiss you," he said.

"You can't," she protested. "What if someone—"

He removed himself from the chair and sat on the edge of her bed.

She felt his warmth against her hips.

He leaned into her.

She closed her eyes and accepted his kiss, his tenderness, his taste, and his love. She accepted all of it. And when the kiss ended, he traced his lips across her cheek and whispered something that made her smile.

He kissed her once more, this time for the last time. Then they looked into each other's eyes and, without a word, everything was said— and still it wasn't enough. It would never be enough.

"You have to go on now," she whispered.

"I know," he said. "After you're asleep." He sat back down in the chair. "Let me see you off to sleep."

That was the last thing she wanted.

"No, you really should go," she whispered.

There was urgency in her voice.

He didn't want to hear it.

"I will," he assured her. "After you're asleep."

And then the pain struck.

It was white hot, like her insides were melting. Doreen didn't want Mason to see her like this, to remember her like this, so she croaked out a "No." And then said the last thing she ever would to him: "You have to go, *now*."

She'd meant it as an appeal, a tender appeal. The pain made it sound severe. She'd almost growled that last word, the "now." Maybe she had. She was about to say something else, something about how much she loved him, but then the pain burst through and wiped the words away. She arched her back, cried out, and clawed for the call button.

6

Stricken, Mason stood like a shot. He'd never seen her like this. The reality froze him in place. The worst was how the pain made him a helpless bystander in the presence of his own wife.

Doreen writhed and clicked the call button.

The nurse answered.

Doreen gasped out a "Help."

Mason reached to caress her. He wanted to be part of her life again, to be her husband, her protector again.

Like he was a nuisance, she pushed him away.

There was only agony now. Doreen was married to that agony and couldn't say what she wanted: *Stay with me. Stay with me and whisper those words to me again, and I'll whisper them back to you. I don't care who knows. Don't leave me. Please don't leave...I don't want to die alone. Oh, God, I don't want to die alone.*

7

It was only after the nurse rushed in that Doreen was able to focus on her husband. He stood by the door looking like a lost little boy.

That wasn't the worst of it.

The worst was knowing that the last time she would ever touch him, she pushed him away.

But she'd done it so the nurse wouldn't see....

She'd done it for Charlie.

Out of the Dark

1

Intellectually and emotionally, Charlie was still seven, still the same age he was the night of the car accident. But the package carrying him now was that of a five-foot-ten, 230-pound man-child with a moral malignancy growing steadily inside of him.

2

There was only one customer tonight, a couple of adulterers who'd parked their cars out of sight by the garbage cans. Without much else to do, Charlie pulled an extension ladder out of some tall weeds and banged it up against the motel sign.

The big, red letters that spelled "Rebel Yell Motel" were so faded you'd have thought the place was closed.

Balancing on the ladder twelve feet off the ground, Charlie chewed a Twizzler and did his best to keep the brushstrokes between the lines. His best wasn't good enough. The work was the sloppy work of a seven-year-old. The glimmering red paint dripped and ran, and Charlie's rage began its re-entry.

It wasn't just the clumsy paint job that infuriated him. It was the memory of who he once was: the "gifted" student, the popular kid picked first for kickball, the cute boy the girls giggled over, the promising child artist.

And now I'm a fat fucking retard who can't even stay in the lines.

On top of all that was the despair of knowing what would happen next. Mason would look at the repainted sign, compliment him, and then say what he always said: *I'll take care of the touch-ups.* Then he'd redo the job and it would look perfect.

It was always like that, always. Like the other day, when Charlie ordered sod for around the pool.

3

Like he did first thing every morning, Mason stopped in the motel office fully dressed...except for his boots. No matter the weather, Mason was adamant about not pulling on his boots until after he'd had his coffee. Even in the rain, he'd walk the whole way from his room to the office in his white socks. Those dirty socks drove Doreen near crazy, which was why he did it. Doreen was pretty as sunlight when she got wound up.

Truth be told, she didn't mind so much.

The moment Mason walked in, Charlie stood up straight, adjusted his glasses, and announced his accomplishment. "I-I-I ordered the-the-the sod. Th-they're delivering it around-round four!" He was all kinds of proud, beaming practically, and feeling like a man who ran things.

"Sod?" asked Mason through a mouthful of powdered donut.

"Yeah, for-for-for around the pool."

Before he could catch himself, Mason frowned, a look Charlie'd seen a million times.

"Wh-what's wrong-what's wrong with that!?" Charlie pleaded, as the all-too familiar warmth of humiliation crept up his face. "You-you-you said to-to always start the-the job from the top and then-and then work our way down!"

"I did tell you that."

"But I'm...but I'm still wrong."

"No, I was wrong to tell you that without explaining exceptions. That pool's gonna need a lot of work: wheelbarrows back and forth, that kind of thing.... We don't want to trample new sod while we fix the pool."

Charlie understood. Of course, that made sense. But he didn't want to be *all* wrong, so he told Mason he'd have the delivery guys set the sod out back.

All Charlie got in return was that face again, which put tears in his voice, "Wh-wh-what?"

Mason hated these moments, hated hurting Charlie, and wished he'd stayed in bed.

"You know what? It doesn't matter," Mason said, using a matter-of-fact voice that made clear he was ready to move on to other topics—like the weather.

"Just-just-ju-j-j-just tell me," Charlie pleaded. "Just tell-tell-tell me. I want to learn."

4

Charlie *did* want to learn, he really did, even though he knew he never would and that the rest of his miserable life would be filled with moments just like this one.

"Fair enough," said Mason. "You can't have that sod sitting around. We won't need it for a while. It'll dry out or rot."

Mason said this like he was talking to a man instead of a child, which always made Charlie feel better.

"Y-yeah, right. Okay. Okay. I-I'll ca-cancel the delivery."

Without realizing he was correcting Charlie *again*, Mason said, "You don't have to cancel it. Just tell 'em to hold off."

Charlie exploded. "Wh-wha-what's the difference! I-I-I'm just gonna cancel the stu-stu-stupid thing! Who cares? *Who cares!?* Who CARES!!!"

Mason surrendered by nodding in total agreement, and during the awkward silence that followed, both would've eagerly jumped into whatever hole was charitable enough to open up.

Misty broke the ice. She jumped on the desk to purr and rub up against Charlie's shoulder. Mason smiled. *Sweet kid's always taking in strays.*

Charlie stroked Misty and was calmed by the thought of strangling her.

5

Charlie wasn't feeling calm tonight. He was messing up the sign and fuming, especially at the thought of Mason's "touch-ups," which would—

Suddenly he switched gears and wished his adulterous customers hadn't blocked the garbage cans. He'd put a whole Salisbury steak from last night's TV dinner out there hoping to attract a dog, a big one he could straddle as he strangled. So right then and there he decided to make the garbage area a "no parking zone." Solving that problem soothed him some as paint dripped from the brush onto his protruding belly.

Now that he was once again feeling like a man who made decisions, Charlie made another one. He was done for the night. *The ladder and the open paint can and the wet brush can stay right here. I'm in charge. I'll do what I want.* And what he wanted was to microwave three pot pies, drink two liters of Pepsi straight from the bottle, and play videogames all night.

The sound of an approaching motorcycle intruded on his reverie. *Might be a customer*—a thought he dreaded. It was always the ones on motorcycles who didn't bother to hide their amusement watching him grapple with counting out their change. So Charlie would know they were laughing at him, those guys always broke out laughing just as they exited the office.

The approaching motorcycle roared out of the black carrying a highway patrolman. Charlie waved. The cop didn't wave back. Charlie's self-pity had a field day with that: *When Mason waves, people always wave back. Mason never looks stupid waving. I always do.*

A metal grate ran along the bottom of the sign, like a shelf. Seething over the motorcycle cop, Charlie carelessly dropped the paint can onto it and the red splashed onto a corner of the sign like blood spatter.

Charlie no longer cared about the sign or the cop or pot pies. He had a new thought.

6

Charlie pulled a Twizzler from his pocket, ignored the lint and grit stuck to it, and popped it into his mouth. Then he *ever so carefully* pivoted himself around on the ladder.

High in the air, with his arms folded and his back against the rungs, he chewed his licorice like a cigar and took a good long look into the night. The stars were out. Charlie never saw stars. He only saw the dark.

He liked how Old Highway 661 led straight into a black cave, into a void that put a chill up his back, a chill he savored. Anything in the world could roar out of that void, and if Charlie could be anything in the world, that's what he'd be. He didn't really want to be Wolverine or

Mason. What he wanted was to be The Thing That Comes Out of the Dark, a dream his fear of God wouldn't allow him to act on.

Last summer, while Mason took his Grandma Dory to chemotherapy, Charlie was left in charge and an old man checked in who was so drunk Charlie had to practically carry him to his room.

As the old drunk lay there sprawled out on the bed asleep, Charlie knew he could smother him with a pillow and no one would ever know. The rummy probably wouldn't even fight back.

As tempted as he was, and as satisfying as it would've been to kill a man, Charlie didn't—and for only one reason: he believed in God.

Charlie didn't want to go to Hell. Hell terrified him. He wanted to go to Heaven to be with his Grandma Dory, with his mom and dad, and Jesus, forever.

This left him with fantasies that were alive with blood-soaked scenes of him terrorizing and humiliating a world that made him feel like a *fat fucking retard.*

Charlie stared deeper into Old Highway 661's black hole and let his mind roam through wicked places.

Yvette

1

Barreling down Old Highway 661, Yvette Lightfoot was low on gas, almost out of cash, and lost—which was how she liked it. She knew she was at her best when cornered, so tonight she'd cornered herself.

Just a few minutes earlier, on a whim (Yvette was big on whims), and with less than an eighth of a tank of gas, she'd exited the freeway by way of a dark off-ramp that promised neither gas nor food nor lodging.

At the end of the ramp her gut said, *Turn right,* so she turned left. That was how she lived her life now. When her instincts said zig, she zagged. A couple more zags put her on Old Highway 661 and the plan was to cruise along until she ran out of gas. Then she'd sleep in her car, and, well, just see what happened in the morning.

After all those years in a suffocating cubicle managing a telemarketing agency, Yvette refused to ever again submit to the grind of a conventional life.

2

Some years back, she'd assumed the happiest day of her life would be the day she quit that job. She'd assumed wrong. Sure, she'd saved up enough money to retire, but only *just enough*—about $260,000. But now, instead of stressing over a job, she was stressing over nickels. She'd emancipated herself from a cubicle only to become a slave to a budget.

That was when she cashed out the retirement account, every penny of it, and then sold everything she owned that wouldn't fit in a suitcase.

Two days later, she pulled into an Atlantic City casino.

"Just be a sec," she told the parking attendant. Slipped him her keys, fifty bucks, and bet all $260,000 on Red 19.

3

Yvette watched that little white ball bounce around knowing she'd walk away a winner no matter what. She'd either be a free woman with $8 million, or a free woman with nothing to lose.

She lost it all.

This left her with only a few hundred dollars and a 1997 Ford Focus with 82,000 miles on it.

That was the best day of her life.

Now she had to live on her wits.

She played it straight at first. Drifted from job to job, town to town. This got dull quick. She was tending bar the first time she lifted a few bucks from the till. Stealing gave her a tingle. She liked that tingle, and took to hustling like a monkey to monkey bars.

For the next two years, she worked and hustled, hustled and worked. Strictly small-time: shoplifting, robbing the register, running numbers in St. Louis. In some rural Iowa town full of sheep-humpers she must've lifted ten wallets from a church coat rack.

It wasn't about the money. It was about breaking the rules and never knowing what would happen next.

There'd been close calls.

Yvette liked close calls.

There was still a warrant out for her in Florida where she'd worked at an electronics store in a Kissimmee mall. One morning, she filled a big cardboard box with tablets, iPhones, you name it. Then she sealed the box, put it on a dolly, and wheeled it right past a security guard specifically hired to stop employees from doing what she was doing.

"Morning, Brady," she said, calm as a blue sky.

"Morning, Yvette. Lemme get the door for you."

She loaded the Ford Focus with the loot, fired it up, and turned West.

Along the way, she pawned the stuff a piece at a time. Now it was gone, she was near broke, the Ford Focus had 143,000 miles on it, and at age forty-eight, she was feeling fully alive as she sped down Old Highway 661.

4

Charlie was still high up on that ladder dreaming of being The Thing That Comes Out of the Dark when a Ford Focus the color of dirt changed its mind all of a sudden and barely made the turn into the Rebel Yell.

He was certain the car was gonna smash straight through the office. Even if it had, there was so much dust, he would've missed the whole thing.

Barely in time, Yvette skidded to a stop, shifted her abused little car into park, and killed the ignition. Before it would agree to shut down, the Ford filed an abuse complaint: KACHUNK, KAFUNG, BABAM, BABAL, BABAHHHhhh*hhhssss*....

While the car complained, Yvette stepped out and marched right into the motel office.

Mesmerized, Charlie watched the whole thing play out like it had nothing to do with him.

The night buzzer went off.

Charlie didn't move.

The night buzzer went off again.

Charlie still didn't move.

The night buzzer popped off five frustrated buzzes in a row followed by a night buzzer rendition of, "Shave and a haircut, two bits."

Charlie's eyes went wide with wonder. *Who is this lady?*

Yvette stormed out of the office until she reached the middle of the parking lot. There, she stopped, put her hands on her hips, and took a long, slow look around.

The idea this glowering woman was looking for *him* never crossed Charlie's mind. He was too mesmerized by this brazen little hellion who he thought kinda looked like Fred Flintstone's pal, Barney Rubble— Barney Rubble in a mini skirt and heels.

At a touch over five feet and 150 pounds, Yvette was indeed built like a thumb topped with spiky bleached hair. She wore a short, tight skirt; high heels, plenty of makeup, and sported a dragon tattoo up and down her right arm. Her best feature was what you'd call an "ample bosom," which she highlighted in a low-cut blouse.

Charlie would've bet a whole bag of Twizzlers she smelled real nice.

She didn't spot Charlie until after she'd lit up a smoke, taken a drag, and relaxed some. Then she popped back to life. "Hey! Hey, you up there!" she shouted.

Not waiting for an answer, she strutted on over, her stilettos kicking up dry dirt as she mumbled, "The fuck...this place...idiot...stupid ladder...room...bullshit..."

Charlie had no sex drive. That was something else he'd lost in the accident. Her cleavage still hypnotized him.

She came to a stop at the bottom of the ladder and looked straight up at him.

"Think you could you stop staring at my tits long enough to get me a room?"

Caught red-handed staring at her tits, a crimson-faced Charlie snapped out of it, turned himself around, and clumsily descended the ladder.

5

As he climbed down with his back to her, she smiled and took a couple of steps back. Wasn't too often she flustered a guy. This made her feel pretty good about herself. She took a drag off the smoke like a young Lana Turner would in this situation and felt even better.

As he bounced down a rung at a time, Charlie tried to defend himself: "I-I-I wasn't staring. I was...I was—" He hit the ground, spun around, and froze. *There she was*, right in front of him.

He could hardly believe she was real.

Yvette looked him up, looked him down, and then up again.

He adjusted his glasses and shifted his feet.

She inhaled some smoke, cocked her head to one side, threw him a half-smile, and then fired the smoke out both nostrils.

He blushed and inspected his shoes. "I wasn't staring at nothing," he said to his shoes.

"It's no biggie," she said. "That's what tits are for. But they do need a room for the night."

Charlie'd never heard talk like that. Not even on the TV. It sure made him nervous...but in a good way.

"A room-a roo—Okay, please-please, follow—come-come with me."

Charlie said *come with me*, but didn't move. He just stood there staring like she'd performed a magic trick and was about to do another.

"This your place?" she asked.

"Y-y-yes. I mean not-not-not yet. It's-it's my grandma's. She's dying of-of a cancer. Then-then it's mine. I'm fixing it up. Painting the sign. Gonna repair the-the pool and-and build a website."

"You retarded, or something?"

And out came the *blah, blah, blah*: "I-I-I used to be-to be normal. But when I-I was younger, my daddy crashed us. He and my-my mama died. My-my brain-my brain got hurt. My grandma lov-lov-loves me, so she took me in. She'll be in-in-in Heaven soon. She's dying."

"Yeah, you said that. Sorry to hear it."

"She's got a cancer," he repeated so he'd have something to say.

Yvette liked what she saw: a jackpot. So the ample-bosomed Barney Rubble in a tight skirt gave him an order, "Get us a room and some ice. I'll get the bottle."

6

Charlie watched her turn around and walk into the lingering cloud of dust kicked up by the mistreated Ford and wondered if what he was feeling was love, or something else.

Body Disposal

1

Ernest had just turned the stolen car onto a gravel road when a drizzle exploded into a downpour. "Of course," he said, with the sour voice of a man resigned to a wretched existence.

It was hot, muggy, almost 3:00 a.m., and there was a lot of work left to be done. This would be an all-nighter.

2

The gravel road turned to dirt, and then it wasn't a road at all. Ernest kept driving. He knew the way.

He caught a glimpse of the water, extinguished his headlights, crept into a stand of trees, and killed the engine.

Before stepping out of the air-conditioning, he blasphemed the pouring rain once more and then entered the sticky swelter of Washington, D.C.'s unforgiving August.

By the time he'd opened the trunk, Ernest was soaked by the rain. A heavy sigh accentuated his plight, if only to himself.

Ernest had had the foresight to unscrew the trunk bulb. When you're on the water at night, the smallest light can be seen for miles. He would do tonight's work without so much as a match.

The plastic hazmat suit would protect him from incriminating hair and DNA, and resembled a black spacesuit: one piece that covered the body head to toe. Ernest knew it would be stifling in that thing, so he considered not putting it on and burning his clothes afterward. Not a good idea. If the cops pulled him over in a stolen car, that'd be one thing. If he was pulled over *buck naked* in a stolen car....

He removed his clothes and shoes. Now that he was naked, the rain decided to ease up enough to allow the mosquitoes to come out and feast. Forcing his sticky, bare bulk into the stiff plastic suit was agonizing work, and once zipped inside, he found himself sealed in a world so suffocating he could smell the chocolate on his breath. Sweat oozed from his pores.

Ernest had never disposed of a body this way before. He preferred to bury or burn them. The meddlesome Old Rich Prick had insisted on this method tonight.

Old Rich Prick was always giving orders just to give orders.

The downpour resumed and Ernest muttered something about God hating him.

3

So much rain lashed against Ernest's plastic universe, it was impossible to see through the blurry face shield and the drops hit like thick drumbeats, *duhn, duh, duhn, duhn, duh.* Looking like a Man from Mars, he wiped the water away and steeled himself to go to work.

First he pulled the plastic-wrapped body of the dead man he called Stark from the trunk and let it drop to the wet ground.

Now rain was popping off Ernest *and* the plastic wrapped around the body. It was loud, too loud. *What if someone hears?* He abandoned the thought. It was too fucking hot to be paranoid.

Ernest dragged Stark's corpse over the wet grass to the edge of the lake and unwrapped him like the package of dead and bloody meat he was. Ernest regretted what came next. *This Stark guy was okay*, he thought. *No cry-babying, didn't stink up the plane, talked to me like a person....*

Then Ernest remembered all the extra work Stark's smarty-pants bank wire move would cause him, all the security footage he'd have to trudge through. Holding on to that thought, he grabbed a four-pound hammer and beat on Stark's face until it was mush and the teeth dust.

He re-wrapped the body and added a black tarp he'd brought along to better camouflage it on the lake's dark bottom.

Then, around the entire Dead Stark package, he fastened heavy chains attached to two cinder blocks wrapped with thick towels. Ernest was a professional. No one would find a floater.

The Man from Mars trotted through the downpour and into the trees to retrieve a four-man raft he'd inflated and concealed the day before. Breathing heavy and starting to get hungry, he dragged out the raft and, with some effort, rolled Stark into it. Then he carefully placed the towel-wrapped cinder blocks on either side of the corpse and dragged the fully-loaded raft into the shallows, where it bobbed without a care.

4

With the rain still pounding him, it was Ernest's turn to get into the raft. Twice he almost toppled over trying. On his third try, with some finesse, he gingerly stepped onto the raft's slippery bottom, and then, ever so carefully, lifted his other foot over the side and *quickly sat*. He made it! He was in! Except, under his giant ass he could feel the lake bottom, which meant his giant ass had grounded him.

He wasn't going anywhere.

Now what?

He had no idea, so he used this time to contemplate the universe's hatred of him and decided to sit there and sweat until he died.

While awaiting the embrace of death, his stomach growled, which led him to think of pancakes and young boys and his million dollars.

His will to live returned.

Ernest knew that if he stood, he'd lose his balance and capsize the whole thing. So, like a dumb dog, he rolled himself over the side of the raft and splashed into the shallow water. Soaking wet, he struggled to his feet, got behind the raft, bent himself over, and pushed it into deeper water, right up to his belly.

From this position, the only way in was to clamber in. His other choice was to swim behind the raft and push it out to where he needed to be: the middle of the lake where the water was deepest. No, too risky. His plastic suit might fill with water and down he'd go.

Somehow, he scrambled into the raft, a sight anyone would've found amusing, even under these circumstances.

5

Using two comically small oars, a woozy-from-the-heat and increasingly hungry Ernest rowed the half-mile to the middle of the lake. Due to the relentless rain, this took forever. He kept having to stop and wipe his face shield. The drumbeat of the drops inside his plastic world was so loud, he wouldn't have heard a helicopter hovering overhead.

He finally reached the lake's center and there, into the dark water, he dropped one chained cinder block and then the other. The weight of the blocks tugged at the chains fastened around Stark's body, which made it easy for Ernest and gravity to roll the body right over the side.

Splash!

"Easy peasy japanesey."

By the time he'd rowed back to shore, heat and hunger had Ernest close to fainting. So he lumbered out of the raft, dragged it next to the stolen car, turned himself around, and walked right into the water—all the way up to his chest. The cool water kept him from passing out and he splashed off the human gore from his plastic suit.

Back on shore, with the cursed rain still battering him, he shredded the raft with a knife, balled up the tatters, and shoved them into large trash bags. Next, he removed the spacesuit and stuffed it into another trash bag. After he dressed in his soaking-wet clothes, Ernest threw the trash bags into the trunk, jumped in the car, fired it up, and turned the air conditioner up, *all the way the fuck up.*

The cool air helped, as did the promise of those all-night diner pancakes. But first the stolen car and trash bags would have to be dumped in different police jurisdictions.

6

Ernest shifted into reverse, made his way out of the trees, and—*stopped.*

In the back of his mind was an itch, a serious itch in need of a serious scratch.

Something was wrong. Real wrong.

I forgot something.

Ernest never screwed around when his brain needed a scratch. He trusted his instincts and switched off the ignition, air conditioning and all.

What did I forget?

The rain spattered against the car windows.

He closed his eyes and mentally walked through every moment of the last couple of hours. He took his time, step-by-step, and when he failed to come up with the answer, there was only one thing to do: he opened the car door and hauled himself out into the rain and humidity.

The air smelled funny, that's how wrong everything felt.

A shiver shot up his spine.

Then the rain stopped, which made the humidity worse.

Then the bugs went quiet.

What the hell?

With his senses sharpened, Ernest listened to the night.... Twigs snapped, trees creaked, branches bristled, water lightly splashed....

His brain itched like crazy.

What did I forget!?

He methodically retraced his steps and whispered to himself: "Okay, this is where I dropped the body. Here's where I changed clothes. I unwrapped him over there. Then I went back to the car to get the pers— the persuader! The hammer! Where's that hammer!?"

A flashlight would've solved this problem in a half-second, a risk he'd never take.

Whenever Ernest got anxious like this, his intestines went to war. Already a gurgling, roiling battle was stirring up his guts, so on top of everything else, he had to take a wicked shit.

Ernest willed himself to ignore the discomfort. If he was going to defy a universe eager to destroy him, he had to focus.

He walked a grid pattern.

Fifteen minutes it took, and it was worth it. Man, it felt good. "Fuck you, universe," he hissed, holding the hammer high above his head like Thor. "Fuck you," he said again, and like Mighty Thor, he hurled the hammer through the air.

The persuader sailed over the lake, surrendered to gravity, hit the water, and sank into the same mucky bottom that now held the pulp of bloody flesh that was once Joshua Mason.

PART TWO

THE DEATH
STORIES

The Old Woman

1

There was no way to know the year of Mason's birth. The concept of time had not yet been invented.

He was born into a clan of a few hundred hunter-gatherers who roamed from water hole to water hole in the vast desert area of what's now called Northern Mexico and the American Southwest. By day, wrapped in animal skins, the clan buried itself beneath the sand to sleep and to escape the blast of the sun. At night they hunted mice, snakes, and beasts that are no more.

This was long before the Aztecs, and even before the Olmec, who came before the Aztecs.

The clan had no language, no name for itself. Communication came in the form of grunts, gestures, and crude drawings in soft sand.

This clan worshipped the moon, for it was the moon that gave them light to hunt and chased away the unforgiving sun.

Brute force and superstition ruled. The men fought constantly over the women and to decide who would lead.

The tribe's true leader, however, was a crone; a vicious old woman with extraordinary powers. When the tribe's precious moon shrank to a sliver and threatened to disappear, only she could bring it back by way of a ceremony that required a human sacrifice.

The old woman put on quite a show choosing her sacrifice. After a beast had been gutted and its smallest bones stirred in her spit, the choice was always a rival of the old woman's or someone who'd displeased her.

This coincidence only proved to the clan that the moon was on the old woman's side.

Dying was no big deal to these primitives, who believed babies proved you returned after death. What they did fear was pain. The Old Woman's sacrifices were disemboweled alive. For this reason, many sought her favor, something she reveled in and abused.

Mason stayed away from the old woman. While he believed in her power to bring back the moon, he also believed remaining invisible was key to survival. He kept to the background. The chorus suited him fine. Always would. Even back then, he'd discovered something so many still haven't: that the most dangerous place in the world is proximity to power.

One day, the old woman took sick, didn't open her eyes for a long time, and a younger woman's magic brought back the moon.

When the sickly old woman woke, she discovered that this clan, who hated and feared her, no longer needed her.

2

Filled with bloodlust, Mason eagerly joined the mob that held her down, splayed her out, and tied her hands and feet to stakes. How he hated the old woman. If the sun didn't kill her, the ants would.

Then, just as he was about to leave her to die, he caught a look in her eyes and saw her for what she was: a terrified and vulnerable old woman. For the first time, he not only saw another person's humanity, he chose to recognize it.

Later that day, as the clan slept under the sand, Mason cut her loose and they ran off together.

He found a cave for them to hide in and, at first, the old woman was grateful, so grateful she offered him her sex. He declined and this rejection put an end to her gratitude. She returned to form: bossing him around, hitting, scratching, and hurling rocks.

He hated her all over again, and nothing would've made him happier than to return from a hunt to find her dead.

After the moon cycled a few times, the old woman fell sick again. The pain of her illness made her meaner. Mason still kept her warm and fed.

Then, as her death closed in, she turned needy and fearful and begged him to remain by her side. She wouldn't allow him to hunt or even to gather water. Although hungry and thirsty, he stayed.

She was practically dead the night the clan's warriors found them. Although outnumbered, Mason still fought in vain to protect her and both suffered painful deaths.

After Mason died, everything went black and silent....

3

The silence of his death was total, and so was the black. Mason hovered in this silent void and then felt its nothingness slowly engulf his body until he was no longer a physical presence. For a time, he floated on this nothingness, feeling as free as he ever had, until a thin shimmer of blue light appeared. The shimmer vibrated and was as tall as a man. Its glow brought with it a sense of peace. He felt an urge to open his eyes. And when he did, he saw the night, the stars, and discovered he was seated beneath a tall Joshua Tree in the middle of the desert.

All of his wounds and scars had disappeared, and so had his thirst and hunger. The calluses on his hands were gone. Two toes he'd lost during a childhood hunt had returned.

Not knowing any better, he returned to the clan.

His reappearance terrified them, proved that their idea of how the world worked wasn't so. This time, they killed Mason slow, and after he died, it happened all over again—as it would every time he died: the black void, the sense of nothingness, the tall blue shimmer, and the Joshua Tree.

He kept to himself after that.

4

Elsewhere in the world, history happened: Alexander the Great, the rise and fall of Rome, Christ's crucifixion, the Renaissance, the birth of Muhammad, the discovery of the New World, wars, revolutions, genocides, plagues....

Mason took no part in history.

5

Like any man, Mason could die. Snakes got him once. So did a fight he didn't start. A lightning strike caught him another time. But he always returned right as rain in that same spot under that same Joshua Tree.

Something Mason was certain of was that, on that small piece of land under the Joshua Tree, nothing could hurt him—nothing in this world, nothing in *any* world.

He just knew that if that lightning bolt had struck him on that spot, he wouldn't have felt it. If an atomic bomb exploded there, it wouldn't mess up his hair. A few feet, either way, he was as vulnerable as any man. But on *that spot*, on that spot *right there*, he was Superman in a universe without kryptonite.

And it was on that spot, under a dark and moonless sky, where Mason returned after a fat man dumped his dead body into the middle of a lake.

6

Mason's nakedness always embarrassed him, so he dressed quickly in clothes he kept in a nearby stash and felt the sharp hiss of instincts scream at him to return immediately to D.C.

Don't wait. Don't screw around. Go before they show up here!

His instincts said one thing; his anguish said another.

It was here where Doreen was dying, and now nothing would stop him from getting to her. And this time he would find the words to convince her to join him.

He pulled on his boots and tried to stand. His legs had other ideas. He dropped to his knees, fell forward on both hands, inhaled a deep breath, held it, and then held it some more. He held it until his head swam and his body chilled. He closed his eyes and held it until flashes from the past popped off in his head....

A wedding veil blowing through the wind.

A giant bow wrapped around a used pickup truck.

The touch of Doreen's hand as she gave him the keys.

The taste of her kiss.

Her body arched in agony reaching for a call button.

He finally remembered to breathe, and when he opened his eyes, he realized he was running—running just as fast as he could.

Night Visitor

1

Doreen woke from a dreamless sleep and wondered if the cancer had eaten up the part of her that dreamt. Through the slits of her eyes, she scanned the room. Everything was a milky blur. She couldn't tell if it was day or night. The quiet outside her door, the lack of activity and nurse chatter, told her it was probably late. But with the rot devouring everything, she no longer trusted her senses.

There was some light, a dim light. Her brain fired off an order to turn toward the window, but her head stayed put. It didn't get the signal.

She reached for a morphine button that wasn't there and then remembered being fitted for an IV drip after the priest performed last rites.

This was when Doreen realized she was about to experience the final thoughts of her life.

Weeks ago, she'd resolved to make those thoughts matter with direct appeals to God prepared in advance.

She gave thanks for her life and for a death that helped her appreciate that life. She apologized to God for feeling alone and told Him that she now knew He'd always been beside her. She had more appeals, but forgot them as her mind rebelled to run off and collect the smallest details of her life....

She remembered Mason's hands—the strong hands of a man who worked for a living—and how his scent changed from morning to night, and yet didn't. She thought of his laugh, and how easily he made her laugh; the taste of his skin, the lines of his face, those dirty socks.

She recalled the day her father taught her to play poker and how they used jellybeans for chips; and a Christmas Eve with her mother; how it was snowing and Bob Hope sang "Silver Bells" over the speakers outside the stores.

She wondered why she didn't think of Charlie, why he was so far from her thoughts, and then heard the sounds of a swimming pool filled with children and saw Maya in a Communion dress so white it looked like light.

She recalled a ray of sun that had woken her long ago in the back of a station wagon and wondered what it was shining on now.

That's right, Doreen remembered. *There was sunlight in my eyes and smoke in Mr. Arthur's. That was more than sixty years ago. Sixty years....*

Then Doreen drifted off to sleep, but only for a few moments. The sound of her own gasps woke her.

She convulsed.

Her eyes wouldn't open.

Her lungs wouldn't draw air.

Doreen had arrived at the moment of her death.

She fought for breath and begged God to accept her soul.

The machines standing guard over her began to shriek.

She gasped and gagged and felt her head swim.

This is it. I'm going to black out, and then I'm going to die and—

The machines went quiet.

The quiet was so sudden, it startled her.

Her lungs suddenly filled with oxygen—beautiful, beautiful oxygen, all she could take in.

She took in one deep breath, then another, and was just about to open her eyes when....

Someone took hold of her hand.

The touch was warm and familiar.

So was the voice.

"It's okay," the voice whispered. "I'm here. I'm with you."

Doreen swallowed hard and her eyes fluttered open.

Across the room, she saw a tall, wavy shimmer of blue light. Its glow filled the dark with reassurance.

Still holding Doreen's hand, Maya gently sat down on the edge of the bed next to her mother. "Don't be afraid of the light, Mom," she said.

Doreen wasn't afraid, and with surprising ease sat up for a better look at her daughter.

"You're so grown up," said Doreen. "You're so beautiful."

Maya squeezed her mother's hand and then told her all the things she'd meant to before the car accident took her life.

2

On that same night, a starlet named Hayley Caldwell died of an accidental fall. She was thirty-three.

Hayley, whose real name was Joan Flatstone, was born in Southern California, and started appearing in television commercials at age four. At age twelve, she landed her own sitcom, *Hey! Hey! Hayley!* Which ran for four seasons on a cable network and reran forever after.

She dropped out of school at sixteen to star in a trilogy of slasher movies: *Die Now!* and its sequel *Die Now—Double Dose!* And the direct-to-video sequel *Die Now—Three Times the Harm!*

Then her career hit a wall.

Hayley built much of that wall herself as she partied away her innocence and millions, kept the tabloids busy, and filed for bankruptcy.

By the time she turned twenty-one, she'd had three abortions, two car accidents, and one divorce.

At age twenty-nine, just after filing for a second bankruptcy, fame returned for Hayley after she won the season on a dating reality show and returned as the permanent co-host.

Although no more than a few million people ever watched, America's fame machine still turned Hayley into a mega-celebrity by way of her turbulent personal life. This included an eating disorder, the claim of being a "rape survivor," and an unspecified stay at a rehab center—all of it seasoned with countless romances, including one with another woman.

3

On the night she plunged to her death, Hayley was trying to save her career after having committed that one sin America never forgives: weight gain.

You see, during her show's hiatus, Hayley discovered she was pregnant. She told no one, had no idea who the father was, and didn't care. Rather than have another abortion, Hayley decided she needed this baby, needed something to love her, and then she gained forty-five pounds.

But after mommy went on a weekend meth binge, the child—a girl—was stillborn at seven months

Luckily for Hayley, her dead baby arrived at the opportune time. Her network contract was up and losing a child guaranteed her the cover of *People* magazine.

This could work.

And then it all fell apart. The day before she planned to release the *tragic news of my miscarriage*, photos of Hayley looking very pregnant and smoking meth went viral online.

Hayley immediately released a statement claiming she was never pregnant. The weight gain, she said, was due to the return of an eating disorder. She announced she had checked into a rehab center and was launching a non-profit to combat body-shaming.

In truth, Hayley was shacking up with Caleb Easton, the fifteen-year-old star of the popular *Die Now!* streaming series.

4

To lose those forty-five pounds and save her career, Hayley hired a personal trainer and went on a meat-free diet (cocaine is plant-based). The extra pounds melted away, and the following day—had she lived—she intended to knock everyone's socks off with her smokin' hot bod.

Hayley and her publicist had arranged for the sleazy celebrity site, Crotcha.com, to take "unauthorized" photos of Hayley walking alone in a yellow bikini along the beach.

In preparation for this photo shoot, Hayley spent weeks with an acting coach so that during this walk she would appear forsaken and vulnerable—but mostly fuckable.

5

The night before her big comeback photo shoot, Hayley hoped to sweat off three more pounds by pedaling up and down Laurel Canyon's steep hills in eighty-four-degree weather while wearing three pairs of sweat pants, a wool hat, mittens, and a heavy parka.

She would never know she'd lost five pounds.

She would never know because a moonless night mixed with amphetamines meant she didn't see the forty-foot drop just inches from where she brought her bike to a stop.

Her right foot hit gravel, her left foot found only air, and into the canyon she tumbled.

If not for the shriek, she might not have been found for days.

6

News of Hayley's death ran every half hour on the cable news and entertainment channels, earned a weekend marathon of *Hey! Hey! Hayley!* reruns, trended on social media, and inspired countless online tributes.

Fans quickly gathered at the site of her death, where a makeshift memorial morphed into a shrine that required traffic and crowd control.

Two girls—aged thirteen and fifteen—committed suicide over the news. The one who hanged herself broadcast it live on FaceTalk and racked up 17 million views.

Hayley's younger sister, Skylar, was so distraught, she released a tribute song and checked into rehab.

7

While America mourned its favorite reality star, Mrs. Doreen Mason died alone of natural causes in a southern Arizona hospice.

The hospice commemorated her death by funneling her body through the cold indifference of a bureaucracy.

The *Lincoln County Gazette* published a short notice announcing that the burial would take place Monday afternoon at the Browning Cemetery.

To protect Charlie, Doreen had made arrangements to deny her true name one final time. The small stone marking her resting place would read: "Doreen Medina."

A Spasm of Hate

1

Under an unforgiving sun during the hottest part of the day, a grim-faced Mason stared down at Doreen's casket and relied on his fury to hide the grief a selfish world wouldn't allow him to declare.

Leaning on his shoulder, bawling like a baby, was Charlie. Mason envied how all the misery poured right out of the boy, which meant he'd probably be okay after a while.

The turnout was small. The presiding priest, who'd never met Doreen, recited a Bible passage.

Two old men stood by quietly, hats in hand, remembering the pretty innkeeper who didn't mind when they flirted and how that generosity had made life on the road less lonely.

A handful of couples from the Church of the Holy Mother huddled together. They didn't know Doreen well, but still felt it proper to see her off.

On the access road, parked behind the hearse, was Yvette, who'd driven Charlie and Mason to the morning viewing and then here, to the afternoon burial. Yvette sat in her car chain smoking and worried about her plans. *This Mason guy might only be the handyman, but he's pretty sharp.*

2

A lot of years had slid by since Mason last attended a funeral. Back then, four men dressed in black had solemnly lowered the casket into the ground using two pieces of rope.

The All at Once, of course, had awarded that honor to a machine, and as Mason watched his wife slowly disappear into the earth, a spasm of hate washed over him that was so intense, he closed his eyes against it and saw the world explode and its pieces hurled into the sun.

After the burial was over and everyone had left, Charlie refused to leave his grandmother alone in an open grave. So he and Mason leaned against Yvette's Ford and watched a machine push a pile of dirt on top of her.

3

Two nights ago, after he'd been murdered in Washington, D.C., and left for dead at the bottom of a lake, Mason ran the whole two miles from the Joshua Tree to his safehouse, where he kept a motorcycle hidden. But the safehouse was forty miles from the Rebel Yell, and by the time he'd arrived and parked the bike, Charlie'd already received the news and fallen apart.

That was when Mason met Charlie's new girlfriend, Yvette.

He'd deal with her later.

The next three days were a blur of making arrangements and phone calls, of consoling Charlie, purchasing them both off-the-rack suits, and keeping a tense lookout for the dangerous fat man.

4

Normally, Mason didn't waste time thinking about the way things should be. But right now, those thoughts were the only thing stopping him from digging through the earth and laying down next to his wife.

The way Mason saw it, he shouldn't have to hide his grief just because others were afraid to die and would hunt him down for his secret. He was no cynic. He knew there were people who would leave him be, people like Angie-the-cashier and, of course, Doreen, who could've joined him and still said no. But those weren't the people in charge, were they?

No, in this upside-down world, power was awarded to the last people who should hold it: those who sought it, along with the greedy, the entitled, the well-connected, and anyone with the correct last name born into it. And about those people, Mason was certain of two things: there was nothing they wouldn't do to get their hands on him, and it was because of them he had to stand here hiding his misery, holding tight to the leash of his anguish, when all he wanted was to claw through the dirt.

5

Hell, even if he wanted to share his immortality with the world (and he didn't), there was the practical matter, the mechanics of it. Mason couldn't it pass it on with a wave of his hand. It was a one-at-a-time process. And if he gave it to you, you couldn't pass it to anyone else. It wasn't a virus. He was it. So who would be the lucky few to win that prize? We all know who: those who rigged the game to win all the prizes, those Mason thought of as the "cream scrapers."

If there was one thing Mason couldn't get over about this society, it was how the All at Once made it possible for the most useless people in the world to scrape off all the cream. He knew that if you built your-self a pile of everyone you see on your TV, they wouldn't add up to the worth of a single plumber, farmer, or coal miner. But if you swept the table clear of those TV people, the world would keep turning just fine, maybe better.

So Mason knew who'd win his prize, and fuck that.

Now imagine explaining his "fuck that" to a congressional committee wielding their "sirs."

You sound selfish and greedy, sir. Like you're full of hate, sir. Like a national security threat, sir.

Oh, the establishment would follow the letter of the law, alright. They always do. And if that letter wasn't already in the law, they'd go ahead and write themselves up a new law making it perfectly legal to hunt him down, open him up, and watch his gears turn.

6

But if they'd listen (and they never would), he'd tell them some hard truths. He'd fan out those truths like a full house.

Anyone eager to wrap their minds around a scenario that only ever ends in a horror show, need only picture a world where no one dies. Forget over-population, focus on human nature.

Let's start with the one thing no one ever thinks of. Not everyone's rich, you know. Most aren't. And for those who aren't, if you take an honest look over their personal horizon in a world where no one dies, there's no retirement, no pension, no social security, no rest. Living forever sentences you to grinding out a living forever. Believe me, I know.

You want to spend eternity in a cubicle pushing papers? You want to dig ditches, cut grass, change oil, wait tables, enter data, deliver mail, sell cars, drive a bus, write code, work in a factory, wash dishes, cut hair, fight fires, groom dogs, mop floors, write briefs, clean teeth, patrol streets, sell homes, stock shelves, make beds, flip burgers, and stand behind a cash register forever?

How about a planet full of assholes? Is that what you want, a world buried in thoughtless, judgmental, unforgiving, forever-young narcissists never compelled to wise up by the coming of the abyss?

Don't you understand, it's the cold truth of dying that forces a man to face the fact there's no endless supply of tomorrows. It's death's unrelenting approach that says you need to become a better man, a better husband and father—now, right now, before it's too late. Now is the time to forgive, to beg forgiveness, to say "I love you," and take hold of what matters.

Don't you get it? It's the harrowing knowledge of our limited time that separates us from animals. You want to live in a world without that? Trust me, you don't.

7

It wasn't as though science never had a chance to look Mason over. Back in '98, a car hit him doing about 25 mph. After Mason woke in the hospital, the doctors had already completed their x-rays and MRIs, had already run a boatload of tests, and found only a concussion. Both days he was there they took his blood. Results didn't lift an eyebrow.

Even so, if it meant he could live in peace with Charlie and openly grieve his wife, he'd agree to their tests. But no matter what he agreed to, it would never be enough to satisfy those who get to decide what's enough.

The cold truth was this: even if he could help them, he wouldn't. Not with his wife in the ground and him standing here forced to pretend she wasn't.

8

A low sun stretched the shadows across the tombstones.

A cemetery worker climbed off his machine to spread a dirty piece of plastic grass over a mound of fresh dirt.

Without a word, Mason opened the car door and slid into the backseat. Charlie piled up front next to Yvette.

As they drove off, Mason tried to relax in the knowledge he would soon return to say a private goodbye.

He had no way of knowing more than twenty years would pass before that day was possible.

Where the Men Talk

1

Under the moon's sliver of blue light, Charlie and Mason traipsed through the desert. Still in their funeral suits, they silently made their way to a spot where Mason lit a fire and they relaxed on a couple of rusty chairs.

Mason had been taking Charlie out to this spot for a long time. Sometimes to sip a cold one and talk things over. Other times, to regard the night in the silent comfort of each other's company. This was the one place where Charlie was allowed to drink, but only the one beer.

Mason didn't care for the taste of alcohol. He didn't drink at all, except here. He believed it was good for Charlie, this ritual of theirs. Men should take young men out for a beer now and again. And drinking just the one set a good example and taught the boy moderation.

2

There was a stiff breeze and every so often Charlie would stop walking, close his eyes, and let the wind slide across his face. This made him feel better. Then, with the ice cooler tucked under his arm, he'd scamper to catch up to Mason.

They arrived at their destination. Mason gathered wood while Charlie used the sleeve of his suit jacket to wipe the chairs clean of blown sand.

After the small fire was crackling and the beers were pulled from the ice, the two men settled in next to one another to honor a silence that felt right.

Charlie looked to the sky and imagined his reunion in Heaven with Grandma Dory. But out of the corner of his eye, he couldn't help but notice how Mason kept rubbing on his face. Rubbing and rubbing, sometimes with both hands, like he was trying to rub something away.

3

Charlie had things to say tonight—well, things Yvette wanted him to say. He didn't really want to say them, so he waited until he'd drained the last of his beer before he said anything.

"Gra-gra-grandma told me all the ti-time there's a Heaven," Charlie said. "That-that she knew that for sure. Th-that she'd seen it, actually sssseen it."

Mason leaned forward so he could set his elbows on his knees and stare down at the earth. After a pause, he confirmed Charlie's report.

"She believed that with everything she had."

"Do you-do you believe that?" Charlie asked. "Do-do you be-believe in Heaven?"

You don't tell a child his grandmother is worm food any more than you tell him there's no Santa Claus, so Mason lied. "Course I believe that," he said.

"You ever seen-seen it? Seen Heaven?"

This time Mason told the truth. "Sure have," he said as he rubbed on his face and remembered that first night when she ran a small hand through her long black hair and asked if he needed change for the machines.

Charlie pressed on. "Wh-wh-what's it look-look like, Heaven?"

"Looks like..." Mason stopped, set his beer in the sand, and stared into the fire.

"Looks like something you can't say goodbye to."

4

Charlie didn't know if he'd ever seen Heaven, but was pretty sure he'd felt it these last few nights with Yvette. The things she did to him...what she let him do to her....

He'd never felt that way before, not even when he looked at dirty pictures on the internet, the ones his grandma tried to block with a computer filter.

Doing those things with Yvette also soothed his rage. This morning, Charlie found a dog rooting around the garbage cans and just ran it off.

It wasn't only the things they did to one another that made Charlie happy. Yvette was also impressed with him.

"You run this motel all on your own?" she'd asked one night in a kind of awe as they lay in bed. "That's a big responsibility," she added. "Most small businesses fail within a year."

Charlie didn't believe that. He knew Grandma Dory and Mason lied to him all the time to pretend he wasn't stupid. He could always tell when they did. But Yvette insisted her claim was true and pulled the statistics up on her iPhone.

"Look here," she said, shoving the bright screen in his face. "More than ninety-six percent of small businesses fail. You're doing better than ninety-six percent."

"My grandma and Mason mostly tell me what to do," he confessed with downcast eyes, hoping she'd keep the compliments coming.

"Listen here," she said, deliberately sitting up so the bed sheet would drop and expose her naked breasts. "You should do more of the decision-making. It's right there on the internet. You're more successful than ninety-six percent. Stop talking yourself down. Just imagine if you took charge."

With no sex drive, Charlie didn't feel lust or passion. He couldn't complete the act and had no desire to please her. Nevertheless, he still couldn't believe a naked woman was in his bed and that he could do whatever he wanted to her. So just because he could, he reached out and grabbed hold of a breast.

Pretending to enjoy his clumsy, sweaty touch, Yvette arched her back, moaned, and clicked off the light.

5

Filled with the memory of how good Yvette made him feel, a grinning Charlie grabbed the neck of his empty beer bottle, reached back as far as he could, and flung it deep into the desert.

Then he remembered all the things Yvette told him to say to Mason tonight, and that good feeling went away.

He didn't want to say them.

He considered not saying them.

Then he pictured Yvette asking him if he'd said them and him trying to explain why he hadn't.

Then he pictured feeling like a *fat fucking retard* for not being able to explain it, so he turned to Mason and rushed through it.

"I-I'd like you to stay on," he said with a firmness Yvette would've been proud of. "B-b-but I got plans and, uh"—the air began to seep from his nerve—"well, uh, if-if you see things my way"—he barely finished this last part—"I-I-I'll, uhm, keep you on as my handyman."

Mason didn't respond. He didn't look at Charlie or even acknowledge what Charlie had just said. Instead, without a word, Mason lifted himself from his chair and walked away into the dark.

Charlie couldn't believe it. *Mason just up and left!* Since Charlie had no idea how to react, he did the only thing he could: sat there and felt stupid. Then he waited. And then he waited some more. Charlie waited right up until he realized he had no idea how to get back to the Rebel Yell. With panic bubbling, he was just about to call out when Mason returned carrying Charlie's discarded beer bottle.

Without a word, Mason reinstalled himself in his chair and dropped the empty into the cooler.

Charlie was too ashamed to say anything. He didn't know why he was ashamed, he just was.

Only after he'd drained his own beer did Mason finally respond: "I'm your friend, Charlie. You shouldn't talk to me like that."

"I-I-I just mean...I mean, I'm-I'm in charge now, right?"

"It's your place now."

"Onaccounta, I hired Yvette as assistant manager." Charlie raced through those words because that was what *he* wanted to say.

Cool as they come, Mason answered, "Well, we're gonna need the extra help once the pool's fixed and the website's up."

Charlie felt better. "Okay."

So did Mason. "Okay."

6

As he stared into the flames, Charlie's good feelings about settling things with Mason slowly twisted into confusion over Yvette. He'd meant to preserve his Grandma Dory's bedroom and yet, to deliberately defile it, that's where he took Yvette to get drunk and have sex. He felt terrible about it and also excited about doing it again tonight. The warring emotions closed Charlie's eyes and he felt himself fall back into that black pool of oil.

Then he broke down crying.

Mason threw an arm around Charlie's shoulder and assured him: "We're gonna get through this, you and I. That's a promise."

Two Lousy Options

1

For just a moment Mason forgot Doreen was dead—just plain forgot. So, when he and Charlie returned from having their beer and entered the motel office excitedly discussing all the projects they had planned, Mason expected to see Doreen standing where she always was, behind the front desk. Yvette standing there instead hit him harder than that car that once put him in a hospital.

After three days of holding it down, he couldn't anymore, wouldn't anymore. So he made a big show of yawning to explain the water in his eyes, said goodnight, turned, grabbed the door, and—

"I'm still taking you to the airport in the morning, right?" Yvette asked with an unearned familiarity.

Mason yanked open the door and answered on his way out. "Meet you around seven."

One more word and his voice would've cracked.

"Good," she called after him, "because we got things to talk about."

He'd deal with her later.

2

Mason locked the door to his room, switched on the air conditioner, turned up the radio, opened the water faucets, closed the bathroom door, sat on the edge of the tub, and stopped holding it down.

3

Room 14 had been his home for more than thirty years—seventeen feet from wall to wall with a queen-sized bed. There probably wasn't a person alive who wouldn't describe it as a D-U-M-P dump. Even so, Mason still appreciated its miracles.

On the wall opposite the bed was a cheap chest of drawers with an attached writing desk. On top sat a small microwave and refrigerator. There was no TV. Mason removed that decades ago for the same reason you'd remove a pipe that pumped sewage into your home.

Laying in the bed, to your left was a good-sized window that looked out on the motel's dusty parking lot. Underneath the window was a built-in heater/air conditioner.

To the right, was a small closet, sink, and his only improvement: a bookshelf filled with books.

4

After a long shower, Mason switched off the radio, air conditioner, and all the lights. In the dark, he opened the drapes, placed his one chair a few feet from the window, and sat down to keep an eye out.

The .38 snub-nose on the nightstand was within reach and brought no comfort.

Mason already knew he'd made a mistake coming directly here that night, that he'd allowed his emotion to override his judgment. Doreen was still dead and he'd lost three crucial days.

If he'd returned immediately to D.C. like he was supposed to, this whole thing would already be over and his pickup would be here instead of gathering dust in a Las Vegas parking garage.

How fast he ran through the desert that night didn't matter, and while he was running he knew it didn't matter. He couldn't save Doreen. You can't save someone who believes only Jesus saves. What the hell had he been thinking? He *hadn't* been thinking, and now he was left with only two lousy options.

Lousy option number one was to wait here for Ernest to show up, in which case the fat man might get the drop on him. And even if he didn't, whatever went down would likely attract all kinds of unwanted attention.

Lousy option number two was to jump on a plane to D.C. first thing tomorrow morning and hope Ernest didn't pass him coming the other way, not with Charlie left here alone and helpless.

What a fiasco.

Mason had already decided on number two.

He'd just have to hope his bank wire move had bought him and Charlie enough time.

It hadn't.

Three Holes

1

Less than two miles from where Mason sat in the dark with a loaded .38, Ernest was digging hole number three.

He'd dug two holes the previous night—one for the dumpy guy always eating licorice. The other for the blonde who looked like Barney Rubble. Once he'd completed those, Ernest assumed all the hole-digging was behind him. But one thing he'd forgotten was just how much the universe enjoyed fucking with him.

A few hours after he'd finished digging those two holes, it was right before dawn when the same guy Ernest left at the bottom of a lake—that Mike Stark guy—suddenly strolled out of the Rebel Yell.

He'd nearly dropped the night-vision binoculars.

"What the wh—?" Ernest blinked a few times, shut his eyes, and rattled his head around like a cartoon character. Unlike a cartoon character, he followed this up with a "What the fucking fuck?" and lifted the binocs for another look.

"Has to be a twin," he told himself as he observed the "twin" slowly circle the Rebel Yell's perimeter.

"What's he do—What's he looking for?"

Ernest knew the universe had its wicked hand in this.

He watched and kept watching until the "twin" returned to Room 14 and shut the door.

He slowly lowered the binocs and didn't move for a long time. He didn't know what to think...and then he did: *Bad juju. Twins are bad juju.*

He could sense the universe pointing and laughing at him.

This unsettling twist of fate also meant that instead of spending a comfortable evening at the Marriott, he was out here digging another goddamned hole.

2

This whole adventure had been a fuck of clusters since day one, and it weighed Ernest down with a sicker than sick feeling he couldn't shake—a feeling like when you pick up the phone in the middle of the night and it's the sister you never talk to saying your name real soft: *Ernest?*

How could that be anything but bad?

Ernest saw himself as a virtuoso when it came to shaking off bad feelings. Hell, he got 'em all the time. When you kill for a living, bad feelings come wrapped in the package. This feeling he couldn't shake—no way, no how. This feeling was different. But he kept right on doing the job, kept right on digging hole number three. No reason not to. Nothing you can do about the universe dangling a piano over your head.

No one gets out from under the piano.

3

What really torqued him was knowing this would've already been over had the Old Rich Prick not interfered.

Old Rich Prick and his Old Rich Prick ego squandered a whole day throwing his weight around.

"Did you not see the pedigree of my guests the other night?" the Old Rich Prick bragged. "You think one of them can't convince a bank to stand on its hind legs and tell us who received Stark's bank wire?"

Big talk, Ernest wanted to scream. *Big fucking talk. People don't deposit money in overseas banks for the free toaster, you idiot. Those banks sell only one thing: secrecy. Muscling an offshore bank to give up a secret is like threatening to kill a guy if he commits suicide. Either way, the guy's dead. Either way, the bank's out of business. So, where's the threat? Enjoy the bupkis, you stupid old prick.*

The Old Rich Prick was always trying to impress Ernest, and Ernest had no idea why. What he did know was that the old bastard was willing to burn up all the precious time in the world if it allowed him to whisper things to influential people like, "We have a problem. Here's what I need you to do."

Old Rich Prick loved having the juice. A good example was killing all these people. There was no need to kill everyone, not really. Nothing could ever lead back to him. The Old Rich Prick knew that, but ordering people dead got him off.

4

While the Old Rich Prick was wasting time jerking off his ego, Ernest tracked Mason's burner phone to Valhalla and obtained a copy of the sales receipt. Unfortunately, Qwik-Shop Inc. deleted its security footage after twenty-four hours, so now it was a matter of waiting for the Old Rich Prick to hand over the Kingdom Key.

The Old Rich Prick would never admit defeat, ever, so after the sun set on any hope of the Beautiful People coming across with the bank wire information, he hit Ernest with some CorporateSpeak about how "We should pursue this on two separate tracks," and early the following morning, the fat man was a VIP at FBI headquarters in Washington, D.C.

5

A cocky young agent named Jerome Something-Something-Ernest-Didn't-Give-a-Fuck handed Ernest a plastic visitor pass and talked too much.

"Ugly building, isn't it?" Jerome said as they strolled down a long corridor.

Silence.

Jerome tried again. "How was traffic this morning? I got here early. Traffic in D.C. is really something, isn't it?"

"We about there?" Ernest asked on behalf of his 350 pounds.

Fucking hallway just kept going, and holy shit was it bright: white ceiling, white floor, white wall on one side, wall of windows on the other. Ernest felt like he was getting x-rayed. Probably was, the sneaky sneaks.

Jerome's keycard opened the doors to a series of rooms that led to a small elevator. Ernest wasn't impressed. He was about to have access to the Kingdom Key and couldn't wait to see if it lived up to the hype.

With an affected flourish, Jerome gestured for Ernest to enter the elevator.

"Jesus Christ," Ernest grumbled and stepped inside.

The elevator had no floor buttons or any buttons. A scan of Jerome's keycard closed the doors and they descended.

"You bring extra socks?" Jerome asked.

Ernest had no idea what this asshole was talking about.

"You're no longer allowed to wear shoes in the Snowden Room," Jerome informed him. "Floor can get kind of cold in there. Someone shoulda told you about the socks."

Silence.

Jerome jabbered on. "That's what we call it now, the 'Snowden Room.' It's not the room's official name. You don't give a room like that an official name, so we call it the 'Snowden Room,' because the heck with that guy, right?"

While Jerome chattered away, Ernest decided that if he was ever given a red button that would kill Jerome in front of his mother, he'd press it four times. Once to kill him, three more times to be sure.

The elevator doors opened.

"I don't have the clearance, so I'll have to leave you here," Jerome explained, adding: "System's automated, pretty easy to use. At least that's what I'm told, so you shouldn't have any problem. Sorry no one told you about the socks." He pointed to a yellow button next to the elevator. "Press that when you're done or need a break. It'll text me and I'll come get you. How 'bout I buy you some lunch?"

"How 'bout you buy me some socks?" Ernest shot back.

Jerome blinked a few times, like a robot processing a new upload. Then the elevator doors closed on his hurt feelings and Ernest found himself alone in a small concrete room with an orange plastic chair and a locker.

On the opposite wall stood an imposing steel door.

6

A recording clicked on. The voice was female and stern: *Remove your belt, shoes, and the contents of your pockets. Place everything in the locker and close the locker door.*

The oppressive recording immediately started over..."*Remove your belt, shoes, and the contents....*"

"Sounds like someone's first wife," Ernest muttered, as he removed his shoes.

As instructed, Ernest put the requested items in the locker and closed the locker's door, which tripped something that slid open that big steel door. On the other side of that door was a short set of stairs that led up to a conveyor belt that carried you through a tunnel made of clear plastic and lights.

Feeling a little vulnerable without his shoes, Ernest cautiously made his way up each step. *This is no place to break a hip*, he told himself, and white-knuckled the handrail before gingerly stepping onto the moving conveyor.

Each section of the tunnel lit up as he passed through, undoubtedly scanning for anything and everything.

At the end of this journey sat a second steel door, which he expected to slide open.

It didn't.

Instead the conveyor abruptly stopped and with a loud *chugah!* All the lights shut off.

Ernest felt his temper rise. *Fucking feds and their*—"Hey, turn on the goddamn lights!" he shouted, and the steel door slid open.

7

Ernest carefully made his way down a second set of stairs, which led to a twelve-foot by eight-foot concrete bunker. Another government-issue orange chair sat waiting for him. Also waiting was a steel desk that blocked access to the other half of the room where an eighty-inch monitor was screwed to the wall.

On the desk sat a pad of scratch paper, an FBI coffee mug filled with sharpened pencils, and a computer mouse. There was no keyboard.

With his feet already chilled from the concrete floor, an excited Ernest took a seat. He grabbed the mouse and the eighty-inch monitor immediately came to bright life with a live satellite shot of planet Earth.

"Zowie," was all he said.

Before him was the key to unlock everything in our online kingdom— the Kingdom Key.

8

Ernest used the mouse to turn Mother Earth to where he could see North America. With a few clicks, he then zoomed in on the state of Nevada. He continued clicking until he was hovering over a live shot of the Qwik-Shop where Mason purchased the burner phone. A few more clicks and he was close enough for the red dots to appear.

Each red dot represented something the government was hacked into, from cell phones to traffic cameras; from email accounts to the cameras and microphones embedded in laptops, tablets, Alexas, baby monitors, voice activated remote controls—all of it, everything everywhere with a camera or microphone.... The FBI not only had real-time access, but in the event the government needed to go back and retrieve something, all the 24/7 audio and video—billions of hours—was recorded, cataloged, and stored forever in a massive hard drive farm hidden beneath the Pentagon.

Clicking on a red dot granted you access to the device, including all of its history. For example, you could watch and listen in real time to what was going on in a home or office through an iPhone or baby monitor, or you could retrieve and review all the audio and video captured and stored from those devices going back to when they first came online.

Ernest found the security camera that covered Qwik-Shop's gas pumps and clicked on its red dot. A menu opened that allowed him to scan the footage. The sales receipt told him the approximate time Mason pulled up. So he rewound the footage a few days—and there it was: video of Mason's pickup pulling up and stopping. The next part was easy. Ernest froze the frame, double-clicked on Mason's license plate, and got what he'd come for: *REGISTERED TO: Doreen Medina, 2764 W Old Highway 661, Browning, Arizona.*

9

Ernest rubbed his cold feet and chuckled at the graffiti penciled on the wall: *Edward Snowden's a pussy.*

The next day, he was out in Arizona digging holes.

Grave Decisions

1

Ernest worked alone, not only because he hated people so much that if you gave him a button that would kill everyone it would make his dick so hard he could use his hard dick to press the button. Ernest worked alone because killing was easy and people liked to complicate things, people like the Old Rich Prick.

In fact, Ernest found killing so easy he was working on a book about how to get away with murder. He had thirty-seven pages in pretty good shape and planned to someday submit them to all the major publishing houses under the pseudonym Clint Camacho.

After all the holes he'd dug, seemed a shame to waste the know-how.

That might not sound like a lot of pages, but Ernest knew that keeping murder simple was the only way to get away with it.

Clint Camacho's 8 Easy Steps to Get Away with Murder

1. Never kill anyone you know.
2. Always dig the hole in advance.
3. Always dig the hole six-feet deep, so no hiker gets his name in the paper after finding the bones that will launch a murder investigation.
4. Make the guy you've come to kill pack his stuff so everyone believes he took off somewhere and is still alive.
5. Force the guy to drive you to the hole.
6. Force him into the hole and put two behind his ear.

7. Bury him with his suitcases.

8. Leave his car near a bus station.

Easy peasy japanesey.

Ernest believed people got caught because they complicated things. They killed out of rage or passion or pride or greed, or they planned out some elaborate, over-complicated scheme. But then the dummies left behind a body!

You want to get away with murder? Get rid of the body. No body, no investigation. It was that simple. But people liked to complicate things, so Ernest worked alone.

2

When he finally finished digging hole number three, Ernest was exhausted and filthy. But before he began the undignified process of hauling his fat ass out of six-feet of hole, he needed to catch his breath. So he jammed the shovel in the ground, sat down in the grave, leaned back against the dirt, and used his teeth to tear open an Almond Joy.

It was at this moment when he decided how to rid himself of that sick feeling he couldn't shake.

Ernest realized that whatever the universe had in store for him, it couldn't be worse than walking around waiting for it to happen. So it was time to force the universe's hand, to get it over with, but on his terms.

So right then and there Ernest chose his own fate. Tomorrow night after he finished filling these holes, he'd fly back to D.C., kidnap a boy, kill the Old Rich Prick, kill that creepy daughter, kill the servants, kill fucking everyone, and then have his way with the boy until the police put him out of his misery.

With that piano swinging over his head, he'd just have to hope he could complete the plan before someone let go of the rope.

A Drive to the Airport

†

The low sun was already too bright as Yvette's abused Ford rolled down a ribbon of sun-bleached blacktop.

The car's insides smelled of cigarettes, cheap perfume, and onion rings. Mason couldn't wait to get out of it. But the airport was forty minutes away and Yvette was in no hurry.

She had things to say.

Mason figured she must've gotten up hours ago to get all tarted up the way she was. Her cleavage alone was a work of art, arranged just so to get what she wanted.

He pondered why she'd try this approach on a man who only yesterday buried his wife, and then remembered Yvette didn't know Doreen was his wife. Then he remembered something else: that the world was a mean and complicated place where no one knew what was rolling around inside of another. And now that he'd remembered that, he decided to be nice about telling her to shove off.

She opened with a sing-songy attempt at charm. "Mason this. Mason that," she sighed through heavy breath. "Charlie's told me all about you."

The combination of his exhaustion and her manipulative tone grinded Mason and threw all that shit about a *complicated world* right over the side. All of a sudden, he had no patience for this two-bit grifter, not with a four-hour flight ahead of him and Charlie left defenseless. So he returned to his original plan, which was to expose and scare the hell out of her, and since it would be especially satisfying to do so while looking her in the eye, the seat beneath him squeaked as he shifted his weight her way.

But now that he was looking straight at her, he saw how she tried to camouflage her sad truths—the truths about her age and weight—under too much makeup and too-tight clothes. And just like that, the pity washed away the anger.

"Since you know all about me," he said, "Tell me your story."

"Well, Charlie and I are in love," she said. "I know it happened fast, and there's a bit of an age diff—"

Mason wasn't interested in that. "I mean, where do you come from, Yvette? What'd you do before you came out here?"

He wanted to hear the lies.

"Well, I grew up faster than I would've liked in Northern California, near Frisco."

Mason cut her off: "'Gold in peace; iron in war.'"

Maybe he didn't want to hear the lies.

Annoyed at the interruption, Yvette responded with a flat, "I don't know what that means."

"Sorry, I—It's San Francisco's motto," he explained. "Doesn't quite fit the city today, I suppose."

2

Yvette had no intention of losing control of this conversation. So she steered it back to what she'd been rehearsing in her head all morning, which meant turning on the charm. "Anyhoo," she chirped, "I want to be a hundred percent honest with you... I'm not proud of my past. And I *do* have one. And I *am* running from it. But I'm looking for another chance. Not a second chance, mind you. Lord knows I've had plenty of those, but a fresh start."

Mason had to admit that wasn't the worst line of shit he'd ever heard, but there was still the issue at hand. "And you see that fresh start in the face of a boy whose IQ barely scrambles over room temperature?" he asked.

"He's not a boy," she said, almost as if she cared. "And if I may say so, he's tired of you seeing him that way."

"Is he now?"

Mason hadn't intended that to sound sarcastic, but it did, and she hit him with a death stare and dropped her act. "Listen," she snarled, "if you're gonna force a choice between yourself and the best piece of ass he's ever gonna get, I suggest you pack your shit right now."

Mason chuckled dismissively and turned away from her.

3

The conversation wasn't going anything like Yvette had expected, which put a tremble in her hands as she pulled the last cigarette from a pack of Winstons. She crumpled the empty pack and tossed it over her shoulder into the back seat.

"How about I offer you a compliment?" he asked.

Her shields went up, but she was intrigued. "What woman doesn't like a compliment? And I am a woman."

"No argument there."

"Oh, my," she said with the unlit Winston bouncing in her lips. "Don't tell me there's an actual red-blooded heterosexual beneath all that disapproval."

He was all smiles now: "With twenty-twenty vision."

She lit her smoke. "Aw, you're gonna make me blush."

"I suspect you haven't blushed in a while."

She didn't find that funny. "You suck at compliments."

"You're good," he lied. "You are. Real good. Problem is you found the wrong mark."

She exhaled a lung full of nicotine. "Do tell."

"Rebel Yell's been bleeding red ink forever," he told her. "Only reason Doreen kept it alive was to give Charlie some stability—something to do, structure, sameness. That place is his whole life. It's his train set. But that's all it is. There's no pot of gold at the end of this long con you think you're running."

She cracked her window and blew smoke out the side of her mouth like a young Kathleen Turner would in this situation. "Oh, is that why Charlie just placed a $5,500 order to fix and reopen the pool?"

She's not dumb, thought Mason. "Like I said, a train set, a mirage subsidized by *my* out-of-town work. Deed to the place isn't worth the dirt under it. It's hardly insured. No point."

4

Her gears turned around and after a few turns she had to admit that made sense. Couple guests a night at thirty-five bucks a pop doesn't exactly add up to buried treasure.

"The good news," he announced, "is that I'm gonna give you a score."

"Are you now?"

"If you want to keep changing dirty sheets until the vacancies convince you I'm telling the truth, feel free. Or you can take three thousand dollars now and go find yourself a more prosperous sucker."

"Someone who makes that kind of offer," she said, "probably has six thousand."

"Dirty sheets or three thousand," he said.

She countered with silence, which was fine by him. While she finished her smoke, he cracked his window and looked out at his desert. All he wanted was to forget about Yvette and the fat man, forget all the killing he was about to do and how it was his fault he'd left Charlie vulnerable.

All he wanted was to get lost out there and wander away the grief.

Yvette stubbed out her smoke and issued a threat: "I could tell him."

Still looking out the window, Mason barely had the strength to reply, "Tell him what?"

"What you just told me about it all being a mirage, a train set."

Without taking his eyes from the passing desert, he replied, "I'm the one putting money into it. Who do you think he'll believe?"

Yvette had no response to that and bought herself some time by opening a fresh pack of smokes. But her shaky hands and chewed fingernails made it impossible to extract a cigarette from the tight pack. She fumbled for a bit and then—"Here, let me," Mason offered.

She handed him the pack. He gently tapped one out a ways and returned it to her. She bit the tip of the coffin nail with her eye teeth and pulled it free. Watching her hands shake as she lit it convinced him to up the offer.

"I can go four thousand," he said. "But you need to be gone before I get back, which gives you plenty of time to write that boy a bittersweet letter he'll cherish forever. That's part of the deal, the letter. That's important."

5

Yvette was tempted but something wasn't right. All the wild pieces of Mason's offer bounced around inside her head. The more she thought about it, the less sense it made.

"What are you even doing out here?" she asked. "You're not related to Charlie, you got plenty of life ahead of you…. What do you care?"

"I've known him since he was a kid, and we both got no one," he said. "And the longer you stay, the harder your leaving'll be on him. And you're gonna leave. Just as soon as you figure out you're digging up a hole filled with more hole, you're gonna leave."

He turned back to the window. "If you want to stick around, that's fine," he said. "This'll stay between us. But when you leave, it'll be empty-handed."

They drove along in silence until Yvette was surprised to hear herself say, "You're kinda being decent about this."

"You're just scratching out a living," he said. "I don't fault you for that."

"You love him that much?"

He didn't answer.

Their single lane of road expanded into two lanes and then three. The All at Once was right up ahead.

Yvette tossed her butt out the window and thought about another revolting night with Charlie, who couldn't get it up, but sure liked her trying. "Got the money with you?"

From the inside of his black denim jacket he pulled a thick envelope. "You go back. You write him a sweet letter. You sneak away in the night. Deal?"

"Okay," she said, and accepted the money.

A few minutes later, Yvette pulled up to the departure gates of Tucson International, a medium-sized airport built with glass and metal curves. One more miracle conjured by the All at Once dead in the middle of a desert.

Without a word, Mason climbed out of the Ford and wrestled his small suitcase from the backseat. Before closing the door, he said: "Appreciate the ride, and I do wish you luck."

She held up the thick envelope. "You knew I'd take four thousand."

"There's *five* thousand there. Make that letter as sweet as you can."

Surprised, and even a little touched by his generosity, she smiled and nodded that she would. Mason closed the door, turned, and got swallowed by the crowd.

Yvette didn't know why, but a feeling came over her that the crowd had snatched him up, kidnapped him, and that he had no say in the matter.

He didn't look out of place, she thought, and yet he did.

6

The airport terminal was humming with traffic and travelers. Signs everywhere made clear you were expected to make your drop-off and move along. Yvette decided she didn't like that rule, so she tapped out another Winston, and lit it up.

It wasn't long before airport security, a thin guy too young for his mustache, tapped her car hood and waved at her to get moving.

Yvette didn't like that, the way he did that without bothering to look at her—as though that was all it took to get people to do what he wanted. So she blew smoke out the side of her mouth like a young Bette Davis would in this situation and stayed put.

"You need to move along, ma'am," Security Man said, still not looking at her.

Ignoring him, she rolled down her window and tapped off some ash.

"Ma'am."

She fiddled with the radio until she found Led Zeppelin.

Security Man was now forced to acknowledge her, to look at her. He set his jaw and approached.

"Move. Now," he ordered.

She replied with a dead-eyed expression that said it all. *Screw you, pal. Screw you and the universe inside your head you live in the center of.*

Rattled by her defiance, Security Man twisted up his face and blurted, "You looking to get a ticket!?"

His exasperation reminded her of Yosemite Sam and Yvette's face broke into a smile as bright as the sun. Then she busted up laughing.

Now indignant, he said, "Okay, if that's the way you want it."

That was a response Yvette approved of. It meant she'd pulled him into the real world and made him face some things.

Just as Security Man opened his ticket pad, she showed him her middle finger and hit the gas.

7

Yvette threaded her abused Ford Focus through the airport's traffic snarl. At the exit she found she could only turn right or left.

Her instincts screamed, *Forget the letter! You have the money! Turn right! Don't go back to that disgusting Charlie! Leave! Run! Zig! Zig!*

While it was true that everything she owned in the world was back at the Rebel Yell, it was also true it could all be replaced with a hundred bucks. There sure wasn't anything of sentimental value back there. Yeah, she'd started her new life with a few photos and trinkets. But more than a few close calls had cost her those—which was fine. The grift left no room for sentiment.

So Yvette did what she'd been doing for years: ignored her instincts and zagged—she turned left, towards the Rebel Yell.

Maybe this time it wasn't only about zagging. Mason had been decent trusting her with the money in advance. That kind of decency can sometimes rub off on a person.

Besides, Yvette liked the idea of the letter, of being remembered forever.

Even if it was Charlie doing the remembering.

Destiny

1

Ernest was feeling fanciful this morning. That was the word he'd finally landed on: *fanciful.* It came to him in the shower while he'd pleasured himself and sang "Puff the Magic Dragon."

The first word he'd come up with was "dandy."

He decided that sounded too gay.

Then he took "fettle" out for a test run, as in, *I'm in fine fettle this morning!* But it didn't sound right. Was it "fettle" or "feddle?" Or was he confusing it with "fit as a fiddle?"

Usually, he would've looked for the answer online, but as many a jailbird can attest, only a fool takes along a cell phone on a murder run. So he went with "fanciful."

Ernest was feeling so fanciful, he called room service and said, "I want a gallon of Orange Gatorade and ten Almond Joys on a plate covered by one of those silver half-globe things."

When room service said it only had the silver half-globe thing, he offered one hundred dollars to whoever made it happen.

Thirty minutes later, Ernest was sipping Orange Gatorade and eating a pile of Almond Joys off a plate with a knife and a fork—like a fanciful man would.

He was also thinking about purchasing a bow tie. Nothing ridiculous, mind you—no polka dots or anything.

2

For the first time in some forty years, Ernest felt in control of his life, and, brother, it felt good, and had since last night when he first decided to kill the Old Rich Prick and tell the universe to go fuck itself.

Even as he'd made that decision, he knew he would have to sleep on it. All kinds of ideas sound great in the middle of the night and then not-so-great in daylight. But when he woke this morning, the thought still struck him as pure inspiration.

Ernest had lost control of his life when he was eight, when his father began selling him to other men for some dope and a bottle of whiskey.

A few years later, he'd killed his father with a hammer and then spent four years in juvie. By that time, he was already large for his age, so he got revenge on his father and the universe by preying on the younger boys. Got to like it, too.

After his release, he found he was a slave to those impulses and couldn't stop himself. Before long, he was sentenced to 140 years for kidnapping a five-year-old boy named Carson.

Carson wasn't the first boy he'd done that to—far from it. But it was the first time he'd screwed up and lost control. Carson lived in his apartment building. Stupid. Never target someone you know, a subject Clint Camacho covered at length in his murder book.

Nearly twenty-three, Ernest entered adult prison with what the cons called "short eyes," the eyes of a kid diddler, and all the cons knew it. He was young then, so instead of killing him like they would today, they turned him out as a punk and passed him around like his father had.

Ernest didn't mind that so much. What he couldn't deal with was the constant prison noise: the 24/7 yelling, fifty TVs and radios always blaring, doors always slamming, toilets always flushing, pipes always clanging, lights always burning. There was no escape, not even at night. He couldn't put two thoughts together.

3

Ernest was thirty-nine and planning his third suicide attempt when he learned of the Second Chance Project. Seemed tailor-made for him. The project offered early release to a con who'd served more than ten years after being sentenced to life as a young man.

To qualify, there'd been a series of interviews, psychological exams, IQ tests, reading comprehension.... They even showed him inkblots. Ernest saw all kinds of sick shit in those blots, but being no fool, he lied about bunny rabbits and balloons.

Ernest loved the testing. Everything was conducted in a conference room, and for the first time in fifteen years, Ernest experienced quiet, heavenly quiet. Better still, the woman asking the questions looked like Angie Dickinson, always wore skirts, and knew how to cross her legs just so.

As Ernest was fond of saying, *Loving the occasional boy don't make me no fag.*

One day Ms. Leg Crosser told Ernest to add a name to his visitor list and to identify this person as an attorney so the two of them could talk in private.

Next day, the name showed up, sat down, and told Ernest the Second Chance Project had narrowed its choices to Ernest and two other cons.

"Whoever survives gets released," the name said.

Said it just like that, like it was nothing.

While Ernest sat stunned, the name gave him the names of the other two, told Ernest they knew all about him, and that whoever survived had a $100,000 a year job waiting outside. The name shook his hand, wished him luck, and *Welcome to Thunderdome.*

The thing was, Ernest knew there was no way he'd get an early release with two shiny new murders on his sheet. Sure, prison killings are easy to get away with—if you got friends: guys to pass the shiv too, guys who can block the guards' view.... But Ernest had no friends. He was a punk.

He did have one advantage. He didn't care if he lived or died. So rather than plotting a murder bound to fail, he decided to let them come to him. Kind of a win-win, if you think about it. If they kill him, they're doing him a favor. If he kills them, it's self-defense and he's sprung with that $100,000 a year job.

So he waited.... Waited weeks, then a month, then two months, and that's when he pieced it together. No one was coming for him. It was another test.

Not doing anything must have been the right call. Few months later, the Second Chance Program fixed his release.

4

After six months in a halfway house, Ernest finally met his benefactor, the Old Rich Prick, who welcomed Ernest onto his estate, took him down those twisted stairs to the basement, and presented him with the gift of a boy.

What Ernest didn't know was that the Old Rich Prick had filmed the whole thing to use as blackmail, and so, ten years and 150 pounds later, here Ernest sat—a walking heart attack with a piano dangling over his head.

But now that he'd decided to kill the Old Rich Prick, those days were over. Ernest was finally free to do whatever he wanted and what he wanted was to die in an orgy of violence and depravity.

"Goddamn, I feel good," he said out loud to no one, and then remembered he was a millionaire. *A full-blown millionaire!* A guy with a million bucks in the bank!

That glorious realization prompted Ernest to stand up from his breakfast, rub his hands together, and pace the room—you know, like a fanciful man would.

Ernest was not only a free man.... He was a free man with a million-dollar problem.

Anne

1

Although it had happened only a few nights ago, Anne had no memory of Mason teasing her about being a pirate or of how she'd stuck a blade in his gut. Like all things in her past, it was a blur.

Thanks to the blackout curtains, she didn't even know if it was day or night.

For a long time, she laid there between the black sheets. The silk felt good against her naked body. The pain felt better. Someone had done terrible things to her last night and she always enjoyed the souvenir of the pain.

She began to crave the drugs and quietly slipped out of bed. She didn't want to wake the person next to her—*whoever that was*.

Her bedroom was a large suite with an attached bath located on the top floor of Demented Tara. Clocks weren't allowed up there. Neither were servants or sunlight. It was a dirty and dark place that smelled of mold and decay. She groped through the dark to the bathroom and closed the door before switching on the light.

Reflected in the mirror was a naked body so pale you could almost see through it, a body peppered with purple and red splotches. Anne rubbed an especially nasty bite above her left breast and savored the sting.

The vanity's top drawer held what evened her out: pills of every shape and color. She knew what she needed and quickly swallowed four reds, three yellows, and two blacks chased down with a thick line of blow.

She was already flying, and the pills had yet to hit.

There was a small stool under the vanity. When she was still a girl, Anne would sometimes sit on that stool, stare in the mirror, and try to convince herself to run.

Sometimes she'd close the door, turn on the hot shower, and try to sweat out whatever it was that made her stay. This was a rich man's house. The hot water never ran out.

After she'd grown into a beautiful young woman, Anne separated herself from who she saw in the mirror and wondered how that woman could live like this.

Then she no longer saw anyone in the mirror.

Today, she wanted to sit among the flowers, so she pulled out the stool, sat down, forced her fingers through the tangles in her hair, and applied makeup that covered the choke marks.

She wouldn't shower. She enjoyed walking around dirty the morning after.

2

Anne no longer thought of Duvall, the young man who loved her so much it made him tremble.

These days, Anne looked like what she was: used up. Back then, she could stop traffic.

Duvall was four years younger, about twenty-four, and as smitten as a young man could be. He was also a talented young executive in her father's D.C. lobbying firm. And as he did to all his promising young executives, the Old Rich Prick sought to shatter Duvall's innocence.

Usually, the Old Rich Prick brought his young men along cautiously. You know, see if they'll cut a legal corner, and then take 'em to a strip club. Encourage them to cheat a client and then take them to a sleazier club for a backroom hummer.

Those were the tests.

The bait was wealth, political power, and media prestige. Want to live in a townhouse, drive a Tesla, own politicians, and be treated like an expert on cable news? All you gotta do is work hard, cut corners, and bring your pretty young wife to a sex party.

Duvall was so enamored with Anne, so obviously in love with her, the Old Rich Prick figured she was bait enough and jumped right over the preliminaries. Invited him to a séance and orgy. Innocent fun. Consenting adults. What's the problem?

Duvall was horrified. Walked right out. Never even cleaned out his office.

But what Duvall had seen that night only increased his love for Anne, and his desire to rescue her.

She agreed to meet him on a bench at the Botanic Gardens. There they held hands among the flowers, and he asked her to marry him. Promised to take her away, to protect her. Said he came from a wealthy family and could give her everything she wanted. Told her he loved her—said it over and over. Promised her a decent life, a clean life. Swore he'd cherish her forever.

He trembled as he said it. His love for her was that strong.

She told him straight out she wanted no part of a decent life. She was exploring herself, she explained, and you can't explore yourself if you put limits on things. She wasn't hurting anyone, she argued. She did plenty of good: donated to all kinds of charities, sat on a couple of boards.

Still trembling, he told her where such things could lead, how there was no bottom, how people get lost down there. Told her it wasn't her fault. She'd been abused and brainwashed. Then he begged her to come away with him. "At least give yourself a chance to clear your head," he pleaded.

"My head doesn't need clearing," she said, and smiled at him as though he were a beautiful fool. Then she kissed him, a real kiss, one of those kisses that promises a young man everything that makes him tremble. Then she wrapped her arms around his neck, pulled him close, pressed her cheek against his, and whispered that she wouldn't go away with him but that he could join her.

She never saw him again.

3

Anne used to think about Duvall all the time. Not anymore. Duvall turned to ash and the ash blew away.

So, she had no idea why she was always drawn to come and sit on this particular bench in the park at the Botanic Gardens.

She didn't look at the flowers anymore. Instead, her head filled with a color so red she could hear it.

4

The color red was roaring in Anne's ears when Mason sat down next to her.

Voice Mail

1

Some fifteen years ago, the All at Once edged a whole lot closer to Mason when certain states began to require fingerprints to obtain a driver's license.

This wasn't something Mason could ignore. Unless you're willing to live beneath an overpass, you need ID in the modern world. But there was no way he would give the government his fingerprints.

Figuring it was only a matter of time before all fifty states followed suit, Mason decided to stock up on IDs. He traveled to the five closest states not fingerprinting, and began a process he'd been refining for decades.

In each of the five states, he did the following:

Figuring he looked somewhere between forty-five and fifty, Mason searched that state's obituaries for a dead male with a Hispanic name who'd currently be between forty-five and fifty. It didn't matter *when* this person died or at what age, only that he was dead, would presently be the appropriate age, and was born in this particular state.

Then, using the dead man's name, Mason rented a cheap apartment. While waiting for the utility bills to arrive, Mason used that same name and address to mail a twenty-dollar bill and a letter apologizing for late payment to several state government agencies. Obviously, the letter was a ruse, but the government would eventually respond with a letter requesting more information. And so, after a few weeks, Mason had what he needed: utility bills and government letters in the dead man's name sent to an in-state address. Using those as ID, Mason had no problem obtaining a hunting license, library card, and voter registration card. Alternately, the hunting license, library card, and voter registration card were identification enough to receive the dead man's official birth certificate.

The birth certificate was the ticket to a legal driver's license.

After that, whenever one of the licenses was set to expire, Mason simply mailed in the renewal fee. Depending on the state, twelve to fifteen years passed before he was required to update his license photo. Since he'd not aged a day, he couldn't do that and the ID expired.

Of those five IDs, only one was still valid.

Sure, he could've started the process over. There were still states that didn't require fingerprints. But after fifteen years, there were new risks, like facial recognition, states comparing records, and what worried him most: what he didn't know.

Had Doreen not gotten ill, he might've figured out a way to safely execute another round of identity theft, but the travel time was too much. His place was with her.

Mason's one remaining legal ID was under the name Martín Gallardo, and Martín Gallardo was about to die in a murder-suicide.

2

"Hope you don't mind me saying so, Mr. Gallardo, but you sure don't look sixty-two," the young lady at the Tucson airport ticket counter had told him earlier that morning as he paid cash.

Although he didn't need it, he still purchased a roundtrip ticket. Post-September 11, a one-way ticket got you flagged.

Mason had no idea what his real name was, or if he even had one. "Joshua Mason" was a name he'd come up with long ago. Before the All at Once, you could carry a fake name for however long you needed. He'd used that name so long it came to feel like his own.

He checked his luggage at the airport: a single suitcase filled with two blankets wrapped around his .38, ten rounds of ammunition, binoculars, and a burner phone.

After he landed at Dulles Airport in D.C., Mason retrieved his suitcase, rented a sedan, and used the burner to call Charlie, who picked up on the first ring and told him everything was fine.

3

After three hours of waiting from as far away as possible, Mason watched through binoculars as a modest-looking car pulled up to the gates of the Old Rich Prick's estate.

The driver, a middle-aged woman, was allowed inside. Fifteen minutes later, this same car pulled out with Anne in the backseat.

Mason followed them to the Botanic Gardens. After Anne got out and entered the park, Mason strolled over to chat up the driver.

"You with Uber?" he asked.

"Lyft," she said. "Can't pick you up, though. Gotta use the app."

He kept an eye on Anne and asked questions of the driver that made it sound like he was thinking of becoming a driver himself. When Anne took a seat on a bench, he handed the driver twenty dollars for her time. This was deliberate. He wanted her to remember him.

Before joining Anne, Mason called Charlie again. This time it went to voicemail, which wasn't unusual.

He still wished it hadn't.

4

Mason sat himself next to Anne on that same bench where a trembling young man had once begged her to marry him.

She didn't sense Mason's presence. Not right away. She was somewhere else, somewhere where the world was red.

"Hello, Anne," he finally said.

She turned to the voice, expecting to see a young man filled with love for her. Instead, she saw....

"I'm the pirate, remember?"

So she could focus on whatever this was she had to deal with, Anne blinked a couple of times to stop her senses from running around like chickens. After they did, she recognized Mason, gasped, jerked herself away from him, and fell off the end of the bench right on her butt.

There was no time to break her fall. She hit the ground so hard she bounced a little.

Mason stood as though he were a concerned stranger and made sure she saw the .38 tucked in his belt.

From the ground, Anne morphed into a helpless maiden, put a pout on her face, and limply lifted both arms. Mason grabbed them and brought her to her feet. She immediately pressed her body against his and wrapped her arms around his neck.

"Thank you, Mr. Pirate," she said looking into his eyes.

He wanted to push her off, but people were watching.

Before he could stop her, Anne's cold, wet tongue was in his ear. Disgusted, he gently grabbed her shoulders and pushed her away. She laughed with dead eyes.

"I'll kill you right here," he whispered.

"But we already killed you," she said. Then she had an idea. "You know, I've never fucked a dead man."

Mason had never seen anything so repulsive.

5

By the time they reached the car, the pills had hit their sweet spot and Anne didn't care about anything. Mason had her sit on her hands before seat-belting her in and she complied. "Ooh, kinky," she said.

Mason snaked through traffic and Anne stared out the window answering his questions the best she could. Told him the servants would have all gone home by now. Told him Ernest was the only live-in servant and was probably around somewhere. Told him a gray plastic thing on the keychain in her purse opened the security gate.

When he asked about her father, she suddenly remembered that he was this morning's lump in her bed. The mental picture made her laugh. "He's home," she giggled.

The questions ended and she watched him pull over to make a call. Whoever he called didn't pick up and he broke the phone into pieces.

"You really him, the pirate?" she asked.

He didn't answer.

He dug the keys from her purse, pulled back into traffic, and dropped the pieces of the phone out of the car window as they fought their way through D.C. rush hour.

The Old Rich Prick

1

The Old Rich Prick's name was Reginald Hartford Gwynne II and seventy-four years ago he was born into enormous wealth.

The Old Rich Prick's father, Reginald Hartford Gwynne I, had been an honest businessman and faithful husband. But like too many self-made men who'd grown up poor, he spoiled his only child by giving him everything, and the boy grew into an entitled and needy young man who then grew into the sadistic Old Rich Prick.

By the time Reginald Senior realized Reginald Junior was a bottomless pit of greed, it was too late. Mr. and Mrs. Reginald the First died in a plane crash, and all the money—billions—went to the twenty-five-year-old bottomless pit.

Like many scions, Junior decided the only way to prove to the world he was no dilettante was to outdo his father. No easy task. With the guts and integrity found in hard work, Senior had spent a productive life delivering affordable energy to millions. He changed those lives, all of them, for the better.

Junior, however, went into *alternative* energy. This repudiation of his father's legacy was now fashionable and therefore the easiest way to accumulate unearned acclaim from the Beautiful People.

But after losing his second billion, Junior was forced to face the fact he was incapable of building or creating anything.

2

Since he couldn't earn respectability, at age thirty-four, he moved to Washington, D.C., to marry it.

The Old Rich Prick's wife, Mrs. Old Rich Prick, was a socialite and boozehound. Four years after their daughter Anne was born, the boozehound died at the hands of her husband. He spiked her drink and then dropped her body off the back of a yacht into the Potomac.

The cold water startled her awake. The last thing Mrs. Reginald Hartford Gwynne II saw before she slipped beneath the dark current was Anne, who watched her own mother die through eyes that were already dry wells.

Now that he possessed *two* inherited fortunes, Reginald lived like a king and purchased access to and influence over the most powerful politicians and media executives in the world. They were available at a much cheaper price than outsiders might expect.

Just as easy was the seduction of his daughter. He filled Anne's vacancy with liquor and drugs, abused, and manipulated her. Soon she was eager to share his bed.

Nothing satisfied the Old Rich Prick more than corrupting innocence. He had everything he'd ever wanted.

Then the Old Rich Prick found Christ.

3

After suffering a near-fatal heart attack in his late forties, the Old Rich Prick was declared dead and during those eighty-seven seconds he saw the face of God, a stern and fatherly God who granted him a chance at redemption.

But Reginald wasn't interested in redemption. What was he supposed to do—turn himself in for murdering his wife and raping his daughter? Blubber a confession to some pimply-faced priest?

Fuck that. Fuck that right up the stovepipe.

The truth was that knowing God disapproved of his sin made his sinning even more satisfying. Defying God kinda got him hard.

But Reginald now knew there was an afterlife, and death terrified him. He was destined for Hell. Oh, yes, straight down.

Thus began his quest for immortality, one that took him all over the world. He met with every specialist in the field, including cranks and quacks. Afterward, he concluded immortality might someday be possible by way of gene therapy, but he'd be dead long before that happened.

Next, he turned to religion, the occult, and spiritualism. He spoke with shamans, oracles, priests, scholars, astrologers, rabbis, imams, Satanists, witches, and faith healers.

After four years of world travel and study, Reginald settled on the truth: *Jesus is it,* he decided. *Christianity is the answer. Serious men practice it; science and archeology continue to validate it.*

More importantly, secular history proved Jesus of Nazareth once walked the earth, claimed to be the Son of God, and was crucified for that claim. Further, this same secular history verified that many of Jesus's disciples chose to die, often horribly, rather than renounce their faith.

Reginald understood no one dies to protect a lie.

Nevertheless, he had no intention of turning his life over to Jesus or of becoming a Christian. But now that he knew the game's rules, he could play it—his way.

4

The rules of Christianity were simple: After death, you either went to Heaven or to Hell. Reginald had zero chance of gaining entry to the former, so he would pursue status in the latter. Rather than be one of those crybabies wailing over how sorry they were as they suffered the tortures of the damned, he would strut into Hell, head held high. *Here's a volunteer ready to go to work!*

Things might go easier on such a man.

The Old Rich Prick wasn't fooling himself. He knew he'd eventually lose this game. Ultimately, God would defeat the Fallen Angel and that would be the end of Hell and everyone in it. Death would someday have its way with him, and *poof,* he'd no longer exist.

But that was a long ways off—billions of years, perhaps—and the void of death was preferable to kissing some Jew-carpenter's ass.

Stairs to Nowhere

1

Barefoot and in a robe so short it exposed pasty white thighs and varicose veins, the Old Rich Prick descended the stairs that led to his front door and foyer. On his mind were everyday things like a cup of coffee, a perfectly toasted English muffin, and the power he held to make three people dead.

He'd just gotten off the horn with Ernest, who'd called from the hotel and was on his way to the Rebel Yell.

The delay, Ernest explained, was digging an additional hole for Stark's lookalike brother. Ernest assumed the Old Rich Prick would want the twin killed.

Ernest was right.

The Old Rich Prick didn't believe all that jibber-jabber about twins having a psychic connection, but the idea of killing a twin intoxicated him. It was like killing an endangered species.

This was what the Old Rich Prick was thinking about when the same "twin" he'd just ordered killed walked through his front door clutching a gun in one hand and his zoned-out daughter in the other.

The Old Rich Prick was so shocked, so disoriented by the sight, he sat down on the stairs—just like *that*, he plopped down on his butt as though a show was about to start.

But the moment Mason spoke, the Old Rich Prick knew, *just knew* this man was no twin and that his Destiny had walked right through his front door.

2

You see, the Old Rich Prick kept video of everything in his house, including the murder of the man he knew as "Mike Stark."

In fact, just last night, while lying in bed with Anne, they'd watched the Stark murder video over and over, like a replay of three-pointers on ESPN.

"You've got lipstick on your teeth," Stark had said to Anne that night. They kept rewinding and replaying it. Couldn't get over how he'd said it.

"You've got lipstick on your teeth."

"You've got lipstick on your teeth."

"You've got lipstick on your teeth."

This allowed the Old Rich Prick to not only recognize Stark's face, but his voice. So, while this angry man holding his daughter waved a gun around demanding to know where Ernest was, the Old Rich Prick realized the glorious truth of what was in front of him.... *My God, this is him. This is Stark! My God, my God, this is him!*

The revelation produced a flush of exhilaration that unrolled itself to reveal his life's purpose. In a flash, everything made sense; his whole life made sense. In an instant, he knew it had all been about preparing for *this* moment, *this moment right here.* He'd sold his soul willingly, and out of appreciation for that sacrifice, the Dark Power had delivered to him this man and the secret to immortality.

In exchange for this secret, the Old Rich Prick could give Stark whatever he desired—money, power, sex, anything.... He had it all, and he would give it all becau—*But-but why is he yelling! Why is he waving that gun around yelling!*

The more Stark shouted, the more the Old Rich Prick's express train to his destiny began to shudder and rattle. He didn't understand.... *Why is he yelling and threatening and sticking a gun in my face!?*

As his Destiny went right on yelling and threatening, the Old Rich Prick fought to keep that train from derailing and waited for the Dark Power to intervene. But the Dark Power did nothing.

I can give this man whatever he wants, and all he wants is Ernest! Why won't he stop yelling about Ernest!?

Sitting on those stairs, the dumbfounded Old Rich Prick tried closing his eyes and shaking his head as though the shaking would remove the disconnect between the man he needed Stark to be—the man who would grant him eternal life and save him from Hell—and this lunatic with a gun demanding Ernest.

Why is he—? Why won't he—? Finally, the Old Rich Prick stood straight up and bellowed, "HE'S NOT HERE!"

3

Mason pushed Anne to the floor and warned her to stay put.

"Yes, Mr. Pirate," she said.

Mason returned his attention to the Old Rich Prick, pointed the .38 at the old man's forehead, and slowly pulled back the hammer.

To fire a double-action revolver, there's no need to pull back the hammer. But it is a helpful gesture in getting the other fella to focus.

"Didn't ask you where he *wasn't*," Mason said, his voice churning with the rage that always came with confronting those who felt entitled to snuff out a life for their own amusement.

At this point, the Old Rich Prick's confidence in his destiny had derailed entirely. He knew what was coming and his words choked on dread and fear: "Ernest is in Arizona somewh—he's—*I have money!*" he shouted and then dropped to his knees. "I can give you anything," he whimpered. "I have power, contacts...."

"I know all that," Mason said.

The Old Rich Prick stared up at Mason. His eyes filled with terror. "I'll give you whatever you want. Please don't kill me. Tell me what you want!"

Mason said nothing.

The Old Rich Prick changed tactics.

"Kill a helpless old man with a gun? Is that what you want?"

At that, Mason chuckled. "Gun's a charity, old man. If you prefer, we can do it slow. Head on down to the basement, chain you to a pole, stick you till you die."

The Old Rich Prick's eyes went wide. "My God, it is you."

"It is."

"Then, please, one last request," the Old Rich Prick begged as he pressed his hands together as if to pray. "A little mercy, please, a little.... You've been there. You've been to the other side. You've seen it. What's waiting for me?"

"There's nothing. I wish there were a Hell for the likes of you. But there's nothing."

"But you come back!" the Old Rich Prick cried. "There must be *something* if you come back!"

"There's only oblivion, and you ain't coming back."

The last thing that went through the Old Rich Prick's mind, other than the .38 slug, was something he'd never felt before: the truth of his own insignificance. He'd built nothing, created nothing; never loved, never been loved. He'd only ever used and destroyed and lied and manipulated and scraped and obsessed, and when he died, he died an old man with pasty white thighs on a set of stairs that led nowhere.

Mason turned around to deal with Anne, but she was gone.

Then she leapt on him.

4

With her legs wrapped tight around his middle, like a crazed animal, she was all over him, shrieking with her long, black hair flying. One hand dug a fingernail into his eyeball, the other beat him over the head with something sharp and porcelain.

The blows and her shrieks disoriented Mason. He spun around and around, and then felt his eyelid rip and blood squirt from his battered head. *Bam! Bam! Bam!* She kept hitting him as pieces of white porcelain exploded off his skull like popcorn. Taking hold of his eyelid, she tried to yank it all the way off, but the blood was too slippery. Still shrieking, she went for his other eye.

Bam! Bam! Then *SMASH!* as whatever she'd been beating him with disintegrated into pieces. Mason stopped spinning. He'd only succeeded in making himself dizzy and was about to black out. Now she had hold of the side of his mouth and was trying to tear it from his face. That was a mistake. The pain surged his adrenaline. His buckling knees stiffened and he stomped backward until, using all his weight, he plowed her into something. The back of her head hit the front door with a thud and her dead weight hit the floor.

Only she wasn't dead. She was spread out on the ground like a ragdoll and laughing through a mask of tangled hair.

Mason realized he'd lost his gun. Certain he was seconds from passing out, with his one good eye, he scanned the trashed foyer's floor.

Anne laughed harder and harder until she was laughing so hard she had to hold on to herself.

Mason found the .38 next to the head of the shattered statue she'd beat him with. He snatched it up and turned.

Still splayed, now Anne was pointing and laughing at him.

Dizzy, Mason slowly lowered himself to the floor to catch his breath.

Anne quieted, propped herself up on her elbows, shook the hair from her face, and threw him a seductive smile. Referring to his one good eye, she said: "Now you really are a pirate."

He pulled a handkerchief and pressed it against his bleeding head and then to his mangled eye.

Still smiling, Anne adjusted herself so she could sit upright against the door. Looking pretty sure of herself, she folded her arms and said, "I'm a girl. Pirates don't kill girls, especially girls who make young men tremble."

Mason rose to his feet. "What is wrong with you?" He lifted the gun and then—

Anne's face...it...*changed*. The fog of the drugs seemed to clear from her eyes. The anger and crazy washed from her face. She blinked a few times as though waking from a nap.

Confused, Mason relaxed his grip on the pistol.

She looked up at him and then slowly looked around the messy room as though seeing it for the first time. Her eyes found her dead father. She frowned, turned her attention back to Mason, and smiled at him.

There was affection in that smile, in her eyes.

Confused, Mason lowered the gun.

She looked to the ceiling, let out a small laugh, brought her knees to her chest, wrapped her arms around them, and told Mason a story.

"I read this book once about a woman, a wife and mother, who wished for nothing more than to go back in time to correct all the mistakes of her past. It was one of *those* books, so her wish was granted. She did it.... She went back and erased her regrets. But again, it was one of *those* books, so this ended up backfiring on her. She was so desperate to correct what went wrong, she forgot to recreate all the things in her life that had gone right. In the end, she found herself alone without her husband and children."

Out of the side of her mouth, Anne blew a stray hair from her eye. Mason found the gesture kind of...beautiful.

"That was the moral of the story: how you shouldn't allow your regrets to stop you from appreciating what's gone right in your life.... It wasn't a very good book. Silly, really. Still, it stayed with me.... It made me realize there was nothing right or good about my life. Nothing to stop me from going back and trying again...."

Still sitting on the floor with her back against the door and arms wrapped around her knees, she peered up at Mason. "Is that something you could do with your magic, Mr. Stark? Could you send me back? There was this boy, you see, and he offered—and I thought maybe you could—"

"No," said Mason.

After a pause, Anne nodded that she understood, let go of her legs, and closed her eyes.

"I'm tired," she said. "So tired."

That was when Mason decided not to kill her, something she seemed to sense.

"But if I can't go back, there's no reason to go forward, is there?"

"You're gonna have to solve your own problems, lady," said Mason.

With her eyes still closed, she lowered her head. Her hair fell over her face, covering it. For a moment she didn't move. Mason waited. Then small pieces of debris fell from her as she slowly rose to her feet.

It was an eerie sight and Mason tightened his grip on the gun.

She stood up, straight up, shook the hair from her face, and he saw that the crazy had returned to her eyes.

Her smile turned smug. Her face darkened. She was determined to get what she wanted and began to advance on him. So Mason gave her what she wanted.

The bullet crashed through her forehead and lodged in her brain. The impact lifted her a few inches off the floor and she hit the ground hard. She tried to move. She couldn't. She was paralyzed. Her eyes wouldn't blink. They were frozen open as if she'd been startled. She could see everything, and as the surface of her eyeballs began to dry and sting, she watched the pirate shove the .38 into his mouth and pull the trigger.

Dead, he fell to the floor, and his blood sprayed on top of Anne's exposed eyeballs.

Seeing the color red always comforted Anne, but she couldn't hear the red and this confused her.

She was wondering why she couldn't hear it when the darkness came, and after the darkness came, she was pulled down through the dirt to the center of the earth where the fire was.

5

The police quickly ruled the Massacre on the Potomac (as the media dubbed it) a murder-suicide.

A driver's license identified the killer as Martín Gallardo. The name led nowhere beyond the rental car parked outside the estate and a roundtrip airline ticket out of Tucson International.

The gun was untraceable; the serial number had been filed off.

A Lyft driver would confirm Gallardo had stalked Ms. Anne Gwynne, one of the two victims. Fearing the police would confiscate it, she didn't tell them about the twenty dollars.

Surveillance video of the shooting yielded no clues other than the shooter was looking for Ernest, a live-in servant whose whereabouts were currently unknown.

While searching the estate, the FBI discovered countless videos of influential people, including much of the FBI's upper echelon, doing terrible things.

The videos were immediately destroyed.

When rumors of the videos leaked, the people in those videos used their power and influence to ensure the media censored, ignored, and ridiculed the truth until it was spoken of no more.

6

Mason had killed himself for two reasons. First, discovering Ernest was in Arizona meant he had to get back to Charlie as quickly as possible, and a suicide that transported him to the Joshua Tree was the fastest. Second, Mason had no doubt the Old Rich Prick's home was loaded with cameras and knew video of the shooter's suicide, *his* suicide, would ensure there was no manhunt.

This time, Mason had bent the All at Once to his advantage—had wrapped it in brown paper and tied it tight with white string.

7

Moments after his suicide, Mason appeared under the Joshua Tree, which was some forty miles from the Rebel Yell, from Charlie. With his pickup in a Vegas parking garage and his motorcycle at the Rebel Yell, he would have to hitchhike.

The closest road was eight miles east. He dressed quickly, and then, just as he had the other night, he ran—ran just as fast as his legs would carry him. And just as it was the other night, he would be too late.

Two people were about to die, and he would never see the Rebel Yell again.

Checking In

1

When Ernest rang the night buzzer, Charlie wasn't watching TV. He was in his TV chair with the TV on, but much too annoyed with Yvette to watch.

Charlie had desperately wanted to spend the night with her, to do those things to each other again. He'd practically begged.

"Too tired," she'd told him. Said it nice, said it sweet, said he'd have to get used to Mr. Monthly, whatever that was.... Said she see him in the morning.

Something wasn't right. Charlie could sense it, and he was simmering.

2

Before arriving at the Rebel Yell, Ernest had been staying at the Marriott in Rio Rico under a false name. While checking out, he asked the hotel to order him an Uber.

He couldn't order the car himself, he'd told them, because he'd lost his stupid phone. The hotel was more than happy to arrange the ride and add it to his bill with a 25 percent "convenience charge."

For his destination, Ernest used an address on Old Highway 661, one about three miles past the Rebel Yell. The address was real, a little office park with a handful of businesses. More than fifty years ago, one of those businesses had been the daycare center where Doreen worked.

Coming from the Marriott, there was no way to arrive at that address without first passing the Rebel Yell. So when the Uber driver approached the dusty little motel, Ernest announced a change of mind. "Why don't you pull on in there," he said. "It's getting late. I'll take care of my business tomorrow."

Now there would be no record of anyone being dropped off at the location on what was about to become *the night in question*.

3

It was late afternoon and the sun was low. Ernest exited the car, ignored the wind whipping dust around his legs, gripped his suitcase, and stared up at the Rebel Yell sign, at Charlie's terrible paint job.

The messy, dripping red paint, especially Charlie's clumsy splash near the bottom, looked like blood to Ernest.

More bad juju....

The wind picked up and Ernest remembered the piano dangling over his head. He knew these hot gusts would sway the piano this way and that, and make it spin around. He pictured the rope fraying and whoever the cruel universe had put in charge of the rope thinking seriously about letting go.

A shiver raced up his spine, which spurred him to contemplate his options. *Why not head back to D.C. right now?* he thought. After all, he realized, he had no personal stake in killing these people. Sure, he enjoyed killing and hated to waste all the sweat equity he'd put into those holes, but he was a free man now, a free man with a million dollars in cash.

Yep, he'd withdrawn his million-and-change this morning and still couldn't believe ten thousand hundred-dollar bills fit in a bag you could carry on an airplane.

He'd secured the money in a locker in a lonely bus station just outside Rio Rico, the same bus station where he planned to abandon Yvette's Ford Focus after he filled those holes.

The locker key was right there in his pocket. *The key to a million dollars!* What a feeling....

The Kingdom Key had told him there were no cameras in or around the bus station. So the plan was to park Yvette's abused little Ford right there, retrieve his million, hop on a bus to D.C., get off the bus in D.C., and start fucking killing everyone.

Easy peasy japanesey.

"The fuck am I even doing here?" he said out loud to himself. "What am I doing in this godforsaken place with its blood-covered signs?"

And with that, Ernest decided to let the people at the Rebel Yell live. But when he turned around, there was no Uber driver, just a swirl of dust where the car once was.

Fuckin' universe.

With no choice, he shuffled his bulk toward the motel office, blinked against the dust the wind was peppering into his eyes, and felt like the last man on earth in the most barren place on earth.

How he hated himself. How he hated being fat and hated whatever it was that made him so evil. As he trudged toward the motel office, the endless indignities that trailed him like a cloud of gnats filled him with so much hate his mind flipped right around and decided everyone here needed to die.

He stepped into the motel office and rang the night buzzer.

4

In his own pissy mood over Yvette, Charlie lumbered up to the registration desk and, without saying much, put his new guest in Room 5.

Ernest went off to his room to wait for dark.

Heat Lightning

1

In Room 3, Yvette re-read what was now a fourth draft of her goodbye letter to Charlie. While she liked the idea of being the kind of someone who'd be remembered forever, getting the words right put cramps in her hand.

Other than that, she was all packed and ready to go. But fearing Charlie might come begging for sex again, she'd hidden the suitcase in the closet. The dark look on Charlie's face when she'd lied about having her period spooked her. She'd seen that look before and knew that a woman who stuck around after a look like that was in for it eventually. She had no intention of finding out what Charlie's face would look like if he caught her with a packed suitcase.

The letter looked good, she decided. Well, good enough. She crossed out a few words, wrote new ones above the cross-outs, spritzed it with perfume, folded it in half, wrote Charlie's name on it, and then concealed it on the nightstand under the latest *People* magazine—a special issue celebrating the life of *Hey! Hey! Hayley* star Hayley Caldwell.

It was time for a smoke.

She grabbed her purse, left the door open, and stepped out to the edge of the creaky, wooden deck. There, she leaned against a thin pillar covered in cracked white paint, dug out a Winston, and lit it up.

2

It was dark now. The only lights were the ones broadcasting the bloody motel sign and the dim, fly-specked bulbs next to each room.

Like it was raising all kinds of quiet hell, soundless lightning flashed far away in the west. Clouds covered the moon and stars, so there was only the lightning, which pop-pop-popped as if the paparazzi had gathered right there in the parking lot.

Mason's motorcycle and Yvette's Ford Focus were the only vehicles in the lot. Mason's five grand was tucked nice and snug under the driver's seat.

"Shouldn't have parked so far away, dummy," she whispered to herself.

After returning from the airport, she'd been thinking about the letter, not escaping, and had parked right in front of the motel office, which was about seventy feet from her room. *Boy, that's a long walk when you're sneaking off with a suitcase.*

She considered moving her car now. If she backed up to her room, Charlie had no shot at stopping her later tonight. She'd be safe as soon as she was in the car with the doors locked.

Yeah, but if she moved the car now, that might bring Licorice Dick running out. He'd want to know what she was up to and she couldn't think of a reasonable explanation.

As she settled herself into the rusty, metal chair next to her door, she thought about walking directly to the car and driving off.

Go, Yvette. Go! You got your purse and keys right here. Money's under the seat. Just go!

She knew that was the right move. But that wasn't how she lived, not anymore. She didn't zig. Fuck zigging. She zagged. Besides, she enjoyed the danger. What she'd gotten herself into here was a *real adventure*. She wanted to hang onto that excitement, at least for a while, so the plan was to switch off her lights around ten and then sit in the dark tingling with this excitement until she saw the glow of Charlie's TV switch off. Then, after an hour or so, she'd take that long walk and speed off to—

"There's no sound," a man's voice boomed from the dark.

Yvette nearly jumped out of the chair.

3

"Oh, sorry," Ernest said from the chair next to his room. "Was just out looking at the lightning."

"What the hell, man?" she said, catching her breath.

"Sorry. Thought you saw me when you came out," he lied. "That lightning has no sound. There's no thunder. How is that possible?" Ernest thought it looked supernatural, like light dancing on a black horizon without music.

"It's heat lightning," Yvette explained. "There's sound. You just can't hear it."

"Not to get philosophical on you," Ernest replied. "But, by definition, something you can't hear has no sound."

"What I mean is that there's sound out there where the storm is. We can see it, but the sound is too far away to travel this far."

Ernest chuckled. "Sounds like you've read a book."

Yvette laughed at that and flicked her butt into the empty lot. Nighttime chat with a stranger during a lightning storm might be just what the doctor ordered.

"Maybe you can help me," Ernest said. "Driving by here the other day, I saw this Indian-looking fella. About fifty. Black denim jacket. Pretty sure I know him. He around?"

Yvette knew the stranger was talking about Mason, but she was in a mood to sound clever. "Gandhi Indian or Geronimo Indian?" she asked.

"Geronimo."

"Yeah, that's Mason," she said. "He's out of town on business. Took him to the airport myself this morning. Pretty sure he's Mexican, though. Heard him speak it once."

4

Whatever, thought Ernest. The fact the twin, this Mason guy, was gone, was all that mattered. Now he didn't have to wait around for him to show up or worry that he might in the middle of things.

There were no other guests tonight. It was time to fill those holes, get ahold of the girl's car, grab his million, get back to D.C., and start killing.

It was just then when a massive crevasse of silent lightning striped its way across the sky directly overhead. Yvette would've sworn the ceiling of the world had just cracked open.

The flash lasted long enough she got a good look at Ernest, and what she saw scared her: a larger, more threatening version of Charlie.

Checking Out

1

Charlie stared at Ernest's gun and said the first thing that came to his simple mind: "You-you want my collection of-of state quarters? I-I-I almost got all fif-fifty of 'em?"

"Throw 'em in the suitcase, pal, along with that clock radio and your bathroom stuff. Toothbrush, razor, and whatnot," Ernest said, waving his .22 revolver.

In his How-To-Get-Away-With-Murder book, Clint Camacho devoted an entire chapter to the reliability of revolvers.

A semi-auto might carry more rounds, but those rounds aren't much good if the gun jams on you. Revolvers don't jam.

Another helpful tidbit from the fat man to the world.

2

The three of them—Ernest, Charlie, and Yvette—were in the small manager's apartment. Yvette was seated in Charlie's big TV chair. When Ernest pushed her into it, the cushion was still warm from Charlie's butt and it felt kind of gross.

The only light came from a TV rerun of *Forensic Files*, which happened to be Yvette's favorite show. And now that Ernest had ordered Charlie to pack his toiletries, she wondered if she might someday star in a future episode—as the victim.

Ernest had assured them he was only there to steal. Didn't want any trouble, he said. Only wanted Yvette's car, their money, and a couple of suitcases full of stuff he could sell.

"I'll drop you a few miles in the desert. No more than an hour walk," he'd promised. "Just need time to get over the border to Mexico." Only he pronounced it "Meheeeko" because he was still feeling fanciful.

Well, Ernest telling Charlie to pack a toothbrush proved all that talk about releasing them in the desert was a lie. Ernest wanted to make it look like they'd packed up and took off, which could only mean one thing.... "You're gonna kill us, you fat fuck!"

Ernest responded calmly. Didn't even look at her. "Only if you don't shut up," he said.

Yvette's instincts told her to do exactly that, to sit there and shut up, so she zagged—stood right up, and shouted: "How you gonna pawn his underwear and toothbrush?" Her voice trembled with fear and indignation. "You're gonna take us out to the desert and kill us. Admit it! ADMIT IT!"

Charlie stopped packing and turned to Ernest. He was interested in the answer to that question.

3

Yvette's open-faced belligerence rattled Ernest. Suddenly, he forgot how to handle this situation, even though Clint Camacho provided the answer right there on page 24:

If the guy you're about to kill asks why you need his toothbrush and underwear, tell him that if you get stopped and searched by the cops, the suitcase has to look like luggage, not a satchel full of loot.

Not being able to remember his own answer to Yvette's accusation frustrated Ernest, so he slugged her. In one quick, fluid motion, he popped her square on the mouth with the butt of his gun. You could hear the hard metal smash into her face. Even before her hands went up, her mouth was full of blood and broken teeth, like warm syrup mixed with pieces of eggshell.

4

Yvette and her bloody mouth fell back in the chair and she looked as helpless to Charlie as a newborn kitten whose eyes still haven't opened. This spiked his rage, smothered his fear, and turned his stammer into something impossible.

"Wh-wh-wh-wh-wh-wh-wh." The word wouldn't come, and Ernest, whose own anger was on the rise, ridiculed him.

"'Wh-wh-wh-wh-wh-wh'—why don't you shut the fuck up and toss those comic books in that suitcase? Because if you don't, I'm gonna kill your bitch, slice her open, and do a jig in her guts."

Charlie was so filled with fury he couldn't move. All he could do was stare at Ernest's throat as the blood roared past his ears.

"Hey, hey, Retardo!" Ernest shouted as he waved his free hand in front of Charlie's face to snap him out of it. "Your call. You tell me what you want to happen next."

Charlie looked to Yvette—to his newborn kitten—and was so ashamed of his inability to protect her, tears squirted from his eyes. He wiped them away with the back of his sleeve, a childish gesture Ernest found so endearing it cooled him off.

"Come on, I swear I'm not gonna hurt anyone," Ernest said, as sincerely as the lie would allow. "Go ahead and toss those comic books in the suitcase, and let's go."

Page 21: It can't look as though the guy you're about to kill packed in a panic. So be sure to rinse any dirty dishes and don't leave behind current newspapers or magazines—things he'd maybe read on the bus.

Charlie was still furious, but the unexpected tears left him confused, so he looked to Yvette for an answer. The blood from her mouth curtained over her chin and down her neck, practically to her perfect cleavage.

She gave Charlie a hard look and shook her head: *Don't do anything.* She knew this wasn't the time to make a move. There might never be a time. Still, it was best to wait and hope for one.

The small exchange wiped away Charlie's fury. He liked how she shook her head like he was smart and would understand what she meant. Not only that, it was a shared moment, something intimate.

Everything's okay now, he told himself. *We're together again. She's my woman.*

Now that they were all made up, Charlie stopped staring at Ernest's throat. He was going to save Yvette by doing precisely what he was told, and after he rescued her, he knew she would never refuse him again.

5

With Ernest and his .22 bringing up the rear, the three of them marched out of the motel office and into the parking lot, where the lightning popped away like a strobe light without rhythm.

Yvette was in the lead and hoped Ernest would forget about wanting her suitcase—the packed one she didn't want Charlie to know about.

She headed straight for her car.

No dice.

"Hold on, sweetheart," Ernest said. "You've got some packing of your own to do."

"Shit," she whispered under her breath, and hoped Charlie was too distracted or stupid to catch on to what that packed suitcase meant.

The door to Yvette's room was still wide open. They marched towards its light.

6

A few minutes later, as Ernest lay dying on the floor of Yvette's room, he could smell the dirty motel carpet and the hot breath of stale licorice as Charlie's teeth sank into his neck and ripped through fatty flesh in search of a windpipe.

Up till then, everything had been *easy peasy japanesey*—going so smooth, Ernest couldn't believe his luck when Yvette pulled her suitcase out of the closet and announced she was already packed.

Then it all went sideways....

7

Charlie had been thunderstruck to discover Yvette had already packed, and as though Ernest wasn't standing right there holding a gun on him, Charlie put his hands on his hips and started demanding answers.

With that stutter of his, you could hardly understand a word—still, the balls on this guy.

Ernest had had enough. "Shut the fuck up and get in the car!" The sharpness in his voice startled Charlie and Yvette into silence. The gun *kept* them quiet. And because he was a professional who crossed Ts and dotted Is, he grabbed the new *People* magazine off the nightstand. You see, someone carefully packing to go somewhere would never leave behind a new mag—Well, you know all that.

Anyway, so Ernest spotted Charlie's name on the goodbye letter hidden under the magazine, and like a guy begging the universe to drop a piano on him, he tossed Charlie the letter and said with a laugh, "Looks like this is for you."

Charlie only needed to read a few words before it was Katy-bar-the-fucking-door.

Charlie was screaming at Yvette, his arms flailing as she screamed right back trying to explain things. All Ernest could do was stand there like he was watching a Rock Hudson/Doris Day remake starring ugly people.

After a minute or so of this, Ernest, ever the professional, calmly closed the door to allow the two of them to hash it out. He figured they needed a little time to calm down.

The only problem was that Charlie wasn't calming down, especially not after Yvette told him it wasn't her fault. Mason had threatened her, she shouted, and then bribed her to leave. Then she screamed something about how if he didn't believe her, the money was right there under her car seat.

Ernest had never seen such rage. Charlie was ready to chew through a brick wall and called her all kinds of terrible names, which got her hackles up. So she poured it right back on him, screaming about what a limp-dicked idiot he was and how the motel was all bullshit and how it and Charlie were total failures propped up with Mason's play money.

Charlie went nuts. He started beating on the wall, punching through the plaster, screaming like something unholy was about to fly out of him.

Ernest had no choice but to step in.

"Okay, okay, you two can settle this walking out of the desert."

He said it matter-of-factly, hoping his tone would bring the temperature down. "Come on, let's get going," he added. And that's when Charlie wheeled around on him.

Ernest had seen some twisted shit in his life, but the look on this guy's face had him thinking seriously about pissing himself.

Ernest wasn't stupid. He wasn't gonna wait for this demented bull to charge. So, to show everyone who was boss, he fired a slug right into Charlie's stomach, right into his fat gut, and immediately realized that was a mistake.

Charlie seemed more surprised than hurt. Then that face of his twisted into something unnatural.

8

Ernest was now regretting bringing the .22, an arrogant decision made under the assumption these two jokers would be easy to push around. If he survived this, Clint Camacho would be adding another tip to his book....

When your prey is compliant, a .22 is perfect for execution-style head-shots. However, when there's only ten feet of dirty motel carpet between yourself and a fat maniac, what you need is stopping power—a .38 or .357.

Things were about to go wild and Ernest only had one move left. He pointed the .22 at the side of Yvette's head and glared at Charlie. "Stay put, or I swear to fucking Christ I'll kill her!"

Charlie's contorted face shifted from dark fury to dark confusion. His eyes spun around.

This is good, Ernest thought, and felt a little less like pissing himself.

The feeling didn't last.

9

Yvette knew this would be her last chance to zag, and wasn't about to pass it up. Defiantly, she turned to face the gun, looked Ernest dead in the eyes, grinned a bloody, toothless grin, and said: "Don't listen to him, Charlie. This fat sack of stupid's gonna kill us no matter what."

Charlie charged.

Ernest put a slug through Yvette's eye, and both she and Ernest hit the floor at the same time—Yvette because she was dead, and Ernest because Charlie was the mad dog on top of him.

Using all his weight, Charlie had exploded into Ernest like a foot-ball player into a tackling dummy, plowing him back into the narrow wall between the door and window, almost driving him through it.

The Rebel Yell, the whole fucking building, trembled like a young man in love.

Ernest bounced off the wall, had the wind knocked out of him, and lost hold of the gun. After the stars cleared, he saw that Charlie was standing over him, his whole body heaving with hate as he pointed the .22 right between Ernest's watery and confused eyes.

Ernest quickly crab-crawled backward until he was able to sit up against the battered wall. He had one play left and shoved his hand into his pants pocket.

Charlie licked his lips, straightened his glasses, and shot Ernest in the thigh.

Bang!

Ernest howled and grabbed the meat of his leg. The slug had found his thigh bone. He screamed in agony and suddenly wanted to live.

"Okay, okay, okay, okay—wait!" Ernest squawked. "It's a million dollars, pal! A key to a million dollars. Cash! It's all there in a locker. I swear!"

Charlie kept inhaling and exhaling, like a 230-pound meat piston embedded with crazy eyes.

Ernest swallowed hard. "Lem-lemme get the key for you, pal. Million bucks, man, a million bucks!" Ernest slowly pulled the locker key from his pocket and held it up to Charlie like it was a ring and he was proposing marriage. "The bus station outside Rio Rico on Third. You know it? Take it. The money's yours."

Charlie answered by firing a slug into Ernest's other thigh. Ernest shrieked in pain and terror, but mostly terror, and the key to a million dollars went flying.

"Please, please, stop," Ernest begged. "I work for a powerful man, he can—"

Charlie fired two into Ernest's gut. The fat man bent over, practically folded himself in half, and whimpered, "Wait, wait, wait!" as the oil-black blood drained from his gut.

Charlie pressed the barrel of the .22 to the top of Ernest's head. Ernest could feel it, feel what so many had felt when he'd done the same to them, and the feeling made him wail like a baby: "Please don't. Please! *Please* don't kill me, please..."

Charlie pulled the trigger.

Click.

The revolver was all shot out.

Ernest raised his weary head and let it drop back against the wall, which exposed his throat. "Get me to a hospital and I'll give you a million dollars. Just get me to a—"

Charlie fell on him.

10

With Charlie's teeth tearing into the meat of his neck, Ernest died inhaling the stench of his own blood, the stink of dirty motel carpet, and the sickly aroma of stale licorice on hot breath. He died desperately not wanting to die, a feeling he'd never before felt.

Most of all, he died wondering how the universe could hate him so much it handed the rope to a *fat fucking retard*.

11

Gut shot with a mouthful of Ernest's gore, Charlie crawled off Ernest's beached whale of a corpse and, on his hands and knees, started to moan and cry like a wounded animal.

He crawled over to Yvette's dead body, laid down on his side, used her bloody chest for a pillow and stroked her face.

"I killed him. I-I-I killed him good."

Her one eye was shot out. The other acknowledged nothing.

The slug in Charlie's gut burned like fire. He stroked Yvette's dead face and cried and moaned and wailed until he realized something—something that exhilarated him.

Ernest had been wrong about many things tonight, chief among them the idea Charlie had lost control.

The truth was that Charlie had never felt more *in control*. For more than twenty years, in a futile effort to control it, and as though it were a god, he'd sacrificed countless animals to the rage. But this time, he'd surrendered to it, he'd allowed the rage to have its way with him, and in doing so, he'd taken care of business—taken care of business like a fuckin' man takes care of business.

Still using Yvette as a pillow, Charlie rolled on his back and stared up at the ceiling to relive the night in his head, which he did, every glorious moment, and as he did, his gore-streaked smile widened and his eyes lit up like sparklers.

166

"Goddamn right," he said out loud. "God-Goddamn right!"

But as the adrenaline slowed and the blood poured out of him, Charlie's eyes began to flutter and to roll to the back of his head. He was dizzy and drowsy and just about to lose consciousness when his eyes shot wide open with the memory of something, of what Yvette had told him about Mason's betrayal; how Mason wanted to take Yvette away from him.

Mason had paid her to leave, she'd said, and then Mason had told her a bunch of lies about how the motel was a cheat, a fake, a big, stupid toy train for a *fat fucking retard*.

Charlie's smile faded. His eyes darkened.

He didn't want to believe it.

It's not true, he thought.

Then he screamed it.

As much as Charlie wanted to stay beside Yvette forever, he had to know the truth. And so, like something rising from the earth, he willed himself to his feet.

The blood draining from his gut was crimson now and soaked his pants past the knee. His mouth was still full of Ernest's flesh. He didn't mind the taste.

12

By the time he found the money under the car seat, found the proof that everything Yvette had told him about Mason was true, Charlie was near passing out. But the discovery, the proof of Mason's betrayal, fired off a final reservoir of hate and adrenaline, enough to allow him to pull a gas can from the shed, empty it out along the front of the rooms, and drop a match.

Charlie watched the fire race along the wooden deck, and then explode in a rhythmic *whoofsh...whoofsh...whoofsh...*on each gasoline-splashed door. As Room 14 burned, Mason's room, Charlie whipped the gas can around like a dead cat and shouted with delight.

The fire grew into a blaze. Glass exploded. Charlie backed far enough away to watch his whole world burn, which filled him with a stew of emotions he could neither understand nor process. When those emotions became too much, bathed in the inferno's slashing light and shadow, Charlie stalked the Rebel Yell's dirt lot like an animal to rage and giggle until the reality of the bullet wound buckled his knees.

Then he saw a white light.

Crouched by pain and weakness, he whimpered and stumbled towards that light, towards the fire. The light was the open door to Room 3—Yvette's room. He crossed the threshold and collapsed on his belly. Now sobbing, he dragged himself over to Yvette leaving behind an oily trail of red.

Before blacking out, Charlie's goodbye kiss left a bloody smear on Yvette's mouth.

PART THREE

THE ESCAPE STORIES

The Car Accident

†

Some thirty years before his son would rip out another man's throat with his teeth, Charlie's dad, twenty-five-year-old Tate Breslin, was getting high on a couch that was way too big for his double-wide.

Even with the help of his running buddies, Cricket and Lenny, it had been quite a show getting that sucker in the trailer. They'd cut off its legs and still tore up that big bitch forcing it through the door.

The whole time they were laughing, high as hell.

Northpoint Hildy had given him the couch so she could stick it to the Rentaroom people, who were coming to repossess it.

Rentaroom was one of those rip-off joints that offered credit to pretty much anyone:

> *You can rent-to-own this 19-inch color television TODAY*
> *for just $25 a week...and after six months, YOU OWN IT!*

Hey, good job, genius. You just paid $600 for a $300 TV.

What happened was this: after Hildy got promoted off the line to shift supervisor, she'd moved into a nicer apartment and furnished the living room through Rentaroom—you know, a TV, VCR, recliner, coffee table, and that couch, that sweet-sweet big-ass couch. The whole set-up cost $75 a week, and after paying $3,900 over twelve months, she'd own it outright.

She didn't mind paying double what the stuff was worth. Her credit was shit. What else could she do? She did mind them repossessing it after she'd paid ten of the twelve months. It wasn't her fault the cannery moved to Mexico.

So while they were hanging out one afternoon, Hildy told Cricket and Lenny she was thinking about selling the stuff and telling Rentaroom to go fuck themselves. She was also thinking about piling everything in the front yard, lighting it on fire, and telling *everyone* to go fuck themselves.

Because of the kind of guys they were, Cricket and Lenny encouraged her to make the second choice. But she wanted to think things over. You see, unlike Hildy-from-the-Depot, who never thought through anything and was always in some kind of jackpot, Northpoint Hildy (as she was called to keep things straight) thought through everything.

So the three of them smoked a Thai stick and drank Colt 45 as she mulled her options.

2

Yeah, Rentaroom had screwed her big time. Hildy knew that. But she also knew she was pissed off at the world, not just them. Here she was, forty-seven years old and right back where she'd started: broke, unemployed, on the dole, and hanging out with these two idiots. She'd run into them at the Split-Level, a dive bar she'd vowed to stay away from after her promotion.

This time last month, she'd been a real citizen: wearing slacks, taking home $415 a week, carrying a clipboard—the whole megillah. She'd even started to look at life different, like maybe she had a future. So she rented a nicer place and drank at a nicer bar, but only on pay nights. Hell, she was even gonna open a savings account after paying off Rentaroom.

But the world had it in for her, and, to be fair, that wasn't only Rentaroom's fault. So Hildy came to a decision: she'd have to return the TV and VCR. Those had serial numbers. But anyone who wanted to bring over their old furniture to trade for her newer stuff—well, they could have it for free. Rentaroom would argue it wasn't their stuff. She'd tell them to prove it.

Lenny and Cricket weren't too hot on the idea. That plan required effort: finding people, hauling furniture. It was more their style to light fires and tell everyone to go fuck themselves.

Hildy disagreed. This was better, she explained. Rentaroom would know she'd screwed them but wouldn't be able to do anything about it.

That was the kind of thing she could sit back and laugh about for the rest of her life.

Lenny and Cricket only sparked to the idea after they remembered Tate. He'd just shacked up with his crazy girlfriend, Maya, over at the Redstone Trailer Park. Tate needed all kinds of furniture.

3

Tate liked the idea but didn't have a couch to trade.

Lenny suggested Goodwill. "Hell, man, you can buy a crummy couch over there for twenty bucks."

No one was surprised Lenny knew this. He had every angle in town nailed down.

But Tate didn't have twenty dollars. What he did have was thirteen dollars and three Marlboro Reds dipped in LSD ("dippers" for short).

To make up the shortfall, Cricket agreed to buy Tate's dippers for the outstanding seven dollars. This immediately became a running joke because Cricket, a notorious thief, was always stealing dippers out of Tate's smokes. So, according to Cricket's worldview, giving over seven bucks for three dippers he could've swiped meant the big-ass couch was partly his.

"How's my couch?" he'd always ask.

Joke never got old.

Tate really liked how the couch sat low to the ground. Cutting off the legs had worked out fine, a perfect place to get high and watch cartoons.

4

Only on this day Tate wasn't watching cartoons. Instead, he was watching his son, something he'd found himself doing a lot more of lately.

Now that the boy was four, Tate no longer doubted Charlie was his. At first, even after the blood test, he'd still had doubts—Maya being Maya and all. But now, when he looked at the kid, Tate recognized himself in the way the boy sat, held his head, and favored his left hand. Charlie was built and moved like his dad.

Thank heaven he looks like Maya, Tate had thought more than once. Little Charlie had black hair, olive skin, dark eyes, and thick eyelashes. An adorable kid, everyone said so. Gonna be a real heartbreaker, they said.

More and more, Tate thought about how he used to pressure Maya to get an abortion. At the time, the last thing he wanted was a kid. He didn't even want a girlfriend, but shaking Maya off was something he could never figure out how to do.

"It's a sin," Maya-the-lapsed-Catholic said of the abortion, "and we can get welfare."

The welfare wasn't much, but enough that they weren't gonna give it up by getting married. Enough that Tate only had to work part-time and could sit around most days getting high on his big-ass couch—something he did as often as possible. This was his happy place.

But, today, Tate was watching his son.

5

Charlie was splayed out on the floor drawing a picture of Tate, Maya, and Charlie, standing out front of their shitty double-wide, smiling and holding hands. Something they'd never done in real life.

It was the drawing's details that grabbed Tate's attention. Kid didn't miss a thing: the trees, Robinson's garbage cans and collapsing tool shed. He even remembered Jerry's four-wheeler and the junk pile in Peterson's yard.

The drawing was crude, the work of a child. The *detail* was something else. Using different colored crayons, Charlie added pockets and cuffs to the pants, and a pattern to Maya's dress. Even Peterson's junk pile looked right. Well, it didn't *look* right—Charlie was only four—but it felt right, the shape and colors.

"They teach you to draw like that in school?" Tate asked.

Charlie answered by bouncing his head up and down like little kids do when they're concentrating. Then he practically floored Tate. After drawing a big orange sun, Charlie grabbed a white crayon and used it to add sunlight in all the right places: on the trees, even the faces.

Light source, Tate realized. *This kid understands light source.*

Tate knew all about light source because he sometimes got high watching this guy on TV who painted landscapes. All the time this guy talked about light source, how it added dimension. Light source is everything, this guy said.

Tate wetted two fingers in his mouth to pinch off the joint and slid in next to Charlie on the floor for a closer look.

6

"Who taught you to do that...to draw the light?"

"No one," Charlie said. "I'm making this for Grandma Dory. She says we got no family pictures."

Grandma Dory was correct. There were no family pictures because there was no family. Tate was a bottom-feeding pot dealer and part-time prison guard. Maya worked for cash hustling drinks at the Split-Level, a dive bar a half-mile down the road. The kid was a welfare check—$385 a month, a little rent assistance, some food stamps.

They lived together, that was all.

This was not the life Tate had planned for himself. He couldn't believe how bad he'd messed up. All this responsibility. *A kid, for crying out loud!* And Maya...a total junkie, and now it was his job to keep her well. And if he didn't, she'd for sure tell the state he was Charlie's father, and then the state would come after him for about a billion dollars in child support, a hassle he didn't need.

Everything was a hassle now.

7

Once upon a time, he and Lenny and Cricket had the secret to life nailed down. They were gonna deal oxy and reefer hot and heavy, but only long enough to buy a used house trailer and set it up on some land owned by Lenny's old man, who was cool with the idea. Then they'd move in, bootleg some cable TV (they knew a guy), and there you go.... What more do you need?

Sure, they'd have to deal a little to keep themselves in weed and groceries, but they had enough burnout friends to remove the risk. It was a perfect plan because it was simple. No bills, no hassles, no Maya, no kid.

With that dream dead, Tate took to dreaming about taking off, to Utah maybe. *There must be good weed and big-ass couches in Utah.* But he never got around to it. That kind of adventure was its own hassle.

Tate didn't think about Utah so much anymore. Charlie was growing on him, especially now that he was something more than a crying-pooping-eating machine. The kid was funny and sharp, a real charmer.

Tate used to hate babysitting. Back then, whenever Charlie'd start crying—which was all the damn time—he'd plop him in the crib, shut the door, put on the headphones, and blaze one up. He'd probably plopped him harder than he should've sometimes.

These days it was less like babysitting and more like the two of them hanging out.

Sometimes, just like that, Charlie would crawl into Tate's lap and fall asleep. And even when he had to pee real bad, Tate didn't move. He let the kid sleep, stared at him, and couldn't believe he had something to do with creating him.

That was when he really wished he could forget about pressuring Maya about the abortion.

8

Tate would always mark the day Charlie drew the light as the day when he began to feel edgy and out of sorts. He didn't know about what exactly, just that all of a sudden he couldn't get mellow or sleep. Lying awake in bed, he'd think about things and try to pinpoint the problem. He even thought about seeing a doctor.

For more than a week, he carried around this unsettled feeling, that and a dream he couldn't shake where he and his boys, Lenny and Cricket, were out exploring a cave. Charlie had a flashlight and was running around like kids do, making the light bounce all over. Everyone was having a good time, talking too loud, laughing.

Then Charlie ran off with the light, deep into the cave, leaving the three of them in the dark. So they took a seat and passed around some smoke. Then Charlie ran back excited, all out of breath—you know, all smiles, and then sped off the other way. Tate didn't worry. No matter how far Charlie ran, he could see the bouncing light and hear his laughter. Then Lenny started talking about reincarnation, which was *always* a big topic of interest when he got loaded.

"We all come back again," Lenny assured them. "Which means we all get a second chance to live our lives the right way."

Then Cricket, who was confused by the whole idea, asked: "Why not do it the right way this time?"

No one had an answer for that, so they broke up laughing.

The next day Tate forgot the dream, but the feel of it stayed with him, making him even more raw and anxious. He wondered if he had lupus. He had no idea what that was; it just popped into his head. On a break, he looked it up in the prison library where there was a set of encyclopedias, and felt better. He didn't have lupus.

Still, everything inside him remained confused, all jumbled. Sure, he'd felt frazzled before. This wasn't that. Those feeling always went away when he got high and dreamt of Utah. Doing those things now only made him feel worse.

9

All this was pressing down hard on him one day while he watched Charlie drink a glass of chocolate milk. The kid was drinking out of Tate's "special glass," this big, ugly blue thing he'd won tossing rings at the State Fair. It held twice what an ordinary glass did, and Tate sometimes liked to make a big thing about how *I'm drinking out of my big-ass glass*, which Charlie found hilarious.

Charlie filled the glass with chocolate milk and struggled so hard to hold on to it, his little arms trembled. Then, after a couple of swallows, he carefully set the glass on the counter, wiped away the milk mustache with his sleeve, and whispered: "I'm drinking out of my big-ass glass." Then he started all over again.

That was when Tate decided to become a good dad, and that's when all those bad feelings went away.

10

Tate thought about telling Maya things had to change. But he knew she'd either blow him off or laugh in his face.

Maya was snorting heroin now. She wasn't on the needle yet, but that next. He'd seen it a hundred times. He also knew Maya didn't respond to pressure. If he brought up her using, she might go on the needle out of spite, as a way to tell him to kiss her ass.

He thought a lot about what it meant to be a good dad and discovered he had no idea how to go about it. It would help if he could talk to someone. He knew some dads, but not one was worth a shit.

The only decent parent he knew was Doreen, but she hated him. *Can't blame her for that.* They'd really screwed her over after she'd trusted them with the motel, which was something else he didn't like to think about.

He liked Doreen, respected her. She was also pretty hot. He considered telling her about his decision to be a good dad, but knew how it'd sound. Like all the times they'd told her what she wanted to hear to get money from her.

He decided not to tell anyone.

11

Three years later, and on the same night she and Tate would die in a car accident and Charlie would be irreparably brain damaged, Maya discovered her first gray hair.

Not even thirty and already gray.

Maya was thinking hard about gray hair and Doreen, her mother, when Charlie chugged over looking for more quarters. He was seven now and having the best time playing video games with Tate.

She filled his tiny fist with as many quarters as it would hold, and he chugged back to continue humiliating the old man at *Mortal Kombat*.

The place was crowded, so Maya was tasked with holding down the booth and guarding the double pepperoni pizza. She was okay with that. She needed time to think.

She was stuck again on step eight, the one where you were supposed to make amends to those you've hurt and betrayed. This was her fourth time walking the twelve steps and her fourth time stuck on step eight.

This go around, she'd been clean six months, and Wanda, her sponsor, said it was better to skip a step than to start using again.

Maya wasn't so sure.

Over these last two years, minus the relapses, she'd been sober eleven months. In the NA meetings she talked a lot about herself, and since she didn't like to wing it, she thought a lot about herself beforehand and discovered she had no idea which way was up when it came to her mother.

Now that her head was clear, Maya remembered every terrible thing she'd done to her mother and was so sorry she could hardly keep the sorry from breaking her back. Just thinking about it made her want to relapse.

But the one thought worse than *not* apologizing to her mother was the thought *of* apologizing. Maya knew that if she told her mom how sorry she was, Doreen would assume her junkie daughter was just running another hustle on her, and the thought of hurting her again like that was unbearable.

This put Maya in a wretched place where she couldn't live with or without making things right with Doreen. Wanda called it a vicious circle. All Maya knew was that she never wanted to get out of bed.

12

Chewing on cold pizza, she watched Tate and Charlie play the videogame and wondered if what she was starting to feel for her husband was love. She'd been crazy for him back in school, eleven years ago. *Eleven years.* She could hardly believe it.

Tate loved her—said he did anyway. She didn't get mad anymore when he said it. She did wonder, though, if he confused love with guilt. Tate hauled around guilt like a bag of anvils.

She hadn't said it back to him yet, hadn't said, "I love you, too." She couldn't remember the last time she'd said that to anyone other than Charlie.

Charlie she loved so much it scared her. Things were better between them. She hadn't lost her shit in a while, so he was a little more relaxed around her. The other day he'd crawled into her lap and fallen asleep.

He was getting heavy, but it was still sweet.

She used a paper napkin to wipe the pizza grease from her hands, grabbed a Marlboro from the pack Tate had left on the table, caught his eye, and signaled she was going out for a smoke. He answered her with a smile, unassuming as ever.

This time of night, the cool, dry Arizona air hit the spot. There was a breeze, and, off in the distance, a lightning storm.

Maya leaned against Pizza n' Play's red brick wall and took a deep drag. The nicotine worked as advertised. She tapped off an ash and watched the families come and go.

Pizza n' Play was the kind of place average families came to on a Friday night and Maya felt a little pride at being a part of that, even though she didn't exactly fit in.

Maya knew how she looked. All these years of living the way she had made a woman look hard, look street.

Truth be told, part of her still enjoyed looking a little notorious. But she'd seen firsthand what happens to hard girls. How they land on the other side of forty and the rough living turns them into something like wrinkled vultures—always perched at the end of the bar, always drinking and smoking and cackling too much.

Maybe it wasn't too late. She was still pretty. Men still threw her a second look—including some of these upright-types at Pizza n' Play.

13

After three relapses, she was starting to think she'd never stay clean. Wanda told her the average addict relapses ten to twelve times before it sticks.

Man alive, seven, eight more times of this...?

Tate up and quit, just like that, nice as you please. Didn't say a word, just stopped. Quit using, quit dealing, started working full-time at the prison. Even got himself a haircut. Real fine citizen all of a sudden, which was his own business until he told her he wouldn't score for her anymore. Boy, she'd put on a real exhibition that day. Lost all of her shit and then threatened to turn him in to the state. They'd garnish his check for back support, she screamed as she looked up the welfare hotline number, grabbed the phone, and started dialing....

"Will you marry me?" he blurted.

"I don't love you," she shrieked, which was true. Then she pulled the phone out of the wall, threw it at him, dropped into his raggedy couch, and wrapped her hands around her head.

Charlie was only five then and didn't know what to do. When mom got this way, he froze, knowing she'd either burst out crying and start hugging him too hard, or shriek if he so much as blinked.

Tate broke through the tension. "Go on out and play," he said, and Charlie did.

With Charlie out of earshot, Maya swore she'd turn him in unless "YOU TAKE CARE OF ME RIGHT FUCKING NOW!"

Tate relented and said he'd score for her one last time. Said he was wrong not to give her some notice, and then apologized. He did that a lot now, *apologized*, and that was something else Maya wasn't sure she liked.

When he returned with the heroin, Charlie was still outside because Maya was inside near crazy. She snorted it right up and went to lie down in the back bedroom, her happy place.

As she floated away, Tate spoke gently. He admitted he'd started her on drugs and said he was sorrier about that than anything else in his life. Everything was his fault, he said, but if they got married his insurance would cover her. He had good benefits working for the state. There wasn't even a co-pay for rehab.

He told her he brought home $612 a week now, so they didn't need the welfare. He asked her what she thought about renting a house in Centerville. He'd be closer to work, and Charlie could go to a better school with a legitimate art program. He promised not to pressure her, asked only that she think about it.

She heard every word, and then spent six months punishing him for every word.

14

After she'd run out of cruel things to shriek and stuff to break, Maya moved in with Trigger-T, an ex-con who said he loved her and promised to keep her high. He didn't love her, but he did keep her high. Then he tried to pass her off to his buddies. She almost didn't make it to the bathroom, where she locked the door and screamed until the sheriff came.

She was sitting in the back of a cruiser, pissed off at it all, when the deputy said he'd take her home and asked where that was.

Tate led her into the back bedroom. She slept three days.

Tate didn't say a thing, not one word about her being gone, or who she'd been with.

The following month they were married by a justice of the peace. Charlie was best man.

Maya stubbed out her smoke on Pizza n' Play's brick wall and wished she'd brought a second one. She would have smoked that second one right up.

15

Cricket and Lenny exited a Qwik-Shop and spotted Maya next door stubbing out that smoke before she headed back into Pizza n' Play. They hadn't seen their former crime-partner Tate in a while and heard he was moving to Centerville.

Tate going straight was no big deal. He was never a dick about it and still lent them a few bucks—at least until they got embarrassed about asking and stopped. Tate wasn't a mark. He was one of them.

They'd stolen that case of beer Cricket was carrying. While paying for rolling papers, Lenny distracted the clerk by chatting her up and, like he was the King of Siam, Cricket walked right out the door with the beer. Lenny'd lost count of how many times they'd gotten away with that, which was why they'd hoofed it all the way out here. Not a good idea to pull that scam too often in the same spot.

Lenny pocketed the Zig-Zags while Cricket stashed the beer 'round back. You don't walk into Pizza n' Play with a case of beer. Even they knew that.

They'd come back for it after they said hello.

16

Charlie kept beating his dad so bad at *Mortal Kombat*, he almost wished he hadn't. But, after each humiliating loss, Tate smiled and shook his head in amazement at his son's skills. Charlie liked impressing his dad.

Charlie was good at pretty much everything. He was in the second grade now and popular; almost always picked first for sports. Girls all thought he was cute.

At a parent-teacher conference—the first one Maya showed up for— Charlie's teacher used the word "gifted," a description she was careful about not carelessly throwing around. Boy, you would've thought Tate had just been handed a million dollars. Couldn't stop smiling the whole way home in the car, which had Maya cracking up...not that she wasn't a little proud herself.

17

Charlie whupped Tate again, this time in just a few seconds. Only half-kidding, Tate said, "I hate it when you do that." Then he busted up laughing, which made Charlie laugh.

They were out of quarters and Charlie grabbed his dad's hand as they headed back for more double pepperoni and Dr. Pepper.

Life was like this a lot now. Anyone paying attention would've described Tate as a doting father. Mom was better, too; still moody, but not mean like before. Sometimes, just because, she'd stoop down, take his hands in hers, and say, "You know I love you, don't you?" Charlie was starting to think maybe she did.

He was excited about moving to Centerville. He'd have his own room in the new house and plenty of space for the easel Grandma Dory had given him for Christmas.

He wasn't so excited about changing schools, but that wasn't until after summer vacation, which feels like a long ways off when you're seven.

18

Tate was genuinely happy to see Cricket and Lenny. With their long hair and stoner clothes, they looked out of place in the family establishment. People stared. Tate didn't care. Maya cared a little.

Charlie didn't like Cricket and Lenny. He associated them with the bad days and thought they were stupid, which they were. Something Charlie did like, though, was watching his dad talk to other guys. Charlie thought his dad was pretty cool when he did that.

As pleased as he was to see his old friends, Tate had changed and things just weren't the same. The handshakes were awkward, the greetings strained: *How you been, bro? Okay. Yeah. Awesome. Good to see you. How's it going? Cool.*

Then Cricket asked how his couch was doing and everyone broke out laughing.

Even Maya cracked a smile and invited them to sit and help themselves to pizza while she took Charlie to redeem the pile of tickets he'd won at skeeball.

The three old friends slid into the booth, grabbed a slice, and it was just like old times as they caught up.

Hildy—not Hildy-from-the-Depot, who was in jail again, but North-point Hildy, the one with the couch—she'd started tending bar at the Split-Level right after Maya quit. She was doing okay, but after too many drinks she'd start cackling about how she'd screwed Rentaroom, a story everyone had already heard a million times.

Confusing his dream with reality, Tate started laughing about that time in the cave when Charlie was running around with the flashlight. Even though this hadn't happened, Lenny and Cricket still laughed as though it had, because there was a lot of shit they didn't remember.

Then Cricket announced they had achieved their life goal. Yessir, got that house trailer, bootlegged cable TV and everything.

Tate suddenly felt the tug of his old life. Lenny sensed it and warned him off. "It actually sucks, man," he admitted. "There's something wrong with the electric. There's no air conditioning and the whole place smells like Cricket farts."

At that, the three of them laughed so hard everyone threw them looks, and Cricket took note that Tate was still the kind of guy who didn't care about those looks—which made him miss his former crime-partner all the more.

Maya caught Tate's eye and waved. She needed him for something. Tate stood. "Don't leave," he said, and meant it, and then headed off to do Dad Duty.

19

What happened next was not an act of malice or even meant as a joke. It was an act of friendship.

20

The cigarette laced with LSD, the dipper, was unmistakably purple. You couldn't miss it.

Lenny grinned as Cricket slipped the purple dipper into Tate's pack of Marlboros. The idea was only to put a smile on Tate's face. To remind him of old times and all the dippers Cricket had filched over the years.

Cricket pictured Tate finding it and tossing it away with a chuckle as he gave his old running buddies a warm thought.

Things had been a little strained tonight, and after Tate moved to Centerville, they'd probably never see him again.

The LSD-laced cigarette was meant as a goodbye gesture, a farewell grace note.

21

Driving home in the dark, Tate didn't see the color of the acid-laced cigarette, and lit it up. It tasted bitter, but pepperoni made everything bitter.

While the acid roared through a system that no longer carried a tolerance for it, Charlie slept in the backseat.

Next to Tate, Maya had her arms wrapped around her knees as she stared out the window into the night and wondered if she'd ever stop craving the drugs. She'd also settled on something: she was going to invite her mom over to the new place for the Fourth of July.

Lost in his own thoughts, Tate worried about landing a promotion. It was time to start saving for a house of their own and the pay increase would make that possible.

Then the LSD told him to steer into the oncoming headlights of a dump truck, and he did.

The coroner's report blamed the accident on Tate for driving under the influence.

22

Doreen would never know the accident wasn't Tate's fault or that he'd matured into the kind of man who stressed over good schools and promotions. She'd never know how sorry Maya was, or how her daughter agonized over finding a way to say so.

Cricket and Lenny learned of the accident, but not what caused it, which was for the best. Over the years, while sitting outside of their trailer with the electricity that never did work right, they'd sometimes pour one out for their old friend and try to remember that day in the cave.

Charlie remembered pretty much everything about that night.

The promise of who he was, of what he might have become, never stopped gnawing at him.

The Hitch-Hiker

1

Thirty-five miles from where the Rebel Yell was still smoldering, Highway 187 was little more than a strip of cracked and lonely asphalt that cut through a cracked and lonely desert—the kind of place that convinced a man he was all alone in the world, especially at night.

When she spotted the hitch-hiker, fifty-seven-year-old Sheriff Zoey Bushnell was looking forward to a comfortable evening in front of the TV with her husband, Quinton, and his latest recipe for beef stew.

Hitch-hiking wasn't illegal in Arizona, and she wasn't the type to roust a man for no reason, especially when she was only two from miles from TV and beef stew. None of that, however, altered the facts as she saw them: a guy in the middle of nowhere without any kind of backpack looking desperate for a ride...right up until he saw her police cruiser.

She considered letting it go and going on home. *Why not?* After all, she'd just finished another sixteen-hour shift. And Quinton had not only made beef stew, there was that sound in his voice that suggested he'd like to do a little after-supper cooking.

But Zoey Bushnell was the sheriff. People of Lincoln County had elected her to three terms, and she took that responsibility seriously.

Please let it be nothing, her mind pleaded as she radioed in her location, hit the flashers, and pulled over onto the dirt.

Eyeing the rearview, she watched the hitcher stop a ways back and spread out his hands like he thought that was a good idea. It was. Now she wouldn't have to fire up the cruiser's loudspeaker and order him back. Bossing people around increased tension, created resentment, and made everything more difficult. That wasn't her style.

Even from here, she could see he was covered in the dust that sticks to sweat. *Someone's been running.*

The cruiser's red and blue flashers swept the dark and empty landscape with their eternal loop. Zoey stepped out of the vehicle and rested a hand on the Glock 19 strapped to her waist.

2

By the numbers, Zoey wasn't a large woman. What she carried was a presence that made her more imposing than her five-foot-four, 140-pound frame. Mainly it was the unmistakable intelligence in her large oval eyes. One look at those eyes and you knew you'd never catch her off guard.

The hitcher's silhouette stood motionless some twenty feet away. Zoey closed the car door, walked around to the cruiser's rear, and clicked on a flashlight. Another way to provoke a man was to shine a light in his face, so she kept it pointed to the ground, approached cautiously, and stopped at ten feet.

That was close enough.

Every cop in the world understood the hazards of stops like this one, especially in the dark. You have to assume the worst—that he's got a gun—so the further away you are, the smaller the target you are. If it looks like he's reaching, you use the one hand to shine the light in his face and the other to shoot the son of a bitch dead.

The second worst case was him charging you—so you now have ten feet of time to shoot the son of a bitch dead.

And Sheriff Zoey Bushnell *would* shoot a son of a bitch dead. Some years back, she'd proved that as a school safety officer when she shot two sons of bitches dead.

Yes, Zoey knew she had it in her to kill a man, and, during moments like this one, that gave her some security. But sometimes, late at night when she couldn't sleep, it made her uneasy about who she was.

There was no sense of security tonight, not in this situation, not in knowing how the fates operate, not when she was only two miles from home and 191 days from retirement. This set-up made her ripe as summer squash to enter the pantheon of ironic stories told late at night over warm beers in dark cop bars.

Remember that lady sheriff, the one who was only two miles from home and 191 days from taking her twenty? Man, what a world.

But the fates could kiss Zoey Bushnell's black ass. She had every intention of surviving to retirement and then living through many years of Quinton's after-supper cooking. So she kept her distance and pointed that flashlight in the dirt.

3

"Everything alright tonight?" she asked.

"Just need to get home," the hitcher replied.

"Where's that?" she inquired, hoping it sounded like a concern instead of a demand.

"Motel in Browning. The Rebel Yell. I'm the handyman there."

Rebel Yell was in Zoey's jurisdiction. She'd just left there. And after watching three bodies whisked off in two ambulances, she'd assigned a deputy to guard the wreckage until morning when an investigation could begin. But now that the handyman had shown up, she knew there would be no beef stew or after-supper cooking tonight.

"Okay," she said, not wanting to give away what she knew. "Mind if I see some ID?"

As the hitcher answered, Zoey casually ran the flashlight over his clothes looking for burn marks. Arsonists seldom get away clean. He was clean.

"My wallet's back there somewhere," he said, pointing a thumb into the desert. "Was camping and got up to go to the bathroom. It was dark. Got turned around and lost. Wallet and everything's back there."

There were two things Zoey didn't believe in: coincidence and jumping to conclusions. But after that pile of shit, those two things were scorpions in a jar.

His story was ridiculous. Man who lives at the Rebel Yell getting lost without his ID on the same night the place burns to the ground with three people in it…? *Yeah, pull the other one; it's got bells on it.*

"Got any weapons on you?" she asked.

"Only thing in my clothes is me."

Zoey clicked her lapel radio and whispered in a request for immediate backup. If she was going to ensure fate kissed her black ass, she couldn't be too proud to ask for help while taking Mr. Bullshit in for questioning.

"Okay, well, I'm going to ask you to wait right there. We'll get you a ride."

4

Mason knew it was best not to say anything. One wrong word could roll him right over the side, but he was too sick with worry for Charlie to wait.

"Something wrong?" he asked.

Mason kept his mouth shut after that, volunteered nothing, and was asked only one more question: "What's your name?" And with that, the All at Once crept a little closer.

While Doreen was alive, Mason could've used any one of his aliases. She knew the drill, but there was only Charlie to vouch for him now, and Charlie wouldn't understand Mason using an alias. So, without knowing Charlie was one of the bodies carried out of the Rebel Yell, he gave the sheriff the only answer he could, the closest thing he had to a real name, the name he hoped would get him out of this jackpot just as soon as she called Charlie: "Joshua Mason."

It wasn't exactly the end of the world. Somehow the mass-marketing branch of the All at Once had already found him. He had no idea how—maybe through the marriage license in Reno—but "Joshua Mason" received all kinds of corporate junk mail. Still, that was different than handing his name over to the government.

5

A few minutes later, two deputies roared up in separate cars and the whole scene changed.

A single set of police flashers gives off a kind of tranquil rhythm. Add two more, and the world goes haywire.

"Hands on your head!"

"Intertwine your fingers!"

"On your knees!"

Mason did as he was told and caught the eye of the sheriff, who at least had the decency to look a little sorry for ambushing him.

Once he was handcuffed, the passive-aggressive taunt of the "sirs" made their appearance.

"On your feet, sir."

"Walk with me, sir."

"Step carefully, sir."

"Watch your head, sir."

Mason was folded into the back of the sheriff's cruiser and during the fifteen-minute drive, Zoey said nothing, which was deliberate. Nothing gets people talking like a long, awkward silence.

This didn't work on Mason, who was coming to the cold realization of what the events of the last few minutes meant. All this hoopla after discovering he was associated with the Rebel Yell...? There was only one explanation. Something terrible had happened, and it had happened because he was once again too late to stop it.

By the time they reached the station, a cold ball of dread had settled into his guts.

6

Mason sat in an interrogation room that smelled of fresh carpeting and paint. In fact, the whole sheriff's station looked like this, like a high school: cream-colored walls, vending machines, motivational posters....

It had been a long time since Mason sat in a sheriff's office. He couldn't remember how long, but there sure as hell hadn't been cream-colored walls and motivational posters.

He could never grasp why anyone would want to work in a place this characterless. Nevertheless, these generic, sterile, windowless buildings were everywhere. And even if there were windows, you weren't allowed to open them.

What's everyone got against fresh air? he wondered.

This was just one more thing that never stopped baffling Mason about this culture. Here was a society where everyone had everything, and still they chose sameness over individualism and variety.

Mason was no Luddite. A lot of good came from the All at Once. He knew that and held no sentiment for the "good old days" of leeches, bumpy carriage rides, smoky cabins, ringworm, and empty bellies. What confounded him was watching the freest, most prosperous culture he'd ever seen willingly embrace conformity.

Everyone's so eager to live the life their TV tells them to, no one stops to think about the wonders that might result if they were to unplug from the mainframe and come up with their own ideas.

The All at Once had fooled people into believing there was safety in conformity, something he saw as a violation of human nature.

7

None of those thoughts were racing through Mason's head now. He was thinking only of Charlie, and how to escape this situation.

The wall across from him was all mirror. He tried to avoid its gaze, but couldn't help wondering who was on the other side giving him the once over.

Zoey

1

It was Zoey giving him the once over, along with a deputy named Ramon Garza.

Garza was a sleek forty-six years old and filled all the way to the top with ambition. Four years ago, when Zoey ran for re-election, he'd challenged her and nearly won. Despite that, they managed to get along, especially now that she was on her way out to pasture and, with all the right people on his side, Garza was certain to win the upcoming election to replace her.

Zoey didn't hold it against Garza. What galled her was knowing that had she decided to run again, she would lose. And it wasn't only Zoey who knew that. They all knew it, the bastards who'd ex-communicated her for the sin of not being one of them.

She loved the job, truly did. Loved being a peace officer, loved being sheriff, just hated the politics.

Everyone wanted to stuff Zoey Bushnell in a box. Everyone wanted to tell her who she was supposed to be. When she closed her eyes and pictured the job, she saw herself covered in ducks pecking away at her, which was the price you paid for refusing to jump into a box.

You're a cop. Jump in the Cop Box.
You're a woman. Get into the Woman Box.
You're black. Climb into the Black Box.
You're a black woman. Here's your tiny Black Woman Box.
On and on it went.

Plenty of benefits came with jumping in boxes, no question about that. When you agreed to become what some group demanded you be, the prizes were limitless. But she wouldn't do it—couldn't do it. Thought of it rubbed her raw.

It was right after she shot those two sons of bitches dead that people started showing up with their boxes.

2

She'd been a school safety officer more than ten years when a twisted soul strolled through a nearby school and shot-gunned everyone he wanted to shotgun. There was no one to stop him. No one in the school was armed. The whole place was helpless and thirteen innocent people died.

Carrying a firearm in a public school was illegal. This law stupidly extended to school security, like Zoey. After the massacre, she was certain common sense would prevail and the rule would be reversed. Nope. Instead, the no-guns-in-school law was stressed and re-stressed, as though the stressing was enough to stop someone willing to shotgun thirteen souls only because he could.

Zoey saw things her own way. She had a duty to protect the kids and worried that all the media hoopla over that school shooting might give other sickos ideas about grabbing a shotgun and going down in their own blaze of TV glory. So, she ignored the law and bought herself a silver .380 semi-automatic with an ankle holster. Every day that gun came to school with her, and many a weekend afternoon was spent getting comfortable with it.

A whole year passed before those sons of bitches showed up. Two cartel vaqueros about to lose a police chase bounced their shiny Hummer over a curb, drove right up to the front door of her high school, and disappeared inside looking for hostages.

Bad luck for them; everyone was in the gym for an assembly. Worse luck for them, Zoey Bushnell and her silver .380 spotted them before they spotted her. And what she saw were two desperados carrying AK-47s and no regard for human life.

Typically, a .380 wouldn't stand a chance against a couple of AKs, but she got the drop on them. Remembering her training, she took a deep breath, released half that breath, stepped out from behind a wall in a shooting stance, and fired off lead instead of a warning.... Kept right on firing.

The vaqueros were too surprised to shoot back, and then they were too dead. She put four slugs in one, two in the other, and shattered the school's trophy case.

Even before all the glass and blood was cleaned up, Zoey was a hero. She was the Big Black Woman with the Little Silver Gun....

The following two decades were about to be built on a lie.

3

Not everyone saw her as a hero. Her illegal gun had saved the day and that angered influential media and political types who enjoyed making examples of those who refuse to conform, especially when that lack of conformity exposed their ideas as foolish.

Immediately, there were calls for Zoey to be prosecuted under the federal Gun-Free School Zones Act. Five years in prison was no joke, so, to avoid adding to her legal vulnerabilities, Zoey lied and said she'd shouted a warning before she'd started shooting. Told everyone that lie: the authorities, her attorney, school officials, media, anyone who asked.

Zoey'd never lied before—not really, not like that. So there was no way for her to know how difficult it was for an honest person to live with a lie, how the shame is like a lump on your neck you ignore hoping it will go away, even as it grows larger.

As time passed, she felt less like a hero and more like what the old-timers called a bushwhacker.

Pictures of those vaqueros were all over the internet, She couldn't help but look. At the time, they looked like dangerous animals. Then as she got older, they started to look different, younger, until they looked almost like boys—the kind of boys who maybe deserved a warning before someone gunned them down.

Maybe they would've dropped their guns.

Maybe they were just scared and stupid.

Late at night, we all count our sins. If Zoey could go back and give 'em a warning, she would.

Talk of prosecuting her ended as soon as those in politics and media decided she'd be more useful joining them in their box.

194

4

Folks who thought it was time to end white political authority in an increasingly non-white state wanted the Big Black Woman with the Little Silver Gun to run for sheriff.

Pro-gun folks wanted the Big Black Woman with the Little Silver Gun to become the face of the cause, make speeches, and TV appearances.

National media asked only questions in search of answers that made them feel good about who they were. So after her first network appearance—a brainless morning show—she turned down the rest.

It was an election year, so candidates from all over called to thank her for her heroism. Even before she'd hung up, there'd be a press release to announce she'd talked with them.

Campaigns cajoled her for endorsements. She said no. How about a photo? No again. How about a job in the new administration? She got an unlisted number.

They all wanted her in their box, wanted her to be who *they* needed her to be. She was grateful for one thing: that she was closer to forty than twenty. Without some seasoning, she would've jumped into one of those boxes and lost herself down there.

5

The only man who came along without a box had been Sheriff Mort "Red" Bingham. He phoned her out of the blue and asked if he could take her and her husband to lunch. Right away, Zoey liked that. Box carriers always tried to get her alone.

She and Quinton met this burly, middle-aged sheriff with a head as square as a checkerboard and face so freckled he looked sunburned. Straight off, he offered her a job, and in doing so, told no lies.

He admitted he'd heard rumblings about the other party running her for sheriff against him. He also admitted he was under pressure to hire more minority and women deputies.

None of the above, he said, had anything to do with the offer. She'd shown sand, he told her, and not only on the day of the shooting, but in choosing to strap on a .380 when the rules said not to. He also respected how she handled the media spotlight. Told her she had poise, and that poise and good policing go together like biscuits and gravy.

Said if she was the kind of woman he thought she was, she'd make a helluva sheriff someday—but not today. She needed experience.

He came right out and admitted experience wasn't a requirement to be elected sheriff. That question was up to voters and she could probably beat him without it. But if she wanted to be an effective sheriff, she first needed to be an effective deputy.

So, even though Zoey knew she was the kind of woman who'd gun down two boys without a warning and then lie about it, the Big Black Woman with the Little Silver Gun became a probationary deputy for the Lincoln County Sheriff's office.

6

Red kept every promise and then some. He did more than bring her along; he mentored her. Next election, he retired and to avoid a box, she ran for Sheriff as an Independent.

Red, a rock-ribbed Republican, still endorsed her and then took all kinds of heat for stepping out of *his* box, which she appreciated.

At the time, people still remembered her as a hero, and she won easily. Since, she'd been re-elected twice and in 191 days, the plan was to retire and live the good life with Quinton, her husband of thirty-six years.

The only thing taking off the luster was knowing they'd beaten her.

7

It all went sour about five years ago when one of her new deputies got into a bar fight with an illegal named Gustavo Piedra.

She couldn't allow her deputies to get liquored up and throw punches, so she fired him. Seemed cut and dried to her, but right away the union started pecking her over the firing. Then the civil rights groups began pecking because the deputy was black. After it was discovered Gustavo was here illegally, a whole other group pecked away as though the deputy's actions shouldn't count because Gustavo had no business being in the country.

Maybe she did what she did because she was angry at the whole bunch. Or maybe it had to do with not shouting a warning all those years back.... Whatever it was, she antagonized everyone when she stuck to her guns about the firing and then gave Gustavo a break.

Even if he was in the country illegally, didn't seem right to up and pluck a man out of the life he'd built, especially over a fight he didn't start. So instead of turning him over to immigration, she released Gustavo after he promised to get his affairs in order and go back to Ecuador on his own.

When that news leaked, half of Lincoln County's big shots wanted her head. Then Gustavo broke his promise and she ended up handing him over to immigration anyway, which infuriated the other half.

She resented losing sleep for doing the right thing and should've stuck to her plan to retire at the end of that year when her second term as sheriff expired.

More importantly, she'd already promised Quinton she would retire, and based on that promise, Quinton had already resigned from a tenured professorship.

But after losing all that sleep for doing the right thing, Zoey decided to stick it to them and defiantly ran for another term. With the mayor, city council, and local media against her, she'd barely won and a chill formed in the marriage that was still there.

These last four years, it hadn't been easy working all those sixteen-hour days knowing Quinton was alone in their four-bedroom home, like a ghost without a purpose. But in 191 days, she intended to swallow the bile of her pride and never stop making it up to him.

8

Garza got off his cell phone and said to Zoey, "Two are dead. The third's in a coma and won't last much longer. All three were shot—the woman right through the eye."

He slipped the iPhone into his breast pocket and knew what would happen next. Whenever the world stopped making sense to Zoey, she'd fold her arms, purse her lips, stare at the ground, and talk to herself.

"What the hell happened out there?" she muttered.

Garza knew not to interrupt.

"Three victims," Zoey said to the carpet, "and a guy who admits he lives at the scene crawls out of the desert carrying a pile of lies about getting lost during a tinkle."

Her eyes lifted to gaze at Mason. "But why would a man responsible for a massacre come right out and admit he lived at the sight of the massacre? And he was hitch-hiking in the direction *of* the motel, not *away* from it...?"

Her eyes moved to Garza. "What do you think?"

"I think that guy looks familiar," Garza said, looking hard at Mason. "Just can't place him."

"Well, it would sure help if you could."

9

Mason was prepared for this. Police custody was one of those situations he'd thought through during those long desert drives. So when the sheriff walked in and started to question him, he had only one word for her....

"Lawyer."

This surprised Zoey, and because she was what you'd call an open book, she didn't hide it. "You want a lawyer? You're not under arrest, Mr. Mason. We only need a few questions answered."

He desperately wanted to know what was going on with Charlie, so he was tempted to answer questions in the hope they'd tell him. But he might say something stupid, which would give them enough to book him, which meant fingerprints and DNA. That was what he had to avoid. Once booked, you're not only in The System, getting yourself released is complicated and time-consuming with court appearances and bail.

He had only one goal—Charlie. If Charlie was still alive, he needed to get them both to the safehouse.

To make that happen, he knew he needed two things: legal representation, and for everyone to know that when it came to his rights he wasn't playing around.

"Lawyer."

"Well, with two dead bodies, that's probably a good idea," Zoey shot back, hoping to rattle him. It did. She watched him coil like a spring.

"You got someone you want to call," she asked, "or should I call the PD's office and get you a public defender?"

The words "two dead bodies" were still ablaze in his head, so he swallowed hard to keep his voice from cracking. "I can't afford a lawyer," he said.

"All right, I'll make the call. You want something to drink while you wait?"

He was parched from all the running. But once he accepted a bottle of water or soda, they'd have his DNA and fingerprints.

"Restroom would be appreciated," he said.

He drank his fill from the bathroom sink and wiped away his prints with paper towels.

Inferno

1

A couple of hours before Mason demanded a lawyer, Maria and her husband Preston were driving home from the movies and had just passed the Rebel Yell when the whole place exploded into a fireball.

Preston caught sight of the flames in the rearview, and like it was reflex, turned the car right around.

"Holy moly," Maria said. She couldn't believe anything could go up so quickly. Preston parked as close as he dared. She dialed 9-1-1. He jumped out of the car.

No point in stopping him, Maria knew. He'd fought for Fallujah and wasn't gonna sit back and do nothing with a motel full of people on fire. Still, she didn't worry too much. He could handle himself.

2

Preston stared at an inferno. But the door to Room 3, Yvette's room, was wide open. A light was on and an empty gas can lay by the door. Through the flames, Preston could see legs on the floor, more than one pair, so he got a running start, dove through the door, and landed hard on the floor near the foot of the bed.

Later he would describe Room 3 as a massacre: blood, gore, revolver, fat guy with his throat ripped out, blonde lady with one eye shot out. Those two were dead, no question.

The third guy was wet with blood from the waist down and laying on the floor with his head on the dead woman, like she was a pillow. He was alive but unconscious.

The wind shifted. The flames now covered the entire doorway, blocking the only way out. Black smoke was already making it difficult to breathe. Preston ripped a sheet off the bed, took it into the bathroom, soaked it under the shower, and wrapped himself with it. Then the Army Vet pulled the wet sheet over his head and grabbed hold of Charlie's legs. Facing forward, like a rickshaw driver, he ran through the fiery door dragging Charlie behind him.

3

This would've worked had Charlie not been such a clumsy arsonist and spilled gasoline all over himself. As he was pulled through the fire, Charlie lit up like a road flare, regained consciousness, and started screaming like a vampire tossed in the sun.

Preston got tangled in the sheet and lost his balance.

Maria didn't hesitate. She leapt out of the car, ripped the wet sheet off Preston, and dropped it on Charlie. The flames were out, but the damage was fatal. Charlie was cooked like Sunday meatloaf. First, he went into shock, then into a coma.

While Preston caught his breath and Charlie lay dying, Maria watched the Rebel Yell's fiery roof cave in on the dead bodies that had once been Yvette and Ernest.

Two Dead, One Dying

1

"We should wait on calling the PD's office. Let him sweat a bit before he's able to hide behind a lawyer," Deputy Garza said, as he followed Zoey into her office. "He might get a little more talkative after a while."

Feeling skuzzy after twenty hours in the same clothes, Zoey settled in her chair and gave Garza a look that said, *We gonna have this conversation again?*

"I'm just saying.... We got three bodies, Zoe. Something like this could go national."

"I know all that, Ray," she said, deliberately using his real name to irk him. Ramon Garza's real name was Ray Garza. Three years ago he'd changed it to Ramon to fit into a box that would ensure he became the next sheriff.

She also knew Garza was excited by the idea of national press coverage, something she wanted no part of. Something else she wanted no part of was playing games with a man's civil liberties. He had a right to an attorney. Period.

To put an end to the conversation, she shrugged apologetically and picked up the phone.

Garza nodded that he understood and retreated.

2

After seventeen years as a public defender, even in the middle of the night, Carmen Estrada answered her phone like a fighter answers a bell.

She hung up, kissed her fourth husband goodbye, and lit out to the Lincoln County Sheriff's Office for another round of Fighting the System.

"Why are they holding me?" Mason asked after a businesslike Carmen entered the interrogation room, introduced herself, and sat down.

"They're not saying much," she replied. "My guess is suspicion of arson and murder."

The words "arson and murder" turned that cold ball of dread in his guts to ice.

3

"You didn't know," Carmen said, surprised. After all these years, she figured she'd been hustled by more criminals than anyone alive, so she knew there was no hustle behind Mason's reaction. This meant she might have an innocent client, a rarity in her profession.

She laid it out for him: two dead, one dying, the Rebel Yell a pile of ash....

Mason had only one question—the only one that mattered—and didn't want to ask it. Asking would mean acknowledging Charlie might be one of the dead. If Charlie was dead, Mason couldn't save him.

"I don't know who's still alive," Carmen said, answering the unspoken question. "I'll find out."

"I need to know that and you have to get me out of here," he said. "That's all that matters right now."

She stood, slipped her notes into her briefcase, and said: "I'm all over it, but they can hold you for questioning for forty-eight hours and this kind of thing is a big deal in this county."

He stood and asked, "You know anything else?"

"I know the victims are two men and a woman and that the survivor was airlifted to the hospital in Rio Rico.... That's it. Sorry."

"What about the...survivor?" he asked, nearly choking on the word.

"No," she shook her head. "He or she has no chance, I'm afraid. Matter of days, maybe hours."

She added another "sorry" and observed Mason slowly sit back down to inhabit a world all his own.

4

"Either charge him or kick him," Carmen said to Zoey. It was a futile demand. She knew that. But a defense attorney is required to say things like, "Charge him or kick him."

"Come on, Ms. Estrada," Zoey said, because that was all that needed saying.

Carmen didn't like Zoey. She was part of *The System*, and above all, a black woman should not be part of *The System*. Still, Carmen respected the sheriff as the rare badge who didn't treat defense attorneys like they were as guilty as their clients. So Carmen said the next thing she was supposed to say: "He's got nothing to tell you, and you don't have anything on him. This is harassment."

Zoey dropped her trump card. "On top of being a material witness in a double murder that's about to go triple, he's already admitted to a crime, so...."

Carmen resented being made to feel like a straight man, but asked anyway: "What crime?"

"Camping on federal land without a permit. He could do six months."

Carmen knew that such an outrageous statement was supposed to explode her into a fit of indignation, but she would never give the fascists the satisfaction.

"Ain't you something," was all she said.

5

After his attorney left, Zoey had Mason moved from the interrogation room to a holding cell, where he joined three other men: an old man sleeping one off and two brothers who didn't look older than twenty. The terrified duo sat together on a lower bunk. They'd been busted selling meth and this was their first prison experience.

The whole place stunk of toilets, cheap wine, and body odor. Mason stood near the steel bars where the air was freshest. He needed to focus.

6

Ever since his first experience with the blue shimmer and the Joshua Tree, Mason instinctually understood two things. That he could make others immortal and that he should never do so. In fact, he'd vowed to never do so, a vow he held on to right up until Doreen ran that hand through her long black hair.

Now there was Charlie, that sweet, innocent boy.... There was nothing Mason wouldn't do to save Charlie. If he could get to him, Mason would make Charlie immortal. He just had to get to him before he died. Mason could not raise the dead.

One way to escape this jail cell was through suicide. Unfortunately, the Meth Brothers looked like citizens—the type who wouldn't stand still while a man tried to off himself. Another problem was the clock. Even if he managed a suicide, the Joshua Tree was some seventy miles from that hospital in Rio Rico and he had no transportation.

Mason tried to focus on solving this problem, but Yvette wouldn't allow it. She kept intruding, kept trespassing, kept accusing.... *You sent me back there.*

Over and over, Yvette whispered the accusation: *You sent me back there.*

7

Ernest and Yvette lay side-by-side on separate stainless steel morgue tables.

She was charred to the bone.

Burnt fat dripped off Ernest in huge globs. Zoey thought he looked like a microwaved Buddha candle.

She'd seen this before. When a meth lab blew, this was the result.

The Medical Examiner only added to the confusion. The woman was shot through the eye with the same .22 revolver found at the scene. Zoey'd already figured that. The surprise came from the revelation that the fat man's throat had been ripped out.

The autopsy ended a little after six in the morning. Zoey had every intention of going straight home and cuddling up next to Quinton's warm body. But waiting back in her office was FBI Agent Jerome Something-Something-Ernest-Didn't-Give-A-Fuck, whose real name was Jerome Byrne.

8

Thanks to the Kingdom Key, Jerome had been sent out to Lincoln County, Arizona, on special assignment to look into this Martín Gallardo, the dead man who'd shot and killed the Old Rich Prick and his daughter less than twenty-four hours ago.

Wanting to know everything possible about the Old Rich Prick's killer—this man who'd executed one of D.C.'s own precious elite, the Deputy Director himself sat in that orange chair in his stocking feet and watched footage from an airport security camera of "Martín Gallardo" purchasing the same airline ticket they'd found on his body.

Hope you don't mind me saying, Mr. Gallardo, but you sure don't look sixty-two.

The FBI already knew "Martín Gallardo" was an alias; no such man existed. So the Deputy Director froze the video of "Gallardo," double-clicked on his face (that actually belonged to Joshua Mason), and after a few seconds of dark computer magic, a menu appeared of every time facial recognition caught that face on video. Using that data, the Deputy Director did a diagnostic pattern search of where that face had traveled. After a few more seconds of dark computer magic, it was obvious he'd always started out from a place called Lincoln County in Arizona. And so, the talkative young Agent Jerome Byrne—who happened to be the Deputy Director's future son-in-law—was put on a plane.

9

Morning had arrived, and along with Jerome's unexpected visit, Zoey was greeted in her office by a rising sun blasting through her window. Her bloodshot eyes watered as she closed the blinds and invited the FBI agent to have a seat. Before she'd settled into her own chair, Jerome had already used three times the words necessary to explain why he was there.

Zoey didn't like the FBI. Jerome did at least seem sincere. That wouldn't last, she knew. No one turned out one-size-fits-all box-dwellers like the Feds.

In his flurry of words, Zoey was able to pick up that an important man had been killed in D.C., that his killer committed suicide, and had probably lived in her county.

"The killer's name was Martín Gallardo," Jerome said. "Does that sound at all familiar to you, the name—you know, Martín Gallardo?"

It didn't, but now that she was sure she could smell her socks, she told Jerome she'd be pleased as punch to set him up at a desk where he could look through her files.

"Oh, I already went through your files during my flight out here. Thanks to the Nationalized Records Act, we have access to all that now. It's all centralized. Went through 'em all on my iPhone. Pretty cool, eh?" He held up his iPhone to punctuate just how cool it was.

"No, it's not cool, but I don't make the rules," she said with as much force as her exhaustion would allow. "But if that's the case, I don't know how else I can help you."

He handed her a manila file, said there were photos of Gallardo inside, and asked that they be distributed to the staff.

Zoey said she'd be happy to do that. "Anything else?"

"Just here to let you know I'll be in your jurisdiction poking around a little bit," Jerome explained. "You know, flashing Gallardo's photo around, that kind of thing. This is your county, so I'm checking in with you. Professional courtesy and all that."

"Appreciated," Zoey said, and accepted the folder without opening it. She then dropped it on her desk and stood in her funky socks to put an end to the pointlessness. "Poke around all you want, and if my office can be of assistance, you know where to find us."

They shook hands and he left.

Exhausted, she plopped back into the chair. It was nearly 7:00 a.m. She lifted the phone to call Quinton.

She wanted to hear her husband's voice, wanted to tell him how much she loved him and that she was on her way home and he should stay in bed because his bones were about to get jumped. She wanted to tell him that in 191 days, every day would be devoted to him, and that the chill in their marriage was her fault, and she knew that, and she was sorry.

She wanted to tell him that right up until she opened Jerome's file and saw Martín Gallardo's photo—a man who was supposed to be dead in D.C., but who was very much alive and sitting in her jail under the name "Joshua Mason."

"Hello?" a sleepy Quinton answered.

"I'll call you back," she said and hung up.

10

Back in that freshly painted interrogation room, Mason again spoke only one word: "Lawyer."

"You don't have to talk, Mr. Mason," replied Zoey. "You do have to listen."

Jerome stood in the corner with his arms folded and couldn't believe he was looking at a dead guy.

"First off, you've already admitted to camping illegally on federal land. That's a federal crime," Zoey explained, "and this federal agent here," she pointed to Jerome, "is about to take you into custody. Now I want you to look at this."

She laid down a photo of the now-deceased Martín Gallardo and said nothing. The self-inflicted gunshot wound blew out the back of his head. The face was still there—*Mason's face.*

Mason stared at his own photo and tried not to react to his worst nightmare roaring to life. After a pause to grab hold of his wits, he stuck to the plan.

"Lawyer."

And then, as though that word held a magic power, Deputy Garza stepped in to inform everyone that Hurricane Carmen Estrada was right outside the room looking for her client.

A few seconds later, she was a Category 5 inside the room saying all the things a defense attorney is supposed to say when her client is questioned without counsel.

"We weren't questioning him," Zoey said, even though she was uncomfortable with semantics. "We were explaining his options. You'd better prepare yourself for an extradition fight. Your client's on his way to D.C."

D.C.? Extradition? Carmen felt like she'd wandered into the middle of a movie.

11

Moments later, after she'd blown everyone out of the room, Hurricane Carmen told Mason the news he was desperate to hear: Charlie was in a coma with the life expectancy of a housefly, but he was alive.

Mason was exhilarated...and prepared.

"You tell them I'll answer their questions if they agree to let me see Charlie. I won't fight extradition. I won't fight anything. But I need to see Charlie, or there's no deal."

"What's this extradition about?" asked Carmen.

"They got a photo of some dead guy in D.C. who looks like me."

"What?"

"That's all I know. And if Charlie dies, the deal's off. Tell them that."

"I appreciate how you feel, but it's a terrible deal," she explained. "There's not a thing you can do for him."

"I know," he said, as though it were true.

Carmen didn't like it, didn't understand it, but she made the deal.

12

In less than ten minutes, everyone reconvened around Mason, which hadn't given him much time. That was probably for the best. He was forced to keep the lie simple. Simple lies are the best lies.

"The dead man in the photo.... His name is Andrew Mason. He's my brother," Mason said.

"Your twin brother? You have a twin brother? I mean, *had* a twin brother?" Jerome asked, as Zoey wondered how it was possible to say the same thing three times in under two seconds.

"We're not twins," Mason answered, knowing his story couldn't be too neat. "He was two years older and a little taller. Lots of people got us confused, though."

Jerome followed up. "Okay, and what was he doing in—"

"Let him tell it," Zoey snapped, like a mother to a child.

So Mason told it....

"My brother showed up at the Rebel Yell day before yesterday to warn me some fat guy was coming to kill me. You see, I was helping my brother launder money through the motel. If you check our accounts, you'll find around a dozen bank wires over the last twenty or so years in the tens of thousands. I'm not proud of that. No one else knew about it. My cut was twenty-five percent. We needed it. But the other day, my brother admits it wasn't what he said it was. I wasn't laundering money for his employer. Turns out, I was helping my brother steal from his employer. Anyway, that's it, that's all I know. I have no idea what happened back in D.C. I didn't even know my brother was dead until you showed me the photo."

"What were you doing in the middle of the desert?" Zoey asked.

"Not thinking they would hurt anyone else, I panicked and took off. Stuffed a backpack, jumped on this shitty little motorbike, got lost, ran out of gas. Stupid. And now Charlie's gonna die. That's my fault. All mine. And I want to tell him goodbye, okay?"

"Who's Yvette Lightfoot?" Zoey asked. Everyone assumed she was the dead woman. The burnt-out car in the lot was registered to her.

"Charlie's girlfriend," he answered.

A long pause ambled around the room.

Jerome had a million questions, but didn't want to get snapped at again.

"Okay," Zoey finally said, "that it?"

"That's all of it."

Carmen was about to say, *Isn't that enough?* when Zoey pulled open the door and called to the officer outside, "Book Mr. Mason for felony money laundering and lock him up."

That wound Carmen all the way up. "Hey, we had a deal!"

"The deal," Zoey said, "was that your client tells the truth, not that he takes a shit in my mouth."

A dazed Mason was pulled from the interrogation room by one deputy. Outside a second deputy took Mason's other arm. What happened next happened in a kind of kind of gauzy slow motion, as though it were happening to someone else.

He was read his rights again.

He was officially informed he was under arrest.

He was fingerprinted.

He was photographed.

He was handcuffed.

He was led through a warren of hallways until they reached a door made of steel bars.

Something buzzed.

The deputy pulled open the door.

He was led past a couple of cells.

They stopped in front of an empty cell.

Someone called out, "Open number three!"

Number three slid open. Mason was gently nudged inside. The cuffs were removed. Number three closed with a *clang*. The deputies walked off. Mason stood perfectly still in the middle of his greatest fear and had no idea what to do next.

Dark Thoughts

1

Hours later, it was the middle of the night. On a top bunk, Mason lay on his side facing a concrete wall with only his anger and a surveillance camera for company.

"Goddamn me," he whispered.

Everything was his fault. All of it. He hadn't immediately returned to D.C. He should have. He'd left Charlie alone and vulnerable. He shouldn't have. He'd asked—no *paid*—Yvette to return to the Rebel Yell and now she was dead.

"Goddamn me," he whispered again and then rolled on his back to stare up at a ceiling covered in obscene drawings, the names of those who'd laid here before him, and someone's idea of prison poetry:

The future lies ahead.
You're lying here instead.
There went another minute.
Where you're not out there in it.

Mason put his hands behind his head, closed his eyes, and let his mind wander through dark places. *Goddamn me, I know better*, he thought. Yes, he knew better, and still he'd allowed himself to care about Doreen and Charlie, and now the government had him locked up and was on the verge of discovering his secret.

Forever ago, a silly little dog named Hok'ee taught Mason the hard lessons of giving a damn. Hok'ee had awakened him to his curse, to the fact that when you live forever, everything you love you'll watch die. Person or tree, you'll see it buried.

When Doreen walked in wearing a scruffy, blue robe and ran a tiny hand through all that black hair, right then he knew he should've run and kept running until he was far enough away to forget her.

Oh, who was he kidding? The moment he saw her, he knew he'd never forget her.

Still, had he run, Doreen never would've grown old or rotted away with cancer. Instead, she'd be with him now, forever beautiful and perfect in his memory.

2

Before Doreen, there'd been others, sure. Man can't live without soft shoulders and perfumed hair and the reminder there's still some tenderness in the world. But he always walked away without leaving behind hard feelings. Okay, sometimes there were hard feelings, but not due to his oath. That he'd saved for Doreen.

The moment he saw her.... He'd always gone the long way around to not get snared like that, a snare that included Charlie, who he loved like a son, and.... *Look at me now.*

Mason rolled over on his side to stare again at the wall and convince himself that eventually he'd get over her.

Eventually...that was the one thing in this godforsaken world he could count on. If nothing else, he'd live long enough to arrive at *Eventually*.

Eventually, a thousand years would pass, and he'd forget all about her.

Another lie.

He'd never forget her, for it was with Doreen where he'd found more than just the woman he loved. He'd found something he never knew existed: his place in the world.

"Goddamn me," he whispered again.

3

While Mason damned himself, Zoey lay in bed listening to the sweetest sound she knew: the sound of Quinton peacefully asleep next to her.

She'd arrived home from work a little before noon. Quinton wasn't there. He filled the time they were supposed to have spent together in retirement at the library researching a book he was sure he wouldn't finish, and if he did, no one would read.

After a long shower, she poured herself a mug of tea and strolled through each room of her house. With retirement about to bring about an end to something, she needed to look back before she moved on.

The house was too big for the two of them. They'd talked about selling, but that's all it was—*talk*. You don't sell the thing that holds the memories of babies crying and little girls running around and teenagers slamming doors and young women saying goodbye to make their way in the world.

You don't sell something that's soaked itself full of your Christmases and birthdays, and all the everyday everydays that add up to a life.

Zoey was proud of her girls. They'd grown into fine women, independent women. One was a registered nurse, another an architect, the third a homemaker. The first two moved out of state. Homemaker stayed right here in Lincoln County.

In 191 days, Zoey would get to know her children and grandchildren better.

Quinton arrived home a few hours later and not in the mood she'd expected, one he had every right to be in. Instead of being angry or hurt—she'd practically hung up on him after all—he was buoyant, full of energy and talk about how well his research was going, how he couldn't wait to start showing her chapters.

After some reheated beef stew and a little TV, they made love, and now she was lying beside a man she adored feeling so good about the future she felt the need to roll over and hold him. But he groaned and pulled away, all the way to the edge of the bed he went. She caught up with him and snuggled in.

The reassurance of his warmth and the comfort of his breathing was something she needed like water needs wet.

4

Quinton was sixty-seven now. When they'd met, he was twenty-nine and already a distinguished professor on the rise. She was a nineteen-year-old waitress fresh off a humiliating breakup. When that guy left her, the wedding invitations had already been mailed. It would've been easier had he died. She never wished that, but it would've been easier.

Quinton pulled her out of dead ground.

Quinton was married then. They snuck around until Zoey forced the issue after getting pregnant. At the time, she was too young and too broken to care he was married. Today, she refused to think about it. The thought she had anything to do with planting another woman in dead ground felt like something that couldn't be true. The idea her marriage was built on a lie, like her career, was an idea she wouldn't tolerate. Too much good had come from it.

5

When sleep finally came, Zoey dreamt it was nighttime and she was walking through a bustling carnival holding on to a kitten she loved very much. Terrified it would escape and get trampled by the crowd, she held it close. Then she came upon a beautiful carousel full of color and light and decided to take a ride. She set the kitten on the ground and convinced herself nothing terrible could happen to something she loved so much.

After the carousel's first turn, she saw that the kitten was gone. Still, she refused to jump off to go and look for it. Doing so, she knew, would be admitting she never should've left it alone in the first place.

With each turn of the carousel, feelings of dread and shame ballooned inside her, until the pressure woke her up.

Filled with all that dread and shame, Zoey lay there a long time and then decided to allow Mason to see Charlie.

6

A couple of hours later, right before he jumped to his death, Mason apologized to Zoey. He was already responsible for so much pain, he didn't want her blaming herself for his suicide.

It was just that he had no other choice.

The Blue Shimmer

1

It was about an hour before dawn when Zoey had Mason released. Mostly in silence, they'd driven south on New Highway 661—but no one called it that anymore. No one remembered the old one. It was simply "Highway 661" now.

"Your story's bullshit," Zoey said as she drove.

Mason sat in the back with his cuffed hands in his lap.

"Ran your name and your brother's. There was nothing," she added.

"Then why are we here?" he asked.

They were here because using human life as a poker chip was something Zoey didn't want to add to the inventory of what kept her up nights.

She didn't say that. The taste of her own virtue was like soot, so she never put it in her mouth.

The sun was just coming up when they arrived at the hospital, the one across the road from the new Starbucks. Zoey brought along a shirt so Mason could hide the cuffs, a courtesy he thanked her for.

Still carrying the silence from the drive, they rode the elevator to the sixth floor ICU.

2

It wasn't the sight of Charlie on the brink of death that numbed Mason. It wasn't the tubes, machines, bandages, or even the artificiality of Charlie's breathing by way of a ventilator. No, it was the smell—the

216

smell of burnt flesh—that no amount of *eventually* would ever allow Mason to forget.

Zoey closed the door to the room and stood quietly, blocking the only way in or out.

Mason composed himself and walked around to the other side of the bed. Behind him was a large window the All at Once wouldn't allow anyone to open.

He was facing Zoey now, which was deliberate. His only chance of pulling this off was to paralyze her with the shock of what she was about to witness.

3

When Mason closed his eyes and appeared to go inside himself, Zoey assumed he was praying.

When he opened his eyes and there was only white and no pupils, she was certain she was seeing things.

When a vertical, vibrating stripe of blue appeared in the center of Mason's white eyes, she thought she was dreaming.

When Mason placed his cuffed hands on Charlie's chest and Charlie's eyes popped open to reveal the same white divided by the same vibrating blue stripe, Zoey was sure she'd gone mad.

And when a tall, blue shimmer of light appeared in the corner of the room and slowly made its way across the floor to the foot of the bed where it collapsed into Charlie like a fallen tree, she was positive she was about to die for witnessing something secret and forbidden.

By the time Zoey pulled her gun, it was over. Charlie's eyes were closed. Mason looked like any man would saying goodbye to a loved one.

The sudden normalness was as disorienting as what she'd just witnessed. Had she dreamt it?

She blinked a few times and was about to re-holster her weapon, when it all went to shit.

4

Mason needed Zoey to focus on him—*not his hands*—so, firmly and quietly, he said, "Sheriff, look at me."

With watery eyes and a shaky hand barely holding onto the Glock, she looked at him, and this gave Mason the moment he needed to grab hold of the plastic tube that ran down Charlie's throat and into his lungs.

Why would he grab that tube? she wondered, and like someone hit with a sudden headache, she felt woozy and closed her eyes.

He again spoke softly. "Shoot out the window, sheriff, or I'll yank out the tube."

The gun drooped in her unsteady hand, tears fell from her closed eyes, and years later—whenever she remembered this—she would wonder about the regret in his voice. But right now, her head was full of hornets and she couldn't process what he was asking of her.

"Sheriff!"

She opened her eyes and watched through the blur of tears as he tightened his grip on the plastic tube.

Slowly and precisely, he said: "Shoot out the window, or I will kill him."

She couldn't do *both*; that was impossible. She couldn't hang on to the Glock *and* form a word. All she wanted was to ask, *What?* That's it. That's all she wanted. Just the one word, the one syllable. But if she said it, she knew she'd drop the gun. It was one or the other, and the hornets wouldn't allow her to choose, so Mason chose for her.

"Shoot out the goddamned window, or I'll rip out his throat!"

She fired three times.

The window shattered into pieces.

The wind blew the pieces back into the room.

Zoey covered her face with her arm, and after she lowered it, Mason was gone.

"I'm sorry about this," she'd heard him say. Plain as day over the wind and glass, he'd said those words.

Mason was killed instantly, nearly cut in half when he hit the edge of a dumpster.

Charlie's status didn't change. The artificial air allowed him to live on...for now.

5

A few hours later, Zoey sat in her office staring at a photo of Mason from thirty-five years ago. He looked no different, not one day younger than the man who went out that window.

Deputy Garza had finally remembered where he'd seen Mason: a family vacation at a little motel in the desert, a long weekend his family remembered fondly as a time filled with swimming and sunburn and orange soda.

Zoey stared at the color photo of twelve-year-old Ray Garza. He wore blue swimming trunks, held a half-eaten hotdog, and did his best to hold a smile against the sun's glare.

Behind him, oblivious to the fact he was being photographed, stood Joshua Mason leaning on a pool skimmer. His face was one of contentment, of a man who'd found his place in the world.

Garza simply didn't believe it was the same guy. "Maybe a relative," he said. After all, to believe anything else would be to acknowledge things aren't what they're supposed to be. So Garza marveled at the resemblance and left it at that.

Without comment, Zoey returned the photo and asked him to close her door on the way out.

6

The hospital room's surveillance camera didn't record the blue shimmer, not the tall one that entered the room and dropped into Charlie, nor the ones that appeared in the middle of Charlie's and Mason's white eyes.

This meant the video backed Zoey's version of things, of how Mason had threatened to kill Charlie if she didn't shoot out the window so he could commit suicide.

7

Now alone, Zoey spun her office chair around to look out at the white sky hanging over the parking lot. Already, what had happened didn't feel real. Still, she resolved to never tell a living soul about it, not even Quinton.

Twenty years would pass before she saw Joshua Mason again, a meeting that would take place in a very different world.

Hok'ee

1

Long after Mason discovered his immortality, days of rain hit the desert and he took shelter in a small cave, one he could barely stand up in.

The rain and dampness were so persistent that nothing would dry, not even wood, so there was no fire.

One morning Mason woke and felt something small and wet against the back of his legs. Sometime during the night, whatever this was had made its way under the animal skins he used for blankets.

As stealthily as possible, he grabbed a large rock to crush the intruder. Then curiosity got the better of him. Snakes were known to seek the warmth of sleeping men. This was no snake.

On top of curiosity, Mason wanted something to eat. He didn't need to eat. The cycle of his hunger lasted only a day. Still, he enjoyed food and this animal felt like it might have meat on it.

So, he carefully lifted the skins for a look and what he found was a black and brown puppy about the size of a gopher.

Mason's movement woke the small dog, but it showed no fear. The pup didn't even look at him. Instead, it lifted its small head, rested its chin on Mason's leg, and fell back asleep.

Mason couldn't believe his luck. Fresh meat had practically landed in his lap. He slowly unsheathed a knife made from animal bone. Then he remembered the wood was too damp for a fire. No meat was preferable to raw meat. He decided not to butcher the dog until he could cook it.

Where the pup came from was no mystery. Various tribes roamed the area and kept dogs to warn against intruders. This one had probably wandered off and gotten lost.

To ensure the pup couldn't escape, Mason lassoed a thin rawhide around its small neck and secured the other end under a heavy rock.

2

The dog didn't mind the leash. Instead, it gleefully rolled over and rubbed its back on the rawhide to claim it with its scent. The pup then chewed away on the leash as though it were a delicacy.

After the chewing and rubbing, the puppy exploded with energy. It scampered as far as the leash would allow and would then stop, crouch, and lift its butt in the air to stare up at Mason—all in a fruitless effort to goad Mason into playing.

Other than meat, Mason saw only a useless, scrawny animal. Hell, the dog's eyes weren't even right. One eye went one way; the other eye went another. And there was mischief in those crooked eyes, unending trouble.

The following night, thunder scared the puppy so badly it chewed through the rawhide and once again burrowed itself into Mason's legs.

Mason began to wonder if the Indians hadn't thrown this crazy dog away.

After that, Mason didn't bother to leash it. There was no need when the oblivious pup was dumb enough to stick around as though the two of them were pals.

3

The rain finally ceased. Eager to eat the obnoxious dog, Mason tried lighting a fire. The wood was still too damp. Frustrated, he threw some kindling across the cave. Thinking this was a game, the puppy dashed over to the sticks, picked one up, brought it to Mason, and dropped it in front of him.

Mason ignored him.

Undeterred, and with its tail slowly waving back and forth, the pup crouched down, growled, and stared up at Mason with crooked eyes that said: *I dare you to grab that stick.*

Unable to stand it any longer, Mason went for the stick, but the pup was too fast. He snatched it up, backed out of Mason's reach, and dropped it to start the cycle over: waving tail, growl, stare.

Now Mason would have to crawl for the stick, which he wasn't about to do. But the pup wouldn't be ignored. It ran around in an excited circle, barking away. When this failed, it switched gears to emotional blackmail: whining.

Desperate for peace, Mason lifted himself off his butt, crawled over, and went to grab the stick again—but again he was too slow. The pup snatched it and backed out of reach.

Determined not to lose this stupid game to this stupid dog, Mason quickly crawled over and tried again. The pup made a fool of him again.

Frustrated, Mason decided to cheat. Knowing it was afraid of noises, he clapped his hands in the dog's face, which startled it. This allowed Mason to snatch the stick, break it into pieces, and throw the pieces outside.

Dejected, the puppy burrowed itself under the animal skins and slept for the rest of the day. This allowed Mason to enjoy a peaceful afternoon watching a fierce sun dry out his desert.

He would butcher the dog in the morning.

4

Mason woke the next morning to find the pup asleep right on top of his chest. *Stupid animal*, he thought. Animals were supposed to sense danger. He'd never come across anything as dumb as this dog.

The pup opened one crooked eye, gave Mason a sleepy look, and went back to sleep with a small sigh. And then, as though that sigh were some sort of signal, without even thinking about it, Mason began to pet the small dog. Naturally, the entitled pup rolled over insisting on a tummy rub.

Mason rubbed its tummy and would never hurt a dog again.

5

Mason named the pup Hok'ee, a Native word for "abandoned," and Hok'ee grew to be no larger than a fox.

Hok'ee was not a useful dog. He only wanted to catch and shake rodents, play his eternal game of Keep Away, and would never stop being spooked by strange sounds, especially thunder.

Nevertheless, over the years, the two of them wandered the desert together and formed a bond Mason never had before, not even with a person.

It was a friendship built solely on Hok'ee's terms. Hok'ee played when he wanted to play, slept when he wanted to sleep, and insisted on sleeping in Mason's cramped legs.

None of this mattered to Mason. Hok'ee was loyal and had a sense of humor. The dog loved to tease and be teased, which swelled within Mason an affection he'd not known was there.

One night a bobcat leapt into camp, one so starved you could see its ribs. Hok'ee immediately ran away whimpering into the dark and the bobcat turned its attention to Mason. It was about to pounce when little Hok'ee rushed back in, ran right up to the starving cat, and went crazy.

Mason had never seen anything like it. Right in the deadly cat's face, the little dog barked and howled and growled and ran around in a frenzy. It worked. Looking more annoyed than scared, the bobcat retreated and never returned.

Mason felt a touch of respect for the little pup with the crooked eyes.

6

Time slid away and Hok'ee slowed. After there was gray in his fur and a white film over his eyes, Mason treated Hok'ee with tenderness, just like he had the old woman. He fed the dog by hand, held him for hours, and resolved to get another as soon as Hok'ee's time was up.

That was how Mason saw Hok'ee, like a knife or animal skin, as something replaceable.

7

One morning Mason woke and Hok'ee was gone. He spent days searching for his companion. And for a long time afterward, well beyond reason, he looked for his old friend wherever he wandered.

Only after Hok'ee was gone did Mason realize he could never replace the silly little dog with the crooked eyes.

Jerome

1

Things like discovering Ernest's throat had been ripped out made it possible for FBI Agent Jerome Byrne to stay off the mood stabilizers.

Jerome was twenty-seven-years-old, burning with ambition to better the world, and had fooled everyone for years.

Every month he had his prescription refilled. The bottle sat right there next to his bed. Go ahead, open it. Count the pills. You'll see that the number of pills corresponds exactly to the date of the refill. Yep, every morning Jerome dutifully removed a pill and just as dutifully flushed it down the toilet.

Jerome hated those meds. Little blue and white capsules muddled his thinking, fuzzed his brain, and filled his mouth with cotton. Muddled thinkers with fuzzy brains and cotton-filled mouths do not become FBI agents.

Jerome had dreams, you see, big dreams for America, and saw the FBI as the fastest way to accumulate the power necessary to make those dreams come true. Politics was for suckers, he believed. Real power, he knew, was found in the unelected, invisible federal bureaucracy. And now, because he didn't take his meds and had learned to focus his mania in productive ways, he was on the road to getting what he wanted.

2

Jerome's teen years had been a time of anxiety and frustration. He'd been a boy overflowing with miseries.

Little things would poison Jerome's head with torment. He'd lay awake nights and obsess over that day's events, over what he *should have* said and done. Big things also tormented him: starving children, pollution, war, poverty, overpopulation, Global Warming, you name it.

Jerome had no control over the world and this threatened to capsize him.

It was in a high school debate class where the bottom of Jerome's despair rose up to meet him. The way Jerome saw it, America's jury system was too important to leave in the hands of everyday people, so he argued in favor of creating professional juries.

He'd spent weeks preparing his case, believed in it, and appealed passionately before his classmates: "Only the accredited and college-educated employed by the government should be allowed to sit on a jury!"

In his head, he heard applause, cheers, huzzahs....

In reality, his opponent crushed him.

After blistering him as a snob, his opponent explained how such a system would become corrupted. And after she pointed out that having a jury on the same government payroll as the prosecutor would be like allowing the New England Patriots to hire the referees, the whole class laughed at Jerome in his Patriots' t-shirt.

He received a C+ and slid into a barrel of depression slathered in black grease he couldn't climb out of.

Jerome's parents found him a doctor. The doctor wrote him a prescription for the little blue and white capsules. The bad days went away...and so did the good days.

Jerome was now a numbed-out mediocrity punching the clock of life.

Two hazy years later, he found a handhold.

At the time, he was where he spent most of those hazy years: zoned out in front of the TV. Nothing made Mom and Dad happier than Jerome zoned out in front of the TV. Didn't have to deal with him then; didn't have to handle him.

Well, the joke was on Mom and Dad. Jerome wasn't watching TV. He was plotting to kill himself. Close the garage door, start the car, lie down in the backseat, die. Everyone freaks out, everyone blames themselves. How sweet would that be?

Jerome desperately needed to be in control, and suicide was the ultimate control.

So no, the little blue and white capsules had not put an end to his mania. They'd only poured thick syrup over it and slowed it some.

But one day Jerome realized that planning his suicide had focused his mind in a way nothing else had, and that this focus had given him a reason to live. The clarity he found in discovering a purpose, even if that purpose was to kill himself, soothed his need for control, and had, ironically, saved his life. This told him that the answer to his problem would be to find something else to focus on, a new objective that would give him a sense of purpose and control. If he didn't, then he'd kill himself.

What ended up saving Jerome's life also charted the course of his life: a 1959 movie starring Jimmy Stewart.

3

Jerome was captivated by the true story of an American hero, an FBI agent who used federal authority to make the world safer and more orderly. Thanks to this hero, the world became more manageable, more under control.

That's how Jerome saw it, anyway.

He purchased a copy of *The FBI Story*, shut his bedroom door, and watched it over and over. The next day something remarkable happened. He strolled into the school library in search of a book about the FBI, and sitting in the middle of a table as though the fates had placed there, was a light-blue hardcover book titled *The History of the FBI*.

He devoured every word.

The book told the story of the Bureau's founding and how its centralized investigative approach helped organize society and make sense of it. It explained how heroic G-Men, empowered by federal authority, made the world safer by enforcing the rules.

Best of all, it revealed how the Bureau could shape the country's laws through the manipulation of events, politicians, and even presidents by highlighting threats to personal and national security. Jerome believed this was the most effective power of all in a chaotic country where selfish people believed they could do whatever they wanted.

Jerome had found his life's purpose. He would join the FBI's patriotic mission in bringing order to a messy world.

His parents loved the idea. Anything that kept them from having to deal with Jerome, his parents loved.

4

So Jerome secretly went off his meds and the Bureau hired him right out of college. Ever since, Jerome had dedicated himself *only* to the Bureau and his mania had never been more under control. There was one lingering symptom: He still talked too much. He was working on that.

But he was living the dream—he sure was. Living it right now on this assignment, and doing so at the direct request of the FBI's Deputy Director—the Number Two Man, and Jerome's soon-to-be father-in-law.

This was an important assignment, a loose end that mattered. The Old Rich Prick had been one of D.C.'s very own, and now all of D.C. wanted to know what was going on.

Was the Old Rich Prick's murder the beginning of something?

Was it a conspiracy?

After all, the Old Rich Prick had video of half of D.C. doing unspeakable things. The FBI believed it had destroyed everything, but what if there were copies? What if blackmail was next, or worse, *exposure*?

So, yes, being sent to Arizona to look into the Old Rich Prick's dead assassin mattered, and the Deputy Director's future son-in-law was on the job.

The Deputy Director's future son-in-law.

5

Yep, Jerome was only a few months away from marrying the boss's daughter.

Truth be told, Jerome wasn't a big fan of the boss's daughter, his fiancée. Her name was Brittany. Everyone was always telling him how lucky he was. Brittany was quite the catch, they said. He wasn't so sure.

Jerome had courted Brittany, not only as a way to cultivate a relationship with the Deputy Director, but as his entrée into the tippy-top of the D.C. social scene.

Didn't work out that way.

You gotta schmooze to get ahead in D.C., and wouldn't you know it, Brittany hated to schmooze, hated parties. She'd agree to go. Sometimes. Always an argument.

She was devoted to him, though. Loved him all the way. Said so all the time. It was just that the two of them wanted different things. She wanted a farm; he wanted a D.C. townhouse. She did frivolous website design; he wanted the power to correct society. She wanted a church wedding; he wanted to get it over with. She loved him to pieces; he saw her as something akin to homework.

Didn't matter. All that mattered was that he was invited to the Deputy Director's house for Sunday dinner and that he and the Deputy Director got along like a house on fire.

6

Finally, the maneuvering had paid off. Look at him now: out in the field on assignment all on his own. And everything about it was thrilling. He loved flashing the badge, wearing the suit, driving the sedan. What he didn't love was the hotel. Carpeting's never clean, especially hotel carpeting. Just thinking about all the bare feet treading across it, the ripped toenails down there in the nap. *Yeesh!*

So Jerome moved to a boarding house. Twelve-by-twelve room with a white floor and whiter walls. Took only a couple of hours to scrub it down and cover the skeezy bed with a mattress pad he'd purchased, along with crisp new sheets and a pillow.

You should see Jerome's D.C. studio apartment. Spartan, simple, ship-shape; four hundred square feet of uncomplicated space. No dirt in the corners. No dirt anywhere. Go ahead, take a look around. Pull out the fridge, peek behind the oven, run a lily-white glove over anything.... Tidy and uncomplicated, and only two metro stops from work, from the J. Edgar Hoover building, from his job at the Eff.Bee.Freaken.Aye.

7

If Jerome were king—and he thought a lot about being king—everyone would live the way he lived. To him, this was a moral imperative. People with large homes, gas-guzzling SUVs, campers, and big yards—people who indulged in all that selfish largesse eating up the world's resources, they disgusted him. How could a great country survive if everyone was allowed to live any way they pleased?

Jerome might never be king, but he had no doubt he would someday be the man in charge—the FBI Director. He really had no choice but to believe that. Knowing he'd ultimately hold that kind of power was the only thing that allowed him to get out of bed.

Hey, so far, so good. Okay, he was still a gofer, the "kid" who escorted VIPs to the Kingdom Key, who was sent to Arizona to put together a secret profile of a dead guy who killed a rich guy.

Sure, it was grunt work, but it was the kind of grunt work given only to those trusted by the FBI's upper echelon, which meant he was part of the upper echelon, and that was the first step toward *becoming* upper echelon.

Some might describe Jerome's attitude toward the Bureau as blind loyalty. But that wasn't true. He knew what he was doing. To him, embracing loyalty was like turning your life over to God. Loyalty was the tidiest and most uncomplicated virtue of all. It clarified the mind and removed the cobwebs of right and wrong, of nuance and conscience.

Above all, he'd never forgotten the lesson from that humiliating high school debate: if reason and facts don't convince people what's best for them, you need power.

8

So, yes, Jerome was thrilled at what he'd uncovered out here in Browning—or as he secretly called it: *HicksVille*. This was supposed to be a simple assignment. Bigshots on the seventh floor only wanted some background on the dead killer, on this Martín Gallardo guy and his associates. But now it was a money-laundering case, undoubtedly involving organized crime!

On top of that, Ernest, the rude fat man he'd escorted to the Kingdom Key just a few days back, was also lying here dead in HicksVille.

What a mess. But it was a mess Jerome had the authority to make sense of, and doing so would almost certainly advance his career.

Who'd ripped out the fat man's throat, and why? Did the dead woman do it, or was the culprit this Charlie guy who would be dead any minute?

Maybe the throat-ripper was still out there!

And what about this Mason guy, the lookalike brother of the guy who killed the Old Rich Prick?

Mason jumped out a window in Rio Rico. The twin brother shot himself in D.C.

Oh, yeah, something was going on out here. Something big. Someone somewhere had something to hide, and it was so big, people were killing themselves to keep it secret.

PART FOUR

THE "PLAGUE" STORIES

Chased by the Devil

1

About a stone's throw from the Joshua Tree, Mason set up a small camp to wait for Charlie's return from the dead.

For shade, he built a lean-to using a blanket and poles. He also brought what he'd need for a fire, which he'd light soon. The sun was already low and the desert grew cold at night. *Nothing like a fire on a cold night.*

2

After Charlie died in his hospital bed, he would appear here under the Joshua Tree, just as Mason did this morning minutes after he jumped out of that six-story window.

It was important for Mason to be here when Charlie returned. He would have to calm the boy, explain things, and assure him everything was alright.

This morning, after Mason appeared under the Joshua Tree, he knew Charlie was on the brink of death and would soon follow. So he dressed quickly and hustled the two miles to the safehouse, where he grabbed up some clothes for Charlie, the supplies for the lean-to, a gallon of water, and a book to help pass the time.

During his hike back, Mason realized Doreen had died only a few days ago, which seemed impossible. It felt like a year, a long year, and this made him as tired as he'd ever been—so tired it took the last of his energy reserves to put together his tiny camp.

There would be a quarter-moon tonight, and as the sun disappeared and the stars began to poke through a sky sliced into thirds of orange and blue and black, Mason lit his fire.

For most of a week, he'd been running and frantic, chasing and desperate, stressed and too late. Now that the scrambling was over and he could just sit here, it all caught up with him. Mason felt like he could sleep forever....

And then he didn't.

A man in a skirmish with his thoughts can never rest.

3

The thought of him and Charlie and Doreen together forever was a thought that taunted.... The only roadblock had been her faith—her ridiculous beliefs.

He was never able to find the words, never able to overcome those superstitions. Truth is, because she was never even tempted by his offer, the whole idea of immortality was nothing more than a hypothetical to her, a lively topic for a philosophical discussion. In fact, until his anger and frustration reared, Doreen enjoyed the intellectual stimulation of their back and forth.

But he wasn't interested in a lofty debate. He was terrified of losing her, so his only goal was to rip her faith to shreds and stomp it into a dust as soft as flour.

That's when she'd leave the room.

None of his arguments, no amount of reason could budge her. She honestly believed that the only way for the two of them to be together forever was in the afterlife, and for that to happen, she had to stay true to what she believed.

His response was to tell her that when you live forever, there is no afterlife, so why worry about it?

She found that absurd. "Eventually, everything will come to an end," she'd say. "Even *you* will come to an end."

"You should hear yourself," he'd fire back. "You make no sense. You tell me faith is required to enter Heaven and then say you and I will be together forever in Heaven. How can we be together if you're floating on some cloud with Jesus while I'm burning in Hell for being a non-believer?"

At that, she'd always respond the same way: "I'm not worried about you," she'd say. "You'll figure it out."

Then she'd repeat it, "You'll figure it out."

There was no smugness in her words. Just love mixed with the kind of denial that comes with love.

It made him want to pull his hair out.

On this topic, the only thing they shared in common was incredulity at what the other believed. Doreen saw no answer other than God to explain the existence of Existence. Mason could only shake his head at that.

"If your God gave us all this," he'd say, "then your God's responsible for creating a sociopathic universe willing to watch a child drown and then toss tragedy around like confetti unconcerned with who gets hit. Your God chose the brutality of indifference over justice or even fairness."

To that she'd say, "You're wrong. I'm not indifferent and I'm part of this universe. You're not indifferent and you're part of this universe. But what you aren't part of is the natural world, so aren't *you* proof there's something more to all this?"

He found that absurd. Of course, he was part of the natural world. Mason saw himself as *different*, not *unnatural*. Perhaps he was a one-in-a-trillion genetic freak or came from another planet where blue shimmers were the norm. Regardless, how was a blue shimmer any more supernatural than the conception of a child or a sunset? There are trees and bacteria that live for thousands of years...why not a person? All kinds of inexplicable things happen in the natural world. That doesn't mean an invisible man's in charge.

So he'd fire the question right back at her, "And this God gave me immortality to what end? For what purpose?"

He never forgot her response, never forgot how, at this point, what had been a spirited conversation edging into acrimony went quiet so she could give the question the weight it required.

"I don't know," she admitted after a long pause. "Maybe God gives us the time we deserve to figure it out."

"Figure what out?"

"That there's a God," she said. "Because with that faith comes salvation."

He found that so ridiculous he could only smile, which irritated her. "You want me to take a leap of faith and join you," she said, "but you won't take a leap of faith and join me."

Other than a shrug, he had no answer for that.

Her eyes softened and then she returned the shrug. "You'll figure it out," she said. "I know you will."

"I won't," he said. "And if there is some deranged puppet master up there in the Heavens, I'm gonna take it personal. Why create a freak like me? To what end?"

"I don't know. I don't," she confessed. "But what might have become of Charlie and I without you...I don't even want to think about it, and that's purpose enough for me."

And so it went, year after year, maddening stalemate after maddening stalemate. The self-righteous part of him assumed that as she grew older, she'd change her mind. *Pretty easy to shrug off a chance to live forever when you're forty-five. Let's see how you feel at sixty-five, seventy-five....*

The better part of him knew she'd never change her mind.

She didn't.

She grew older; then she was old. She grew sicker, then she was gone. But through it all she held to her superstitions, and Mason was forced to helplessly watch age and cancer rot her away when he had the power to stop it.

Those nights when he'd lie there next to her full up with the fear of losing her, he'd try to convince himself that if he went ahead and did it, she'd be able stay with him forever without having betrayed her faith.

What he could never talk himself into was betraying her.

There were times when he resented her for leaving him, for inhabiting him against his will and then abandoning him in favor of her God. She'd chosen something over him, and knowing that captured the corners of his emptiness with wounds and jealousies.

4

After darkness fell, the disarray of his thoughts could no longer mount a challenge to his exhaustion. Next to the campfire, Mason drifted off into a dreamless sleep, and was sleeping still when Charlie began to scream.

5

Charlie's coma had been a peaceful one, like floating easy and free deep beneath a warm ocean.

There, in that liquid tranquility, the outside world—with all of its slights and humiliations—no longer existed. He felt only a little pain from his wounds, like a mild sunburn. Through his closed eyes, he could barely tell the difference between night and day.

The muted beeps and hisses coming from the machines that kept him alive sounded faraway and soothing, as was the sensation of the artificial air pushed in and out of his body by the ventilator. Up and down went his chest. Up and down, with no effort required from him.

The whole time he'd laid there, the only clear sound he'd heard were three gunshots: *Pow! Pow! Pow!*, which disrupted his tranquility and made him appreciate this place all the more.

Charlie was content down there, his anger sated by the settling of scores. He'd avenged Yvette by killing Ernest. He'd avenged Mason's betrayal by burning down the Rebel Yell.

Down in the dark deep, Charlie clutched the pleasure of his night of vengeance. Down there, he was safe. The world was at long last helpless to wield against him its unending insults and snubs, or to take back his status as a man revenged.

6

When death arrived to take Charlie, there was no mistaking what it was, and he welcomed it. He would now enter Heaven a winner.

As death pulled him deeper beneath the warmth and into something purely black, the light faded along with the sounds of the machines, and he felt no pain, not even the sunburn.

Deeper and deeper he was pulled, until it was so dark he'd never seen such darkness. He loved this place, the serenity of it, the perfect black, and after he left his body and was no longer something physical, he felt like a spirit hovering in space.

A tall shimmer of red light appeared. Not a blue shimmer. Charlie's shimmer was bright red and tall as a man. The shimmer vibrated and hovered and told him to open his eyes.

So he did.

7

Charlie's screams startled Mason awake, and he immediately realized he'd fallen asleep and that poor Charlie was out there naked, confused, and terrified.

Upon opening his eyes, Mason made the mistake of looking directly at the fire. The impression of the firelight blotched his vision. As he snatched up the blanket he'd been laying on, he tried and failed to squint away the orange phantom.

Charlie was in a stark panic, ping-ponging around in the night like a rat in a hot box. Mason couldn't see him, couldn't see anything, only orange, but the sound of the screams told him where Charlie was—everywhere.

Mason called out Charlie's name and told him to join him by the fire.

8

After Charlie opened his eyes, he saw it was dark but nowhere near as dark as the perfect black of death. He sensed he was back in his body—well, *a body*; it didn't feel like his body.

One by one, Charlie's five senses came to life: he could see the stars, smell a nearby fire, taste the dry air, hear the wind, and feel its coolness against his exposed skin. The sand under his bare bottom felt gritty and uncomfortable, as did the bark of the Joshua Tree against his naked back.

Then, off in the distance, he saw flames.

Where am I?

He stood, realized he was naked, and groped about in the dark until he caught his foot and tumbled to the ground. Lying on the rough sand, his eyes were again drawn to the flames.

Am I in Hell?

As he lay there, his panic began to spike, and with it his anger at being yanked from the black serenity. Then his rage and terror mixed into something primal, and he began to moan and shriek. He was supposed to be in Heaven, not here.

Not here!

Filled with all that fear and fury, he lifted himself to his feet and— froze in place.

The Devil's here!

He could feel it, feel Satan's presence, and after the Devil called him by name and beckoned him to the fire, Charlie panicked and ran blindly in circles, howling and shrieking curses at his betrayer, at God.

Then the Devil—the Devil *himself!*—caught Charlie in a blanket and said, "I got you. You're okay, I got you."

Just before he lost consciousness, like a surge of hot electricity, Charlie felt his hatred of God detonate through his body.

The Safehouse

1

Mason didn't believe in God, religion, politics, or country. Instead, he broke the world into two groups: *Those Who Wish to Be Left Alone* and *Those Who Push People Around.*

He was a lifetime member of the former. He'd seen it too many times.... How *Those Who Push People Around* brought only misery and ultimately war to *Those Who Wish to Be Left Alone.* He'd seen it happen within families and tribes, in cities, and across continents. So he knew the warning signs.... As *Those Who Push People Around* started to grow in numbers and a self-righteous certainty about how the other fella should live, speak, worship, and think, oppression and violence soon followed.

Everyone talked about wanting world peace. But no one was willing to do what was necessary to achieve it, which was simply this: *Mind your own goddamned business.* How difficult was that? Well, if you read a history book, you'll see it's impossible.

Human nature being human nature, one tribe's always gotta bully the other. One group's always certain its ideas are superior and won't tolerate others doing anything different.

In the never-ending war between *Those Who Wish to Be Left Alone* and *Those Who Push People Around,* Mason sometimes joined a side.

Just as often, he didn't.

He'd fought against Indian tribes that sought to subjugate and enslave other Indian tribes. He'd fought against the European and American invaders in what became known as the War for the American West. But he had nothing to do with America's Civil War, a war he saw as one between two sides of the same *Those Who Push People Around* coin: slavers and invaders.

Wars don't come any stupider than that.

Mason was awed by the zeal of *Those Who Push People Around*, the energy and time they committed to their grotesque cause.

He had all the time in the world—literally—and still couldn't imagine wasting even a day bullying someone to do things his way. And that's what worried him most. Pushing people around was their religion, and there was no stopping them because their only morality was whatever furthered their wretched cause.

That's why, decades ago, he'd built his safehouse.

Signs were all there as the electrified wonders of the All at Once perverted what had been a healthy pluralist society into a centralized mass-culture controlled by a powerful few who had all kinds of ideas about how everyone else should live and think.

To increase their numbers, *Those Who Push People Around* recruited from the ranks of the insecure, the neurotics, the snobs, the entitled, the smug—anyone with a hole inside of them that could only be filled by lording their superiority over someone else. Then, with the ultimate goal being domination, things started out with a shame-on-you attitude directed at *Those Who Wish to Be Left Alone*. Before long, this attitude was stoked into a superior disgust, which was then juiced into a hate that inevitably led to a certainty that the desire to be left alone was so dangerous it justified violence.

In the past, there'd been no need for Mason to hide under the ground. There was still plenty of country to get lost in during the Civil War.

Well, no more. The whole world was mapped, monitored, and patrolled.

Underground was the only place left.

2

Mason's safehouse was nothing special—the equivalent of a bomb shelter shored up with wood beams and corrugated steel.

He'd chosen the spot for a good reason: it was the closest to the Joshua Tree with a water spring. Best of all, it was featureless and wouldn't attract attention. There was no shade, no nothing, and only he knew of the spring. To the outside world, it was just another piece of arid, barren flatness.

A camouflaged hatch opened to a shaft and ladder that dropped twelve feet to a short tunnel. That tunnel led to a steel door that opened to about seven hundred square feet of living space with a ceiling just high enough for Mason to stand in.

The main area held a living room and small kitchen area with a hand pump connected to the spring. There were two small bedrooms, a storage room, and a small bathroom with a toilet, sink, and cold shower.

Mason had dug out a sizable septic tank for waste, and with the money made from selling his life, stored a cache of non-perishable foods, spare parts, firearms, cash, ammunition, fuel, and the thing that meant most to him: books that filled shelves throughout the place.

Concealed solar panels delivered just enough power for some light and two small circulation fans that moved air through secreted shafts.

Nearby, he'd camouflaged a spot for his motorcycle and pickup, both of which were now lost.

Night after night, over two decades and using only hand tools, he'd dug out and outfitted this secret space. A normal man would consider such a thing impossible. Well, nothing's impossible if you have time. With enough time, you can move a mountain from one spot to another.

He'd shown the safehouse to Doreen only once. All she said was, "Well, let's hope we never have to use it," which said it all.

3

While Charlie slept in one of the safehouse's bedrooms, Mason spent two anxious days walking its crude wooden floors. He'd pace until exhausted, sleep some in a way that never felt like sleep, and then pace some more.

Mason's nerves were a tangle of opposites, of relief mixed with inquietude. He was relieved Charlie was safe, but nervous about who might emerge from that bedroom.

One of the blessings of the Joshua Tree was how it brought a person back to perfect health. The moment he caught Charlie in that blanket, it was apparent the boy was no longer overweight. He would also no longer require glasses.

What unsettled Mason was that he had no idea how Charlie's personality would change now that his brain was perfectly healed and would function as though that terrible childhood car accident had never happened. When he woke up, Charlie would emerge from that room a man with a normal, healthy, working brain.

Mason felt feather-headed worrying over such a thing.

How could that be anything other than a blessing?

Discovery

1

The corpse Charlie had left behind, the body that died of a gunshot wound and third-degree burns, underwent an autopsy. FBI Agent Jerome Byrne attended and asked the medical examiner to check the contents of Charlie's stomach for human flesh and blood. Traces of both were found and a DNA test proved the blood and tissue in Charlie's stomach belonged to Ernest. This confirmed it was Charlie who, like a wild animal, had ripped Ernest's throat out—with his teeth.

Jerome was stunned and elated by this news. He'd only requested the tests out of his need for orderliness, which required thoroughness. He'd never expected it to pay off like this. *What a discovery!*

Jerome then had Charlie's DNA and fingerprints added to all the local, state, and national databases. Even if Charlie had acted in self-defense against Ernest, which was how it looked, Jerome figured someone capable of such a barbaric act might have done something in the past. If so, his DNA or fingerprints might match some unsolved crime, maybe even a homicide.

Nothing matched, which was fine. That wasn't the point. Thoroughness was the point. Squaring things away was the point.

2

Jerome flew back to Washington, D.C. and spent three days writing a stellar report on his findings.

Coming to conclusions was not his job. That was the job of the Deputy Director. Jerome's only responsibility was to present the facts in a way that allowed the upper echelon to reach their own conclusions, which they did....

As far as the FBI was concerned, the killing of the Old Rich Prick was resolved. Everyone connected to it was dead. Martín Gallardo, Joshua Mason, Charlie Breslin, Ernest, Anne, Yvette, and the Old Rich Prick were all dead, which was a great comfort to the Bureau. A small task force was assigned to look into the money laundering Mason had confessed to, but that quickly went nowhere and the case was closed.

Jerome's report was subsequently filed and forgotten.

Jerome had done what he was told, kept his mouth shut, and remained discreet. He didn't rock the boat or ask questions or in any way attempt to bring color to the bureaucratic gray that defined the Bureau.

Jerome's future was a bright one.

Rebirth

1

Charlie, with his lean frame, 20/20 vision, and perfectly healed brain, could hardly conceal his exhilaration as he ascended the safehouse's ladder, pushed open the hatch, and stepped out into the bright heat and harshness of the desert.

Charlie had slept three full days before he recovered from all the stress of dying and returning from the dead. He then spent two suffocating weeks underground with Mason, who tried everything to convince him to stay—something Charlie never intended to do.

After they'd climbed out of the shaft and into the sun, Charlie offered the man he hated a stiff hug and a false promise to stay in touch.

So desperate was he to escape Mason's clutches, Charlie had to control the urge to bolt into the desert, to run as far away from Mason as he could and into whatever his new life had to offer.

Instead, he stayed cool and presented the front Mason needed to see: *Don't worry, I understand everything you told me. I'll take it seriously, and I'll stay in touch.*

During those two weeks underground, Mason had tried to explain and teach Charlie about the world and what it meant to live forever. Charlie played along and pretended to care, even though Mason's *lectures*—as Charlie saw them—were what he hated most about the man; all the lofty wisdom and condescension.

Well, that was all behind him now. Charlie was a free man with a fully-functioning brain. He was trim, he was immortal, and he intended to take advantage of everything life had denied him, most of all his independence.

2

After this awkward goodbye, Charlie departed with a week's worth of food and water on his back, along with three thousand dollars and some camping equipment.

He walked a long way before looking back and, sure enough, there was pathetic Mason, still watching him. Charlie tossed him a wave, Mason waved back, and Charlie resumed his march west.

Once safely out of Mason's sight, Charlie stopped, put up a lean-to, and dozed in its shade. Then, after dark, he packed up, turned right around, and headed east.

He made his way through the dark desert without any fear of getting lost. Now that his brain functioned, he had no problem comprehending what Mason had taught him about reading a compass and using the stars as guideposts.

On his third night of walking, Charlie arrived at his destination: the black and sooty wreckage that once was the Rebel Yell.

3

During his journey, Charlie had wondered how he'd feel about returning to the place that had been his home for so long. But now that he was here, other than admiration for the damage a gallon of gas and a match could do, he felt nothing. No nostalgia, no wistfulness. He'd already forgotten about Yvette.

He thought only of the task at hand.

Two hours later, after pulling it out of the parking lot rubble, Charlie had Mason's motorcycle running. He pushed it deep into the desert and taught himself to work the clutch and gears. The rest of the night was spent getting comfortable operating it.

Just before dawn, he drove out to his "den," to that fetid pile of dead animals. There, he shut off the motorcycle, stepped off, and looked down at his life's work. He stared for as long as the stench would allow and finally felt *something*: embarrassment at the desperate childishness of it all. For a moment, he felt the old fury, the resentment and rage at a world and a God that had driven him to such humiliations. He closed his eyes tight until the murder fantasies receded.

It was daylight when he found the spot where he and Mason would sometimes sit and drink a beer under the stars. Here he felt what he always felt when his thoughts turned to Mason: a galling sense of inadequacy.

Charlie slept hard that night and dreamt of fire and death.

4

He didn't worry about being recognized. Lean-bodied, normal-brained Charlie looked and acted nothing like the *fat fucking retard* who'd shopped at this Qwik-Shop a thousand times before. So he topped the motorcycle's gas tank and purchased a pre-paid iPhone.

The iPhone was necessary for internet access. Among other things, he had to know Arizona's motorcycle laws. He had no driver's license, no ID of any kind. The last thing he needed was to get pulled over for something avoidable, like not wearing a helmet.

Lucky for him, Arizona required only eye protection on a motorcycle. He went back inside and purchased a pair of sunglasses.

As he cruised along the new Highway 661 under a cloudless sky, Charlie realized how different the world looked through a normal brain. Things like how the mile markers corresponded to the exit numbers now made sense. He suddenly understood how the left lane was for passing and the right for slower vehicles.

For the first time, he was able to comprehend the logical patterns that ruled everyday life.

A few miles outside Rio Rico, he purchased a large canvas bag, strapped it to the bike, and filled it with canned goods, water, three bags of Twizzlers, and thrift shop clothes.

Then he stopped at his favorite comic book shop, where he was once again humiliated. As he stared at the rows of brightly colored books splashed with muscle-bound men in spandex—a sight that had once delighted him—the embarrassment of who he'd been returned, as did a sense of resentment toward a world that had made him that way.

The iPhone directed him to where he could buy a metal detector. He purchased the most expensive one, along with flashlights, plenty of batteries, a miner's light that strapped to his forehead, a battery-powered lantern, a short-handled shovel, a large bucket, and a screen to sift debris.

By the time he had everything loaded and secured, it was past dark. He fired up the bike, flipped on the headlight, and cruised back to the Rebel Yell.

It was clear and cool, a perfect evening for a motorcycle ride. Charlie motored through the night and never looked at the stars, which still held no interest for him. Instead, he focused on the black and a future that was limitless.

Limitless.

He was a free man. Free from the brain damage. Free from Mason. Free even from death.

He could now do whatever he wanted, and that's exactly what he intended to do—*whatever the fuck he wanted.*

First, though, he would return to the Rebel Yell, find that locker key, and retrieve Ernest's million dollars from a bus station in Rio Rico.

The Bus Station

1

Walter Roma's IQ didn't quite reach 90, something that was both a blessing and a curse. The curse was that his world had never expanded beyond the small efficiency apartment where he lived alone and the bus station where he worked alone. The blessing was that he had no curiosity beyond that world. The curse was that he would never experience a great romance. The blessing was that he had no desire to.

Walter was sixty-seven years old, had worked the overnight shift at the Rio Rico bus station for forty-one years, and would not live to see tomorrow.

2

Walter took seriously a job most found demeaning. When his shift ended, the bathrooms were clean, the floors were mopped, everything that had a place was in that place, and the register balanced. Walter might require a little more time to peck out register transactions, but the money was always there, every penny.

He manned the 11:00 p.m. to 7:00 a.m. weekday shift. Most of that time was spent behind the ticket counter. From there, he could keep an eye on everything. And that's where he was, eating his usual lunch of a peanut butter sandwich, when Charlie strolled in.

3

After three terrible nights digging and sifting through the wreckage, Charlie had finally found Ernest's key to a bus station locker that was supposed to hold a million dollars in cash.

Throughout those miserable nights, Charlie had tried not to think about the likelihood of Ernest hoping to save his life with a desperate lie about a locker full of money. But now that the moment of truth had arrived and he was about to find out, Charlie was thinking real hard about that likelihood and those thoughts had put him on edge.

In fact, it was only after he began to seriously consider the possibility of the money *not* being there that Charlie realized how much his plans depended on the money. Without it, he would have no idea what to do with himself.

After all, the only thing that had motivated him to inhale ash night after night was the dream of the glorious future that came with a million-dollar windfall. He had it all planned out: He would take classes to learn how to invest. Then, to ensure the money lasted forever and he would never again be dependent on Mason or subjected to the humiliations of a job, he would.... Well, he wasn't quite sure what he would do. He only knew he was free.

But only if the money was there.

4

The heat of the fire had melted away the locker key's plastic grip. This was a problem. The locker number had been stamped on the grip. Also, with no grip, Charlie would have to turn the key using a pair of pliers, which might attract attention. With those complications in mind, Charlie's working brain told him it was best to do this in the middle of the night.

Buzzing with adrenaline and anxiety, Charlie entered the bus station, hardly gave the old man at the ticket counter a look, turned a corner, and there it was: a wall of twelve lockers—four up, three across. Nine of the lockers still had keys. So if indeed there was a jackpot waiting, it had to be in one of the other three.

Obviously, Charlie could try all three, but that would look suspicious and that old man was already eyeing him. There was also a security camera. If he got lucky and guessed correctly on the first try, no one would be the wiser. *But which locker was it?*

"You, ah, need some help with something over there, son?" the old man behind the ticket counter called out.

"I'm okay, *Dad*," Charlie spat over his shoulder. Then he changed his mind and turned. "You know what, I do need something. You got change for that soda machine?"

"Sure thing," said Walter as Charlie approached. "And I meant no offense, sir. Jus' the older I get, the younger everyone else looks."

"I understand, old timer," Charlie sneered and handed Walter two singles.

Although Walter had used this cash register thousands of times, he still hesitated before making a commitment. Charlie watched the old man hit a button. Stop. Search. Hit a button. Stop. Search. Hit a butt—

"First day on the job, eh?" said Charlie.

Guileless Walter heard it as a sincere question and stopped hitting buttons. "No, sir," he said with a big, toothless smile. "Forty-one years. Be forty-two in June."

As Walter prattled on about how the company had sent him a certificate and a fifty-dollar bonus for his fortieth anniversary, Charlie looked at the old man—the very first person outside of Mason he'd had any real contact with since his return from the dead, and felt a wave of superior revulsion toward every fucking person in the whole fucking world.... *This worm. This toothless fucking retard boring me, holding me up, complicating my life, my plans, my jackpot!*

And then, it hit. Holy fuck did it hit. For the first time since what he'd christened "his resurrection," the oily-black rage swamped Charlie. Only this was different. Now that his intellect had returned, it mixed with the oil to create a black stew of loathing and righteousness, of the certainty of his own supremacy and the resentment at it not being recognized and respected.... Walter's face, with its grotesque nose hair and chapped lips prattling on about a worthless life, surged in Charlie a violent contempt for all humanity. Then a bubble of spit flew from Walter's ignorant mouth and landed on Charlie's hand, and that's when Charlie realized two things: that he wanted to murder this man and that the thought of murdering him had given him his first erection.

Ding!

The register drawer flew open.

"Hey, here we go!" Walter smiled with accomplishment. Then, just as carefully as he'd pressed those buttons, Walter counted out eight quarters. Charlie wasn't paying attention. He was too confused and distracted by the emotions thundering through him.

"You okay, young man?" asked Walter, holding out the quarters.

"Yeah," Charlie said after his eyes focused. "Yeah, I'm fine." He took the change. "Thanks."

5

In a plastic chair facing the lockers, Charlie sat in a daze trying to make sense of what he was feeling. Churning inside of him was a toxic jumble. Most confusing was his potent sexual desire—something he'd never felt before.

Not knowing what else to do, he closed his eyes and pictured all the things he'd done to Yvette in his grandmother's bed. Then he pictured his hands around her neck, squeezing and squeezing, her face turning redder and redder until it morphed into the face of the old man behind the ticket counter. But this fantasy wasn't enough. He wanted blood. He needed to defile and—*SCREEEeeeeeccch!* Charlie's concentration was shattered by Walter, who'd dragged a mop and bucket out of a utility closet. Then, with short, awkward steps—and in the most irritating way Charlie could imagine—Walter banged and scraped and clanged the bucket across the floor into the men's room. Blissful quiet returned with the closing of the bathroom door.

The interruption had snapped Charlie out of his dark confusion.

Now he felt a little queasy and his throat was dry. He strolled over to the soda machine, dropped six quarters, and pressed his selection. The cold root beer soothed his thirst and he returned to his seat.

After a few deep breaths, he was able to focus again.

Which locker?

Figuring Ernest wouldn't put the effort into bending his four hundred pounds over to reach the bottom row, Charlie eliminated that locker. That left lockers two and three. Number two was on the top row. Number three was in the—*Wait, the old guy's gone*, Charlie realized. *Now's my chance!* Working quickly, Charlie pulled the blackened key from his jacket pocket, gripped it tight in the pliers, stood, and—Walter exited the bathroom and returned to his seat behind the ticket desk.

Charlie sat back down and seethed.

"Sure you don't need some help over there?" Walter called over.

Charlie exploded: "SHUT THE FUCK UP, OLD MAN! JUST SHUT THE FUCK UP, YOU FUCKING BUG!"

Stung by the fury and cruelty, Walter said, "Hey, you don't—"

Charlie stood like a shot and turned toward him, eyes blazing.

"I said, shut the fuck up."

6

Over the years, Walter had been robbed a few times. That was scary for sure, but nothing like this guy. The look in his eyes....

A few weeks back at the library, where Walter liked to kill time paging through books, he'd looked through one about the occult. So, yes, Walter had seen Charlie's eyes before.

The sheriff's number was right there on a piece of paper taped to the desk next to the phone. It was useless. Walter was afraid to move, afraid the sound of him lifting the phone would—

Charlie suddenly came around the chairs. Walter nearly gasped. With *those eyes*, Charlie came straight at him. Walter leaned back and lifted his sandwich like a shield.

Staring at something beyond old men, beyond walls, Charlie advanced on Walter, and then abruptly turned and left the bus station.

The sandwich dropped to the desk.

7

Walter was just about finished cleaning the women's bathroom when he heard the noise: *Thud! THUD! Thud! Thud! THUD!*

Then the noise stopped.

Still spooked by the memory of Charlie, Walter decided not to investigate. Probably the garbage man outside or—*Thud! Thud! Thud! THUD! Thud!* This time the thuds were accompanied by spine-chilling howls.

Thud! Thud! "Fuuuuuuck!" *THUD!* "Fuck-fuck-fuck YOUUUUU!" *Thud!* "Cocksucker!" *Thud!* "COCKSUUUUCKERRRRR!"

With a trembling hand, Walter carefully leaned the mop against a sink and slowly made his way to the door, which was thrown wide open so anyone who needed him would know where to find him.

When the old man finally released his breath, it came out in a stutter.

He switched off the light and carefully peeked out the door, using just part of one eye. And like a crazed animal, there was Charlie yanking wildly on one of the locker doors. He'd already pried one open. Now he was working on the other, but the lock held, so he was yanking on the pried corner—*THUD! Thud! THUD!*—and screaming curses like something unholy.

Finally, it popped open. Walter watched Charlie greedily reach inside, snatch a heavy bag, unzip it, look satisfied at its contents, wheel around, march straight towards the women's room, *toward him*, abruptly turn, and exit the building.

Walter didn't move. Didn't breathe. Frozen in confused terror, he waited and then waited some more. After it felt safe enough, he flipped on the light and then *quickly flipped it off*—the dark was safer. He didn't move. He waited and waited until he could wait no longer. Then, as quietly as possible, Walter stepped into a stall, unbuckled his pants, and sat on the commode to silently relieve his aching bladder.

Sitting there, he kept imagining Charlie bursting in and beating him over the head with a hammer.

Charlie didn't burst in, but fearing any noise would attract him, he didn't flush. Walter cautiously lifted his pants, buckled up, and gingerly stepped out of the stall. There, he stopped. He listened. He stepped to the door for another peek. A woman and her son, who looked to be about six, stood waiting for him at the counter.

"Can you help us with some tickets to Phoenix?"

The wave of relief that came over Walter was so strong, tears brimmed his eyes. "Be-be just a sec," he said.

8

Dragging the mop and bucket behind him, Walter said to his customers: "The, ah, five-oh-five to Phoenix arrives in a little more than an hour. That, ah,"—Walter took a quick look around to make sure Charlie was gone—"that suit you?"

"Yes, thank you. Is there someplace we can get breakfast while we wait?" she asked.

Walter stepped up to the counter feeling almost normal. "Yes, ma'am. You take a left out the door here. When you hit the corner, make another left. You'll see the café right there. Tell Jessica ol' Walter sent you. She'll treat you extra special."

"Thank you. And we'll be sure to be back in time."

"Oh, don't fret," Walter said, as he smiled at the little boy, who turned shyly away and grabbed his mother's hand. "Been here forty-one years. Know all the drivers. I can hold them a bit for ya'."

"Well, thank you," she said, "but we'll be back in time."

"The tickets come to forty-six dollars even."

She handed him a credit card. He carefully hunted and pecked his way through the transaction. The kid mouthed to his mother, *I'm hungry*. She answered with a look that told him to behave.

Walter handed her the tickets.

"Thank you," the woman said.

"Now don't forget to tell Jessica ol' Walter sent you."

"Oh, we won't," the woman said at the door.

Smiling and waving at the shy boy, Walter added, "And don't fret if you're a little late. After forty-one years, I can talk to the—"

They were gone.

Walter enjoyed his job. He surely did. Meeting nice people like that. Helping them out. And Jessica always took extra special care of his customers. And if he had to ask the Phoenix bus driver to wait a little to help out some nice folks, he was happy to do just—

"Where's the videotape?" demanded Charlie as he stepped out of the men's room.

Walter'd forgotten all about Charlie, all about his meanness and wicked eyes. And now here he was, like something out of last night's nightmare.

"What?" squeaked Walter.

"The security camera. Where's the tape or hard drive, or whatever the fuck?"

"The-the-the camera's a fake, mister," Walter said. "It's nothing. It-it-it's just plastic."

"Don't you move."

Walter didn't move. He should have. He could have. He could have run out the door and kept running, but he didn't.

Charlie dragged a chair under the camera, stepped on it, and easily pulled the camera from the wall. There were no wires. It was junk. Still standing on the chair, Charlie motioned for Walter to move to his left. Walter had no idea what he meant. Amused by Walter's stupidity, Charlie grinned and motioned again. Petrified, Walter still didn't move, couldn't move.

"Sir," Charlie said laughing, "I just need you to please step to your left."

"What?"

Like an infinitely patient parent to a child, Charlie again motioned for Walter to step to his left.

It took a moment, but Walter figured it out and took a tentative step to his left.

Now Charlie could see the mop bucket.

"Thank you," said Charlie. Then he carefully lined up his shot and launched the fake security camera into the air. Like it was in slow motion, Walter watched the camera arc, feel the pull of gravity, and splash into the dirty water.

Charlie smiled at his perfect shot. He was still smiling when he stepped off the chair, grabbed Walter by the shirt, and pulled him into the women's bathroom.

9

Fifteen minutes earlier, Charlie had stormed out of the bus station with a million dollars under his arm and his mind twisted into a raging knot of competing impulses.

The money should have been enough, should have satisfied him. It didn't. It didn't mean shit.

It was the key that had set him off. That goddamned key. He'd spent night after night rummaging through filth to locate it, only to have the fucking thing snap off in the lock.

Charlie's growing fury didn't want money. What it wanted, what it *needed* was to crush that old man, to choke the life from him, to stomp his face into soup, and then stomp everyone's face into soup. What stopped Charlie was that one thing that had always stopped him: his very real fear of God, of Hell, of burning forever.

Frustrated and confused, Charlie had grabbed up the money and left Walter behind. Once outside, he'd walked and walked trying to sort through his roiling mind. After exhausting himself, he sat on a curb, put his head in his hands, and began to cry. He bawled like a baby and cursed God for persecuting him.

After he'd cried himself out, Charlie sat there and fumed through his favorite fantasy, the one where he stormed into Heaven, got right up into God's face, told Him off, and demanded to—

And then it hit him....

It hit him so hard he almost laughed....

How could I have been so stupid...?

This was the moment when it all changed, everything; when Charlie realized he was something beyond man, beyond God.

You have to die to meet God, Charlie thought.

I'm immortal....

I'll never....

He quickly wiped his eyes and jumped to his feet to double-check his logic.

He spoke out loud into the night....

"I-I'm...." He paused and tightly closed his eyes to pull the answer together, to think it all the way through. "God judges you *after* you die.... You have to die...to be judged...and I...God can't...judge a man...who never dies.... And I'm never...so God can't...."

His eyes opened with the look of a man who'd just been told the tumor was benign; the look of a man who—after so much stress and worry—can hardly believe the good news. But the news was true and Charlie knew it, and just like that, the agony of his conflict vanished and he was free.

"You have to die to be sent to Hell," he said with a grin. "And I'm never going to die, so...I...I can't be sent to Hell...."

Charlie felt dizzy with delight. All the dark confusion disappeared and was replaced with clarity. He was now a man without a worry in the world.

"God can't touch me. He can't...." Charlie began to laugh. "Oh, my God, I'm free. I'm-I'm free!"

Exhilarated by his emancipation from a God he still believed in but no longer feared, Charlie snatched up his money, turned right around, and ran back to the bus station to finish his work.

10

From Walter's bulging eyes, tears swelled, fell, and streamed down Charlie's wrists.

Charlie held tight to the old man's throat. In a euphoric trance, Charlie was someplace else. Killing animals was nothing, he realized. *This* was rapture. *This* was power.

My God, thought Charlie, *I was so ridiculous planning out a life of, what, candy and videogames?*

He laughed out loud at himself and Walter's body went limp. Charlie didn't notice. He squeezed harder to hang on, his thumbs digging into the dead man's Adam's apple.

God can't touch me.

He released Walter's neck.

God can't touch me!

The dead man flopped to the ground.

GOD CAN'T TOUCH ME!

Still in his trance, Charlie stepped behind Walter, dropped to his knees, sat Walter up, wrapped a forearm around the dead man's neck, and squeezed and squeezed until he felt Walter Roma's neck...*give*.

Breathing hard from the effort, Charlie released the body. It hit the floor and he absently kicked it out of the way. Then he sat there a while catching his breath and staring at Walter's dead, limp, stupid, vacant, simple face. In it he saw his own face. Not Resurrected Charlie's face, but *fat fucking retard* Charlie's face—the Charlie the world had humiliated for so long.

Charlie got to his feet and stomped and stomped until Walter's face was mush.

Then Charlie began to cry, cry for himself and all the injustices inflicted on him. He cried a long time, right up until he heard the air brakes of a bus pulling up outside.

With a face blazing with childish self-pity and fury, he looked at the corpse he'd just defiled and thought, *They all deserve this, every goddamned one of them.* He wiped his nose with his sleeve, picked up his bag of money, and walked out.

11

When Charlie exited the bus station, he didn't know how he would go about it. He only knew that by the time he was done, they would pay, *every goddamned one of them.*

A Pointless Quest

1

A few months after Charlie killed an old man in a bus station, Mason crossed the Texas border into New Mexico searching for something that could not be found.

Somewhere out there was Doreen's only remaining connection to the world, and even if Mason did happen upon it, there would be no way of knowing that he had.

With Charlie gone, this was all Mason had left.

2

He'd never expected Charlie to leave the safehouse, not like that, and when he did, Mason was left snake bit with rejection.

Charlie had every right to leave, to endeavor to find his way in the world. Mason had just never gone beyond picturing the two of them together. He'd planned to spend years counseling Charlie, filling him with the wisdom of his books, guiding and teaching him.

Charlie's brain had healed, but in so many ways, in too many ways, he remained an immature thirty-six-year-old boy.

Still, Mason couldn't blame him. Charlie'd been trapped in a disability all his adult life. And now that he wasn't, the opportunities were too many to hold him.

Whenever he thought of Charlie's rejection, which was often, Mason chided himself. How stupid it was to assume a young man gifted with the return of his mind and good looks would want to spend years underground reading books yellowed with age in the company of a man yellowed with age.

And so, on top of everything else, Mason felt the fool.

He did his best during the two weeks they did have together, but he could tell very little got through. Charlie was too excited to sit still and listen, too eager to venture into what life held for a trim and handsome young man who no longer stuttered.

At first, Charlie had a million questions, mostly about his new "powers." The added value Charlie put on passing immortality to others gave Mason relief in knowing Charlie could do no such thing. But once all of his questions were answered about the Joshua Tree and overseas bank accounts and false identities, Charlie's mind went elsewhere.

The boy fidgeted while Mason explained the necessity of remaining hidden, guarding his secret, and not getting snagged in the barbs of the modern world. Charlie's eyes glazed over as Mason stressed how important it was to mentally prepare for what it meant to live forever. Charlie studied the ceiling as Mason made a case for why the two of them should remain in the safehouse until the authorities forgot about them.

After Mason had spent his arguments and repeated them too many times, Charlie made his own case—the arrogant case of a child about why it was important for him to face the trials of the outside world on his own.

"I agree with you," Charlie said. "I do need to grow up, and the fastest way is by making my own mistakes out there."

Mason knew that was a lie, but believed it was the calculated lie a boy tells a father to gain his independence before he's ready.

He couldn't very well kidnap Charlie, and while he foresaw countless complications with him on the loose, he imagined nothing that couldn't be remedied by Charlie returning to the safehouse to hide out until whatever the calamity was had died away.

In his own arrogance, Mason assumed Charlie *would* soon return, and do so with the fidgets and eye glaze slapped from him by a harsh world.

3

Mason had a little over twelve thousand dollars in cash stashed away and offered half to Charlie, who, in a boastful manner that again pained Mason with the truth of the boy's immaturity, asked for only three thousand.

Charlie also rejected Mason's offer to guide him through the desert to a town. He asked only to be pointed in the opposite direction of the Rebel Yell.

"I understand I have to stay away from people who know me," he said, gripping his compass and backpack.

Mason told Charlie of a post office box in Las Vegas and implored the boy to stay in touch. He again told Charlie he loved him and assured him he would always be here for him. As they embraced, Mason sensed Charlie's resentment and was confused and lacerated by it.

After Charlie disappeared over the horizon, Mason returned to the confines of his safehouse. The wave of grief that hit him over the loss of his wife came as no surprise. What he hadn't anticipated was a restlessness that became intolerable.

4

As the weeks passed and it became apparent Charlie was not coming back, an aching unease told Mason he did not belong where he was and demanded he go someplace else. Where, though? Where could he possibly go?

All he wanted was to lose himself in the mourning of his wife. But the restlessness wouldn't allow it, and soon drove him out of the safehouse and into the vast desert, into that place that, in the past, had always allowed him to wander about and process his thoughts into something manageable.

This time, the desert offered no consolation. The wasteland felt alien, and as he roamed through the heat and sand, his hope that the restlessness would pass, that *Eventually* would kick in, was in vain. The restlessness only worsened, and soon he was a spinning compass in a world with no north.

5

It wasn't the grief he wished to escape. Mason had no desire to put an end to his sorrow. Grief was all he had to fill the place Doreen had opened inside him. Grief was all that remained of her. What he hadn't foreseen was not being allowed to grieve, and the awful discovery that his only place was with her—which left him with nowhere to go.

He could think of only two places where some part of her might still be. One had burned to the ground. The other was her gravesite, a place he dare not visit. He'd only barely escaped the All at Once's clutches with a preposterous lie about a lookalike brother followed by a desperate jump out a six-story window. He'd also shown a county sheriff too much.

If he was spotted—No, it was unthinkable and might put Charlie at risk.

There was only the desert, so he wandered and waited for the turbulence inside him to ebb, only to have it throb into something so sharp he was certain he'd go mad.

He took to running across the flats, running and running until his insides burned, until the sharp stitches in his side, the heaving of his lungs, and the sand in his eyes gave him something to think about other than the restlessness of his misery.

And then one morning, while on his knees attempting to catch his breath, he remembered Doreen telling him of a camping trip she took as a girl.

6

They'd been married more than twenty years when she first recounted to him her two weeks with Mr. and Mrs. Arthur. And after she'd told Mason of orange soda, warm days, sunburn, and a dog named Kiefer, he stared at her as though she'd performed a marvel.

"Why are you looking at me like that?" she asked, her eyes still misted with recollection.

She was always to him an unexplored island, exotic and unknowable, replete with treasures yet to be discovered. Throughout their life together, what she shared of herself would be introduced only at the appropriate time, and each release of her reserve would be greeted by him for what it was: a unique and precious gift.

The story of the Arthurs had come about in the most unexpected way, during one of their sour debates over religion.

With a sting of sarcasm, he'd challenged her to describe Heaven, a challenge she had accepted. But, to do the question justice, Doreen took the time required to properly gather her thoughts before answering. And after she'd related the story of her two weeks with Mr. and Mrs. Arthur, she realized she couldn't remember the name of the campground, only that it was somewhere in West Texas or New Mexico—which was why, if Mason did find it, he would not know that he had.

He could only trust that if he visited every campground in West Texas and New Mexico, one would be the place that meant so much to his wife it was her vision of Heaven. And so, after having waited in vain for Charlie to return and nearly going mad in the desert, Mason had retrieved his pickup from that Las Vegas parking garage, hitched a used camper to it, and launched a futile search for a place that could never be found.

7

At dusk, he pulled into the Fire Lake Campground, the third on a list of more than forty. He paid cash for a month's rent, which included a discount for not using the camp's electricity. He didn't need electricity, only water and sewer. He carried his own propane for heat, hot water, and cooking,

Within an hour, he'd detached the tiny camper, leveled it out, connected it up, and was sitting by a fire trying to picture a four-teen-year-old Doreen waving to him as she passed by walking a dog named Kiefer.

Sometimes he could almost see her.

In his dreams, he did.

He'd stay in this place for as long as he'd remained at the others: until the restlessness forced him to move on to the next. In the meantime, he'd look for day labor to subsidize his dwindling money.

The camper was modest and cost only a few thousand dollars. He used it only to sleep, to shower, and to make the occasional meal. Twelve feet wide and eighteen feet long, it held a tiny bathroom on one end and a double bed on the other. In-between was a galley kitchen and eating area.

His only additions were shelves for books that no longer brought comfort.

8

When not out working or looking for work, Mason could be found by his fire or walking the grounds, a phantom sentenced to wander a place he did not belong.

"Heaven Is a Campground"

1

Some sixty-five years before Mason began his futile search for a place that could not be found, fourteen-year-old Doreen woke from a deep sleep and lifted a hand to shield her eyes from a ray of early morning sun.

Disoriented by the light's intrusion, she didn't know where she was. To focus better, she blinked a few times, and then observed that she was under a blanket in the back of a station wagon. This strange scene only added to her confusion, so she propped herself up on her elbows for a better look. The station wagon's back door was swung wide open, and it was the sight of Mr. Arthur putting up a tent that brought it all back. She was on her first vacation ever, and they'd driven all night to get here.

She didn't want to risk waking Indusa, who was fast asleep next to her, but Doreen had to pee so bad she had no choice. As delicately as possible, she pulled back the blanket and gingerly slid herself forward on her butt until she reached the open door. After her stocking feet safely touched down on gravel, she turned to grab her shoes and saw, to her relief, that Indusa hadn't stirred.

Doreen barely knew her new friend. As high school freshmen with a couple of classes together, they were only acquainted, so it was a surprise when Indusa approached her last week in the hall to invite her along.

Indusa was a foreign exchange student from Kenya. Before returning home, her sponsor-parents, Mr. and Mrs. Arthur, arranged for her to accompany them on their annual two-week camping trip and suggested she invite a classmate.

Doreen's "yes" was immediate. Aunt Patsy's permission came by way of a, "Yeah, sure, have fun."

2

At the sound of the final bell, excited students streamed out of the school to begin their summer vacation while Doreen, as instructed, made her way to an outdoor bench near the gym.

Books were her constant companions, especially the classics: *A Tale of Two Cities, Robinson Crusoe, Tom Sawyer....* She settled in and opened *Little Women*, which she was reading for the third time.

Still plagued with baby fat, Doreen was one of those girls no one noticed. She was mostly okay with that, even though she'd had her share of unrequited crushes, which can be tough when you're fourteen. Still, if given a choice to participate in one of the end-of-school celebrations going on around her or sit here and watch them from afar, she'd choose to watch.

After Indusa joined her, they became fast friends over a shared love of books and *77 Sunset Strip*. They talked about losing Elvis to the army and Indusa's home in Africa, a place she was eager to return to.

Mr. Arthur pulled up in a blue station wagon towing a small white and red camper rented just for the occasion.

Indusa was black, so Doreen shouldn't have been surprised to discover Mr. and Mrs. Arthur were black. She still was.

Mr. Arthur was in a huff and hurry, brusque and impatient; he wanted to get on the road. It was a long way from Arkansas to New Mexico, and he intended to arrive by morning.

Although Mr. Arthur knew in advance Doreen would have to return home to pick up her suitcase, the detour still irritated him. He didn't say so. He didn't have to. Doreen could sense it.

As he wordlessly tied her suitcase to the roof of the car, she wished she hadn't come.

Mr. Arthur drove the whole way, all through the night, stopping only for gas and to let Kiefer out, a big, fluffy, yellow dog of indeterminate breed he doted on.

During the long drive, Kiefer lay in the backseat between the girls.

Mr. Arthur was a big guy, mid-forties, clean-shaven with just a touch of gray in his flat-top. A bit thick around the middle, he wore glasses like Buddy Holly's.

Mrs. Arthur was a thin woman of forty, quiet and polite, pretty as all day, but frail. Makeup couldn't hide the dark circles under her eyes. She'd loaded a cooler with sandwiches and little cartons of chocolate milk, like the ones you get in school. When not asking if anyone needed anything, she was content to look out the window at the passing world.

Doreen noticed that every now and again, Mrs. Arthur touched Mr. Arthur like she had to. She could be looking out the window and then, like she wasn't even thinking about it, she'd reach over and grab his hand or rub his arm, as if to make sure he was still there.

Sometimes he did the same with her.

Once they hit the freeway, Mr. Arthur relaxed, and like he was sorry about the suitcase episode, kept telling Doreen how happy everyone was she came along. He even played "I Spy" with the girls and let them choose the songs on the radio, which they had fun with.

Pretending to be in anguish, Mr. Arthur would say something like, "Come on now, how about some Louis Armstrong or Nat King Cole?"

The "Backseat Girls," as he came to call them, teased right back.

"Nat King who?"

"Never heard of him."

"I think the pilgrims listened to him."

3

Darkness fell and the station wagon was making its way through a lonely part of East Texas when Kiefer released a quiet whine to announce it was time for a pee.

Mr. Arthur pulled over and shut off the car, headlights and all, which made everything dark and quiet.

While he patiently walked Kiefer, Doreen stretched her legs under stars so bright they didn't look real.

"You can't see stars in town, not how they really look," Mr. Arthur told her from a crouch as he stroked Kiefer, who lapped up a bowl of water. "All the electric lights dim 'em out," he explained. "This here is what stars look like."

4

As his headlights sliced through the night, Mr. Arthur announced he was taking back control of the radio and tuned in to what he called a "Border Blaster." XERO-AM was one of a handful of independent stations armed with a powerful transmitter aimed at America and deliberately built on the Mexico side of the border to avoid FCC regulation.

Doreen had never heard anything like it. The disc jockey spoke in slang, laughed at his own jokes, reassured listeners Pat Boone records were not allowed in the building, declared Little Richard the "True King of Rock 'n' Roll," and played "Tequila" three times in a row. The Backseat Girls rolled down the windows, bounced to the rhythm, and shouted "Tequila!" to the jackrabbits and scorpions.

When Mrs. Arthur started to doze off, Mr. Arthur went to turn down the radio. She shook her head no, snuggled into him, and closed her eyes. He put one arm around his wife, lit up a Pall Mall with the other, and drove on through the night, steering with his knee.

Doreen fell asleep to The Platters singing "My Prayer." She'd heard it a hundred times before, but out here in a blue station wagon under unreal stars with a pillow named Kiefer, it was the prettiest song she'd ever heard.

5

Crouched down, securing the tent with a Pall Mall hanging from his lips, Mr. Arthur looked up at Doreen and blinked through the smoke stinging his eyes.

"Morning," he whispered.

Doreen didn't have to say anything. Her small hops lobbied on her bladder's behalf. But he didn't do what she expected, what most adults would do: make a joke or a thing about it that would embarrass her. Instead, he pointed to the bathhouse and went back to his work.

She quickly pulled on her shoes, didn't bother to tie them, and hurried off, blind to everything but her discomfort.

The bathhouse made a favorable impression. White tile, roomy, sparkling clean—it even smelled okay. Doreen was no fan of public restrooms, but decided she could live with this one.

She was even less of a fan of public showers. Gym class was its own kind of horror for a heavy girl. So she was relieved to discover the bathhouse offered individual shower stalls that even included a private place to undress before you stepped under the water.

There was something thoughtful about that.

The Wecota Lake RV Park was nothing like Doreen had imagined. Instead of sand, rattlesnakes, tumbleweeds, and giant lizards, it was green, practically lush, with tall leafy trees to keep the heat off you.

She took her time making her way back to the station wagon. The sun was still low, and except for the whispering leaves and the crunch of her footsteps on gravel, everything remained quiet and still.

It was a Friday morning, and only about a quarter of the 265 sites were occupied. Still, Doreen had never seen so many RVs and travel trailers, and had no idea there were so many styles and colors. Some were big; some were small. Some you drove; some you pulled. Some looked like extravagant castles. Others were simple little pop-ups.

Each sat on its own spacious, shady lot complete with picnic table, fire ring, and plenty of room to relax with your family.

Doreen noticed how each campsite was a place all its own, cozylike, reflecting the personality of its occupants: American flags, team pennants, colored lights, hammocks, flowers, chimes, pinwheels, gnomes.

Some posted signs that said "Happy Campers Here" or "Heaven Is a Campground."

The handful of early risers who came out in the dawn light to enjoy that first smoke and cup of coffee all threw Doreen a wave and a smile as though they appreciated her taking the time to pass by.

6

Indusa and Mrs. Arthur were still asleep when she returned. Now that she was fully awake, Doreen saw that their campsite was right up against the lake the park was named after.

Doreen and Mr. Arthur spoke in whispers.

He explained that he and Mrs. Arthur would sleep in the camper. The tent and sleeping bags were for the Backseat Girls and not to concern herself with the heat. The desert cooled at night. If anything, he said, she would welcome the extra blankets he'd brought along. "And don't worry," he told her, "the tent is critter-proof." After a beat, he grinned and added, "Well, almost," which made her laugh.

He untied her suitcase from the car's roof and surprised her with a job offer: fifty cents a day if she'd take Kiefer on a few long walks. She'd be happy to do it for nothing, she told him. She knew right off she wanted to explore this place.

"No, no," he said. "Indusa gets an allowance, and you'll have more fun with some change in your pocket. You'll see."

7

Doreen's walks with Kiefer became her favorite part of the next two weeks.

As she strolled through this self-contained world where everyone was friendly and still minded their own business, where everyone paid their own way and was still eager to help a neighbor, Doreen filled herself to the brim with a sense of contentment.

She walked Kiefer five, sometimes six times a day, long walks, exploring every inch of the place. She couldn't get enough.

She observed that most of the families were black and Hispanic. When you live in the segregated south, that's the kind of thing you notice.

In-between the walks, she and Indusa filled their leisurely days enjoying everything the campground had to offer: a big outdoor pool, miniature golf, and horseshoes. At night they whispered and laughed themselves to sleep. When you're fourteen, you whisper and laugh about everything.

Mr. Arthur was right, the desert did chill at night, and Doreen would never forget the cozy feeling under all those blankets.

8

After the sun began to set on that first night, a line of weekend campers streamed in until almost all 265 sites were occupied. After dark, every-thing came alive with the glow of fires, the smell of wood smoke and outdoor cooking, and the *thunk* of beanbags missing the hole and hitting wood. The air vibrated with different styles of music and with animated conversation and laughter from families who wanted nothing more than to be together.

Saturday night was the same, and Doreen got a wonderful feeling being a part of that. Sitting outside by the fire, she and Indusa laughed at Mr. Arthur's bad jokes and waved at everyone who passed by.

It was like this every weekend, and Doreen looked forward to those Friday and Saturday nights like Christmas morning.

The feeling didn't last. Come Sunday, a sort of gloom came over everything. The weekend was over. It was time to pack up and go home. Time to return to all the things you came here to forget.

Those first two dreary Sundays, Doreen didn't have to worry about going back to the things *she* wanted to forget, so while she felt bad for those who did, she was relieved for herself.

As she walked Kiefer past the empty spaces that just the night before had been filled with good times, she wondered about the people who'd come and gone, who they were, and what they did back home. She was sorry they had to leave and tried not to think about when she would be one of them.

9

Mrs. Arthur slept in most mornings, so Mr. Arthur made breakfast, a rotation of eggs, pancakes, sausage, grits, even biscuits.... He told the Backseat Girls *man food* was good for them.

When the girls returned from what they got to calling their *late-morning swim*, Mrs. Arthur, always cheerful, always on the edge of exhaustion, had a stack of sandwiches and potato chips waiting.

Until she got a proper tan, Mrs. Arthur gave Doreen a cream that smelled of coconuts. That and an aspirin before bed soothed the sunburn.

When she was up to it, Mrs. Arthur would make a big supper. The camper had a small oven, so there was spaghetti and garlic bread smothered in butter; red beans and rice, macaroni and cheese—and not from a box. But when she wasn't up to it, Mr. Arthur grilled up some ribs or burgers.

Every night after supper, Mr. Arthur faithfully paid Doreen with five dimes, which was deliberate and thoughtful. Everything in the game room cost a dime, and so did the machine outside the camp office that sold the coldest bottles of orange Fanta you ever tasted. The soda was so cold that when you popped off the cap, steam came out the top.

On her good days, Mrs. Arthur liked to sit in the shade and read a hardback book. But on her bad days, she stayed in the camper. It didn't take long for Doreen to figure out that when the camper door was closed and the small air conditioner was running, that meant Mrs. Arthur wasn't feeling well and to keep her voice low.

10

Other than helping with meals and caring for his wife, Mr. Arthur did only one thing: under the camper's canopy, in a simple lawn chair that faced the lake, he puffed Pall Malls, read a stack of paperback Westerns, and drank ice-cold water from bottles stored in the cooler next to him. On the other side of him was Kiefer, always Kiefer.

For two weeks, Mr. Arthur was a gracious host constantly looking after his wife's comfort. But when his time was his own, all he wanted was to sit in that chair by the lake, relax, smoke cigarettes, throw a tennis ball for Kiefer, and pore through his pile of Louis L'Amour books.

On some nights, after everyone was asleep, he'd quietly step out of the camper, build himself a small fire to ward off the bugs, and get lost in his thoughts.

One evening, he came out while Doreen was still awake and sat himself down right outside the tent. She didn't know what to do. She didn't want to spy, but she also didn't want to disturb him. She stayed quiet and watched the orange glow spread across his broad face every time he took a drag off his cigarette.

His eyes were so sad she got sad.

"Hi, Mr. Arthur," she finally whispered.

"Hi, sweetie," he whispered back.

"Thank you again for bringing me."

"You having a good time?"

"Yeah, it's great." Tears streamed down Doreen's cheeks. She didn't know why.

"Maybe you could come back next year and walk Kiefer again for us." He dropped his smoke and ground it out with the toe of his shoe.

Doreen wiped away the tears and steadied her voice, "Yeah, I'd like that."

"Goodnight, sweetie."

"Goodnight, Mr. Arthur."

He lit another Pall Mall and stirred the fire.

11

On their second Saturday, the campground put on a pig roast. The animal had been cooked underground all night in a pit covered with rocks. A flier advertised potato salad, corn on the cob, watermelon, ice cream, a live band, and more! *Free!*

In the center of the camp, next to the big building that housed the laundry and game room, as well as the office, ice cream shop, and camp store (which was like a general store with everything you'd need), there was a large open field for Frisbee and baseball.... It was there where everyone gathered in front of the bandstand with lawn chairs and blankets.

Mrs. Arthur was all set to go. She stepped out of the camper in tan slacks and a white blouse looking as pretty as a woman can. Mr. Arthur couldn't stop looking at her, couldn't stop smiling. Then something went wrong. Air just seemed to go out of her. Embarrassed, she leaned into her husband and apologized.

Mr. Arthur told the girls to go on and have fun.

They did, and when they returned, the air conditioner was on.

Later that night, long after dark, Doreen and Indusa sat at the picnic table playing Monopoly by a lantern's light when Mr. Arthur quietly exited the camper with Kiefer.

He paid Doreen her five dimes and added a dollar bill. Said he appreciated all those extra walks. Before she could respond, he walked off with Kiefer and didn't return until after Doreen was asleep.

Early the following morning, Mrs. Arthur was all dressed up again, this time in heels and a printed dress that looked a little big on her. Mr. Arthur looked smart in a suit and tie. Indusa was still asleep, so Mrs. Arthur invited Doreen to come along with them to church.

"We'll stop for breakfast after," she said.

Doreen said she thought she'd better stay back.

For the rest of the morning, she wished she'd gone with.

12

That final week flew by so fast that, before Doreen knew it, she was in the backseat of the station wagon headed back to Arkansas.

Indusa was excited. She would fly home in a couple of days.

Doreen never wanted to leave, ever. Even so, during that final week, she refused to let her growing apprehension ruin her good time. Instead, she hid those anxious feelings away somewhere.

Mrs. Arthur had enjoyed some good days and Doreen sometimes sat with her in the shade. They talked some, but mostly sipped orange soda and read their books.

From what Doreen could piece together, Mr. and Mrs. Arthur had been married thirteen years and had no children of their own. He'd fought in the Pacific, got sunk once, and spent eleven days in a raft with a handful of other men before being rescued. Now he worked six days a week in a machine shop, sometimes seven, and plenty of double shifts for the overtime.

They owned a small house and every year he'd burn up all his vacation days so he could relax for a couple of weeks in a camp that was kind of a secret from the world, except for those who knew it wasn't segregated.

Indusa told Doreen that Mrs. Arthur seemed fine at the beginning of the school year and had no idea why she'd gotten sickly.

The drive home was quiet. Doreen slept most of the way. It was after dark when the blue station wagon towing the white and red camper pulled up to Aunt Patsy's house. Everyone was exhausted, the goodbyes subdued....

Other than thank you, Doreen didn't get a chance to say all the things she wanted.

13

Years later, when she was working as the night manager at the Monument Resorts that allowed Maya to sleep in the back office, Doreen received a corporate memo inviting her to join the company's executive training program.

Very few who applied were accepted. But Doreen had not applied. Her general manager thought so highly of her, he'd done so on her behalf.

With that letter, she held in her hand a golden ticket that meant a move to Phoenix, a housing allowance, and a big raise. Within two years, she'd be earning $75,000 a year as an assistant general manager. Within five years, she'd double that as the general manager of her own location.

Doreen never even considered accepting, and had you told her those two weeks with the Arthurs were the reason, she would've accused you of overthinking things.

But the truth was that Doreen spent her entire professional life seeking to recapture the feeling of her time with the Arthurs, and to her great credit, never for herself. She sought only to grant those memories to others.

In one way, she'd succeeded. There were plenty of people who fondly remembered a leisurely week at a little motel in the middle of the desert. They might not remember the name of the place, but there was a game room and swimming pool, and, *Oh, man, you shoulda' seen the stars.*

In another way, though, she'd failed....

If someone had ever warned Doreen that all the effort she put into recreating those two weeks for her grandson, for Charlie, and that sheltering him and spoiling him and shielding him from the struggles and setbacks of the natural world would contribute to all the terrible things about to happen.... Well, no one would've been so cruel as to tell her something like that.

14

Doreen stood on Aunt Patsy's front lawn and watched the Arthurs drive away. She would never see them again.

That night she slept hard, straight through to noon.

First thing, she called Indusa. They talked for only a few minutes. Yesterday, they were best friends. Today, they ran out of things to say.

They traded addresses and promised to write. Doreen's first letter came back "undeliverable." She never knew why. Maybe she'd screwed up the exotic overseas address.

If Indusa wrote her, Doreen never received it.

A week later, Doreen called to talk to the Arthurs and told Mrs. Arthur she wanted to thank them again. The truth—which she didn't confess—was that she missed them something terrible.

Doreen had more to say, but Mrs. Arthur sounded so tired the conversation didn't last long.

A month later, the number was disconnected.

Doreen tried to find the new number, but there were too many Arthurs in the book and she didn't know their first names. She considered sending them a letter, but didn't know the address. She even thought about getting in touch with the RV park but couldn't remember the name of the place.

So the Arthurs took up residence in the memory of a lonely teenage girl, and then a grown woman, and then an old woman who died alone across the road from a new Starbucks.

The Murders

1

The clock radio clicked on at 9:00 a.m. It was tuned to a news/talk station still in full-freakout mode over a terrible massacre in a Pittsburgh nursing home.

Like everything else in the world, Zoey didn't care about any of that. Without opening her eyes, she slapped the snooze button and went right back to sleep.

Ten minutes later, she slapped it again.

Ten minutes after that, it was 9:20, and she knew FBI Agent Jerome Byrne would be by at ten. If she had any chance of looking presentable, it was time to get her ass up.

She'd already slept twelve hours and still it felt like bowling balls were tied to her eyelids. With some effort, she sat up and dropped her bare feet onto the cold hardwood. She sat there a long time trying to convince herself she was awake enough to safely lie back down, but only for a minute or two.

Forty minutes later, the doorbell woke her.

Zoey stumbled out of bed and, through the closed door, told Jerome to go and get himself a cup of coffee down the block. She'd meet him in twenty minutes.

"No problem," he said, and after his footsteps faded, she leaned against the door and wondered how it had all fallen apart so quickly.

2

A few months ago, while she'd been boxing up twenty years of her professional life to make room for her replacement, newly elected Sheriff Ramon Garza, Zoey felt like a fool—but in the best possible way.

Over the previous weeks, as her looming retirement began to feel more and more real, she'd remembered something her mother used to say: "The fight was so bitter because the stakes were so low."

As a girl, she'd heard that whenever she squabbled with her brother or her father grumbled about work.

The fight was so bitter because the stakes were so low.

In fact, her mother said it so often that, to Zoey, it came to sound like a banality spoken by someone with nothing else to say. But now, at age fifty-seven, Zoey recognized its wisdom and wished she had sooner.

Four years ago, she'd promised her husband she would retire. She then broke that promise to run for another term as sheriff, and for what? To prove to people who didn't matter that they couldn't force her out.

Talk about "low stakes."

Talk about being a fool.

She was proud of her work as a peace officer, but that was separate from the political nonsense. Looking back now, she wondered why she'd ever allowed herself to care so much about things that didn't matter.

The fight was so bitter because the stakes were so low.

It was then that Zoey realized the truth of what she'd done: burnt off four of her golden years to make a point to an insignificant subculture of local politicians, reporters, and bureaucrats.

Well, that was behind her now, and as she closed the boxes and prepared to enter the third act of her life, she found it liberating to no longer care about things that didn't matter.

Quinton mattered.

Her husband mattered.

Two weeks later, she lost him.

3

Turned out Quinton had not been spending his days at the library. Instead, he'd been falling in love with another woman.

Zoey's broken retirement promise had set him adrift, and during that time, he'd—as he put it—*met someone*. One thing led to another, and now it was Zoey who was adrift.

The divorce was finalized last week, the home she loved was empty and for sale, and she blamed only herself.

So she slept, and then slept some more in this generic condo with its bare white walls and piles of moving boxes she couldn't bring herself to unpack.

Unpacking would make it real.

Zoey wasn't ready for real.

4

While he waited, Jerome sipped his iced matcha tea latte and found it comforting that this Starbucks looked exactly like the ones back home. He appreciated the stability of sameness, of one-size-fits-all.

In both his personal and professional life, Jerome had done quite well in the months since he last visited "HicksVille." Currently, he was working directly for the Deputy Director—who was now his official father-in-law—and his job was that of an all-around fixer, the guy who tidied up for the Bureau. That was why he'd been sent out here again. Something desperately needed tidying up.

5

About a month after Charlie Breslin died of a gunshot wound and third-degree burns, his fingerprints were found at the scene of a brutal murder at a bus station. Because Charlie was tangentially connected to the murder of the Old Rich Prick, Jerome was tasked with looking into it. After a thorough investigation, it was decided that, although odd, the only possible explanation was that Charlie had somehow left his prints behind prior to his death. The prints were fresher than they should have been, but stranger things have happened.

But then, just two weeks back, someone strolled into a Pittsburgh nursing home and bludgeoned thirteen old men to death with a pipe wrench. This *someone* also dipped his hand in the blood of one of his victims and left a handprint on the wall.

When those prints matched Charlie's, all hell broke loose.

You should have seen the alarms go off on the seventh floor when the local police matched the nursing home killer's prints to Dead Charlie. The Old Rich Prick and all the potentially explosive video connected to him simply refused to stay buried.

Jerome was immediately put in charge of ensuring that, whatever was going on, it did not blow back on the Bureau. The first thing he did was convince the Pittsburgh police the fingerprint match was a computer error, which didn't change the fact that the prints did indeed match.

Then Jerome was sent back to HicksVille under orders to figure it all out *and* ensure things remained contained. The media were in a frenzy over the nursing home killings and had already dubbed the killer "The Plague," as in: *He swept through the nursing home like a plague.* For this reason, no one could know why Jerome was really out here, which required delicate handling as he re-interviewed everyone, like former Sheriff Zoey Bushnell.

Specifically, Jerome was here to exhume Charlie's body, double-check his fingerprints, and ensure this "Plague" lunatic hadn't done something nutso like sawing off Charlie's hands.

Well, the exhumation was completed two days ago and the results only deepened the mystery. Charlie's body was still buried, he was still dead, his hands were still attached, and his prints still matched.

6

The Kingdom Key was of little help.

Coming and going from the nursing home, the "Plague" carefully used a cagey mix of disguises, public transportation, and car switches in underground garages.

All the cameras in the world couldn't nail down someone who got lost in crowds, changed clothes, and was sly enough to enter a parking garage in one vehicle and exit in another.

The vehicles the Plague left behind were no help. To avoid face-to-face contact, the cars had all been purchased online under phony names using Bitcoin and the seller instructed to leave the vehicle in a lot with the keys under the seat.

Whoever this "Plague" was, he was smart, had resources, and paid attention to detail. He also craved attention. Leaving behind a bloody handprint was a signature and proof he was looking to become famous.

But why was he using Charlie's fingerprints? Where did he get them? That's what had the Bureau freaked out.

While everyone on the seventh-floor sweated and stressed, Jerome found it exciting. Of course, he kept that excitement to himself. But the truth was that this was the most significant case in the world, and he was secretly running down its most crucial lead.

7

Fieldwork sure beat what he'd spent most of his time doing, what everyone else derisively called the "ship work," a play on the term "shit work."

"Ship" came from the acronym S.H.P.S., Bureau jargon for "second high-placed source."

When not serving as the Bureau's fixer and bagman, or illegally delivering money and who knows what all around the world, Jerome was stuck in his office on the phone with political reporters pretending to be the anonymous "second high-placed source" needed to confirm whatever story the Bureau wanted blown up in the news media.

Sometimes he confirmed a truth. Mostly it was lies. Jerome didn't care. He was serving his country, serving the cause. The media also didn't care about the truth, but did want the protection of a "second high-placed source" in case the story backfired.

What a thing it was to sit back and watch the lies he'd confirmed roar to electronic life. The explosion Jerome detonated would almost always consume the news cycle until whoever the FBI wanted ruined was ruined, or whatever lie the government wanted the public to believe was believed.

Jerome slept just fine, thank you very much. He was serving a greater good, which filled him with enormous satisfaction and no small amount of patriotic pride.

His mania had never been so sated.

The one downside was how much he despised the people he worked with. Whether it was his Bureau colleagues or media contacts, he found them vain, insecure, and concerned only with status. This disgust eventually put an end to his surfing of the D.C. cocktail circuit. Instead, he was either at work or home, which wasn't so bad, even though his new wife, Brittany, was a bit of a handful.

Jerome needed things to be just so and while Brittany did her best to accommodate him, she was wired different: looser, frivolous. For example, she didn't care that there was only one way to properly load a dishwasher or if long showers wasted water. She refused to separate trash for recycling. She enjoyed '80s music and slasher movies, hated politics, goaded him into racing during their morning jogs, wore frilly dresses, and seduced him in the shower. In other words, a silly, silly woman.

Her website business was doing well, he had to give her that. But she refused to apply herself and expand it by taking advantage of her father's connections. She also wouldn't work more than forty hours a week and was always on him about his long hours.

"Life's short," she liked to say, and he agreed, but for a different reason. He intended to use his time to whip this country into shape.

Still, Brittany was growing on him. She made him laugh and they were trying to have a baby. While it was true the idea of a messy baby upending his orderly life gave him the willies, the Deputy Director— aka the father-in-law—wanted a grandchild, and that was the one man Jerome had to keep happy.

8

Zoey finally arrived looking harried and rushed and set her plain old black coffee down with a half-hearted excuse about having just gotten over the flu.

She installed herself in one of Starbucks' heavy wooden chairs and—stopped.

"What is that?" she asked, looking at Jerome's half-finished iced matcha tea latte as though it had asked her for sex. This was a reasonable question about a green liquid poured over ice and topped with plant life.

"It's good. You should try it," Jerome said. She surprised him by grabbing it and taking a sip.

"Not bad," she admitted.

"That's what I'm here for, Sheriff, to expand your horizons."

It was already apparent to Zoey that Jerome had matured and gained some composure since she last saw him—a thousand years ago. That was how her old life felt, like something that had happened so long ago it might've happened to someone else.

"So what's this about?" she asked and almost added *so early in the morning*, before catching herself.

Jerome answered by effortlessly repeating the elaborate lie he'd been telling everyone in HicksVille, about how the Charlie Breslin/Joshua Mason case had blossomed into a money-laundering investigation involving organized crime, and how he was looping back to fine-tooth old ground.

"A thankless job," he said, "but what are you gonna do?"

Jerome was a practiced liar, but after what Zoey had seen in Charlie's hospital room with Mason and the blue shimmer, she knew he was lying. And because she couldn't abide being lied to, she blurted out, "Bullshit. What's this really about?"

Even before she'd finished saying it, Zoey knew she'd said too much. By expressing her certainty he was lying, she'd tipped her hand that she knew something worth knowing. And just like that, she'd cracked open a door that could pull her right back into the world of the blue shimmer when all she wanted was to go back to bed.

9

Although it was apparent from the look on her face that she regretted saying too much, Jerome stayed cool. "Why do you say that?" he asked.

An awkward silence ballooned between them. Hoping to pressure her into spilling, he sipped his drink and let that silence keep right on expanding, which was something the talkative Jerome from last time never would've been able to do.

"Nothing," she eventually replied. "Sorry. What do you want to know?"

With that, she'd left Jerome two choices: he could either stick to his lie about money laundering and learn nothing from her, or he could risk taking Zoey into his confidence and hope she'd do the same with him.

Ninety-nine people out of a hundred, Jerome would've stuck to the lie. But Zoey he liked, respected. She was good people, good police. He might've only dealt with her that one time, but he'd worked with enough bad ones to know the difference, so he took a chance.

Jerome set down his exotic drink and grinned sheepishly. "Thought that was a pretty good cover story," he said.

Hoping another awkward silence would provoke her into talking, that was all he said.

Zoey couldn't hear that silence, not with *Dummy! Dummy! Dummy!* screaming in her brain.

After that long pause failed to crack her, Jerome finally relented, "Hey, whatever it is, you can trust me."

She answered with a fierce glare that was equal parts accusatory and fear, which startled him. *I blew it*, he thought. *What a stupid thing to say.*

He was about to make things worse with an apology when her glare dissolved. She was studying him now, sizing him up, and in those large, intelligent eyes, Jerome saw a woman desperate to commiserate with someone she could trust. Instinctively, he knew that to become that person, he would have to make the first leap of faith. So he did, and in doing so, walked into a world there was no returning from.

"You remember the murder at that bus station outside Rio Rico a few months back, the night manager?" he asked.

"I remember."

"There was a connection to Charlie Breslin."

That cleared the *dummy-dummy-dummies* right out of her head.

"What kind of connection?"

"Charlie's fingerprints were all over the scene."

Watching her closely, Jerome was dumbfounded when, instead of skepticism or disbelief, a strain of worry spread across her face. Her hand trembled as she sipped her coffee. She peered over the steaming brim and said, "That murder happened *after* Charlie Breslin died...."

It wasn't a question.

"A few weeks after," he confirmed.

Zoey slowly set down her coffee, laid her hands in her lap, took in some breath, and turned to stare out the window at a line of cars waiting at a stoplight. How she envied the people in those cars, their everyday lives, and the contentment that comes with not having driven your husband into another woman's arms, with not knowing the world contains blue shimmers and things that return from the dead.

The light turned green, and, with all those lucky drivers safely on their way, she asked herself out loud, "Why would he kill a bus station manager...?"

Jerome was flabbergasted. Anyone else would have said, *That's impossible* or *Those must be old fingerprints* or *There must be some mistake*. Instead, as though a dead man running around committing a murder was plausible, she was sitting there wondering *why* he'd done it.

His insides jumped and buzzed like a live wire skipping over a pond, but he answered with an even-keeled voice. And, as Jerome spoke, Zoey watched the cars stream by and realized the world of the blue shimmer was preferable to this world, the one where she was discarded and obsolete.

"It looks like the killer had a key to one of the lockers," Jerome said. "But the key was charred, weakened by fire, and snapped off. We found the broken piece in the lock of a locker that had been forced open. The assumption is that the night manager tried to stop his murderer from breaking in and, well...."

Zoey turned away from the window to size up Jerome with a new face, a cop's face. "Do you have any idea what was in the locker...what he was after?" she asked, feeling necessary for the first time in months.

"No," Jerome said. "No security cameras, no witnesses."

Zoey processed what this might mean while Jerome sipped his green tea and tried not to explode into a million questions.

After what seemed like forever, she looked him dead in the eyes, and because he was able to hold her gaze, she told him everything—of the blue shimmer, and how Mason summoned it with empty eyes, and how the shimmer floated across the room and fell into Charlie like a dead tree.

After she finished telling the story, he told her everything, including the discovery of Charlie's bloody handprint at the scene of the Pittsburgh nursing home massacre.

My God, Zoey thought, *Charlie is the Plague*.

10

In the years that followed, whenever Jerome looked back on this moment, the thing that would surprise him most was how he'd believed everything Zoey had told him, and how he immediately understood how to exploit Charlie's reign of terror.

The Thing That
Comes Out of the Dark

1

Charlie had decided to keep Mason's motorcycle. He enjoyed the open air much more than the confines of a car, especially on a night like this one.

After the nursing home killings, while roving the country with no destination in mind, he'd committed two additional massacres. Each time, the rage had told him where to stop, and wherever that was he then enjoyed the thrill of a working brain as he plotted out the intricate details of his next rampage. And after the planning came the most satisfying part, that moment when he allowed the rage to have its way with him.

But now the time had come to stop the aimless roaming. Charlie had bigger plans. *The Thing That Comes Out of the Dark is about to go national*, was how he liked to put it. He was headed for Chicago. There, he would set up a base of operations—*a den*—a home that would allow him to hide in plain sight and take things to the next level.

Behind him, clutching his waist was the woman he'd just married. Vicki wasn't pretty or intelligent, but life was easier with everything in her name, especially the bank accounts. She was also devoted as a puppy, put up with rough sex, and never inquired into his secrets.

She'd do for now.

Charlie avoided the oppressive light of day and major highways. He rode only by night on these back roads.

In the daytime, they slept in cheap motels, places that should've reminded Charlie of home, but didn't. He no longer thought of the past.

2

Charlie leaned the bike into a sharp curve, came out of it, hit a straight-away, and poured on the speed. But up ahead, the road was flooded with an eerie white light. Not knowing what he might run into, Charlie down-shifted, slowed, and found himself cruising past a backwoods revival meeting.

A large, white tent sat in the middle of an open field filled with parked cars lit by portable lights. A huge banner proclaimed, "JESUS SAVES!" and the sight of it rattled Charlie to where he almost lost control of the bike.

"Dammit!" he hissed, as he righted the machine and gunned it to escape.

"Goddammit!"

He accelerated out of the light and disappeared into the black tunnel of night.

Charlie ripped off his helmet, jammed it between his legs, and let the wind cool his face and dry his sweat.

As the moonlit trees whipped past, Charlie increased the bike's speed and then closed his eyes.

With his eyes closed, he leaned back and rode on—free from fear, free from death, free from God's judgment, free as a man could be.

Four Years Later...

1

Four years had passed since that fateful coffee shop meeting between a retired sheriff and an ambitious FBI agent. Four years had passed since Charlie had decided to "go national" and settle down in Chicago.

And now, after almost five years of searching for a place that could not be found, for that last connection to Doreen, and although there was no way for him to know he'd found it, Mason *had* found it.

Upon his arrival at the Wecota Lake RV Park, there'd been no jolt of recognition, no spark of intuition. It was merely one more campground on his list. And although the world had gone through many changes over these years, the Wecota Lake RV Park looked very much like it did when Doreen spent two weeks here with Mr. and Mrs. Arthur some seventy years before. There'd been some updates. The camp had WiFi, the soda machine offered fruit juice and water, and the game room was more about video than pinball.

Nevertheless, it was still 265 spaces on twenty-eight acres; still a place Doreen would recognize.

2

On a typically bright and clear New Mexico afternoon, Mason pulled his creaky pickup into a gleaming, new Qwik-Shop. After switching off the ignition, he stepped out into a hot day and found himself standing alone in a platoon of twenty glimmering gas pumps.

The only sound came from the hum of cars moving along a nearby interstate. It was the sound of people on the go. That's what Mason wanted, to be on the go. Only he didn't know where to go. After all this time, the restlessness still refused to tell him where he belonged.

He was working part-time for the owners of Wecota Lake RV, good people who paid him a fair wage that included his rent. They owned the mulch piled in the bed of the pickup. What Mason owned was a pile of problems that grew taller by the day.

During these last few years, the All at Once had progressed with remarkable speed, and he was now a man out of moves.

Hoping to clear his head and feel the sun on his face, Mason strolled through the forest of gas pumps until he was out from under their massive metal canopy. The sun felt good against his skin, but it wasn't enough, so he walked the length of the parking lot to where the asphalt stopped at a patch of perfectly green grass that had no business growing there. He then crossed the lawn and stopped where the grass met the desert. He stood there a moment and stared out at the dry vastness he'd once called home.

His hands found their way into his pockets and he wondered about Charlie, where he was, what he'd been doing all these years; if he'd found a place for himself, and why he'd not reached out since leaving the safehouse.

Mason still couldn't understand the boy's rejection. He spent a lot of time looking back trying to figure out what he'd done wrong. Maybe he'd pushed too hard. That was probably it. In his own way, with his brain freshly healed, Charlie was just entering his rebellious teen years and Mason had practically smothered him, planned out his whole life, and told him he'd have to remain underground and read books.

Filled with a wave of regret, Mason closed his eyes, lifted his face to the sun, and muttered, "Stupid, stupid, stupid."

He closed his eyes tighter, as though such a thing could erase his mistakes, all of them, and then he opened them to again stare into the desert in the hope it would beckon him and once again become what it was: the place where he belonged. If it had, he would've dropped everything right there and disappeared into the desolation. But it didn't, so he turned around and found himself looking down at a plastic sprinkler nozzle buried in the lush grass. He wondered why the nozzle was black instead of green and why people went to all the trouble of growing grass out here. He then wondered why he wondered such things and decided it was time to enter Valhalla.

3

He made his way across the hot asphalt and marveled at how rapidly Qwik-Shop had expanded its operation by buying up all the independents and small chains. Like dandelions, Qwik-Shops were everywhere now. This one had opened last month.

A notice taped to the door offered a familiar and foreboding greeting....

After the first of the year, we will no longer accept cash.
Credit and debit cards only.

—Have a Qwik-Shop Safe Day!

These warnings were everywhere. All the major chains were phasing out cash and Mason had no idea what to do about that.

He couldn't obtain a credit or debit card without opening a bank account, and no one was allowed to open a bank account anymore without one of those new federal IDs. Worse yet, to get a federal ID, you had to surrender your fingerprints and DNA. Even if he were willing to do that—and he wasn't—he'd have to hand over his current driver's license, a long-expired fake.

With a quiet *whoosh*, the electric doors slid open and Mason got his first look inside Qwik-Shop's latest model. The new ones were twice the size of the old, and so automated, only one employee was required per shift.

He felt the familiar cool air envelope him, only it now came with the bludgeoning sounds pulsing from television monitors that hung everywhere to blare out the latest headlines from the Qwik-Shop News Channel.

4

As was always the case these days, the breathless reports focused almost exclusively on "The Plague," a story the media and much of the public were obsessed with beyond anything Mason had seen before. And whenever the media seemed ready to move on to something else, the Plague struck again. Only last month, he'd rampaged through a boy scout camp killing eleven with a pipe wrench and again left behind what was now his signature: a bloody handprint.

After all this time—after all the massacres—the authorities claimed they still had no idea who the Plague was and that no one had seen his face. One thing was certain: the Plague had media savvy. Year after year, into that mercenary electronic maw, the Plague delivered fear and blood, hysteria and slaughter, and that one thing the media craved above all: an evolving narrative speeding towards a terrible climax.

Over the last year, the Plague had zenithed the media frenzy by releasing videos online. With a digital camera strapped to his head like a miner's light, the Plague gave the public a first-person view of his bloody rampages. Each massacre concluded with the gore-soaked Plague stepping in front of a mirror dressed all in red, including an executioner's mask. On the mirror, the Plague would leave his signature—a bloody handprint before the screen went black.

Jerome Byrne, the FBI special agent in charge of the Plague task force, claimed everything possible was being done to pull these videos offline. Even if that were true, the videos were still everywhere and they were unspeakable.

Then there was the fact the Plague targeted only males, society's protectors. The public had never felt so vulnerable.

We're doing our best, said the authorities.

This is a national crisis, cried the politicians.

The government offered everyone free security cameras and told Americans to respect local curfews, have patience with police checkpoints, and remain home as much as possible.

5

Mason tuned out the headlines. There were never any new developments in the Plague story, just the same ones repackaged, repeated, and reheated into fear porn.

Besides, he had his own problems.

Still, like he always did in Valhalla, Mason walked the aisles and marveled at what the All at Once had wrought now.

Slowly creeping through the store were two cylinder-shaped machines as thick as fire hydrants that stood about four-feet tall. Mason guessed they kept the tiled floors gleaming. Another device, this one as tall and thin as a coat rack, zipped around scanning barcodes. Mason had no idea what that was all about.

The only other human in the place was no older than nineteen and, like everyone else in the All at Once, staring intently at her phone.

Like a tennis referee, she sat in a tall chair overlooking a long counter with a dozen automated cash registers.

"Welcome to Qwik-Shop," she said without looking up.

Mason didn't waste time with a response. Instead, he stepped to one of the registers and selected the necessary prompts to prepay for his gas. Then he fed six twenties into the machine. This triggered a recording, a woman's robotic voice:

Dear valued customer. Please be advised that for your convenience and safety, Qwik-Shop will no longer accept cash after the first of the year. If you have any questions, please seek out one of our associates, and have a Qwik-Shop safe day.

Mason decided he had some questions.

"Excuse me, miss?" he said to the tennis referee.

She was too hypnotized by her phone to respond.

He tried again. "Ma'am, I have a—" He saw the problem. Earbuds were snugged in both of her ears.

He caught her attention by stepping into her line of sight and waving. She removed a single earbud and took a moment to focus on the real world. Her smile was stiff, her annoyance at being interrupted obvious.

"Did you need some help checking out, sir?"

These people and their "sirs," thought Mason.

"No," he said, "but I am wondering how I'm supposed to pay for gas after the first of the year. You won't take cash and I don't have a credit or debit card."

"Oh, that's no problem," she said, sliding out of the tall chair and hitting the ground. "I'll give you one of our cash cards."

The tennis referee stepped to the counter and hit a button that twirled a display filled with plastic cards stamped with the corporate logos of all the major chain and online stores. She snatched up the one stamped with Qwik-Shop's red logo and handed it to him.

"These are totally free," she said, "and they work just like a debit or credit card."

Mason stared at it. "I don't understand."

"Here, sir, let me show you," she said, and impatiently snatched the card back. She then flipped it over and pointed to the QR code on the back—which looked to Mason like a Rorschach test. In a way, it was.

"You just like download the Qwik-Shop app to your phone," she explained, "click on 'add funds,' scan this QR code, and then you can transfer money from your bank account directly into the card. It's like, super easy."

Mason stared at her as though she were an iced matcha tea latte.

Eager to get him out of her hair, she said: "If you wanna give me your phone, sir, I can get you all set up."

"I don't have a bank account," he said, "much less a phone. I just want to buy gas next year."

"Oh," she replied. "You're kinda like old school, huh?"

"Any ideas?"

"Honestly, no."

"None of this makes sense," he said mostly to himself.

"No, actually, it does, sir," she replied with the arrogance of youth creeping into her voice. "Paper money's full of bacteria and we'll all feel safer with the elimination of cash, especially at night."

"You've been robbed?" he asked with genuine concern.

"No," she said. "But we'll feel safer."

6

As soon as Mason lifted the gas nozzle, the monitor embedded in the silver pump burst to bright life and blared out the latest breaking news from the Qwik-Shop News Channel.

There was no escaping this shit, and now, almost every major retail corporation had its own news channel.

Mason ignored the breathless anchor's "breaking developments in the Plague case," shoved the nozzle into the pickup, and stared at his rear license plate—another problem he couldn't solve. His tags expired next month and there was no way to renew them.

One more stomach knot.

Last year, he'd spent all his residual cash to install an updated exhaust system and only barely passed the emissions test. The emission standards were even stricter this year and there was no way he'd pass. In a few weeks, Doreen's wedding gift to him would no longer be street legal.

Gas cost $23.48 a gallon, so those six twenties—the last of his money until he got paid—wouldn't get him far.

He replaced the nozzle in the pump, which shut off the breaking news (that wasn't *breaking* anything), grabbed a squeegee, and was cleaning his windows when a sleek yellow convertible crept up without a driver. It was one of those new ESDs, or "electric self-drivers," that were all over nowadays.

7

Already some 15 percent of passenger cars were ESDs, which allowed the former drivers to use their newly-acquired free time to ignore the road and stare at whatever screen hypnotized them most.

Almost a quarter of delivery and commercial vehicles—mail trucks, semis, and the like—were ESDs, and there was no one at all in those.

ESDs were easy to spot; they never went even one mile per hour over the speed limit.

The federal government was eager to move everyone into these "safe" and "clean" vehicles, and offered all kinds of incentives: tax breaks, rebates, zero-interest loans. For those who weren't interested, the government doled out backdoor penalties, such as emission standards older vehicles could never pass.

There was no one at the wheel of this yellow convertible, a sight Mason was sure he'd never get used to. But in the backseat a young couple sat arguing.

"How can you not love this car?" the exasperated young man asked.

"That's not the point," the girl replied. "You should've asked first."

He barked a command: "Ignition off! Open my door!" The convertible obeyed. The man extricated himself and left the girl with one word: "Fine."

She folded her arms and turned away from him in a pout.

He pulled a debit card from his wallet and inserted it into a Qwik-Shop electric charging pump. "You know," he finally said, "all I wanted was to surprise you and now you have to go and be like this."

"Oh, so you bought this *for me*," she shot back.

"I bought it for the both of—Hey, what is this?"

"What's wrong?"

Squinting, he leaned into the pump's monitor reading something. "This thing ate my debit card," he said. After some more reading he turned to the girl. "They suspended my card over that FaceTalk post. I have to delete it to get my card back."

The girl reached into her purse, retrieved a debit card, and handed it to him. "I told you not to post that," she said.

"It was a joke," he said, and slid her card into the pump.

"Well, I told you that if you—" He lifted the thick, black charging plug and the Qwik-Shop News Channel blared to life, drowning out their argument.

Finished with his window washing, Mason returned the squeegee and noticed the ESD owner's t-shirt. It was black with a big, red executioner's hood across the chest. The Plague had a logo and this guy was wearing it.

What a world, thought Mason.

Mason jumped into the pickup, fired it up, and was about to drive away when, all of a sudden, *every* monitor on *every* gas pump burst to electronic life with a "Breaking News Announcement!" And so did the young couple's iPhones.

The spat forgotten, the two of them stood hypnotized by whatever the news was.

Mason drove off.

8

He merged onto the freeway and passed another one of his soon-to-be problems: a federal toll booth still under construction. These monsters were going up everywhere, and once operational, you could only pay your toll with a digital pass. No cash allowed. Without the digital pass that required the bank account that required the federal ID that required your fingerprints and DNA, you wouldn't be able to drive the interstates without being ticketed for unpaid tolls.

Mason kept his eye on the road and tried not to think about it.

9

By late afternoon, there was a steady flow of weekend camper traffic filing into the Wecota Lake RV Park.

Mason unloaded the mulch and spread it under a stand of trees that separated the outdoor pool from the miniature golf course.

It was near dusk when he finished the rest of his work.

Before heading back to his camper for a shower, he climbed into the bed of the pickup to sweep out the stray mulch. Finished with that, he leaned on his broom to look out over what was now a familiar sight.

Just as it had been when Doreen was here all those years ago, the camp was coming alive with weekend campfires, conversation, laughter, and the sound of children playing.

It was when the day began to dim that he missed her most.

Lucy

1

Later that same evening, long after Mason had retired from his nightly fire, Lucy Stockton and her small RV rolled into Wecota Lake RV Park.

To be more precise, it was Lucy's middle-aged son who rolled her in, and then abandoned his elderly mother for two weeks; left her alone with a few hundred dollars and a peck on the cheek.

Lucy was Scot-Irish, eighty-one-years-old, and looked like a Q-tip. A puff of regal white hair sat atop a pleasant, deeply-lined oval face and rail-thin body. She had perfect posture, liked everyone she met, and wore wire-rimmed glasses thick enough to magnify pale blue eyes that frequently appeared bewildered.

An ungrateful family saw her as a burden.

"We rented you a camper for a couple of weeks," her son had told her, even though he'd charged it to her credit card. "And got you a nice spot by the lake less than fifty miles from here. You deserve a vacation, Mom."

After Lucy's husband died, her deadbeat son and his family of five moved in uninvited and were now putting her out. Things had gotten tense. She didn't know why, but maybe a couple of weeks away would help. So she went along with the ruse and thanked them.

2

Mason immediately noticed Lucy's camper. It was hard not to spot the gaudy billboard-on-wheels slathered in advertising promoting the company that rented it out. Rental RVs covered in advertising weren't uncommon. What caught Mason's eye was that the RV looked as though it had been parked and abandoned.

The first thing most people do is unroll the camper's awning, set up a grill and lawn chairs; that sort of thing. There was no sign of life here. Lucy's son hadn't even bothered to extend the handrail next to the stairs.

At night, as he sat by his fire, Mason saw life moving about inside the rolling commercial. Lights came on, shadows crossed the shuttered windows. A few days would pass before he saw its occupant, and only then after she needed his help.

3

The sun was down, the night cool, the fire comforting. The campfire was where Mason spent his evenings until the need for sleep arrived and where he was when the door to Lucy's RV opened.

As soon as he saw her tiny, shaky foot hit the first step, he dashed over. "Hold on," he called out, which she did as he extended the handrail.

"Thank you," she said, with a grateful smile and touch of Irish lilt. She gripped the rail and descended the remaining steps without a problem.

"You're welcome," he said.

"You're the young man who works here, aren't you?" she asked. "I was just coming to see you. There's a water leak, and I called the RV company, but they can't come out for a couple of days."

"Sure. I can have a look."

"I don't mean now," she protested. "You're probably having your supper. Maybe in the morning?"

"Now's a perfect time."

Mason liked Lucy straight off. It was apparent she was unassuming and kind. The inside of her RV revealed she was something else: lonely.

The RV was clean, too clean. The only sign of life was some knitting on the bed and a few word-search books stacked neatly on the counter.

What really hit Mason was a photograph—a picture of Lucy, looking a few years younger, with an old man, who was obviously her husband. They were outside some sort of medical facility—a hospital or nursing home. She sat on a bench. He sat beside her in a wheelchair with an oxygen tube attached to his nose. They were holding hands and smiling through the terrible knowledge he wasn't long for this world.

4

There was a small leak where the plastic water supply line screwed to the back of the toilet. The threads had been stripped. Mason didn't have the parts to replace the connection, so he wrapped the threads with plumber's tape, screwed the line back on, and it held.

"Oh, thank you," she said, clasping her hands. "I'd been wiping up that water and wiping up that water. It was no problem, but I was worried it might damage something and cost my son his deposit."

"I'm right next door," Mason said as he retrieved his tools from the tiny bathroom's floor. "You need anything, you just come on over."

He meant it, too, which felt strange. Over these past five years, he'd received plenty of offers to get to know someone better. He begged off when he could, grinded it out when he couldn't, and even went so far as to move along if someone refused to let it go. Lucy's company he already enjoyed.

On his way out, he noticed that the TV hanging over the foot of the bed was broadcasting a blue screen.

"You having trouble getting a signal?"

"Oh, it's no problem," she said with a wave of her hand. "I don't watch anything. I sometimes keep it on for company."

The camper had an aerial that would pick up a few local TV stations. He had her hooked up in a few minutes.

She again clasped her hands and then offered him one. "I'm Lucy Stockton," she said with a wide grin.

"Joshua Mason," he replied, and shook her warm hand.

5

The following night, Mason poked at his fire and watched Lucy's shadow move about inside the garish camper until the thought of her alone with word search books became too much.

He knocked on her door and invited her to come over.

She lit up with surprise. "Be there in a jiffy," she said and then asked, "How do you take your coffee, Joshua?"

"Well, uh, black is fine."

Then, like a magician about to make a rabbit disappear, she twinkled her eyes and lifted a bony finger that said, *You're gonna love this.*

A few minutes later she arrived with two mugs brimming with steaming coffee on a small tray. A "special recipe," she told him, and as the two of them got to know one another, Mason realized it was some of the best coffee he'd ever tasted.

Lucy had recently graduated high school and was about to enter a Catholic convent when she met her husband Gerald while lunching at the roadhouse his father owned in Santa Fe.

It was love at first sight. They were married six months later and for the next fifteen years—along with waiting tables, doing the books, perfecting her coffee recipe, and producing the son who'd abandoned her here—she played piano in the roadhouse and sang torch songs.

"I was quite the looker in my time, I'll have you know," she told him.

That was the first time Mason had laughed in a long time.

6

Every night after that, she'd toddle over with what he came to call "Lucy's Miracle Coffee" and then he'd ask the questions required to hear the story of her life.

After the roadhouse closed, Lucy and Gerald managed a local chain of restaurants. There were then twelve blissful years of retirement before he took sick.

"We did a lot of things," she told Mason one chilly evening. "Traveled to a lot of places. Gerald called it 'creating memories.' But I don't ever think about those trips."

She folded her arms against the desert chill and stared at something beyond the fire. "We had a small sun porch off to the side of the house." She paused to remember this place, to summon a picture of it in her mind. "That's what I remember, not the trips or the cruises.... We never did anything special out there. It's just where we always were. Gerald in his chair watching a ballgame, me next to him, knitting or reading.... We talked all the time out there. I don't remember what about. Everyday things, I guess. Nothing special things, like married people do. That's what I miss most, those nothing special days."

A pause.

"Had someone told me at the beginning that Gerald and I would have fifty-three years together, I would've been thrilled. Then those years, they...."

Firelight glinted off her moist eyes and some time passed before she added, almost bitterly, "People who've seen too many movies think there's something romantic or poignant about it. There isn't."

"No," Mason said. "There isn't."

Surprised, she turned to him.

He kept his eyes on the fire.

"I was married," he admitted.

After a pause he turned to her. "Doreen, that was her name."

And with that, little by little, over the following days—without revealing his secrets—Mason told of his life with Doreen.

It didn't flood from him. He wasn't built that way. It came in pieces and parts and chunks. And with each word, the terrible restlessness within him abated.

7

On their last night by the fire, Lucy said, "I had this aunt with a heart defect. She ended up living a good long life, but before the corrective surgery, and on two occasions, she was pronounced clinically dead. She told me that both times she died, she was reunited with her grandparents and a dog she'd loved as a girl."

Lucy smiled at the memory and its meaning, and then placed her hand on Mason's arm. "We'll see them again," she said.

Mason's face spoke for his skepticism.

"You don't believe that?"

"Dunno," he shrugged.

"You think my aunt was seeing things, or maybe telling a small child a comforting lie?"

"No, no," Mason said, shifting uncomfortably in his chair. "All kinds of people've experienced what your aunt did. But she was never really dead, was she? She came back, so there had to be something going on with her."

"Like what?"

"I guess you might call it a death dream. Maybe, before we die, we slip into a state of unconsciousness and dream what we hope the afterlife will be."

"That's actually kind of nice," she said.

"It is," said Mason, working up a grin. "Until everything goes black."

She threw her head back and laughed. "You'd make a great Irishman—a poet and a cynic." She stood and stretched until she was on her tiptoes. Then she dropped back down and announced an end to the evening, "It's late, and my son's coming for me early."

He stood and said, "I'll be up to see you off."

"Well, just in case...." She offered her hand, and he took it. "It was nice to meet you, Joshua."

"You as well."

She gathered her coffee mugs on the small tray and smiled a grandmotherly smile that told Mason she would miss him.

Still smiling, she wheeled around, took a couple of steps, and then stopped.

She was deciding on something, and after she'd decided, she turned back around and said, "May I impose on you one last time?"

"Sure, of course."

She set down the tray and then lifted a necklace over her white hair. Two items hung from it: a Crucifix and a ring. She opened the tiny clasp and removed the ring.

"This was Gerald's," she said, and then paused to control her emotions. "This was his wedding ring. I see you don't have one and I'd like you to have it."

"I can't acce—Good heavens."

"You want to know what my son's going to do with this after I die...?" Her voice edged into a hurt and anger Mason hadn't heard from her before. "He's going to pawn it for a few dollars. So if you would take it, I'd know it was out there and that would be a comfort."

Mason didn't know what to say. So she gently took hold of his wrist, opened his fingers, and placed the ring in the center of his palm.

He stared at it awhile and said nothing. Then he looked at her and said, "Doreen and I, we never got the rings."

"It should fit," she said.

It did.

8

Mason woke earlier than usual the next morning. It was still dark. As coffee warmed on the camper's propane burner, he stepped outside to get a preview of the day.

Lucy's RV was gone.

By that afternoon, he'd sold his camper for gas money and was on the road headed back to Arizona, to his safehouse.

Fifteen years would pass before he ventured out into the world again.

The Birthday Boy

1

Just after dawn, on the day Charlie turned thirteen, Mason exited Room 14 to stretch and yawn under a sky streaked with oranges and yellows. He grimaced at the sight of only two cars in the lot, which was the norm these days.

Even with Doreen working that second job, they were behind on the mortgage. To save expenses, she'd recently sold off the games in the game room and closed the pool.

Fully dressed—except for his boots—Mason finished stretching and, in his white socks, strolled along the creaky wooden porch, passing all the rooms. He then walked around the office to the back door that opened into the kitchen of the manager's apartment.

It was a small kitchen with harvest gold appliances from the seventies, wooden countertops and cabinets, and a round metal table with three chairs (the fourth sat in front of an easel in Charlie's small bedroom).

The screen door squeaked as Mason pulled it open. He was careful not to let it slam and wake Doreen.

Charlie didn't bother to look up from his comic book and bowl of cereal. No point. He knew who it was. Mornings had gone exactly like this for about five years now. "M-m-morning," Charlie said.

"Yeah, good mor—" Mason paused as though confused. "Who the heck are you?"

The comment surprised Charlie and prompted him to look up from his comic. After he figured out Mason was teasing, he smiled. He loved it when Mason teased. "I-I-I'm Charlie!" he said and started laughing.

"Don't play games with me, mister," Mason replied with a stern look. "Charlie's a little boy, and I know the difference between a little boy and someone who's all grown up."

"*I'm* Charlie!" he said laughing and pointing to his chest for emphasis.

"You better tell me what you did with Charlie."

"I'm Ch-Charlie! I'm Charlie!" he said, laughing harder.

"How can you be Charlie when you're all grown up?"

"That's right, I'm all growed up. I-I-I'm thirteen today!" the delighted boy said, as though turning thirteen was quite the accomplishment.

"Yes, you are," Mason said with affection. "You are thirteen—a teenager. I can hardly believe it. Happy birthday, son."

"Do-do I really look-look more growed up?"

Mason looked him over as though giving the question serious thought, which cracked Charlie up all over again. "Well, you're certainly not the little boy I first met," Mason said honestly.

Charlie went back to his comic book. Mason headed for the stove, where there was fresh coffee. No matter how late she returned from mopping floors at the mall, Doreen still got up to set out Charlie's breakfast and make coffee for her secret husband. Then she'd go back to bed for a couple of hours.

Mason poured the coffee and caught Charlie sneaking a peek at his dusty socks.

"My-my grandma's gonna g-g-get mad again," Charlie said, relishing the prospect.

Mason replied with a shrug.

"Why don't you just p-p-put your boots on?"

Now it was Mason's turn to point to *himself*. "Because I'm a free man in a free country. I'll decide when I put boots on."

Charlie could only shake his head at the wonderment of such ideas. "She's gon-gonna be mad," he repeated before disappearing behind the comic.

Mason took a sip of coffee and said, "Got you a birthday present." Charlie's head popped up like a turtle. "I'll give it to you tonight."

"Why n-n-not right now?" Charlie asked. It was his turn to tease.

"I don't have it yet."

"Why not?"

"I'm gonna take you to school and pick it up after."

"Why didn't you-you pick it up yesterday wh-while I was at school?"

"Did you forget I'm a free man in a free country?"

Charlie looked again at Mason's socks. "Man, she's-she's sure gonna be mad."

"Better eat your cereal," Mason said, glancing at the plastic clock on a wall covered with faded wallpaper. "We gotta be on the road in ten minutes." Charlie set down the comic and was concentrating on spooning cereal into his face when Doreen walked in, looking exhausted in a robe and slippers.

2

By this time, Doreen and Mason had been together twelve years, married for eleven, and Charlie'd been with them a little over five. And when it came to keeping the marriage secret, most especially from Charlie, Doreen and Mason didn't play games. There were no stolen looks, no in-jokes or winks, no cute stuff. Mason was an employee and family friend, that was all.

Still, even after so many years, one thing Mason couldn't control was how his heart skipped a beat whenever Doreen entered a room, and how it sunk seeing her so exhausted. These days she was always tired and he could only do so much to ease that burden, which threatened to drive him mad with frustration.

3

"You're up, Grandma!" Charlie said.

"Of course I'm up," she said, blinking the sleep from her eyes. "It's your birthday." She kissed the top of his head. "Happy birthday, sweetheart."

"Thank you, Grandma," he said through a mouthful of Cheerios.

"Morning, Mr. Mason," she said flatly as she opened the fridge and grabbed some orange juice.

"Morning, ma'am," he replied and then averted his eyes. He loved watching her, but couldn't. So he used his peripheral vision as she pulled a glass from the cupboard, filled it with juice, took a sip, and dropped a slice of bread into the toaster.

"We'll have a little party tonight, okay," she said to Charlie with her back to him. "Just be the three of us...that is, if you'd like to join us, Mr. Mason."

Before Mason could answer, Charlie said, "He's gonna gimme my p-present tonight!"

She turned to smile at Charlie and leaned back against the counter. "You'll get all your presents tonight. A cake, too," she promised.

"Alright!" Charlie cheered.

"If it's okay," Mason said. "Thought I'd take him to school, pick up those shower curtains over at Sheffield's, and then, since I'm in town, take an early lunch. I want to hit the library."

That made Charlie sit straight up. "Don't f-f-forget my present!"

Mason grinned. "...and pick up Charlie's present."

"You might want to pick up some new socks, too," she said, eyeing his feet, and Charlie broke out laughing.

"You be quiet," Mason said to Charlie, who obeyed, but not in spirit. Instead, he made a big show of closing his mouth, but then pointed at Mason with a spoon dripping milk and mocked him with silent laughter.

Doreen shook her head at the two of them.

Her toast popped, so she turned to deal with that and answered Mason. "Library's fine, but I do need some painting done this afternoon."

"Sure thing," he said. "I'll be back in plenty of time."

Painting was code, an invitation for an afternoon tryst while Charlie was in school.

Charlie finished his breakfast and took his dishes to the sink.

With Charlie's back to them, Mason stole another look at his exhausted wife. She was working herself to a frazzle seven days a week, and he was now at a point where he'd do just about anything to put a stop to it.

4

"You-you-you read too much," Charlie said as he stared out the pickup's window at the passing desert. "The library's boring."

"You read comic books all the time."

"Yeah, but comic books are cool. Books are boring." To emphasize this point, Charlie leaned over, closed his eyes, and snored.

"Maybe you'll feel different when you get older."

Charlie sat up like a shot, spread his arms wide, and said dramatically: "I'm already thirteen. What more do you want from me!?"

Mason busted out laughing.

5

Charlie enjoyed making Mason laugh because Mason never faked it. Charlie could tell the difference, like when his teachers faked something just to make him feel better. Mason never did that. He only laughed when something was funny.

"Actually, you might think what I'm doing at the library's pretty interesting. They got a new computer over there that's hooked up to this thing called the World Wide Web. They're holding a tutorial on it."

Charlie didn't respond.

"You know what that is? You ever hear of it?"

Charlie shook his head no. He wasn't interested.

"Yeah, me neither," said Mason. "I'll let you know."

"Okay," Charlie said, still not interested.

6

Mason dropped Charlie off in front of the Browning Public School where the boy received special education. He then headed over to Sheffield's Department Store to pick up the shower curtains, fourteen in all, one for each room.

Sheffield's was an eighty-seven-year-old, family-owned business that wouldn't live to see to eighty-eight. The All at Once's Walmarts were already on the move.

At the Browning Public Library, the librarian gave Mason and a handful of others a detailed tutorial on what she called the "internet." Even back then, when it was agonizingly slow, Mason understood he was looking at an astonishment.

Before the end of the following year, he would discover the Dark Web and the means to sell his life, which would finally put an end to Doreen working herself to death.

7

Done *painting*, Mason and Doreen lay in his bed catching their breath.

"Bet you miss smoking right about now," she said.

"We were both smoking a minute ago," he said.

Her laugh was unguarded and sexy, and he pulled her next to him so he could feel her soft skin and naked breasts against his bare chest. Holding her like this, he could inhale her perfume, feel her sweat, and sense all the life and beauty within her.

She absently rolled her fingers on his chest and began to drift off.

The sound of a car woke her. She jumped out of bed stark naked and peeked out the window.

He sure liked looking at her. He sure did.

"Mailman," she said, disappointed it wasn't a customer.

She fell back into bed.

"I suppose I should get those shower curtains up," she sighed.

"Come on," he said. "I can take care of that tonight. You got Charlie's birthday party. Then you gotta go to work. Why don't you give yourself a break for a few minutes?"

"Okay," she replied, already sounding sleepy.

As she slept in his arms, he tried not to think about the gray in her hair.

8

Charlie's party was held around back in the picnic area Doreen built a lifetime ago. No one except them used it anymore.

Mason grilled cheeseburgers while Doreen brought out a cake she'd covered with thirteen candles and a sparkler, which delighted Charlie. The fact it was still daylight didn't stop him from snatching up the sparkler and running around the desert with it. Mason would never forget the sight of it, the innocence.

Doreen was in her work uniform, yellow and white polyester, and couldn't stay long. She wanted to attend a late Mass before her shift at the mall began.

After the sparkler burned out, Charlie ran back all smiles and out of breath. "I-I-I think it's present time, Grandma. Wh-what do you think?"

Doreen answered by handing him a nicely wrapped box, which he ripped open and gasped at the sight of: "Playstation!" he shouted. He quickly set it down and ran into her arms. "Thank you, Grandma. Thank you! Thank you!"

With Charlie's hands still wrapped around her waist, she put hers on his shoulders and gently leaned him back so she could peer down into his face, and in that face she saw Maya, saw everything the maternal side of her cherished and loved. That was why, after telling Charlie a hundred times they couldn't afford a videogame console, she'd sold the last valuable thing she owned: the wedding ring from her first marriage.

"You're welcome," she said. "And it comes with two or three games, and there's—"

"I-I-I know! I know!" He gave her another quick hug and then snatched the box so he could hold it in the air and look up at it as though it were a mysterious treasure.

"Can we-can we set it up tonight?" he asked Mason. "And you can p-p-play me!"

"Sure thing," Mason said as he removed the burgers from the grill and slid them onto the buns.

"You've still got a bedtime," Doreen said.

"I know, Grandma," Charlie said like he was annoyed, which cracked Mason up.

The three of them settled in for a rare meal together. The conversation was easy and full of laughter. Charlie knew all about his Playstation and kept telling Mason how cool it was and what a good time they were about to have.

Charlie was so excited, he was halfway through his cake before he remembered something—"Hey," he said to Mason with yellow frosting on his chin, "wh-where's your p-p-present?"

"Where's *my* present? Someone got me a present?"

"Ha ha. Ver-very funny. That's not-not what I mean."

Doreen watched her two men—which was how she thought of them—and then remembered the time. She had to leave in a few minutes.

"Did-did you forget to-to go and buy my-my present?" Charlie asked. Now he really was worried.

"Course not. I'll be right back." Mason pulled himself out of the picnic table and disappeared around a corner.

After Mason was out of earshot, Charlie turned to Doreen with a conspiratorial face. "Do you-do you know what it is?"

"I do," she said.

He leaned in and whispered, "You can tell me."

She pointed behind him and said, "Look for yourself."

Charlie turned as Mason rounded the corner carrying a small puppy. The boy was speechless. His wide eyes and slack jaw did all the talking.

The pup was black, brown, and yellowish, all mutt—a castaway Mason adopted from a shelter.

The dog reminded Mason of Hok'ee and Doreen of Kiefer.

Still speechless and not wanting to spook the pup with any excited movements, Charlie slowly got up from the table to meet his new friend.

"Hello, little puppy," Charlie said, as he gently stroked the top of its small head.

With Charlie distracted, Mason and Doreen broke their rule.

"I love you," she mouthed.

He replied with a wink.

Charlie named the pup Wolverine, "Wolfie" for short, and forgot all about the Playstation, at least for the night.

9

Under a starry sky, Charlie and Mason sat on metal chairs outside the motel office.

Wolfie was in a deep and peaceful sleep on Charlie's lap.

"You know why Wolfie can sleep on your lap like that?" Mason asked with a low voice so as not to wake the dog.

"Why?" Charlie whispered.

"Because he already feels safe with you. He already trusts you enough to close his eyes and sleep. He knows you'd never hurt him, or let anything else hurt him."

"I would nev-never h-h-hurt Wolfie," Charlie whispered, and at the time he meant it as much as he'd ever meant anything.

"Dogs are a big responsibility," Mason continued. "You're responsible for a whole life now. Not only that, you're about to be the single most important thing in Wolfie's life; the center of his life, even if he's not the center of yours. That means you have to be kind to him, take care of him, play with him, and love him. If you don't, you'll break his heart."

"I'll love-love Wolfie forever," Charlie whispered.

"I know you will."

There were no customers tonight, so it was just the two of them. After taking in some comfortable silence, Charlie asked quietly, "Did-did you-you ever have a dog?"

"Long time ago, I did," Mason answered. "Little mischief-maker named Hok'ee."

"What ha-happened to him?"

"He got old." After a pause, Mason added, "Sometimes when dogs get old, they go off to die on their own."

"Why?"

"I don't know. Might be that's how much they love us. They want to spare us that part."

Charlie started to cry.

Mason put his hand on the boy's shoulder. "What's wrong?"

"I don't want Wolfie to die."

"That's not something you have to worry about for a long, long time."

Charlie used the back of his sleeve to wipe his nose. Then he leaned over and kissed the sleeping pup on the top of its small head.

PART FIVE

THE LAST STORIES

Charlie's Wife

1

Only a few weeks had passed since Mason sold his camper and entered the start of what would be fifteen years of underground seclusion in his safehouse. By this time, Charlie had become the most efficient of murderers and Vicki, Charlie's wife, once again found herself living with the dread of knowing he would soon return home.

2

All her life, Vicki Pearce had been The Ugly Girl.... Her head was too big for her body and topped with dirty blonde hair the texture of straw. Her nose spread across her face like it had retired from boxing with a losing record. She stooped when she walked, was flat-chested, and, except for bony hips that protruded like something from a cartoon, painfully thin. Her arms appeared to be three inches too long and came to a stop at thick hands better suited to a working man.

Her childhood had been hell.

In grade school, the boys announced her presence with animal sounds and pantomimed vomiting. The girls dubbed her "Clyde," after an orangutan in a Clint Eastwood movie.

In high school, the girls continued to call her "Clyde," but now the boys took her to the quarry or behind the local Qwik-Shop. They knew they could have their way with Vicki Pearce, and sometimes they took turns.

You see, even if it was a bunch of drunken and desperate boys thrusting away on top of her and walking away with glassy eyes filled with self-disgust, in that moment Vicki Pearce was wanted.

After high school, she became a whiskey-voiced barfly and the town slut, the last woman chosen at closing time. Drink and drugs could only blur that self-hate for so long, and at age thirty, she was institutionalized after a suicide attempt. Upon her release, she gave up on everything—drugs, alcohol, even the hope of escape through suicide—and resigned herself to a solitary life of getting by. Seven years later, she was living alone, still clean and sober, and mopping floors at the local community college. There she met Charlie—handsome, charming Charlie.

He was taking a couple of financial courses and would sometimes join her outside on her smoke breaks. He was funny and flirtatious, ridiculously good-looking, and, at first, Vicki refused to allow herself to believe he might actually like her.

On their first date, he spent the night. On their second, he said "I love you." A few weeks later they were married and the months-long honeymoon that followed was something beyond her dreams. Together, on Charlie's motorcycle, they traveled the country. It took a while for her to get used to his nighttime schedule and she didn't like him disappearing for days at a time to "go to work," as he put it. But Charlie was still nice then. He'd only hit her a few times.

3

A few years ago, after they'd purchased a house on the outskirts of Chicago, things began to change. He'd beat her for laughing too hard or for not laughing enough. He'd beat her for teasing him or for patronizing him.

Sex was the worst. No, that wasn't the worst, that wasn't even close to the worst.

Early on, when they were still dating, after they'd made love and he was stroking her bare back, Charlie told her she was beautiful. At that moment, Vicki felt more love than she'd ever felt for anything or anyone. So she told him about the cruel girls, how they'd called her "Clyde."

Now Charlie called her "my monkey."

That was the worst.

4

God, she hated him.

There were no good times anymore. There was only the horror show of walking the edge of a straight razor to humor him, to stay alert to his mood swings, and to make damn sure to convince him she was having fun...and an orgasm.

Life with Charlie was exhausting and wretched, and were it not for the oasis of his long absences, she would have long ago killed herself.

Each time he returned, he'd force her back on the heroin, but as soon as he left, she'd stop. Withdrawal was grueling and worth it, worth all four days of the puking, shitting, yawning, sweating, twitching, and insomnia.... As sick as she was, Vicki would still lift herself out of bed to start cleaning. Until the drugs sweated out of her system, she scrubbed her house into a home. This she saw as a purifying ritual that delivered her into a clean life.

5

When he was home, Charlie partied 24/7, so when he finally left to "go to work," the house was a greasy explosion of bottles, pizza boxes, cans, wrappers, needles, dust, grime, vomit, dirty dishes, dirty clothes, roaches, filthy bathrooms, and unchanged linens. Everything stunk, everything was tainted and stained, so no matter the weather, Vicki threw open windows and scrubbed and scoured and then scrubbed and scoured some more.

She pulled everything from the cabinets, from the closets. She pulled out the appliances and cleaned behind those. If only fire could remove Charlie's filthy presence, she would clean like fire—every corner, every shelf, the floors, the walls, even the lightbulbs.

Everything except Charlie's office.

She never entered his basement office. Not once. Not ever. That was off limits. That was a death sentence. Oh, he'd tried to trick her. Sometimes he'd deliberately leave the door wide open. But she wasn't stupid. Nobody was that stupid.

6

Vicki had no idea Charlie was the Plague. By now, she certainly knew he wasn't what he claimed—some sort of freelance consultant. Between his sadistic cruelty, his secrecy, and all that money, she was certain he was a criminal. Nothing else made sense. Why else would he want the house, his car, bank accounts, and all those safe deposit boxes stuffed with cash in her name?

7

After she'd finally kicked the skag and purified the house, Vicki could live a clean life, so she did. Every morning, she'd wake before the dawn and make a mug of tea. Then, as the sun rose, she'd sit out on her stoop and watch her middle-class neighborhood come to life. Off to work, off to school, off to run errands; shoveling in winter, mowing in summer, raking in fall.... The simple innocence of it all.

Then it was time for a walk, a long, brisk walk accompanied by an audio book—always a classic. Something like *Crime and Punishment* or *Moby-Dick*, Shakespeare or Hemingway. *To improve the mind*, she thought.

She'd lunch at a small deli where the staff knew her and greeted her warmly. This was followed by a nap and an evening of old movies. She loved old musicals, especially the ones where Fred chased Ginger and sang about the way she looked tonight.

The days would fly by, and as Charlie's inevitable return loomed, dread slowly filled her insides.

She prayed he would die in some terrible accident that would allow her to keep the money and live like this forever. But he always came home, and upon his arrival the routine never changed. He'd want sex, something to eat, and then he would sleep for a long time, at least a day, sometimes two, and while he slept, she was expected to prepare for the relentless party that would begin the moment he woke.

Narcotics had recently been legalized and were sold through government-run dispensaries. There, she'd spend thousands on a smorgasbord of heroin, meth, crack, coke, pills, peyote, you name it. Then she'd fill grocery carts with liquor, junk food, and Twizzlers—lots and lots of Twizzlers. All over town, Charlie's "monkey" would pick up the latest videogames, sex toys, and whatever else he demanded. And then, like a lumbering monster returned from the dead, he would rise, and the horrible, exhausting, loud, frenzied, empty orgy would begin and not end until it was time for him to leave again.

8

As bad as things had always been, they were worse now.

During their first year in Chicago, Charlie always came home exhilarated, like a man returning from a job well done. He still smacked her around and lost his temper, but he could still be fun, even tender. No more. Now he came home exhausted, edgy, even haunted, like a man returning from an unjust war.

The change was sudden. After Charlie found a little gray in his hair, he snapped. *We all age*, Vicki thought. *He'll get over it.* Not Charlie. He obsessed over the fact he was aging and with every gray hair, buried himself deeper and deeper into the escape of drugs and self-pity.

Vicki could feel it all building toward something inevitable and awful, toward an end, a terrible end. But when the end came—when Charlie burst out of the bathroom and advanced on her with the loaded shotgun—it didn't feel terrible at all.

Knowing she was about to die came with an exhilarating sense of freedom, and she was able to scream "You puny-dicked faggot!" just before her head came off.

Surrender

1

Charlie was aging.

He'd suspected it for a while, but there was no question about it now. The crow's feet and flecks of gray that continued to appear in his black hair didn't lie; and the magic of the Joshua Tree wasn't going to save him.

Again and again, he'd overdosed on heroin in the desert (his favorite way to die) and returned beneath the Joshua Tree only to discover the same forty-two-year-old man with graying hair staring back at him.

Had Charlie known he would someday die of old age, which he now knew was his fate, he never would've killed all those people. There was no going back. His soul was damned, pure and simple. Mason was Satan and Satan had tricked him into selling his soul with lies about immortality.

Redemption was out of the question. His sins were too great and he didn't regret them. Not one. Not a single one of the sixty-seven men and boys he'd killed during his rampages.

As far as the public was concerned, he'd killed almost two hundred. It seemed as though the FBI was blaming him for every unsolved murder in the country. That was fine with Charlie. The notoriety had made him the number-one media star for years. Charlie loved the idea that his own government had helped him reach his goal. He was now, without question, The Thing That Comes Out of the Dark.

2

Charlie closed his eyes and felt his head swim as the drugs put a shine on everything, even his doomed soul.

The music's not loud enough, he thought, so he pulled the door open. "Turn it up!" he shouted. "Turn it all the way the fuck up!"

He slammed the door shut and his "monkey" did what she always did—exactly what she was told. The booming thrash metal melded with the drugs and, like the air was seeping out of him, Charlie's whole body slowly drooped to the floor. He sat on the cold tile, leaned back against the tub, and let his head fall back.

Through blurry eyes, he stared up at blue shower rings and remembered Mason talking about a blue shimmer. *Blue. Mason's shimmer was blue, blue, blue, BLUE!*

Charlie's shimmer wasn't blue. Every time he died, his shimmer was red. That was the difference, he knew. That was why he was aging.

Then Charlie had a new thought, one he liked a whole lot: *It wasn't Mason who tricked me. It was God who tricked me. Fucking God.*

Charlie didn't know if that was true and didn't care. He needed to blame someone, so why not God? Besides, the idea of being God's victim made Charlie feel superior to God. God was the persecutor. Charlie was the persecuted. So who held the moral high ground now?

3

Oh, how Charlie loved the drugs. Ask any junkie why they do it, and they'll tell you they're on an impossible quest to recreate that very first high. Well, thanks to his internal system recycling every twenty-four hours, Charlie had no fear of addiction, so every high *was* the first high.

The heroin warmed his face, buzzed his ears, and gave him the power to focus on the positive, on the fact that a man who's already damned has nothing to lose. So he closed his eyes, bounced his head to the music, and mentally walked himself through the plan one more time.

Step one was in his pocket: a cell phone.

Step two was in his lap: a sawed-off shotgun.

"God fucked me," he whispered through spit bubbles that popped and ran down his chin. "God fucked me and now I'm going to fuck God's creation."

Charlie laughed.

Charlie stood.

Charlie made his phone call.

Charlie exited the bathroom, racked the shotgun, and blew off Vicki's head.

4

It was late February and Sharice and Lincoln despised one another, which made an already tough job even tougher. For eleven months they'd been stuck together in this WIND-TV van, which meant eleven tense months of sitting and waiting.

Lincoln was the cameraman, Sharice the producer, and their job was to be in this van, night after freezing cold night, waiting for the police scanner to deliver a shooting or car accident or whatever other horror Chicagoans might enjoy over their morning coffee.

Chasing a story at least moved the clock. Waiting like this was the worst. Time refused to budge. It just sat there with a sullen look on its face.

5

At first Lincoln had been excited about working with Sharice. A former Miss Chicago, she was so hot that whenever he thought about how hot she was, his mind spelled it H-A-W-T.

On the first night they'd worked together, he'd shaved, ironed a shirt, and sucked in his gut the whole shift. He knew he had no chance with her. She was twenty-two, he was forty-six and twice divorced, but that's how H-A-W-T she was.

Then she opened her mouth and kept opening her mouth, and by the end of the first week he was spelling it V-A-P-I-D. By the end of the second week, he'd stopped the shaving and ironing. By the end of the month, he'd even stopped holding his farts. Instead of stepping outside, he'd just let one rip. *This one's for you, princess.*

This allowed them to arrive at an unspoken accommodation. She stopped talking, he stopped farting, and now they were in their usual position: sitting in a truce of stony silence watching the clock not move.

6

It was about halfway through that night's shift when Sharice's cell phone rang.

"Hey, Carla," she answered. "What's going on?"

While Carla spoke, Lincoln watched Sharice's face slowly expand into a state of shock. Then she turned to him with a look that could only be interpreted one way: *You are not gonna believe this.*

But Lincoln *did* believe it. Carla was the overnight news director and she never used the phone. Whatever this was, it was so big that Overnight News Director Carla did not want it going over the radio.

"Yeah, okay, good-good-good," Sharice said. "Gimme the address." Her hands shook as she punched the numbers into the van's GPS system. "But how'd you verify it was him?"

Beat.

"No shit."

Another beat.

"No shit?!"

With her hand still trembling, Sharice finished inputting the address, pressed "enter," and told Carla, "We're leaving now. Yeah, right now. We'll beat the cops, no problem."

She hung up.

Lincoln was set to explode. "What?!?"

"It's-it's the Plague. He's gonna turn himself in."

And with that, the excitement drained right out of him. "Oh, please. It's a prank."

With both hands, Sharice grabbed the front of Lincoln's wrinkled shirt. "He FaceTalked Carla and blew off some woman's head with a shotgun. Carla saw the whole thing!"

Before Lincoln could even process the madness of that, Sharice let go of his shirt and yelled, "Let's go!"

With his adrenaline starting to pump, Lincoln pressed the dashboard's "BEGIN DRIVE" prompt and the van took off with all the power of...a broken golf cart.

Man alive, Lincoln hated these ESDs. Not one mile over the speed limit would they go. Not one yellow light would they run. A career story was six miles away, the streets were empty, and here they were, put-putting along at twenty-five miles per hour. All he could do to protest was close his eyes, fold his arms, and fume.

Oblivious to this outrage against human nature, Sharice worked on her makeup. All she'd ever known were ESDs, and was therefore too young to remember the thrill of barreling down city streets in pursuit of journalistic glory.

7

But as soon as they pulled up to the address of a nice, quiet, dark house in a nice, quiet, dark neighborhood, it was obvious they had indeed been pranked.

"Too good to be true," Sharice said flatly.

"There goes your Pulitzer."

"Eat a dick."

Lincoln was just about to let one rip when they saw the flames.

"Whoa," said Lincoln, as a paralyzing chill vibrated his body.

Sharice didn't hesitate. "Get the camera! Get the camera! Get the camera!" she said, as she shot out of the van.

The fire started on the first floor and burned so quickly that by the time Lincoln was filming, the flames had made their way upstairs.

In the years that followed, Lincoln would be interviewed countless times about this moment, and would never fail to give Sharice the credit. Just the thought of being in the same zip code as the Plague scared him to pieces. But she held it together. A total pro. Told him where to stand, how wide she wanted the shot, even put her hand on his shoulder to calm him down.

Had she not done that, the moment the Plague's front door flew open, Lincoln would've ran to his mother's house.

The Plague had killed hundreds—all males—which, for obvious reasons, terrified Lincoln all the more.

And now, there he stood, big as life. Looking exactly like he did during his last four rampages, which the Plague had recorded and broadcast online. Head to toe, he was dressed all in red, including that executioner's mask.

If that wasn't bad enough, the Plague was holding a fistful of decapitated corpse.

This headless body bounced down five cement steps as the Plague dragged it behind him like a laundry bag.

By now the house was a fireball, the heat exploded some windows, and there was the far off sound of approaching sirens, which meant competing news outlets were on the way.

At the bottom of the steps, the Plague dropped the corpse and just stood there.

"Get close on him," whispered Sharice.

"Are you crazy? Look at this shot!"

It *was* a helluva shot: the red-hooded Plague standing in front of an inferno with a headless woman at his feet. Blowing a shot like that could cost him his job.

Like the seasoned pro she was destined to become, Sharice gave his arm a reassuring squeeze and whispered, "He's gonna take off the hood."

She was right, he did, and Lincoln got the shot, a shot that would become as iconic as any in history.

8

With his dark eyes blazing hate, Charlie had revealed his face to the world.

Charlie's Prophecy

1

Early the following morning, the greenspace outside the Cook County Courthouse was already a carnival.

People ate steaming churros, shouldered children, and thrust selfie sticks like broadswords to broadcast live on their social media accounts. TV cameras were everywhere. Police directed traffic. Media trucks created a Great Wall. Satellite dishes reached for the sky, as though attempting to escape the madness.

The talk was too loud, the laughter too frequent. Political slogans were chanted and every familiar face that entered or exited created a melee as people fought for position to obtain autographs and photos.

The biggest hit of the day was a chimp named Macbeth who wore a red executioner's hood, did back-flips, and posed for photos.

Souvenir stands sold t-shirts emblazoned with the Plague's red executioner's mask—which was now as famous as any mask worn by Hannibal Lecter or Jason Voorhees.

There were a few people—too few—who had the decency to look over this spectacle as though it signaled the beginning of the end of the world.

Of course, the "Plaguers" were there, some two dozen members of a small but growing and vocal cult who identified themselves with neck tattoos of the Plague's red mask.

The media loved the Plaguers, couldn't get enough of them, and a Plaguer spokeswoman, who'd become a familiar face on cable news, spewed her usual talking points into a bank of hungry cameras and microphones.

"We certainly don't approve of his methods," she explained. "But the Plague kills only males and the patriarchy must come to an end."

Conveniently forgotten in those talking points was the fact that, less than twelve hours ago, the Plague had decapitated a woman, his own wife, with a shotgun.

The Plaguers saw the Plague as a real-life superhero, someone who did what he wanted, believed in nothing, consumed national media attention, spread chaos, and successfully eluded the authorities.

2

Of course, the Plaguers had no way of knowing—not that knowing would have made any difference—that the FBI task force in charge of the Plague case (headed by Special Agent Jerome Byrne) had identified and located Charlie years ago. But in order to keep public fear stoked, nothing had been done to stop him.

Had the Plague not surrendered himself, a federal government eager to increase its control over a terrified population desperate for security, would've allowed him to rampage for however long he wanted.

3

As the Plague's court appearance neared, the crowd grew so frenzied that by the time it was all over, the greenspace would be stomped into mud and its four small trees destroyed by memento hunters who'd stripped and snapped them bare.

Inside was little better.

4

The largest courtroom in the Cook County municipal building was so gorged with the clamor of humanity, one columnist would later describe it as "a jar of ants shaken by a malicious boy."

The gallery was packed with hundreds of Chicago residents who'd waited outside through a cold and drizzly night for the chance to witness history.

The jury box was jammed with reporters and cameras from all over the world.

The bailiffs demanded quiet. No one listened.

The judge entered, took his seat, and pounded his gavel. No one cared.

It was only the opening of a door that delivered silence.

Led by three guards, the Plague stepped into the courtroom with a face full of smug defiance and a look in his eyes that said he had a secret. In the ten hours since his arrest, Charlie had not said one word, not even to his attorney, a young woman who waited for him behind the defendant's table.

The Plague was dressed in prison orange, which many found unsettlingly close to the red garb he'd worn during his recorded massacres.

The guards—two men and one woman—were in over their heads, and knew it. All three had dreamt of becoming police officers, but were too heavy to qualify.

As instructed by the judge, the guards stopped for a few moments to allow the media to get their pictures.

The Plague stood there. His presence transfixed the room. With his lean build, salt and pepper hair, and dark eyes, Charlie had the undeniable charisma of a leading man. No one breathed. No one blinked.

Then the judge ordered the media to stop with the pictures and the room quieted. The only sound was the rhythmic *click-clank* of Charlie's handcuffs and ankle chains as the bailiffs led him to the defendant's table.

5

This spectacle wasn't confined to the courtroom. The whole world had come to a stop. People everywhere were glued to their screens. Many felt a sense of relief it was over. Too many, though, felt a sense of loss.

For five years, fed by a craven media selling fear for both profit and at the behest of the government, millions had embraced the adrenaline rush of every real and manufactured twist and turn in the Plague case. But the story was coming to an end and many realized they had nothing in their lives to fill that hole.

For the time being, though, they pushed those feelings aside. This was their moment. Climax had been achieved. The Plague had been apprehended and here he was....

Charlie was nothing like anyone had expected. How could he be? No one could live up to all those years of hype, certainly not a trim, nice-looking man in his early forties.

Charlie's good looks alone would have swelled the ranks of the Plaguers. But it would be the fulfillment of his coming "prophecy" that would, at long last, give millions of godless Americans their god.

6

Click-clank. Click-clank. Click-clank. Charlie took his position next to his attorney, a young public defender named Tammy Brazil who'd been temporarily assigned to handle the bail hearing. She offered her client an uneasy smile. He stared right through her and then turned to face the judge.

The hearing was a formality. There would be no bail for the Plague.

The judge called for the rubber-necking spectators to be seated and after everyone complied, he began the formalities.

Representing the state was the camera-hungry district attorney, who identified himself for the record. Tammy Brazil identified herself for the defense. The charges were read against "John Doe" (other than the FBI's upper echelon, no one knew Charlie's true name). There was one count of homicide and one count of arson. More charges were expected to be filed later.

And then came the moment everyone was waiting for—would the Plague speak?

"How do you plead?" the judge asked the defendant.

Charlie said nothing.

The judge waited.

Tammy side-eyed her client.

A spectator cleared his throat.

The judge waited some more.

Tension stretched across the room.

Tammy whispered, "Do you want me to—" and Charlie finally spoke. One word only, with a voice that was calm and certain. "No," he told her, and then went silent again.

The crowd stirred.

The judge gently tapped his gavel.

The crowd quieted.

"I need a plea, counselor," said the judge.

Tammy swallowed hard and turned to her client.

Charlie just stood there.

"Counselor?"

As confused as anyone, Tammy said, "Your honor, my client doesn't want—"

"ON EASTER MORNING, I WILL APPEAR AT HOLY LIFE CATHE-DRAL HAVING RETURNED FROM THE DEAD."

Charlie hadn't screamed or shrieked those words. Instead, from somewhere deep inside, the words had thundered from him, and, after making that terrible promise, he again went mute.

Eyes widened.

Mouths swung open.

A chill slithered up the room's collective spine.

Even the judge, who'd seen it all after eighteen years on the bench, was spooked. But he was also determined not to let this proceeding turn into a circus.

"Is your client going to enter a plea," he asked, "or shall the court enter one for—"

"ON EASTER MORNING, I WILL APPEAR AT HOLY LIFE CATHE-DRAL HAVING RETURNED FROM THE DEAD."

Each word boomed from the walls, boomed through television speakers and ear buds. And this second helping of that blasphemous prophecy unnerved the world even more than the first.

Before the silence could get too eerie, the judge again banged his gavel, called for order, and decided some levity might break through the tension.

"Young man," he said, "you can't return from the dead if you're not dead."

There were a few chuckles.

Only a few.

"So how do you plead?"

Silence.

"Counselor?"

More silence as Tammy looked on helpless.

The judge had had enough. "The court will enter a plea of—"

This time Charlie turned himself around so he could look directly into the eyes of the world through the television cameras.

"ON EASTER MORNING, I WILL APPEAR AT HOLY LIFE CATHE-DRAL HAVING RETURNED FROM THE DEAD."

"Okay, okay, that's enough of that," said the irritated judge. "The court will enter a plea of 'not guilty.' Now get him out—"

And that's when Charlie made his move.

7

The world watched as Charlie calmly turned to his attorney, lifted his cuffed hands in the air, spread his chained arms apart, and then threaded poor Tammy through those arms, trapping her in his embrace. He yanked her close and tilted his head as though to kiss her, but instead tore into her throat with his teeth.

For a moment, the swiftness of Charlie's move froze time. Everyone looked on in shock, like it couldn't possibly be real.

One reporter wordlessly stepped onto a chair for a better look, while a number of spectators, in a sort of trance, brought out their phones to record the event.

A woman was heard to say, "Will you look at that."

And then the place detonated.

As though the floor were giving off electric shocks, people screamed and shrieked, stumbled about and thumped into one another.

When the bailiffs finally rushed over to pull Charlie off his shrieking attorney, it was too late. He had her in a bear hug and the roly poly bailiffs only got in each other's way.

Already there was so much blood, the floor was slippery with it, and the bailiffs couldn't capture the leverage necessary to pull Charlie from his doomed victim.

Blood spritzed and splashed out of Tammy's neck as she squealed in pain and terror. Only after Charlie found her vocal cords did she go quiet.

Then it became a scene from a grisly silent movie comedy: three chubby guards slip-sliding on a blood-covered floor, one trying to pull Charlie off, the other two beating him with nightsticks. Then the biggest one lost his footing and all three tumbled to the ground like bowling pins.

One guard then made the mistake of pulling Charlie to the floor with them, which only increased Charlie's advantage. He was now dead weight on top of his prey, and even though Charlie knew she was dead, he kept chewing and tearing as though she wasn't.

Finally one of the bailiffs pulled a gun, shouted at everyone to get the hell out of the way, and blew out the side of Charlie's head.

Charlie's gore hit a network anchor, who would broadcast throughout the day and night without cleaning himself off.

Enough of Charlie's skull had been blown away that his brain slowly oozed out until it was stopped by the floor.

His glassy eyes stared off into oblivion.

The Plague was dead.

8

On Easter morning, I will appear at Holy Life Cathedral having returned from the dead.

And six weeks later, on that Easter morning, Charlie fulfilled his prophecy.

Fifteen Years Later...

1

Almost exactly fifteen years after Charlie's world-shaking act of Easter morning blasphemy, Mason arrived at the outskirts of Tucson looking like hell. The desert's heat, sand, and wind had ravaged his appearance. His clothes were near rags, which was actually a good thing. After fifteen years of seclusion, Mason had no idea what kind of world he was about to enter and looking like a bum was the safest way to find out. If there was one constant throughout history—if there was one surefire way to remain invisible and unbothered—it was to assume the role of the unwanted, of the castoff.

Walking to Tucson had not been the original plan, nor, for that matter, had he planned on leaving his safehouse at all. Just as he was not the type to slow at the scene of an accident, Mason had no desire, not even after fifteen years, to take the temperature of the world.

As a witness to the past, to the rise and fall of many civilizations, Mason knew the All at Once was not immune from the arc of history that proved affluence was followed by decadence was followed by decay was followed by collapse.

Long before he'd sold his camper for gas money and retreated underground, this civilization's decay stage was well underway.

He'd ventured out of his safehouse for only one reason. After fifteen years of days spent underground with his books and evenings spent wandering about the desert, his restlessness had returned—not like before, nothing like that. But something within said the time had come to sit by Doreen's gravesite and lay his hand on her marker.

The increased desert patrols had forced him to take this route, which was more than fifty miles out of his way. The original plan had been to head straight to Browning, and he'd spent nearly two weeks trying. But he would only get so far before the Bureau of Land Management patrols showed up. His knowledge of the area allowed him to elude arrest, but past a certain point there were no hiding places, just miles of wide open space. Luckily he knew of a route to Tucson with plenty of caves, caverns, gullies, and crevices.

2

As he made his way into one of Tucson's outlying suburbs, one change was already apparent. The city had experienced enormous growth. A skyline that once had shown off only a few tall buildings was now bursting with skyscrapers, and the outlying suburbs had sprawled out for miles.

What truly surprised Mason were the crows. The sky was full of them—hundreds and hundreds of blackbirds that swooped above the city.

Only they weren't crows.

Once he was close enough, he saw that they were mechanical, that they were drones—a countless number of drones. Some as small as kitchen blenders, others as large as his long dead and rusted-out pickup truck. The sky was positively alive with their to and fro, their landing and taking off.

3

He entered a suburb that was not here fifteen years ago, and it was nothing like he expected. Instead of a leafy neighborhood filled with single-family homes, schools, and parks, it was jam-packed with bland, square, twenty story apartment complexes built of colorless cement and embedded with small, barred windows.

There were no sidewalks and no lawns. Block apartment after block apartment crowded out everything and were built nearly to the edge of the narrow roads that cut through their bulk.

Mason had no choice but to walk in the street.

Almost no one was outside and those who were dashed inside or ran off at the sight of him. There were no parked cars and the only sound came from the sky, the hum of the busy drones darting about like bees gathering pollen.

What purpose the drones served baffled Mason, until one, as big as a washing machine, landed in what was labeled a "Delivery Zone."

Attached to each apartment building, these "Delivery Zones" were about the size of a two-car garage and surrounded by steel bars, like prison bars.

As the drone approached, the Delivery Zone's metal roof slid open. Using its three propellers, the drone slowly descended into the cage and delicately landed on four sturdy legs. Then, as though giving birth, and right there on a concrete pad, its bottom opened to release three boxes slapped with a yellow logo for something called "Bigtime Inc." After a quick scan of each box, the drone leapt back into the air, off to its next delivery, and the roof slid closed.

Mason had no idea what he'd just witnessed until a heavyset man—in sweatpants, socks, and t-shirt—stepped out of the apartment complex and into the Delivery Zone. There, using what looked like an iPhone, he scanned one of the box's barcodes, snatched it up, and disappeared back inside.

A few seconds later, a woman came out and did the same.

A pale and pierced teenage girl claimed the third and final box and gasped when she caught sight of Mason watching her. Then, as though realizing she was safe behind those bars, she shot him a smug glare and disappeared inside with her prize.

4

Mason aimed himself toward downtown and witnessed dozens of these deliveries. They all happened the same way. The drone landed, gave birth to its loot, and someone—usually in pajamas or sweat pants—would scurry out to retrieve their prize. The only thing that changed were the logos on the boxes. Along with "Bigtime Inc.," he saw "Food-Stuffs Co.," "Everything Inc.," "Qwik-Shopper," "Pleasure Planet," and "Dreams Delivered." But that was it, only those six.

5

If human life had not sometimes stirred outside the block apartments, Mason might have mistakenly believed he was walking through some sort of penal colony. Occasionally, he'd pass people like himself dressed in rags. Unlike him, they looked like drugged-out zombies and they prowled the streets in small packs. Wherever he or they went, windows closed and people scurried into their secure buildings.

Also, there were the driverless ESDs that slowly and quietly whirred through the streets, while their passengers sat transfixed by electronic screens. The vehicles seemed to all begin and end their journey in the secured garages beneath each apartment complex—which explained the lack of parked cars.

Mason's only friendly interaction came from an old man sitting on the back of a convertible ESD as though he were the king of a homecoming parade. He had frizzy gray hair, a long gray beard, and when he spotted Mason, a big smile burst across his face and he waved like a homecoming king.

Mason was too startled to wave back. The old guy didn't seem to mind.

6

Eventually Mason made his way into an older suburb that looked just as deserted. All the single-family homes that once stood here had been demolished and replaced with those ugly and massive apartment buildings. What had been an idyllic neighborhood complete with lawns, leafy trees, parks, and playgrounds, was gone forever.

He passed some schools and small businesses, all of them vacant and shuttered. At the site of what once was a synagogue, unmanned and massive 3D printers fabricated another block apartment.

7

The only other sign of life came from a noticeable police presence. There was no way to tell if an actual person was inside the patrol cars. The windows were blacked out. The car itself was pure white, except for a black "FPD: Federal Police Department" logo and a light-bar attached to the roof. Much to his surprise, the police didn't bother him or any of the zombies. They were free to roam and menace, which explained why everyone remained locked up.

8

The closer Mason got to downtown Tucson, the worse things got.

By way of filthy streets, Mason walked through vast tent cities teeming with drug addicts, alcoholics, stray dogs, prostitutes, mental cases, discarded children, criminals, and gangs. It was like a giant refugee camp and it sprawled for miles.

Here there was no police presence, no law whatsoever. In the wide open streets people fought, got high, had sex, defecated, and raged against whatever demons lived inside their heads.

Other than sex, the only commerce came by way of what fueled this horror: federal drug and alcohol dispensaries, where government-issued debit cards could be used to purchase everything from heroin to whiskey to lottery tickets, and it all came cheap.

And it was here where the bizarre symbol was omnipresent. In the suburbs, Mason had seen it on a random banner hanging from a window or a decal stuck to a door. But here the logo of the red executioner's mask was everywhere.

Banners and pennants stamped with the blood-red symbol flew from the ragged tents. Mason spotted it on t-shirts, shoulder patches, tattoos, and most especially the graffiti on the burned out and vacated buildings that hovered over this endless cauldron of human disaster and depravity.

The graffiti blared things like:

THE PLAGUE LIVES!
THE PLAGUE IS MY SHEPHERD
HOLDOUTS=HERETICS
CRIMINAL HOLDOUTS MUST DIE!

Looking down on all of this were the glittering skyscrapers with their outdoor malls and cafes, their leafy terraces and plush helicopters, their rooftop gardens and pools. Mason couldn't get near those, not with eight foot walls surrounding the entire area, FPD troopers everywhere, and official signs declaring it an "Executive Safety Zone."

Mason had seen enough.

He turned south.

9

It was dusk when he reached Tucson's outskirts. Here he found that every road out of town was wide open but deserted. Here the signs said:

WARNING
You Are Leaving the Federal Safety Zone
Your Government Cannot Protect You Beyond This Point
WARNING

Outside the Safety Zone's immediate limits, like a threat to anyone who dared stray beyond those limits, were burned-out homes on both sides of the weed-choked interstate. For miles and miles, fires that had obviously been allowed to rage, had ravaged neighborhoods that once reached into the horizon.

Other than the infrequent ESD, the interstate was itself a ghost. What had been four lanes of well-lit, well-traveled highway was now dark and still and slathered in graffiti:

JESUS PLAGUE SUPERSTAR
THE PLAGUE DIED SO WE CAN LIVE
HOW GREAT THOU PLAGUE
BURN THE HOLDOUTS!

Hours later, after he'd made his way past the burnt-out suburbs and into a rural area, Mason saw no more of the graffiti or Plague logos. Here, everything was slowly and inevitably being reclaimed by the desert. Mason was surprised by his reaction to this new reality. Here, the All at Once was getting its ass kicked. Here, the desert he loved was erasing the asphalt and strip malls he hated. Wasn't that what he wanted? It was; at least he thought it was. But now that it was actually happening, he felt something he'd never felt before: a lament for a lost civilization.

Maybe that had to do with Doreen. The world she'd known—the world that had once held her—was gone, and with it another piece of her.

10

That night Mason camped in one of those places he'd loathed more than any other. They'd once been everywhere. Those bloated, congested commercial strips, those four-lane nightmares of cars and commerce right off the interstate; those endless strips choked with retail signs, chain restaurants, box stores, gas stations, outlet malls, stoplights, and gridlock.

Well, those days were over. Everything here was shuttered and dark and left to rot. Broken windows, sand-smothered parking lots, nothing but the wind. The only life came from the desert animals who'd come to reclaim the land of their ancestors.

Mason sat by his fire behind a shuttered Qwik-Shop and wondered how this had happened so quickly and where Charlie might be.

That night Mason dreamt of Hok'ee and Doreen, of Lucy giving him the ring; of a tall, blue shimmer that turned into a red shimmer that turned into a bloody handprint. He dreamt of his books crumbling to dust in his hands, and then watched his hands vanish, leaving only the wedding ring, which hovered high in the air like a sun.

11

He was about thirty miles south of Tucson and five miles north of Browning when he finally saw another person. Not everyone had moved into the city. Out here, about 5 percent of the homes were still inhabited, and the people in them watchful and wary of strangers.

As he passed by, out of each occupied house, at least one resident would grab a firearm and step out the front door, but never in a threatening manner. Most didn't even look at him. Without a word, they stood there with a rifle or shotgun pointed at the ground.

After he passed, they would go back inside.

Here the graffiti was different:

GOD BLESS HOLDOUT AMERICA!
HOLDOUT OR DIE
HOLDOUT HAVEN
FUCK THE FASCIST FEDS

12

When Mason reached Browning, he found more of the same: a scattered population that never threatened, but made clear that, if he wanted trouble, he'd be handed all he could carry.

He walked through Browning's boarded-up downtown and turned east. Here he found fields of crops, barns, windmills, livestock, and people on horseback.

They're really making a go of it, he thought, but that was all he thought. After having lived here for so many years, another man might've felt like he'd arrived home.

Not Mason.

Doreen was his only home and his pace quickened as he approached the graveyard.

Home Again

1

Former Sheriff Zoey Bushnell had come to see for herself.

To be granted a travel permit, that wasn't what she'd told the government. As far as the FTB (Federal Travel Bureau) was concerned, she was here to visit her husband's gravesite. Having died just prior to the official implementation of the Safety Zones, where everyone was cremated, Quinton had been buried in Browning.

Granted, she did want to pay her respects, but her daughters were the real reason she'd left the comfort of the Phoenix Safety Zone and spent five hours in the backseat of this slow-moving ESD.

Over the past few years, all three of her daughters and their families had fled to a Holdout community in Wyoming and were urging her to join them.

That was a big ask for a seventy-seven-year-old woman who lived in a nice condo, had friends and a routine. Zoey was no Philistine. She enjoyed TV, digital books, and those wonderful apps that brought restaurant food to your door. Only a crazy person would give that up to live the rustic life of a Holdout.

I'm too old to play Little House on the Prairie.

What's more, if she left the Safety Zones, she'd lose her pension, her Social Security, and savings. Money was all digital now, cashless. You couldn't stuff it in a suitcase.

Nevertheless, she'd made this trip because she *was* considering it. She missed her family, especially those grandbabies. The thought of sharing what was left of her life with them, even if it was a life without reliable electricity, was tempting. FaceTalk wasn't the same.

The biggest hurdle was her pride. Joining the Holdouts would be an admission she'd been fooled by the government's fear mongering about *those dangerous Holdouts*. She'd even allowed the FTB's dire warnings about the horror of the lawless Holdout territories to give her nightmares. So far, though, other than a wave hello, no one out here paid her any mind.

2

With his successful "resurrection" on that terrible Easter morning, like a ghastly god, Charlie had proved to the world the supernatural was real and that only he held its power. After that, nothing was the same, and to further terrorize the country, Charlie launched a five-year murder rampage—but only in rural America.

The rural cops said that wasn't true; that the FBI was lying, was blaming every unsolved rural murder on the Plague.

No one listened, and people were so terrified and outraged by the ineffectiveness of local policing, that the federal government took over *all* policing. Then the government's message was this: *Move to the cities. Together we're safe.*

And so, the great migration began.

Knowing what she knew about Charlie, something she'd told no one other than Special Agent Jerome Byrne twenty years ago, Zoey had been among the first to flee to the city—which had worked out fine. Instead of being herded into those block apartment buildings, she'd scored a nice condo.

Then Charlie's murder-spree stopped. Just stopped. The government took credit, but warned everyone to remain in place lest he return. That was ten years ago. No one has seen or heard from Charlie since.

3

"Make that left up ahead there," she told the ESD. Feeling nostalgic, Zoey wanted to cruise past her old house, the one she'd shared with Quinton and her daughters.

"For your safety, that is an unauthorized area," said the ESD's soothing female voice.

Zoey didn't argue. There was no point. Government satellites controlled ESD navigation and the government decided where you could and couldn't go.

A few miles later they passed her old sheriff's station. "Can you at least slow down?" she asked the car. "Slowing down," was the cold response. The ESD's electric motor downshifted. Zoey peered out the tinted windows at her past, a long-abandoned sheriff's station. Then Zoey thought of something. "Hey, roll down the windows."

"Rolling down."

With a quiet whir, the windows descended and Zoey was hit with a burst of something she'd not enjoyed in forever: fresh, country air.

She closed her eyes and inhaled a deep breath. The familiar aromas filled her head with so many memories she felt dizzy.

4

With the wind in her face, Zoey took in the familiar sights of Lincoln County and realized how much she'd missed this.

Out here, there were no electric screens, no drones, no white walls, and none of the nonstop *safety alerts* blaring through everyone's phones.... Just a simple drive down a country road on a sunny afternoon.

"You probably won't get within five miles of Browning," the BTS clerk had told Zoey. "Those Holdouts don't maintain anything. They live like animals."

Another lie.

These roads had seen better days, sure. The brush on either side could use some trimming. But they were clear and the Holdouts she passed—who were either on foot, horseback, or in horse-drawn wagons—ignored her or waved.

She leaned back and without realizing it, dozed off.

5

"You have arrived safely at your destination," said the mechanical voice.

Zoey opened her eyes just as the ESD powered itself down. She'd slept hard and wondered for a second where she was. Then she saw the cemetery.

6

Zoey was expecting brush, weeds, and garbage. Instead, the Browning Cemetery, which was about the size of a shopping mall parking lot, sported neatly cut gut grass and four large flower beds bursting with color.

Someone was taking care of this place.

Under a hot, late-afternoon sun, Zoey approached Quinton's small marker. When the memories arrived, she welcomed them. The good and the bad.

She placed some plastic flowers and was about to leave when she spotted the reason the cemetery was so well tended.... About a hundred feet away, pushing a manual lawn mower and sweating under the sun, was a man in blue coveralls.

It was a long drive back, but she wanted to thank the man who was taking such good care of her husband's resting place.

When Zoey saw that this man was Joshua Mason, she let out a gasp and stopped in her tracks.

7

Mason looked up from his work and smiled at her through an unassuming face covered in sweat and dust.

"Hello," he said.

All at once, a million things flashed through Zoey's mind. For starters, she'd always been certain it was Mason and his blue shimmer that had brought Charlie back from the dead, that monster who'd—*Wait*, she thought. *My God, is Charlie here?* Feeling vulnerable and alone in the middle of a cemetery (of all places), her eyes darted from tombstone to tombstone expecting to see a man dressed in red bearing down on her.

To regain her senses, she closed her eyes, swallowed hard, and took a deep breath. Then she opened her eyes and said calmly, "You're Joshua Mason."

"Yes, ma'am. Is there something you need?"

She walked right up to him.

"You don't remember me," she said.

It wasn't a question.

Why would he remember her? Her black hair was now white and cropped close. She'd lost twenty pounds, which improved her health but deepened the lines in her face. She was an old woman now, an old woman growing angrier by the second.

"I don't. I'm sorry," he said. "I've only been here a few months and there are a lot of faces and names to rem–"

"I'm the sheriff who shot out a sixth floor hospital window so you could take a leap."

It didn't take long for his eyes to flash recognition, but before he could speak, she did.

"I got older," she said. "You didn't."

His eyes fell to the ground. As sheriff, she'd seen that look a hundred times—the look of a guilty man. But the cop that still lived inside Zoey wasn't interested in a confession. She wanted the perp.

"Where's Charlie Breslin?" she demanded. "And don't you lie to me. I know what that whole scene was about. You brought him back from the dead."

He lifted his eyes to meet hers and admitted it. "I'm sorry you had to see that, Sheriff."

"Where is he?"

"No idea. Other than a few weeks after all that, I haven't seen him."

"You haven't seen him? You don't know where he is?"

"No. Why?" he asked. "Have you seen him?"

Zoey looked to the sky for help and her anger grew. "Don't you think you should've kept a better eye on him? Don't you feel even a little responsible?"

"Responsible? He's a grown man. He wanted to live his life. What do you care?"

"What do I care!?" And then it hit her: *Mason didn't know.* He really didn't know. He had no idea what Charlie had become or what he'd done or—*Wait a minute. That's impossible.*

"Where have you been all this time?" she demanded.

"Why?"

"Tell me."

"You've seen Charlie. You know where he is."

"I have no idea where Charlie is," she said. "What have you been doing all this time?"

"Well, not that it's.... I was in the desert. So what?"

"All this time?"

"All *what* time? A long time."

Feeling a little dazed, Zoey stared into the distance.

"What are you not telling me?" he asked.

Zoey took a few breaths to compose herself. Then she turned to Mason and recognized another face—the anguished face of a parent who'd lost a child. She now knew Mason had no idea what Charlie had become or what he'd done.

That left her with a decision.

Should she tell him or not?

Easy choice.

She let him have it. Both barrels.

He didn't believe her, said she was crazy, and that's when she told him she could prove it.

The Temple
of the Red Plague

1

From the floor to the tip of its three spires, the temple stood at nearly two hundred feet and was constructed entirely of red marble. At the top of a grand staircase, eighteen-steps high, stood its wide-open entrance, a thing so grand a bus could zoom through without breaking a sweat.

Inside was 35,000 square feet of majestic, open space. And as though this were a church and not a wicked place, its endless stream of visitors spoke in hushed and reverent tones that reverberated off red walls.

There were only four pieces of art inside. One hung over the entrance. The others were embedded in each of the three remaining walls—colossal mosaics fabricated from small tiles; detailed images of The Plague, of Charlie Breslin's handsome face and malevolent eyes.

Below those images stood marble altars covered in melted black and red candles.

Although never given an official name, this profane palace became known as The Temple of the Red Plague, and its most striking feature lay right beneath your feet.

The floor was constructed entirely of thick glass and below that glass lay the preserved and burned-out ruins of the Rebel Yell Motel.

2

Takoda Woodie was fifty-nine-years-old, a grandmother, and increasingly concerned about the man in the blue coveralls.

When the man in the blue coveralls first walked in, he took only a few steps before he stopped. This wasn't unusual. First-timers were often overwhelmed by the size of the place. But then the man in the blue coveralls didn't move. Not for a long time. He stood and stared as though his eyes were lying to him.

When he finally did move, he looked dazed and unsteady. Takoda assumed he was drunk. This also wasn't unusual. The idiot Plaguers she sold her goods to were often bombed out on one chemical or another.

Takoda watched as the man in the blue coveralls stumbled along the temple's perimeter and then stopped at each image of the Plague to lay his hand on it. The look on his face never changed. He was still a man who didn't believe his eyes.

Now the man was staring down at the ruins beneath his feet and oblivious to the danger metastasizing around him. There were more than two dozen Plaguers roaming about, and they were becoming increasingly agitated by the man in the blue coveralls.

Normally, nothing would have pleased Takoda more than to watch a mob of Plaguers beat one of their own senseless. But something told her this man was different, that he wasn't one of them. So she pushed her cart across the marble expanse and parked it next to him.

He didn't notice.

Instead, he stared through the glass floor at what had been the kitchen of the manager's apartment. There among the ash and blackened wood lay a harvest gold stove and refrigerator, and a melted piece of plastic that had once been a cheap clock.

3

Takoda shoved a red kerchief in the man's hand and whispered, "Let that hang from your pocket."

The man in the blue coveralls blinked a few times and then focused on Takoda's wide, lined, and pleasant face, at her long gray hair and eyes that burned with urgency.

Now that he was close, Takoda thought he looked like a little boy who'd witnessed his dog get hit by a car.

There was no time for introductions. The Plaguers' stares were now glares. They were huddling, whispering.

"You got to let that hang from your pocket, mister," she said. "You got to fly the colors or you're gonna get jumped."

"What?" he said, like she was crazy.

"Look around, dummy."

It took a moment for the man in the blue coveralls to focus, and when he did, the growing hostility around him was unmistakable.

To a person, the Plaguers were young, dressed in red clothes ripped by trendy designers, and carrying thousand-dollar phones. Some were pierced. Some were tattooed. All were full of themselves.

It was the look on their smug faces, the arrogant mix of phony outrage and superiority that got his blood up. The man in the blue coveralls wanted to shred them, all of them, strip them to their bones, and when the Plaguers began to advance on him, he—

"Hey, it's okay," Takoda said, lifting her hands in the universal gesture of surrender. "It's his first time. He's a little overwhelmed is all."

The arrogant faces weren't so sure. Neither was the man in the blue coveralls. Both wanted blood.

With one hand still in the air, Takoda used the other to tuck part of the red kerchief in his back pocket.

"It's fine," she assured them with an even voice. "He didn't know."

Half-satisfied with the red cloth that represented fealty and half-intimidated by the crazy man in blue coveralls staring them down, the Plaguers disbursed.

4

"You shouldn't be in here if you don't know the rules," Takoda said.

"I don't give a fuck about the rules," said Mason.

"Well, then, you're welcome," she said and pushed her cart all the way across the temple and out the door.

Mason's eyes returned to the floor, to the wreckage of his past, to the ghastly truth about Charlie—the monster he'd created. His head began to swirl. Then the whole place swirled and Mason fell to his knees. The last thing he saw before blacking out was the kitchen table where a little boy named Charlie once ate Cheerios and read comic books.

5

Outside on the marble stairs, Mason sat with his head down.

"Take some deep breaths," Takoda told him.

He did and felt better.

She gave him a bottle of water from her cart. He saw the price and said, "I don't have ten dollars."

She waved him off.

"Thank you," he said, cracking the bottle. "And thank you for coming to...and...for before."

"Thank you for saying thank you," she replied.

He sipped his water and watched Takoda do a brisk business with the Plaguers, who were showing up in increasing numbers. They purchased candy, the occasional "Temple of the Red Plague" souvenir t-shirt, but mostly they wanted the red and black altar candles. Payment was completed by touching the watches strapped to their respective wrists.

Mason scanned the dirt parking lot, what had once been an empty piece of desert where Charlie ran around with a sparkler on his birthday. Zoey sat waiting in the back of her ESD. He lifted a hand. She returned the wave.

There was a lull in the action, so Takoda took a seat.

"You're not one of them," said Mason.

"I just take their money," she said.

He turned to look her over and said appreciably, "Navajo."

"Born on the rez, gonna die on the rez," she answered. Now it was her turn to study him, but it did no good. "Your people.... I don't know. South of the border, that's for sure. Way south, I'd say."

Mason shrugged and drained the last of the water.

A convoy of three, shiny ESD SUVs turned into the dirt lot and parked. Nine Plaguers exited those vehicles, all dressed alike—up to their necks in red. Somehow they managed to look intimidating and ridiculous.

"Things this crazy where you're from?" asked Mason.

Nine smug faces and eighteen drugged-out eyes started up the stairs.

"Nothing changes on the rez," she said.

"That's good."

"I didn't always think so," she confessed. "'What's wrong with progress?' I used to wonder. But now that I see all the loco in progress.... There's wisdom in holding on to the old ways."

The red-clad mob brushed past them.

Takoda looked at the low sun and stood. "Time to go," she said, covering her cart with a tarp. "Neither of us should be here after dark."

Mason got to his feet. "What happens after dark?"

As if to answer that question, a pickup rolled in with a live goat in the back. The driver, a heavyset woman covered in tattoos and wearing a red cape, used a leash to pull the goat from the truck and lead it to the stairs.

"I've never been stupid enough to find out," answered Takoda.

Mason turned himself around to stare up at the temple.

"It was just here one day," she volunteered. "The real mystery is why here?"

"No one knows?" Mason asked.

"Place was owned by an old woman and her brain-damaged grandson. That's all anyone knows. What could they have to do with the devil?"

6

The sun was nearly gone and the sky was the color of a bruise. With its soft, electric hum, the ESD crept along Old Highway 661.

Mason sat in the passenger seat.

Zoey sat in backseat knowing she'd made a mistake. The silence coming from Mason felt like something violent.

Me and my big mouth.

Had she not said anything, Mason might never have discovered the truth. There was hardly any internet among the Holdouts to reveal Charlie's face and the government had never made Charlie's name public. She'd let her temper get the best of her and tossed a grenade into a decent man's life.

And that was the least of her sins.

From the moment he'd returned to the ESD carrying the truth she'd shoved in his face, Zoey knew something terrible had been unleashed. She didn't know what exactly. What she did know was that this time she would accept responsibility. Wherever this runaway locomotive was headed, she'd be there, right there, at the end of the line.

7

"You need to tell me everything," Mason said without turning around.

From the backseat, she did. She told him everything, all of it: of the bus station and the massacres, of Charlie's wicked courtroom prophecy and his fulfillment of that prophecy on an Easter morning that changed everything forever; of how no one has seen or heard from Charlie in more than a decade.

It was dark when she finished and Mason remained quiet for a long time—right up until they pulled up to the cemetery and stopped.

The ESD announced their arrival and shut down, lights and all.

In all that dark and quiet, Zoey listened to the crickets and waited for what she knew was coming. The knowing had given her time to come up with an answer. So after Mason asked, she said, "There's one person who might be able to help."

Confrontation

1

Had Zoey not known this was Jerome Byrne sitting across from her, she wouldn't have recognized him. That lean, young, overeager FBI agent she'd last seen two decades ago was now fifty pounds overweight, balding, jowly, and obviously quite comfortable with political power and the lavish surroundings of his four bedroom, D.C. townhouse.

When Mason looked at Jerome, all he saw was a sack of shit.

2

The years had been good to Jerome Byrne—at least professionally. He was now the FBI's Deputy Director, and the presidential candidate who was currently way ahead in the polls had pledged to make him the big kahuna: the Director-Director.

All those years as the agent in charge of the Plague case had blasted his career into orbit. Jerome had gone above and beyond to panic the country into something shipshape, and for his loyalty to the cause of the state, his climb into Washington, D.C.'s upper echelon had been swift and sure.

There were still the Holdouts to deal with, but those chess pieces were headed in the right direction. In the upcoming election, the Safety Caucus—a bipartisan group of Republicans and Democrats—was expected to win enough state legislatures to amend the U.S. Constitution. The amendments necessary to "legally" bring the Holdouts to heel were already written.

Jerome had remarried six years back. She was a young and pretty senator's daughter named Rebecca who knew how to properly load a dishwasher.

When Brittany asked for the divorce, Jerome didn't argue. When she demanded custody of the three kids, he didn't resist. When she fled with the kids to a Holdout community in West Virginia, he let her. Serving his country was what mattered, and personal dramas—like ugly custody battles—damage careers.

Jerome didn't miss Brittany or the kids. He didn't think of them at all. Well, sometimes he did...the holidays mostly.

Even though she'd ambushed him, Jerome was glad to see Zoey. He had no idea why. He didn't like anyone else, not even his new wife. Zoey he'd always liked. His affection for her had never waned. That was how she knew where to find him—the Christmas cards.

3

When Rebecca entered, Jerome had been where he always was this time of night, sucking on Tums and working in his study. "There's someone at the door who says she knows you...a Zoey Bushnell?"

At first, Jerome was delighted. "Zoey!" he said with a grin. Then the instincts that had served him so well launched a flare. *What could she want?* He decided that whatever it was, he didn't appreciate being caught off guard.

"Tell her I'm not here," he said. "She can email me."

Rebecca understood and exited.

A minute later she returned.

"She told me to tell you she brought someone with her. A guy."

Jerome looked up from the computer, removed his glasses, felt his blood pressure spike, and popped another Tums.

"Who?"

"All she told me was that 'he's the man who created Charlie Breslin.'"

4

The greetings had been awkward.

Mason and Jerome didn't shake hands.

Zoey gave Jerome a quick hug, but Jerome couldn't take his eyes from Mason, who looked exactly like he had in that interrogation room a generation ago.

Purely by reflex, Jerome's Machiavellian mind began to plot a series of moves to use Mason's immortality to America's advantage.

Uncomfortable and confused by the silent tension, Rebecca gestured Mason and Zoey to a large leather couch.

Jerome settled behind his imposing desk.

"I'll leave you to it," Rebecca said, and closed the door behind her.

"So what can I do for you?" asked Jerome.

5

While Mason listened, Zoey told Jerome the whole story and ended it with this: "And you're the only person I could think of who might know something."

"Why would you want to find him?" asked Jerome.

"Are you joking?" said Zoey.

"There's nothing funny about this," said Jerome. "In our business, when a serial killer stops killing, we call them dormant. The Plague's been dormant ten years. What makes you think you should poke someone like that with a stick?"

Zoey's hackles shot right up. "He murdered over two hundred peop—boys, children.... You can't count on someone who lives forever to remain dormant forever." She turned to Mason for back up. He was no help. He sat there like a spectator at a ballgame.

"Hey," said Jerome, leaning forward on his desk. "I hunted that maniac for years. No one has to remind me what he did. Every time he killed, that was on me. But that's the thing.... You *can't* stop him. Have you thought about that, about the fact you can't kill him? Because thanks to that man"—Jerome pointed to Mason, who didn't respond—"Charlie will only rise again from the dead. Yeah, sure, you can try to lock him up, try to control him—you don't think we thought of that? But eventually he *will* find a way to escape through suicide. Wherever he is, he has stopped, he is dormant, and that's the best outcome."

Zoey couldn't believe what she was hearing. "You're supposed to be a cop!"

"I am a cop! *Safety* is my priority," he said and then leaned back in his chair with an air of triumph. "What's yours?"

6

Right then, Jerome was pretty proud of himself. He'd put on a helluva show. He had to. The presidential election was three months away and the voters were focused on what the government wanted them focused on—bringing those dangerous and unpatriotic Holdouts to heel. The last thing this country needed was a distraction; much less the surprise return of the same Plague the government had taken credit for stopping.

Yep, Jerome's masterful, on-the-fly performance mixed with the exact right amount of personal umbrage and impeccable logic had strangled this potential complication in the crib.

At least that's what Jerome was thinking until Mason asked: "You about done?"

And because he'd been luxuriating in his slam-dunk rather than formulating additional arguments, Jerome had no response. So, yeah, he was done.

"Good," said Mason. "Let's save everyone's time and get to it. You know what I am. You know what I'm capable of. So you're either gonna give us everything we want, or I'm gonna burn you to the ground."

Jerome went cold. After a few speechless moments, his gears managed to turn a little and came up with this: "You weren't around," he said with a less than confident voice. "You were underground *hiding*. You don't know how it was. And now you want to risk launching him on another murder spree?"

Mason was having none of it. "Would you prefer to launch *me* on a murder spree?" he said. "Because mine starts with coming across your desk."

Jerome suddenly felt something he hadn't since losing that high school debate a lifetime ago: bulldozed, bested, embarrassed.... Jerome's professional and social status held no sway with this belligerent man. He'd never faced such a thing. And that wasn't the worst of it. The worst was knowing this man could see right through him, and that what he saw was the truth: that without the shield of state power, Jerome was nothing, not even worthy of respect in his own home.

With his face flush and throat tight, Jerome managed to croak, "You still haven't explained how you'd stop him."

Before Mason could fire back, Zoey stepped in.

"Okay, okay, that's enough," she turned to Mason. "This is not the way we—"

With his eyes still on Jerome, Mason reminded her, "You opened this box, Sheriff."

"I did," said Zoey. "That's true. But how you intend to stop him is a good question. Or can you use some of that blue magic of yours?"

Despite everything, Mason broke into a smile and then chuckled. "There's no magic," he said, shaking his head at the ridiculousness of it.

Now that Zoey was on *his* side, Jerome got a second wind: "Then how do you intend to stop someone who can't be stopped? What's your plan?" he demanded.

"To come across that desk if you don't start talking."

She wasn't sure why, but Zoey now believed Mason did have a plan, so she joined Mason in staring Jerome down for an answer.

7

Jerome knew where Charlie was. Hell, he'd always known where Charlie was. The only question was—should he fess up, or spill just enough to get them out of his house? After a few mental calculations, he realized he had no choice. Mason was an obvious madman who would never stop complicating his life until he got what he wanted. And if Mason ever discovered Jerome lied to him.... No, there was only one thing to do.

"An island," said Jerome. "You'll find him there."

"An island?" said Zoey.

"How do you know?" asked Mason.

Jerome couldn't tell them the truth—that not long after Charlie moved to Chicago, the FBI had located him and chose not to stop him. Put simply, it had been decided that the massacres—while unfortunate—were worth the good that came from exploiting the panic.

"Twizzlers," said Jerome, which *was* true. Traces of Twizzlers had been found in a few of the vehicles Charlie had abandoned in those underground parking garages. From there it was a matter of manpower and the Kingdom Key.

Since he couldn't tell them that, Jerome made up a pretty good lie. "The garbage cans behind the house in Chicago survived the fire," Jerome said. "It was obvious he enjoyed this candy, so we kept an eye on purchases and followed up on anything promising."

"And Charlie had the candy delivered to his island?" guessed Zoey.

"That's right. And with the help of satellites and drones, we're keeping an eye on him. He's there now and he's not bothering anyone and you two should leave this alone."

"And *where* is *there*?" demanded Mason.

There was a pause as Jerome sucked his Tums and recalculated his options. Then he arrived at the same dead-end conclusion: that he had no choice but to tell the truth, so he did: "The Pacific. About one hundred and twenty miles off the coast of Florida."

"That's not an answer," said Mason.

"I'll give you the coordinates," said Jerome.

"We'll need travel permits, a boat," said Zoey.

"Fine," answered Jerome.

Zoey turned to Mason: "This could be over in a few days."

"No," replied Mason. "I'll need time. And from *you*," he pointed at Jerome, "I'll need a lot more than travel permits."

"Fine," Jerome said again and took solace in this lost round by reminding himself he was playing the long game.

Jerome wasn't done with Mason, not by a longshot.

8

So much time passed, Zoey began to think Mason had changed his mind about going after Charlie. Then, one morning, there he was at her condo's front door.

She'd expected an argument about her wanting to come along. But all he said was, "You still sure?"

"I'm sure," was her answer. And she was. Like Mason had said himself, she'd opened this box.

He nodded and they were off.

That was the thing about Mason, she realized. He didn't say much. But his silence never radiated tension or anxiety. It was just...*there*. Something was going on inside of him. She didn't know what, but believed it was their best chance of surviving this.

If only she had a gun.

Guns weren't allowed in the Safety Zones, not even if you were a former sheriff. So, once they were in open water, Zoey took a methodical inventory of the boat—a thirty-foot cabin cruiser—and didn't find so much as a steak knife.

Her instincts told her not to ask Mason about it. Whatever Charlie had become, Mason had once loved him like a son. It seemed cruel to suggest they might have to shoot him down. Then the thought made her laugh. *If we kill him, he'll escape*, she realized. *Can't risk that.*

Then the thought gave her a chill and she stopped laughing.

Nevertheless, she *was* enjoying herself, especially the blunt edge of the fear. Head to toe, Zoey Bushnell, even at seventy-seven, was and would always be a cop—a protector. As they motored past Cuba, she felt the setting sun on her back, the spray of saltwater in her face, and decided she would leave the Safety Zone and join her daughters in Wyoming.

Think I'll take up fly fishing, she thought, and then pictured herself knee deep in clear river water surrounded by tall trees and grandkids.

So she wouldn't have to think about not having a gun, she held tight to those thoughts.

9

Zoey was wrong about Mason. There wasn't anything going on inside of him. There was nothing down there. The moment he'd discovered the truth about Charlie, he knew what had to be done and that getting it done meant he would have to shut himself down.

So he did.

The only way through it was through it, so he numbed himself to everything but the task in front him.

He hadn't expected the old sheriff to come along, but arguing with her might have cracked the dam he'd so carefully constructed inside of himself. *She'll probably get killed*, he figured, *but that's her decision.*

Mason had made some decisions of his own: He was no longer Charlie's grandfather. He was no longer Doreen's husband. He was no longer anyone or anything. He was Whatever Was Needed to Bring It to an End.

10

The last of the sun disappeared. The boat's auto-pilot pegged their arrival at just before dawn.

Mason settled in behind the wheel, folded his arms, bowed his head, closed his eyes, and felt only one thing: the hard steel of the .38 pressed against the small of his back.

The Island

1

It was still dark when Mason killed the engine and dropped anchor about a thousand yards from where the GPS said Charlie's island was supposed to be.

Zoey peered over the bow, looking for land but saw only night.

"I don't see it," she said, and suddenly the idea her old pal Jerome—who'd blossomed into a fleshy, duplicitous D.C. rent-seeker—had sent them on a snipe hunt crossed her mind.

Mason stepped into the tender. "You don't have to come," he said.

She went.

2

The tender's electric motor was reassuringly quiet and had taken them about five hundred yards when a moonlit silhouette came into view. The island wasn't much: long and narrow and almost cut in half by a large lagoon. The wind had bent the scattered palm trees into wild-haired aliens stooping to pick up nickels. The shore was all jagged rock.

Zoey, who wasn't enjoying the fear so much anymore, said, "Maybe we should circle around and see what we're dealing with."

Mason agreed without saying so.

What they were dealing with had been ravaged by hurricanes.

Moving through the silence of this windless night, they slowly motored past three separate piers battered and broken into kindling. The house was something else. At one point, it had been a stunner, a dream home, really—a spacious A-frame with massive windows and decks that offered spectacular views of the lagoon and then the ocean beyond; the kind of place where you sat in a chaise lounge knowing you had it all. Now it resembled something that had barely survived being stepped on, something that wouldn't withstand a whisper, much less another hurricane. The windows were all shattered and there was enough moonlight to see that the inside of the house looked like the whole place had been picked up and shaken.

The one beach was covered in litter blown from the house: shingles, siding, glass, trash. The beach was exposed, but was the only place to tie up and come ashore.

3

Dawn was right over the horizon and there was no sound to cover their trek across ninety feet of open sand—no wind, no waves, just that eerie quiet.

Zoey snatched up a two-foot piece of plastic pipe.

It was better than nothing.

For the first time, Mason looked anxious and nodded approvingly at Zoey's plastic weapon.

They slowly advanced on the house.

The front door would never open. The frame was bent to hell. They didn't bother with it. There was no need. The patio door on the other side of the house had been blown out. They crouched and hurried over to a deck covered in broken glass. In all that terrible stillness, each step— each *cruunckssshht* of glass—sounded like the scream of a bank alarm.

Zoey peered inside through the patio door and saw only black. *It's so dark in there*, she thought. *Why didn't I bring a flashlight? And why the hell didn't I bring a gun?* She knew why. A flashlight would give away their position. A gun might kill Charlie, which meant he would escape and the chances of ever finding him again were zilch.

Those sounded like good reasons on the boat. Not so much here.

One more step, just *one* more, and she'd enter the Plague's world. She knew Charlie could've easily seen their approach and be in there hiding, waiting....

Zoey didn't blink. She didn't dare. A blink would give Charlie enough time to run screaming out of the dark.

A spasm of fear numbed her already chilled skin and tasted like metal. "I don't think he's here," Zoey said to no one.

Mason was already inside.

4

Mason didn't realize how light it was getting outside until he stepped into the dark of this blasted-out house.

Zoey crept up next to him. She was practically vibrating.

She had guts, he had to give her that.

He whispered to wait for their eyes to adjust to the dark. She white-knuckled that pipe and swallowed hard.

All around them water dripped. Other than their breathing, that was the only sound.

The stink was the worst: rotting garbage and mold.

"I don't think he's here," Zoey whispered a second time.

Mason didn't answer. His eyes had adjusted enough to see they were in some kind of media room. On the far wall hung a moldy movie screen and broken speakers. The floor was covered in Blu-ray discs, Twizzler wrappers, CDs, liquor bottles, crack pipes....

"Charlie, Charlie," Mason whispered with disgust, as he stepped over a shattered Playstation console and bizarre sex toy.

Zoey was right behind him and for a third time said, "I don't think he's here." Now she was saying it like a prayer.

"He's here," Mason assured her. He kept walking. She stayed put.

After a few steps, he sensed her absence and turned.

She shook her head. *No way*, that head shake said. *No fucking way*.

He gestured for her to stay put and then disappeared into the tunnel of a dark hallway.

Filled with shame and a fear heading into dread, tears streamed down Zoey's face. She was certain death was about to come screaming out of the dark, so she begged a God she'd never given much thought of for help....

And that was when she heard the scraping sounds.

5

Mason quietly made his way down the dark hall and the dam he'd built inside himself began to crack. It was all so awful. How was it possible it had come to this? How could that sweet boy—how could he have done those things and live in all this wretchedness? Mason had to stop thinking about it. *He had to.* One more thought and he'd freeze like Zoey, and then crumple.

Stealthily he moved from room to room, and every room was as wrecked as the last, except one—the room where Charlie lived and slept.

On the floor lay a dirty mattress, dirtier blankets, clothes, empty water jugs, sex books, wrappers....

There was one spot that was clean and organized: a small desk with a chair and mirror. On the desktop sat a dozen or so tiny glass bottles. Mason snatched up a few but the windowless room was too dark. He couldn't read the labels. He jammed them in his pocket and kept searching.

6

It was a long scrape was followed by a quick bump.

It sounded like this: *Scraaaaape-bump. Scraaaaape-bump.*

Fate was taunting Zoey Bushnell.

It had to be fate. There was no other explanation. Every time Zoey came up with a logical reason to dismiss the noise, fate shot her down.

Scraaaaape-bump.

Must be the wind.

There's no wind, Sheriff.

The house is settling.

Settling houses creak and groan, Sheriff.

An animal, then.

You're being ridiculous, Sheriff.

She resented how fate kept calling her "Sheriff," kept mocking her with her former title. It was cheap and manipulative. Fate was baiting her, daring her to ignore her duty.

I'm old, retired, used up. I've done my duty.

You opened this box, Sheriff.

Stop calling me Sher—

Bump-bump-bump.

A pause.

Bump! Bump! BUMP!

And then came the: *Mmmmhhhhh!! Mmmmmmhhhh!*

The noises were human; they were coming from the front of the house.

Zoey headed straight for them.

7

Mason would never forget the beauty of it.

Like a dream spun by Norman Rockwell, about fifty yards away and backed by the golden light of a rising sun, sat the silhouette of an old man in overalls holding a fishing pole off the end of a shattered pier.

After what he'd just seen, all the wreckage that symbolized a life devoted to depravity and excess, Mason didn't trust his senses. *How could this be true? How could something so—*what was the word? *So...so eloquent...survive here...?*

He watched the old man reel in his line and cast it out again.

The sight was hypnotic, and Mason stepped out the back door for a closer look.

8

The noises stopped, so Zoey stopped.

Winded from stress and moving so quickly, she stood in the middle of what had been a living room. Long ago, water had caved in the vaulted ceiling. Trash was everywhere. The stink was worse. It came from a charred dog in the fireplace, its face a black and frozen document of the horror and pain of being burned alive.

Zoey covered her nose and made her way through the garbage and glass to a blown-out picture window. It was light out now and the outdoor air was fresh. She took deep breaths and looked out over what was still an impressive view: palm trees, the lagoon, a calm blue oc—

What is that?

A white pole was sticking straight up out of the lagoon. That wasn't odd. It could've been a flagpole or signal light. What *was* odd was what the pole was attached to. She craned her neck and through some scrub saw what looked like.... Well, whatever it was, it glinted.

Careful not to cut herself on the jagged glass, Zoey lifted one leg over the window frame and then the other and stepped out onto the deck. Her view of the lagoon was no better here.

She crossed the deck to the beach and passed what looked like a pile of burnt suitcases—*like a suitcase bonfire*, she thought, and kept walking. The ground dipped for a bit and then rose, and that's when she saw it. Dotted throughout the lagoon were big, black, underwater shadows—like great white sharks frozen in place.

The sight of it stopped her right there. It was...*unnatural.*

This is wrong. Very wrong.

She remained statue-still as the numb and chill returned to grab hold of her body. That was okay with Zoey. She didn't want to move. Whatever this was, she didn't want to know.

This is bad. This is bad. This is bad.

Then she felt something. A presence. It was directly behind her. It was Charlie. Who else could it be? She could feel his humid breath on the back of her neck. She closed her eyes, steeled herself, and spun around. Her vision was blasted with the color red. She whipped that pathetic piece of pipe through the air before realizing her eyes were still closed. She opened them. There was nothing. No one. No Charlie, only that house—that crooked, battered, unspeakably awful house.

Did she really want to go back there?

No.

She turned back around.

There it was, a lagoon filled with eerie shadows.

Deep breath.

Another.

One foot in front of the other.

Okay, now we're walking. Now we're—*Oh, my God.*

At the water's edge there was nothing to block her view. She saw it all: the lagoon and the vast ocean beyond. And since the water was blue and clear, she could see what created those shadows.... Sunken boats. Dozens of them. Speedboats, sailboats, rafts, fishing boats, skiffs, cabin cruisers, wave runners—all of them laying there dead under the water.

The odd-looking pole that had drawn her here was the mast of a sailboat. The glint came from a window on that sailboat, which hadn't sunk all the way. On its way to the bottom, something went wrong. It had shifted and settled on top of another boat.

9

As Mason approached the old fisherman, the bottles in his pocket clanked to the rhythm of his stride.

The old fisherman heard this and turned.

Mason stopped.

He didn't know what to do.

So he waved.

There was a pause, and then another pause, and then the old fisherman waved back.

Mason resumed walking and the old fisherman reeled in his line and laid the pole on the pier.

Then, like you'd expect an old fisherman to do, he slowly got to his feet, slid his hands into the pockets of his overalls, and calmly waited to meet his guest.

10

Zoey didn't understand what she was looking at, what this graveyard of ships meant. Or maybe she did and chose not to.

Mason, she thought. *Mason has to see this.*

She turned and walked back to the house as quickly as her seventy-seven-year-old legs would allow. Once she reached the deck, she stopped. No way. No way in hell was she going back in there. She came up with a new plan, a better plan. She would circle the outside of the house until she found Mason or Mason found her, or—

Scraaaaape-bump.

Zoey'd forgotten about that.

Scraaaaape-bump.

MMMhhhhh!

And so, Sheriff Zoey Bushnell climbed back into the house.

11

The old fisherman had tears in his eyes and said, "Hello, Mason."

Mason had tears in his eyes and said, "Hello, Charlie."

Charlie looked awful, like an aging drag queen. Mason now knew what the bottles in his pocket were. But no amount of makeup or hair dye could cover up the fact Charlie was aging, or that he looked fifteen years older than his fifty-six years.

Mason had no idea how or why Charlie was getting older.

And then, just like the little boy he once was, Charlie wiped away his tears with back of his sleeve and Mason's dam shuddered and buckled.

"I'm sorry," Charlie said, sobbing. "I'm sorry about everything, all of it. I'm so...."

The two men embraced.

Charlie kept repeating how sorry he was.

Mason kept telling him everything would be okay, and then noticed there was no bait on that fishing hook.

12

The noises were coming from the kitchen, and what a hideous sight the kitchen was.

Scraaaaape-bump.

Everything was covered in black mold.

MMMhhhh!!!

The smell made Zoey's eyes water.

Scraaaaape-bump.

"Where are you!" yelled Zoey.

Bump-bump-bump-bump-bump.

The floor. The sound was coming from under the house.

Bump-bump-bump-bump-bump.

There! Under the kitchen table—a hatch! She dropped the pipe...

Scrape-scrape-scrape.

...and slid the table out of the way. She grabbed the hatch's handle and...

MMMhhhh!

...lifted it.

The smell.

My God, the smell.

The stench of death practically knocked Zoey over. She stumbled back gagging and then did fall, right on her butt.

Mmmmmmhhhh!! Bump-bump-bump. Mmmhhhh!

She groped around for the pipe. It wasn't there.

Scraaaaape-scraaaaape

Zoey got on her hands and knees, crawled over to the hatch, peered down, and saw....

In that fetid hole was a man and woman.

Both were gagged and tied.

Both had been bled white and had no arms.

The man was using his head to *bump-bump* the wall.

The woman was using her head to *scrape-scrape* the wall.

Lying in front of them, in a gruesome pile covered with flies, were their arms and a hacksaw.

It took only a half-second for Zoey to put it together: Charlie was luring people to his island.... He was torturing them, murdering them, burning their suitcases and pets, and sinking their boats.

13

Still hugging Mason, Charlie blubbered, "I want to go home. I just want to go home."

Mason gently pushed Charlie off him, gripped both of his shoulders, and looked him in the eye.

"That's what I'm here for, son, to take you home. We're going home."

"I love you, Mason," said Charlie.

"I love you too, son."

Charlie's thick makeup was smeared and streaked from wiping away tears. He looked freakish, grotesque. The sun revealed the gray roots in his dyed-too-black hair. He wouldn't stop crying.

"It's okay," said Mason. "It's really okay. We're going home."

"I burned it all down," Charlie wailed. "Oh, God, the things I've done! What I've done...."

With one hand Charlie rubbed his eyes in shame.

With his other hand, Charlie grabbed hold of the loaded Beretta hidden in the pocket of his overalls.

Mason was reeling. The thick makeup, the house, the aging, the hair dye, the murders.... It was too much. Too heartbreaking. Mason's dam wasn't going to survive this. How could it when all he could picture was that kid, that beautiful kid who joked and teased and ran around with sparklers. How was it possible that this pathetic, broken freak in front of him was that kid? But this freak *was* that kid and nothing would ever change that. This was Charlie, the boy Mason loved and would always love. Most of all, Charlie was part of Doreen. The only part left.

Mason felt his chest heave and he let go of a sob.

Charlie slipped his finger onto the Beretta's trigger and—

"Get away from him!" screamed Zoey as she burst out the back door. "Get away!"

Somehow, on those seventy-seven-year-old legs, she was running.

Mason and Charlie exchanged surprised looks.

Then Mason turned to face Zoey.

Charlie, trying not to laugh, pulled the gun, and hid it behind his back.

"There are people...boats...all the boats!"

Mason didn't understand. He took a few steps toward her. "What? What is it?"

"The people!" she shouted. Her wide eyes darted between Mason and Charlie.

"What people?"

Mason took a few more steps toward her. Behind him, Charlie was grinning. And why wouldn't Charlie grin? Things were about to get good.

Zoey ran up to Mason crying. "The people, there are...."

Mason grabbed her shoulders, "What peop—" And then all questions were answered when that armless couple stumbled out the back door, their faces covered in white terror, the rest of them covered in their own gore. The shock of sunlight was too much. They screamed and fell unconscious into a heap.

Silence.

Godawful silence.

Mason understood everything now. The fisherman act was a trap. The bait on that hook was Charlie, and Mason had bitten.

Paralyzed with the horror of it all, Zoey shifted her eyes from the couple on the ground to Mason to Charlie, and at the sight of Charlie she screamed, "No!"

Mason turned.

It was too late.

Charlie had the Beretta snugged under his chin. One pull of the trigger and he'd escape.

Time stopped.

No one moved.

Nothing moved.

Then Charlie threw Zoey a "fuck you" wink and that was that.

14

She was too old to go at him, but Sheriff Zoey Bushnell did anyway, and before she took two steps, Charlie shot her down. The bullet ripped into her chest. The force of it spun her around and she hit the ground face first. She laid there, her mouth moving without saying anything. Through eyes glassed with hate, she stared up helplessly as a grinning Charlie pointed the Beretta's barrel to the side of his head and placed his finger on the trigger.

Mason no longer cared about Charlie. He dropped to his knees next to Zoey. "No, no, no, no, no," he kept saying.

Zoey inhaled a raspy breathy and exhaled an order: "Stop him."

"You didn't have to shoot her," said Mason, as he gently turned her over and applied pressure to the bloody hole in her chest.

Zoey pushed Mason's hands off her and hissed, "No! Stop him!"

"I can't," said Mason.

"He can't, you stupid old bitch!" said Charlie. Then he wriggled his gun in the air and said, "This is my ticket out."

"You didn't have to shoot her," Mason repeated.

"YOU LIED TO ME!" screamed Charlie. "Look at me! I'm old! I'm gonna DIE and I'm gonna go to HELL because of YOU!"

Mason said nothing.

"You gave ME the red shimmer! The RED one! And kept the blue shimmer for YOURSELF!"

Mason had no idea what Charlie was talking about. His eyes dropped to the ground.

"Stop him," Zoey pleaded. "Stop him...."

"I can't," Mason said again.

Zoey was dying, but Charlie still taunted her. "I'm gonna pull this trigger and then, like A GOD, I'll wake thousands of miles from here! Then I'm gonna find everyone you love, you old bitch. All of 'em!"

Zoey began to cry.

Mason never took his eyes from the ground.

"No one will EVER find me!" Charlie screamed and put the gun to his head. Then he looked at Mason and made a quiet promise: "And after I'm done with her people, wait till you see what I do next."

Mason looked up at him.

Charlie smiled.

Charlie pulled the trigger.

And—

The gun jammed.

It was a semi-automatic, not a revolver. Clint Camacho could have told him this might happen.

Zoey's eyes widened with hope. But....

Mason didn't move.

Charlie pulled the trigger again.

Nothing.

Mason *still* didn't move.

Charlie pulled and pulled and pulled that trigger, and to Zoey's growing horror, Mason let him.

"Oh, why won't you stop him?" she pleaded. "Why, why...?"

But rather than tackling him, which he could've done easily, Mason allowed Charlie to try and un-jam the gun by removing the magazine, replacing it, and then yanking away at the slide. As Charlie cussed and yanked, Zoey wept and Mason stared into the horizon.

Infuriated, Charlie finally gave up and hurled the useless gun into the water.

And that's when Mason made his move.

15

Still kneeling by Zoey, Mason pulled that .38 out from under his shirt and pointed it at Charlie.

This confused Charlie. *Why would he help me like this?*

And it enraged Zoey who, weak as she was, clawed away at Mason's arm for the gun.

"You bastard," she hissed. "You lying bastard. You came to help him escape!"

Mason pulled himself free from Zoey's weak grasp, stood, leveled the gun on Charlie's forehead, and pulled back the hammer.

"What are you doing?" Zoey cried out. "What are you—You bastard, you lying—You're helping—What are you do—?"

Zoey couldn't finish the question, so a confused and delighted Charlie finished it for her.

"Yeah," Charlie asked with a grin. "What *are* you doing?"

"You'll find out," said Mason, and then he blew out the back of Charlie's head.

Charlie's body hit the ground like a sack of dry cement.

"I trusted you," Zoey whispered.

Mason knelt beside her. "He'll never hurt anyone again," he said.

"But he...."

"He'll never hurt anyone again," repeated Mason, and then he explained everything.

16

It was pitch black when Charlie appeared where he always appeared after dying: under the Joshua Tree. He could feel the bark against his bare back, a comforting feeling.

He laughed at the memory of Zoey's betrayed face when Mason pulled that gun. He also felt a little less hate toward Mason; he felt grateful, even.

Warmed by those thoughts, Charlie groped about for his stash of clothes, found it, dressed, pulled on some boots, and stood.

Boy, it's dark, he thought.

Above him there were no stars, no moon. *Cloudy*, he figured and waited for his eyes to adjust to the night. But they didn't adjust. He couldn't see a thing.

He put a hand to his face.

He couldn't see his hand.

As he stood there waiting to see something, *anything*, his confusion grew into suspicion and fear.

Am I blind? And then his fear did what it always did: generated rage. He pawed at his face and eyes and said to the darkness, "He blinded me! Mason blinded me!"

Charlie took a few careful steps and groped around with his hands. He groped and groped until his hands landed on something...*strange.*

What is this?

He didn't believe what he was feeling.

A book?

He ran his hands to the right. Then to the left. There was no mistaking it. This was a bookshelf.

What?

His hands fell to the shelf below. Here he felt different items. He quickly grasped each one to identify it: Jar. Another jar. Stack of cans. Manual can opener. Tin cup. Cardboard box. He slid his hand up and inside the box and felt batteries—tons of batteries.

A flashlight! Thank God!

He dropped it.

Breathing hard, Charlie got to his knees and felt around in the sand. *Where is it! Where*—He had it and clicked it on and discovered....

He was not blind.

This was worse than blindness.

Bars.

All around him: steel bars.

Still on his knees, Charlie whipped the light around.

Bars.

Bars.

Bars.

He spotted a small, battery-powered lantern on a table next to what looked like a cot.

He stood and grabbed for it.

Its light illuminated everything and....

Charlie saw that he was in a prison cell.

In the middle of this prison stood the trunk of the Joshua Tree.

Above him: bars.

All around him: bars.

What about below?

Charlie dropped to his knees and began to dig and dig.... And there he found more bars.

There was no way to dig under or out.

And there was no way to escape though suicide. He would only return to this prison with his own rotting corpse for company.

Charlie screamed.

No one would ever hear his screams.

To camouflage the prison he'd built around the trunk of the Joshua Tree, Mason constructed an artificial dune and covered it with two feet of sand, which served as perfect soundproofing.

17

Nothing could be done for Charlie's armless victims. Mason made them as comfortable as possible until they died of shock and blood loss. He then buried them and the corpse Charlie left behind in the island's gravelly sand.

He carried an unconscious Zoey to the tender and then lifted her into the cruiser. He was taking her down into the cabin when she protested.

"No. Put me in the back," she whispered through half-closed eyes. "Sit me up. I want see the water."

Once she was situated with a blanket over her shoulders, Mason asked, "Is there anything you need me to do?"

"My family's in a Holdout community in Wyoming. Let them know."

Mason promised he would and then stared at her, his face filled with conflict. He was trying to come to a decision and couldn't, so she made it for him. She shook her head no. "I'll die the way God intended," she told him.

18

As Mason cruised them back home, Zoey watched Charlie's island grow smaller and smaller. It was almost out of sight when she slumped over and died.

19

Mason secured Zoey's body in the blanket and gently slid her into the ocean. He stood there a long time staring at the water. Then he looked up and all around. There was nothing. No land anywhere.

And it was here, in this desert of water, where Joshua Mason let go of the dam inside of him.

Prison

1

Sitting in the Kingdom Key's orange, plastic, government-issued chair, Jerome fast-forwarded through two-days of overhead drone video covering a large dune in the middle of the desert with a Joshua Tree sticking out of it.

And then it happened.

Sucking on his ever-present Tums, Jerome's eyes went wide as he saw a man approach the dune—and that man was Mason.

Jerome bit down on the Tums, slowed the video to normal speed, and watched Mason lift the door of a secreted hatch, climb down inside the dune, and secure the hatch behind him.

"Gotcha."

2

It had taken Mason two months to build Charlie's prison, and while doing so, he'd been careful not to be tracked. Mason had scrutinized each piece of material and equipment hauled out to the Joshua Tree—the bulldozer, steel bars, welding tools, everything—for tracking devices. To avoid drones tracking the delivery of those supplies, Mason requested a dozen trucks and sent eleven of them on wild goose chases.

Satellites could've easily tracked all twelve trucks, but not even the Deputy Director could command satellite time without involving other bureau personnel.

Nevertheless, Jerome had still outsmarted Mason.

After personally approving Mason's travel and purchase permits, Jerome ingeniously had a tracking device installed in one of the hundreds of batteries Mason ordered. The tracking device was connected to a timer powered by the battery. Assuming—correctly, as it turned out— Mason would regularly check for tracking devices and get comfortable after some time passed without finding one, the tracker was scheduled to remain dormant for three months. Then, after it went live, a drone was launched to the location.

But by then, Mason had already built and camouflaged Charlie's prison, so the drone only recorded the dune and Joshua Tree. At first Jerome was discouraged. Something had obviously gone wrong with his plan. But his instincts told him to hang in there, to keep an eye on that dune. Week after week, the drone hovered over that spot. Week after week, Jerome painstakingly reviewed the drone's footage. And now, his persistence had paid off.

Jerome possessed Mason's secret.

3

Jerome decided to keep this extraordinary find to himself. Only after he'd kidnapped Mason and put him into a medically-induced coma would Jerome reveal to the world that he had found the secret to immortality.

What a day! he thought as he leaned back and placed his stocking feet on the Kingdom Key's desk.

Why it had only been four hours ago that the new president-elect had summoned him to a private lunch. Even though Jerome had just eaten a large meal, he still accepted the president-elect's invitation and of course he ate that second lunch right up. Sure, it had given him a heartburn from hell, but it was more than worth it, for it had finally happened. After so many years and so much sacrifice, the incoming President of the United States had said to him, *I want you to be my FBI Director.*

Grinning from ear to ear at the still-fresh presidential memory, Jerome tossed two more Tums in his mouth, folded his arms over his expansive belly, belched, began to plot his exploitation of Mason, grunted, and then dropped out of his orange, government-issued chair and hit the concrete floor.

4

After locating and informing Zoey's family of her death, Mason returned to the Joshua Tree to keep another promise, the one he'd made to his wife about being at Charlie's side when Charlie died.

5

Thirty-seven years after the events on the island, Charlie Breslin did die, peacefully in his sleep at age ninety-three.

Not once during those years did Charlie speak, not a single word. When not sleeping or brooding, Charlie sometimes read the Bible searching in vain for a loophole.

Sporadically, in the living area he'd constructed for himself right outside Charlie's cell, Mason tried to engage him, but Charlie refused to respond or to even look at him.

6

Mason cut away the bars with a welding torch, wrapped Charlie's body in a blanket, and, in a non-descript spot, buried the body six-feet deep so the coyotes couldn't get to it.

But as though it were some kind of payback for all those animals he'd tortured, the coyotes did get to Charlie, as did the other desert animals.

They didn't eat Charlie. His meat was sour. Instead, they ripped him to shreds and spread those shreds throughout the desert where all the pieces of Charlie rotted into nothing under a merciless sun.

The Death of Time

1

Mason would never understand where the red shimmer came from or who or what had decided Charlie was unworthy of eternal life.

Mason would never know that FBI Deputy Director Jerome Byrne had been almost entirely paralyzed by a devastating stroke. Bed-ridden and no longer able to control anything, including his bowels, Jerome blew his brains out.

And like the rest of the world, Mason would never discover the origins of the virus.

Early rumors claimed that in what had become a bitter and violent war to bring the Holdouts to heel, the federal government created the virus to destroy the Holdout's crops. There were doubters, though, and they made some sense. The risk that such a virus could spread to the vast corporate vegetable and insect farms (meat had long ago been outlawed) that kept the Safety Zones fed was simply too great.

Whatever it was, wherever it came from, it didn't matter. The virus put it all to an end. In less than five years, all plant life on the planet died, followed by the animals, insects, and then people—even the bacteria vanished.

And so there was only Mason, and although time itself had died with the humanity that invented it, he was certain it had taken years for the stench of all that death—something he'd not experienced since the buffalo slaughters on the Great Plains—to dissipate.

2

Mason filled this lonely time with his books, until time turned those books to dust, along with his clothes. Naked now, except for the gold wedding band, he began to wander about and explore the great cities of North and South America, until time turned the cities to dust. After the oceans dried up, he explored their bottoms and caves.

He was walking along the deepest part of the Mariana Trench when the sun turned a dark blue and began to pulsate.

He understood what this meant, and hoped his death dream would be of her.

3

At the same moment the world exploded, Mason closed his eyes and felt himself blasted into dust. Along with every other living thing, the Joshua Tree had long ago died. So it was on the chunk of desert that once held the tree where Mason reappeared as it hurtled him through the airless vacuum of space toward the blazing blue sun. Mason lifted himself to his feet knowing that once his sacred piece of land entered the sun's blue fire, he would die and never return. So he closed his eyes and thought of Doreen, of her black hair and soft skin, of her perfume and her laugh. He knew that whatever remained of her would die with him, and at that moment, he longed for her more than he ever had before.

He closed his eyes tighter and concentrated on her face, on the first time he saw her, on the way she ran a small hand through her long black hair.

He prayed and prayed for his death dream to be of her.

If I could see her one last time, he prayed. *Please*, he prayed, *please, just let me see her one last time.*

And then he laughed.

You'll figure it out, she'd told him so many times during their bitter arguments over the existence of God. *You'll figure it out*, she'd said.

Well, he still hadn't figured it out. But as he stared off into the beautiful vastness of the Universe before him, he wondered who it was he'd just been praying to.

You'll figure it out.

His longing for her was now so great, he fell to his knees, and as much for his own sake as to honor her memory, he stared up at the infinity of space and said out loud the closest he could come to a prayer.

"If you are real and one of my sins is not believing in you," he said, "I hope you can forgive that along with the others."

4

The pulsating blue sun was now so close it filled his field of vision and its blazing heat began to melt the sand beneath his knees. Then the heat crystallized the sand into countless glass shards, and like a thousand laser beams, those shards reflected the sun's blue light up and into Mason's naked body, where it invaded him and then exploded into pinpricks of light firing through his pores.

As he sailed through space toward a fiery death with the blue light bursting from him, Mason slowly rose to his feet, clenched his fists, and felt an awesome power course through his body. This power grew and grew until it detonated his whole being into....

Black.

5

The Universe was gone—the stars, the sun, the planets, all of it had disappeared. There was nothing now, only a great expanse of...*nothing*.

Mason could hear himself breathing and felt panic rising in his chest. The void terrified him. He felt a scream building in his—*But wait*.... Out there, off in the distance, hovering and vibrating in the black.... The blue shimmer.

As Mason ran toward it, he realized he was fully clothed and looked down at his scuffed cowboy boots as they clomped across a surface he could not see.

When he looked up, he stopped dead in his tracks. There, next to the shimmer, sat an Old Man on a stool. The Old Man had frizzy gray hair and a long gray beard and looked familiar. Mason couldn't quite place him, and then remembered the Old Man who sat on the back of that convertible, the one who'd waved to him like a homecoming king.

Maybe this was him.

Maybe not.

Probably not.

"What is all this?" asked Mason.

From his stool, the Old Man answered by thrusting out his hand. With a playful grin, he slowly opened it. Sitting on his palm was a red sphere. The Old Man beckoned for Mason to take it from him.

Mason wasn't so sure.

The Old Man gestured that it was okay, to go ahead and take it.

Instead, Mason took two careful steps back. He wanted a better look at his situation, at where he was. He slowly turned himself around, all the way around. But there was nothing to see out there, nothing anywhere. There was only the Old Man on the stool, the blue shimmer vibrating and hovering beside him, and the red sphere in the Old Man's hand.

The Old Man appeared to read Mason's mind and shrugged as if to say, *What else are you going to do other than take this from my hand?*

Mason almost laughed. Something about the Old Man *was* reassuring, so Mason stepped forward and accepted the red sphere. It was no bigger than a plum and he could squeeze it as though it were made of rubber.

"What is this?" Mason asked.

The Old Man answered by gesturing for Mason to throw it.

"What?"

The Old Man furrowed his brow and emphasized again that Mason was supposed to throw it.

"You want me to throw it?"

Delighted that his message had been received, the Old Man smiled and tapped his nose with an index finger.

"Okay," Mason said, sounding a little unsure.

The Old Man didn't like that and shook his head. He didn't want an *unsure* throw from his guest. He raised a fist to emphasize strength, to tell Mason to put some effort into it. Then the Old Man pantomimed reaching way back and really letting it fly.

So Mason did just that and the red sphere sailed out of the blue shimmer's light and into the black where it disappeared, landed, bounced a few times, and rolled to a stop.

Silence.

More silence.

Waiting for something to happen, the Old Man turned himself around on the stool, leaned forward, and stared intently at where the ball had disappeared.

Mason didn't understand any of this.

"Is that all you wanted me to—?"

The Old Man placed a finger to his lips.

Confused but resigned to the fact the Old Man was in charge here—wherever *here* was—Mason remained quiet and waited.

Then the Old Man rubbed his hands in anticipation. Mason thought this was the oddest death dream anyone ever—and then he heard it....

Something out there was making a light *tap-tap-tap* sound, followed by a scurrying, and it was coming straight at them.

"What is that?"

The Old Man didn't respond.

Tap-tap-tap, scurry-scurry-scurry, closer, closer, closer.... Mason didn't like this, didn't like standing here, didn't like—

And then out of the dark and into the blue light trotted a little dog carrying the red sphere in its mouth. Mason let out a gasp. His eyes filled with water.

It was Hok'ee.

Grinning with pleasure, the Old Man folded his arms and watched the reunion.

Hok'ee trotted over to Mason, dropped the red ball at his feet, and looked up at him with those crooked eyes. His tail wagged and he said hello with a yip.

Overwhelmed, Mason dropped to his knees. Hok'ee immediately leapt into his lap and licked his face with so much energy, Mason ended up on his back laughing like a boy with the excited dog romping all over him.

6

Over and over, Mason threw the red ball for Hok'ee until the pup had had enough and flopped down on the ground in a happy pant.

The Old Man, who'd enjoyed every moment, now stepped off the stool, gently placed a hand on Mason's shoulder, and pointed to the blue shimmer.

Mason understood that he was to wait and watch the shimmer.

The Old Man waved farewell, left the stool where it sat, and ambled off into the black.

The blue shimmer hovered and Mason watched it and waited.

Then Hok'ee let out a bark.

Mason looked down and saw that his old friend was also watching the shimmer. And then the little dog with the crooked eyes let out a different bark, one Mason recognized; a warning bark that meant something was coming. Mason turned to see what it was and out of the blue shimmer stepped Doreen.

7

At the sight of him, she stopped and smiled, and then her eyes filled with mist and all the love she held for him.

"It's me," she said.

And it *was* her.

It was the woman he loved looking exactly like she did the moment he fell in love with her.

Mason couldn't move. Couldn't speak. So Doreen ran a small hand through her long black hair and ran straight into his arms.

He pulled the familiar feel of her body into his.

The smell of her hair, the taste of her kiss, the feel of her skin....

This was home.

He gently cradled her face in his hands. Then he kissed her again and then again and then studied her face a long time.

They stared into each other's eyes until they both broke out laughing.

"It's you," he said.

"It's me," she said, and then she slowly slid her hand down his arm and intertwined her fingers in his.

"Come on," she urged, leading him to the blue shimmer.

He hesitated.

He had to know.

"Is everyone here?" he asked.

She turned to him and shook her head with regret, and he understood that he would never see Charlie again.

"But Maya's here," Doreen said. "My daughter's here."

8

Mason stared at the shimmer and nervously squeezed her hand.

"It's okay," she assured him.

He nodded, took a few steps towards the blue shimmer, and stopped. Then he turned around.

"You coming?" he asked Hok'ee.

The little dog with the crooked eyes snatched up his red ball and dashed over to them.

Doreen stooped to scratch his ears and asked, "Well, who is this?"

"That's my partner," Mason said. "That's Hok'ee."

"Well, Hok'ee, you and Kiefer are going to be great friends."

Doreen stood, gently took hold of Mason's elbow, and guided him into the blue shimmer.

"It's okay," she assured him.

"I know it is," he said, and then he disappeared into the other side.

With a quick leap, Hok'ee followed.

"I can't wait for you to meet Mr. and Mrs. Arthur," Doreen said, and then she too disappeared into the other side.

9

In the vast emptiness of the black, the blue shimmer hovered alone and gave off its vibrating light.

Because he had not been eavesdropping, some time passed before the Old Man returned, and when he did it was with the face of a man satisfied with a job well done.

With a youthful spring in his step, he snatched up the stool, stepped into the blue shimmer, and disappeared into the other side.

The stool was no longer necessary.

The waiting was over.

His children had all come home.

Acknowledgments

WITH SPECIAL APPRECIATION

Jane Arnold, Adam Bellow, Alex Marlow, Julie Nolte, Josh Silver.

WITH APPRECIATION

The editors and staff at Post-Hill Press, Al Arnold, Zack Arnold, Robert Avrech, Kim Benson, Mike Binder, Jeremy Boreing, Andrew Breitbart, Victoria Dougherty, Aleigha Kely, Andrew Klavan, David Limbaugh, Faith Moore, Ralph Nolte, Ben Shapiro, Roger Simon, Larry Solov, Steven J. Wolfe.

About the Author

John Nolte is a Midwesterner by birth, a Southerner by choice, and spent the first two decades of his working life as a bill collector. While barely scraping a living as a screenwriter in Hollywood, he met Andrew Breitbart, who hired him as the very first editor-in-chief of what is now Breitbart News, where Nolte still writes almost daily. Nolte is currently semi-retired in the Blue Ridge Mountains of North Carolina with Julie, his wife of thirty-three years, his two dogs, and a Blu-ray collection that will never be large enough.